MASK OF F

Maureen O'Brien

To Darling
Doreen
With much love,

Maureen O'Brien
Jan '98

Constable · London

First published in Great Britain 1998
by Constable & Company Ltd
3 The Lanchesters, 162 Fulham Palace Road,
London W6 9ER
Copyright © 1998 by Maureen O'Brien
The right of Maureen O'Brien to be
identified as the author of this work
has been asserted by her in accordance
with the Copyright, Designs and Patents Act 1988
ISBN 0 09 478090 0
Set in Palatino 9pt by
SetSystems Ltd, Saffron Walden, Essex
Printed and bound in Great Britain by
MPG Books Ltd, Bodmin, Cornwall

A CIP catalogue record for this book
is available from the British Library

For Michael, as always.

Thanks to Claire, my editor, and Imogen, at Constable. And to the Kentish Town CID, especially DCI Arnie Cooke, DI Alan Pink, who looked after me so well, and DC Miki Volpe whose pipe and blazer (though no other characteristics) were an inspiration. And most of all to DI Julian Jeneson, who read the manuscript and gave advice, criticism and encouragement.

1

A BAD SMELL

It was Saturday. He shouldn't have been in the office at all. But weekend duty suited him these days. It occupied his errant mind, it kept him off the scotch, and it forced him to attempt the nursery slopes of the mountain of paperwork.

Niki Cato was on duty with him, a cynical little Geordie who wore a beard and smoked a meerschaum pipe, even played the violin in the police orchestra. He moaned constantly about the mean CID car allowance, said he was there because he needed the overtime.

Not that it mattered to John Bright which of them was on duty with him; their hostility was an inconvenience, no more, an added weight on the side of getting out, finding something else to do. Since the end of his affair with Millie, he didn't know where his heart had gone, but it wasn't in policing any more.

The morning ground on like toothache. Cato was down in the canteen, indulging in tea and tobacco and the fantasy that he was Sherlock Holmes. Weird to see the CID room empty, silent. No one round the big tables, no coming and going, no phones ringing. Bright groaned. He pulled another report off the top of the pile. No matter how many he dealt with the heap remained as high. Like the villains, they just kept coming.

Then at half-past three a call came in to the crime desk. A young copper had found a body. 'A house in Leverton Street, sir. Looks like a suspicious death.' And Bright was out of there like a man shot from a cannon. He didn't give the paperwork a backward glance. He called Cato on his mobile but got no reply.

Leverton Street was five minutes away, the other side of Kentish Town Road. He walked, zipping up his scruffy old bomber jacket against the sleet. Not four o'clock yet and nearly dark. This was one of those winters that went on and on. Surely by now there should be some sign of spring?

He didn't need to be told which house the body was in; the smell nearly knocked him off his feet. Even the small crowd gathered outside kept its distance. The uniforms in the police van grinned at him. It was all right for them, they didn't have to go in.

'You guys the first on the scene?'

The big one laughed. 'Not us, guv. Babyface over there. Rookie's luck.' A young lad in uniform was coming out of the shiny yellow door. He had

7

blond hair and skin like a baby. Laughing Boy stuck his head out of the van window. 'You don't look very well, constable.' The lad's face was paper-white.

'You the one who found the body?' Bright said.

He nodded, seemed to be finding it hard to speak. Bright took him a few yards up the street where he could breathe.

'Sir. Two neighbours called the station, a Mrs – '

'Forget the notebook, constable.'

'Oh. Yes, sir. Well, the council inspected the drains and they couldn't find anything wrong.'

'When?'

'Yesterday, sir.'

'So why weren't we called till now?'

'Well, these two neighbours got together this afternoon, sir, and decided they were fed up with nothing being done so they – '

'A-ha.'

'Phoned us, yes, sir. So I was sent to check, being in the vicinity. I went over the neighbour's wall and broke in at the back.'

'Why not the front?'

'Didn't want to draw attention, sir. Didn't want to spoil any evidence.'

'Any sign of a previous break-in?'

'No, sir. All the locks intact. Front and back.'

'Where's the body?'

The lad looked sick. 'In the bath, sir. Upstairs.'

'Male? Female?'

'I think female.'

'You think.'

'Yes, sir.'

'A-ha. How old?'

'Can't tell, sir.'

'Christ. Cut wrists, anything like that?'

'No, sir.'

'Any other injuries?'

'There's a bit of a cut on the head, sir, but it doesn't look like it could have killed anybody.'

'Drowned?'

'Not much water, sir. But it might have drained away, I suppose.'

'Who lives in the house?'

'A girl, woman, in her thirties. Neighbours haven't seen her around for over a month. Sir – '

'Name?'

'They don't know but, sir – '

'How long's she lived here?'

'About three years, they say.'

'And they don't know her name.' Bright stuck his head in the window of the van. Laughing Boy was still grinning. 'You.'

'Yes, guv?'

'Take this lad's place guarding the house.' That wiped the grin off his face. 'Sit in the van, lad, the pong's not so bad there. I'll want to talk to you later.'

'Sir.' The lad hung back.

'A-ha?'

'I, er, I threw up, sir.'

'Where, constable?'

'In the back yard, sir.'

'There's blokes wouldn't have made it as far as the yard, believe me.' Bright went back to the house.

The stench came right up and belched in your face. Like a fog it filled the space before your eyes. He forced his senses to function, his brain to take note: yellow front door; lock intact; no break-in. Yellow stair carpet? What kind of person chooses yellow stair carpet? White walls, stripped pine handrail. All new-looking. New paint. He took the edge of the white-painted stairs, two at a time, avoiding the carpet, not touching the rail. The smell got worse.

The back bedroom was neat, the bed made, everything in its place. The front bedroom was a mess, bedclothes tangled, stuff on the floor. He clocked that for later use. The bathroom was right there ahead of him. It wasn't like the rest of the house: cracked greenish tiles, worn grey lino, old green fittings. He didn't go in.

The body was stuffed into the bath, knees up against the side, head bent at an angle. The hair was black, long and thick. Strands of it adhered to the enamel, most spread like luxuriant vegetation over the edge of the bath. The gash, on the back of the head, was small but deep. It hadn't made much blood: a splash on the wall-tiles, a blackened crust in the hair. A blow fly crawled round the edge of the crust, but only a few maggots littered the wound like faintly moving grains of rice. A greasy brown gravy barely two inches deep souped round the swollen limbs in the bottom of the bath. The flesh, liquefying, had run back into it.

Nothing he could do here yet. Except use his eyes. And his brain. No hope of that in the miasma of this sick stench. He went out into the street. Laughing Boy stood close to the house. Even with a wad of tissues clamped to his snout you could tell he wasn't laughing now.

Bright ducked under the cordon of blue and white tape and walked up the street to the van, gulping mouthfuls of hard cold air that didn't shift the smell. It clung to the mucous membrane, he'd never get rid of it. Babyface said, 'You all right, sir?'

'Just glad I missed lunch.' He got on the blower to mobilise the SOCOs. And the pathologist, Dave Rimmer, would want to see this for himself. They told him Dave was doing a post-mortem. That meant he could be hours yet. And where was Cato? Little twerp. What was he playing at? 'Cato, get your ass over here.' He shut off the phone. 'I'm going back in.'

'Sir.'

'What, constable?'

'The neighbours say she's an actress, sir.'

'Who?'

'The victim, sir.' Something in Bright's look stopped him. 'Er, I mean the woman. The – the woman who lives in the house. She's on the telly. I tried to tell you, sir.'

Silence. Bright looked at him, small brown eyes suddenly sharpened. 'Are you taking the piss, constable?'

'Taking the piss, sir?' The lad was new. His face showed he didn't know.

'I don't believe this.' Bright got in the van and sat. He crossed his arms on the steering wheel and rested his forehead on his arms. He wanted off this case. It was a bad joke. He didn't want to be around for the punchline. He didn't want to be around. He jabbed the number for the DCI. Listened while he got transferred to the switchboard.

Someone tapped on the window. He looked up. Cato smirked through his facial undergrowth, waving the meerschaum pipe. 'Hear it's another actress, guv. Just up your street.'

He looked at Cato, expressionless. He shut down his mobile, climbed out of the van.

The street lights were on now. Faces hung in the air with hollow eyes, lit from above. Laughing Boy came almost at a run. 'Okay if I do the victim's fingerprints, guv?'

'Need the twenty-five quid, do you, Joker?'

'Come in handy, sir.'

'What have we got on the owner of the house?'

'She's on the telly, guv.' He smuggled Cato a grin. Cato gave his little smirk, cute little beard a-quiver.

'Anyone round here know her name?'

'No, guv.'

Bright sighed. 'Visitors. Anyone seen going in or out in the last month or so?'

'No.'

'Ask that Nosy Parker over the road.'

'Nosy Parker, guv?'

'The one with all the lights off.'

'Oh. Tried it, sir. No one home.'

'The curtains just twitched.'

10

'Oh.' Laughing Boy lumbered across the street, trounced but glad to escape from the smell.

Bright turned to Babyface. 'Hey, lad.'

'Sir?'

'Would twenty-five quid come in handy in your life?'

'Well, yes, guv.'

'Think you could fingerprint the corpse?'

'Oh hell, sir.'

'Think about it. Yours if you want it.'

'Yes, sir. Okay, sir. Right.' He looked sick but would do it, not for the dosh but to redeem the mess in the yard. 'Thanks, sir,' he said. The only one not taking the piss.

Cato stood in his chic little navy blue overcoat and his yellow scarf puffing on his meerschaum. 'Put that thing out before you come in here.'

'Thought I'd help to fumigate the place, guv.'

He had a point.

The kitchen was at the front at the bottom of the stairs. Biscuity walls, blue and yellow Provençal tiles. Clean. New. A wide arch and shallow step led down to the living-room at the back. Sliding glass doors with the forced lock opened on to the little square garden with its thick mat of wet winter leaves, a dirty London brick wall all round it six feet high.

'Fresh vomit here, guv!'

'Yeah. No connection with the case.'

'Yours, guv?'

'If you like, Niki. If you like.' He left Cato out there.

The phone, on a long cord, stood on the edge of the kitchen work surface, by the arch to the living-room. No address book. No papers lying about. He couldn't do a thorough search till the SOCOs had been and gone. He chafed at the delay.

'Christ, John. You know how to pick 'em.'

'Where'd you get the disguise, Jack?'

Jack Craig the photographer was unrecognisable in a pollution mask. 'I feel like one of those joggers in New York. Doesn't alleviate the smell much and it interferes with the viewfinder but what the hell, you only live once. Understand she's an actress, John.' The mask hid his mouth but not his eyes.

'Don't jump to conclusions, Jack.'

'Well, she's about to have her portrait done whoever she is. Where is she, then?'

Bright waited till Jack had finished in the bathroom before going up. The bedroom was a mess. In the shock of the flash bulb the stains on the

11

tumbled sheets stood out clear. 'She had fun anyway,' Jack said. 'Before she popped her clogs.'

'Let's hope.'

Bright switched on the light. Its yellow glow showed a pine chest with a stone jar of dried flowers, a water-colour landscape of an English village: red roofs, pollarded willows and a white road winding away. Nice white linen on the bed, with big lace pillows. Two of them on the floor.

'Nice,' Jack said. 'Shame she got the chop.'

Bright said, 'Don't bother too much with the back room. Hasn't been touched.' He went downstairs. No use the rest of the SOCOs arriving till Jack had done. He sat in the van and shut his eyes, tried not to think.

The SOCOs arrived. In their white paper space suits, blue plastic shoe bags, shower hats, face masks, they piled out of their vehicles into the house. Bright tried the pathologist again.

'Dr Dave won't be free for at least an hour, inspector. He'll be with you as soon as he's finished here.'

Kitchen dusted and done, the space suits crawled over the living-room.

'Anyone find me an address book yet?'

A couple of the ghostly figures looked up and shook their heads.

'Anyone finds it, let me know.'

'Here's your victim, guv.' Cato handed him a big black album. 'It's got to be her, look. Height, colouring, everything.'

Bright opened it. Page after page, ten-by-eight, black and white, the same face. A strong face with a vulnerable mouth and a lot of dark hair. *Kate Creech* was printed in the lower margin of some of them. *5 feet 7. Dark brown hair. Blue eyes.*

'Thought a lot of herself, eh, guv?' Cato said. 'A whole book of glossies, just of her.'

'Requirement of the job, Niki.'

'Well, you'd know, sir.' Cato took the dead pipe out of his mouth and carefully examined it.

Bright looked at the back of a picture. *Agent*, it said, *Diana Sutcliffe* with an address and a number. 'Get me the agent's home number, Cato. Quick.'

He bounced on the balls of his feet, rattled the change in his pockets, watched the men go systematically through the room, till Cato handed him the phone.

'Diana Sutcliffe here.'

'I believe you represent Kate Creech.'

'Yes?' Puzzled: Saturday evening, strange time to call. 'Who is this?'

'I'm John Bright, Kentish Town CID.'

'Oh God, something's happened to Kate.'

'Can you tell me when you last saw Miss Creech?'

'Well, yes. Last week.'

12

'Last week?' Bright did a fast rewind in his head. 'You sure about this?'

'Yes. On Tuesday. I went to see the play.'

'She's in a play?'

'Yes.'

'And you saw this play last Tuesday?'

'Yes!'

'And she was – all right?'

'All right? She was wonderful! Well, she'd a bit of a cold but you'd never have known!'

'Only, her neighbours haven't seen her around for a while.'

'Well, no, they wouldn't have, she's been in Coventry for eight weeks.'

'Coventry?'

'Yes. She's doing *Medea* at the Belgrade! Tonight's the last night. Please tell me. Has something happened to her?'

'No, Miss Sutcliffe, I don't think anything has happened to her.' Not a dead actress in a bath of her own gravy, just a live one with a bit of a cold and someone else dead in her house.

Suddenly he didn't care how late Dr Dave was. The later the better. 'Cato. Get a couple of Coventry uniforms to identify this Kate Creech. They'll have to wait till after the show. Find out what time it finishes and let me know. I want to speak to her, find out how soon she can get here.'

'To the station you mean, guv?'

Bright raised an eyebrow but didn't speak.

The pipe wobbled on Cato's lower lip. 'You're not going to have her view the body here?'

'If it's still here when she gets here.'

'You can't do that, sir.'

'Don't worry, Cato, I'll give her the choice.'

'Sir, it's right against the rules – '

'Actors are as nosy as we are, they like to know the details. And they don't like rules.'

'Sir, she's not a suspect even, yet.'

Bright's mouth made a small movement. 'That's right, Cato. She's not. Not yet. And before you go off duty get me a WPC over here. To take care of her. Case she's a bit upset.'

Cato's pipe was going cold in his hand. 'Sir, why are you doing this?'

'I want her to see it. Before the guys in the morgue have had time to tidy it up. And I want to see her face when she sees it. You got some objection to that?'

Cato looked at his cold pipe, put it in his mouth. Took it out.

'Gonna have a little word with the DCI, that what you're thinking, Niki?' Cato's face showed Bright had hit the mark. ''Cos do, by all means. There's nothing I'd like better than to get off this case, believe me. You want the

13

team to be taken off a murder? 'Cos that's what'll happen. How long since you had a decent murder? You want that, you have a word with the boss.'

Cato pursed his little mouth amongst the whiskers but said nothing.

'So, you objecting to my methods, Cato?'

'No. Sir.'

'That's all right, then. And I'll want you to witness my conversation with this Creech. Just so's you know I'm not breaking any rules. So stick around.'

2

A SHOW CLOSES

'Many matters the gods bring to surprising ends,' the chorus chanted.

And the most surprising end is the end of this run, Kate thought.

'The things we thought would happen do not happen. The unexpected God makes possible.'

Thank you, God.

'And such is the conclusion of this story.'

Under the swell of the ethnic drumbeat Kate climbed out of her chariot in the flies. She helped her dead children out and guided them down the rickety stairs in the dark to the wings, waited for the final curtain to drop, then piloted them on to the stage. She seemed to bow for ever, head swimming, till the safety curtain came down.

'Good applause tonight, Kate.'

'Yeah.'

'Tumultuous even.'

'For endurance, Ken.'

'Aren't you the least bit sad it's over, babe?'

'Ken, I can honestly say there is nothing but rejoicing in my heart.'

Ken placed a hand on her forehead. 'You're not well.'

'I'm fed up with acting, that's it.'

'You don't mean it really.'

'Oh, Ken, I do.'

'No. It's the illness talking.'

Actors stood about on stage, wigs in their hands, pulling pins from their hair, scratching heads itchy from constraint, laughing, discussing future plans.

'Are you going home tonight, Kate?'

'No, I'd better not. I've still got a slight temperature, I think.' She was

14

dripping with sweat. But tomorrow at last she could go home to her own bed and get well. She walked down the concrete corridor towards her dressing-room. Ken laid his arm across her shoulders. 'Did Michael come?' she said.

'No.' Ken shrugged his shoulders sadly. 'He's working at this all night gay café in Soho. He hated missing my last night, though. Nice to be loved, isn't it?'

'Frankly I can't remember, Ken. Is it?'

'Ah, no, has he left you, babe?'

'Not him. Me. I'm the one who goes. It's always the same.'

'You didn't want him, then.'

'It's not that.'

'What is it, then?'

'I don't know. As soon as it looks like getting serious, I'm off. It's weird.'

She sounded low, without her usual sardonic edge. He stopped outside his dressing-room. 'Come back with me, Kate. I'll be all on my own. You won't even have to talk. You can curl up on the back seat. It'll be nice and warm, I've got the heater working again. I'll drop you off right outside your lovely yellow front door.'

'Dear old Ken. Thanks but I've just got to drop into bed.'

'In a couple more hours it could be your own bed.'

She looked longing a moment but said, 'I'm not even properly packed.'

'Kate!' The little ASM handed her a folded piece of paper. 'Message for you. Came while you were on.'

She didn't glance at the message. She had to get out of the drenched costume, dry herself down, scrape the make-up off her face. She was in her own clothes and had started to pack up the accumulated debris of the run of a play: the first night good luck cards, the hair pieces, the rolls of cotton wool, the cough medicine, paracetamol, honey and lemon, throat lozenges, dressing-gown, make-up box, make-up-stained towel. She emptied the dying flowers out of the cracked vase and washed it. She picked up a handful of used tissues to sling them in the bin. Among them she noticed the forgotten message: *Ring the Kentish Town police* and a number.

The police? The Kentish Town police? She found some change and shivered at the pay phone by the stage door. *My house.* Everyone sooner or later got burgled in Kentish Town. *It must be my house.*

Jack, the director, squeezed her shoulder as he passed heavy with bags. 'Sorry to dash off, Kate. Sure you don't want a lift back to London?'

She couldn't answer. Shook her head.

'Well, if you're determined to spend another night in the cells.' He kissed her cheek. 'Bye, love. It was great. Keep in touch.'

15

'This is Kate Creech. I had a message to call you.'

'Hold on a minute, please.'

She piled more coins into the machine and waited, drumming her fingers on the wall, moving from foot to colder foot.

'Hello. That Kate Creech?' A horrible nasal grating South London voice.

'Yes.'

'Detective Inspector John Bright, Kentish Town CID. Where are you speaking from?'

'The theatre pay phone.'

'Coventry, that right?'

'Yes. What's happened? Is it my house? Has it been burgled?'

'Why should you think that?'

'Well, it's the first thing you – Has it been broken into?'

'It hasn't been broken into, no.'

Now she was convinced it had been burned down. 'Has there been a fire?' she said. He didn't answer and she thought, *It has been burned down.*

'How soon can you get here?'

Oh, it's not my house, it's Lizzie. 'It's not my sister, is it?'

'Your sister?'

'Has she had an accident?'

'Was she staying in your house?'

'No.' Kate was bewildered. 'No, she lives in Bristol with her daughter.' *Oh God, let Maisie be all right.* After playing Medea for four weeks you knew the things that could happen to children.

'Bristol,' he said. 'What's her name?'

'Lizzie.'

'Her surname.'

'What? Oh! Creech! Lizzie Creech. Are you saying Lizzie's – ?'

'As far as we know she's fine.'

'As far as you know?'

'Has there been anybody staying in your house while you've been away?'

'No. Can you tell me what's happened, please?'

'Lend anyone the keys?'

'No!'

'On the way back could you try and remember all the people who've ever had keys to your house?'

'Why?'

'It's important.'

'Please tell me what's happened.' She was like Medea on her knees to Creon, the tone of her voice changed. 'Please.'

'We've found a body,' he said.

'A body?'

16

'A-ha.'

'In my house?' There was a silence. She felt she was in an underpass: dim light, distant echoes, a long way to the exit and darkness closing her in. 'In my house?' she said again.

'Any idea who it could be?'

''Night, Kate. See you in London. Give us a ring.' Jude, leader of the chorus, squeezed past with Gregory, the body beautiful who'd played Jason. His hand stroked across her shoulder blades. She shivered. They went on down the underpass, disappearing into the dark.

She didn't speak so he went on. 'Female, five seven or so, lot of dark hair. In the bath.'

'In my bath?'

'Sound like anyone you know?'

Another silence that went on and on.

'Miss Creech?'

'Oh.'

'What?'

'It's not Lizzie. It's not my sister,' she said.

'How do you know?'

'She's short. Five fourish. Her hair's red. She's all right. Oh.'

'When can you get to the police station?'

'I was going to come home tomorrow. But I can come tonight.'

'Go straight to the police headquarters. It's just off – '

'I know where it is.'

'Not to your house.'

'You're telling me I can't go to my own house? Why not?'

'We don't like people to identify bodies till after they've been tidied up a bit. It'd be a bit upsetting at the moment, love.'

A mutinous silence. He asked her if she was coming by train. She said, 'Do you know any English city you can get out of by train after nine o'clock at night?'

He said, 'Come in the morning if you want.'

'No, thanks. A friend will give me a lift.'

He said, 'There's a police officer on his way to the theatre now. Please identify yourself to him.'

Identify myself. 'Ken? Ken!' She ran back down the dressing-room corridor. Her illness had left her, just as it did when she went on stage. She banged on his door. He was on his knees zipping up his big theatre bag. 'Oh, Ken, thank God. Does the offer of a lift still hold?'

She'd begun packing this morning before the matinée. Stripped of adorn-ments the theatre flat looked like a cell in a reformatory, Blue-Tack spotting

17

the walls like a disease. Outside, the gangs that prowled the shopping centre by night bellowed and wailed. A city with the heart ripped out of it twice, first by the war then by the planners. She'd been glad to be leaving. Now, the world beyond had become a stranger place, a lunar landscape where fissures opened under your feet. A woman had been found dead in her bath. *A woman who isn't Lizzie. A woman who looked like – Don't think that. Just don't think.*

A dim lamp lit the theatre car-park. An unmarked car zoomed to a stop and a policeman uncurled like an eel from the driver's seat. 'Are you Miss Kate Creech, love?'

'Yes.'

'And do you normally live at – ' He got out his notebook and carefully read her address aloud.

'Yes.'

'And where are you going now?'

'This is Ken Driscoll. He's – '

'I can confirm she's Kate Creech, officer.'

'He's giving me a lift back to London.'

'I see. Well, you drive carefully, sir.'

Kentish Town Road. Winos huddled in the dark of the doorways. Litter everywhere, spilling out of the unemptied litter bins, whipped along the street by the wind. She wondered why she liked the place. She'd wondered this before. Everything was closed, even the Iraqi supermarket. It was midnight now. Ken's old car had made good time. 'Don't take me to the police station, Ken. Let's go to my house.'

'But Kate, he said the police station – '

'No one's got the right to keep me out of my house.'

3

BRIGHT FACES FACTS

The pathologist came out on to the landing. The lab liaison guy squeezed back against a cluttered chest of drawers. 'That it, doc?'

Dr Rimmer stood a moment in the bathroom doorway shaking his head.

18

He was a tall rangy man with a long, kind, sad face. Cared for the bodies like children. He sighed. 'Yes, that's it.'

Bright followed him down the stairs. 'Well?'

Rimmer was in the hall taking off his gear, the white paper suit, the plastic shoe covers. 'Well, John, the gash on the head was made with something heavy and sharp, something maybe like a brick though there's no sign of any residue, something harder than brick but with a corner to it, I'd say.'

'That the cause of death?'

'Won't know till we look at the lungs, but the blow was made from above and behind.'

'Possible it was an accident?'

'It would have to have been a very strange one.'

'And nothing lying round that looks like a possible weapon?'

'I've seen nothing. Who was she, do you know?'

'No.'

'Not the owner of the house?'

'No.'

'Oh. Where is the owner of the house?'

'On her way back from Coventry.' Bright looked at his watch. 'I hope.'

'Coventry? Who sent her there?'

'Appearing in a play.'

'Oh, dear, John.'

Bright breathed out heavily. He squinted at Rimmer, one eye half closed. 'A-ha.'

'You pick them or they pick you?'

Bright shrugged. 'How long's the bathing beauty been in the water, Dave?'

'God knows. More than a month.'

'Why aren't there more maggots?'

'Winter. We're lucky.'

'There's no heating on in here. That mean there's been no heating on for over a month?'

'Looks like it.' Rimmer stepped outside the front door. 'Smells almost as bad out here.' He got into his car. 'See you in an hour or two, John.'

'Cato.'

'Sir?' The soft voice and softer step on the pavement. Somehow the clever little prick always managed to be outside the range of the smell.

'I want the thing that made that gash on the head.'

'Sir?'

'Something heavy and sharp, harder than brick but that shape. Sharp corner or corners. Get the uniforms on it.'

19

'You want to start now, guv?'

'And where's the WPC I asked for?'

Cato went out, reaching into the snappy blazer pocket for his pipe.

Bright stood in the garden. Either the smell was fainter or he'd got used to it; he could smell the cold sooty air of a London night. Someone breathed behind him. The young bobby stood there.

'You do the fingerprints?'

'Yes, sir. It – wasn't so bad, sir.'

'A-ha.'

'I'm supposed to search the garden, sir.'

'Yeah.' Bright rubbed a hand over his face. The boy hovered. 'Go ahead, constable.'

4

HOME SWEET HOME

She'd expected arc lights, police cars, crowds in dressing-gowns and curlers. But there was just a cordon of blue and white tape saying *Police do not cross* and some lights on in her house. Then she opened the car door.

'Christ! No wonder someone called the police, this smell's a crime in itself.' Ken found a bundle of tissues and covered his nose and mouth.

Kate turned away and put both hands over her face. She found her make-up towel stuffed in the top of a carrier bag on the back seat, pressed it over her nostrils and mouth. If this smell got inside you you'd never get it out.

She ducked under the tape. A very young policeman came out of her front door. 'You can't come in here, madam.'

She tried to thrust past him but he blocked her way. She said, 'This is my house,' but the towel muffled her words. The numbness she felt, *if you can feel numbness, if that's not a contradiction in terms*, was the residue of her sleep in the car, the shock of the smell, and a preparation for the horror, whatever it might be, to come.

'What's going on, constable?' The nasal South London voice she'd talked to on the phone.

The young policeman started to explain.

The voice interrupted. 'Okay, lad. Let her pass.'

The young policeman moved out of her way. She crossed the threshold.

The odour, evil, sweet and dense, seeped into her eyes, her ears. It probed the pores of her skin. She wanted to run from it and hide.

A man stood at the top of the stairs, small, wiry, wearing a scruffy leather bomber jacket. He held a wad of tissues over the lower half of his face. His small brown eyes flickered with sharp points of light. 'Kate Creech?' The voice was his. 'Detective Inspector John Bright. I told you not to come here. I told you to go to the police station.'

'This is my house.' She found she couldn't say more. The towel filled her mouth. Her rehearsed speech died into its folds.

'I advise you to go to the station and wait for me there. It's not a sight for the squeamish.'

She found herself walking towards the stairs. A nattily dressed man with a beard came out of the kitchen. She thought he was going to stop her. She said. 'I've got to know – It's my house.'

Leather Jacket said, 'See what I mean, Cato?' The bearded bloke stood behind her in the hall. He didn't answer him. 'You heard me tell her to go to the station, that right? But if you're absolutely determined, Miss Creech. Come on up. Be my guest.'

The smell rolled down the stairs like fog off a mountain. You climbed up into it, into the centre of it, ingested by it. At the top of the stairs he jerked his head towards the bathroom door meaning she was to go in there. She walked ahead of him along the landing, olfactorily mesmerised, and stood in the doorway.

A bunch of greyish white balloons was crammed into the bath. They were the source of the smell. She took a step into the room and saw that the balloons had a head, a sort of head, with thick black hair plastered about it. The head was at an odd angle, curled to one side. Each part of each limb and each section of the torso was grotesquely swollen and had the texture of rubber, whitish, streaked with green.

She stood there some incalculable time then turned to look at the sharp brown eyes above the wad of tissues. He blocked the doorway. He didn't mean her to get out, but he shifted when he saw her eyes. She went past him on to the landing and leaned over the stair rail. The walls, and everything surrounding one spot on the yellow stair carpet, started to go black.

But she stared at her hands gripping the banister rail. She concentrated on them. She didn't throw up and she didn't pass out. The centre spot of light enlarged. The black receded. She stood up straight.

'Well, now she's here, Cato, she might as well identify the victim for us. Don't you agree?' Leather Jacket lifted an eyebrow to invite her back to the bathroom. She didn't resist: *let's get it over with.* She stood looking.

'Remind you of anyone you know?' His voice was muffled by the tissues.

The flesh of the face had started to recede, dragged backwards, downwards. The part of the body in the inch or two of water had liquefied into a brownish greasy gravy. *Remind you of anyone?* She couldn't even shake her head.

'Come on, Miss Creech. You telling me this is a total stranger? In your bathtub? In your bathroom. In your house.'

She moaned into the towel, 'let me out of here' the only distinguishable words.

'You can't identify who this is?'

'Please.'

The eyes, little stones with jagged lights, stared so hard at her they seemed to squint. He turned and nodded at someone behind him on the landing. The bearded one glanced at the thing in the bath then took her arm and started to lead her downstairs.

'Hang on a minute.'

They turned. Leather Jacket was standing in her bedroom doorway. 'Come here.' He turned on the light.

Her beautiful peaceful bedroom. What had happened to it? A hurricane? He put on a bedside lamp and she saw the stains on the sheets. She gazed at him. His amused rat eyes gazed back. Her head shook. She couldn't stop it and couldn't speak.

'This the way you left it?' he said.

Her head stopped shaking. 'No.'

He switched off the lights. 'Okay, let's go.'

People moved about in the downstairs rooms. She couldn't see them; she felt their presences.

Next she was sitting on the low garden wall in the night air of the street. The smell was slower here. Quieter. It didn't rush at you so hotly, it didn't thrust its fist down your throat and pulverise your intestines. Leather Jacket was talking into a mobile phone. A car drove up, then another. Curtains twitched in the dark house opposite. Two doors away a baby started to cry.

Leather Jacket brought a young woman over to Kate. He said, 'This is WPC Edgley.'

'Hi.' She was small. *She'd be good at judo, I suppose. Her centre of gravity is low.* Her thoughts were like that, snatching at random for anything that wasn't the thing in the bath, the mess in her bed. Ken's car had gone. She said, 'Where's Ken?'

Leather Jacket said, 'Your friend Mr Driscoll? He's gone to make a phone call. He'll meet you at the police station.'

A van drove up. Two figures pulled a stretcher out of the back.

'Mortuary van's here, guv.'

'Show them up, Cato.'

The mouth tightened under the little beard but he didn't falter. 'This

22

way, gentlemen.' He seemed to be waving a meerschaum pipe. She must have imagined that.

More men got out of the van. They went into the house. She visualised their feet on the yellow stair carpet. Everyone had told her it was a crazy colour. Well, they were right. *The isle is full of voices*: her thoughts, and all these men talking to their little black boxes and the little black boxes talking back. She shivered. 'What are we waiting for?' she said.

'Cold?' His little eyes were amused. 'Want to go back inside?'

She didn't bother saying no. 'What time is it?'

'Round half twelve.'

'Sir. Sir? Excuse me, sir.' The lab liaison officer tapped Bright on the shoulder. Two men came out with a stretcher. He stood to one side to let the stretcher pass. The thing on it was wrapped in a plastic sheet. The smell intensified for a moment as it passed. They put it into the van. The van drove off.

'Neighbours who reported it thought it was you in there.'

'Me?'

'Hadn't seen you around.'

She was surprised they'd noticed: her absence, not the smell. 'Me.'

'That's what we all thought. Till we rang your agent.'

'Diana – ' She stood up. Her brain made a dizzying gyration in her skull.

'It's okay. WPC Edgley told her we'd contacted you.'

She sat down again on the wall. A night breeze sliced into them like a knife. They shivered.

A car pulled up. Bright said something to Edgley, the policewoman, then walked to a car and drove off. Edgley took Kate's arm and guided her to another car.

5

THE ARMS OF THE LAW

Silvery plants round the police station garden glowed in the dark. Inside, the graceful Victorian building had been partitioned into many small spaces. She was put into one on the left labelled *Waiting-room*. Two black boys sprawled on a bench. One of them, perhaps twelve years old, had a fresh deep cut down the side of his face. The other, younger, was crying, wiping his nose with the back of his hand. Kate sat on the bench facing them but they never looked at her.

Edgley came back and took her into a room on the right, a long narrow room with a frosted window on to the street. A long table almost filled it. She left her there. Kate sat looking at the wall, trying to keep her head as blank as it. No thoughts must come there. *No thoughts.*

The door opened. Edgley said, 'Would you like a cup of tea?' She had a posh diffident voice, sounded like the daughter of NW1 intellectuals. It must have given them a shock, her becoming a policeman, Kate thought. She said, 'Can I go to the loo?'

'Hang on.'

'I've been doing that for two hours.'

Edgley disappeared, unsmiling. Kate waited in the white silence. Edgley came back. Kate followed her among partitions. 'I've got to come in with you. Don't lock the door, please.' She looked surprised when Kate didn't object.

Kate washed her hands. The smell clung. The smell of her house. She didn't look at her face in the mirror. She didn't want proof of her existence. Not tonight.

Leather Jacket stood in the doorway of the narrow room. 'Right? The constable's going take down a few particulars. Won't take long.' A black policeman in a bright white shirt sat at the end of the table. He looked fresh and clean. 'Sit down, love.'

She sat.

'What's your name?'

'Kate Creech.'

'That's Miss or Mrs?'

'That's Ms.'

He looked up. Leather Jacket's little brown eyes sparked. 'That's *Muz*, Winston.'

'Oh. Right, sir.' When they got to profession he said, 'Actress, huh? You on the telly then?' Leather Jacket shifted against the door. Winston moved on to the next question.

A knock. A hand passed in a polystyrene cup. The tea was thick and gravy-brown. Though she couldn't drink it she put her hands round it. But warmth doesn't penetrate polystyrene. The room wasn't cold but she was. While she answered the questions Leather Jacket never took his eyes off her. They were half closed but you could see the metallic points of light.

The questions came to an end. Leather Jacket said, 'Thanks, Win.' 'Win' got up with his papers. 'Get me a copy.' The nasal rasp like a metal file. 'I want it, like, yesterday.'

'Yes sir.' Very correct.

'Sir' sat down in Win's chair. He put his hands on the table. They were small square capable hands. For the first time she felt threatened. Acutely personally threatened. She didn't know by what.

'Aren't you going to drink that?' He took the cup and gulped. 'Christ,' he said. 'Get us some coffee in here, Edgley.'

Edgley veiled a look and went out.

'The coffee-flavoured piss is better than the tea-flavoured piss, that's as much as you can say for it. I'm new to this nick, haven't got things organised yet.' His voice made rings round her head. Rings of sharp wire. 'You're an actress then.' His mouth made an odd movement. 'There's a thing now.'

'It's a job like any other.'

'A-ha, that right?' He looked at her and looked away. 'What show were you doing in Coventry?'

'*Medea.*'

'My Dear?'

'It's a Greek tragedy. Medea's the name of the – heroine.'

'A-ha.' She'd have sworn he smiled only not a muscle in his face had moved. 'What part were you playing then?'

'*Medea.*'

'I see.' He seemed to be mocking her but there was something else there that puzzled her. 'Didn't she kill her kids or something?' he said. Kate's surprise must have showed. 'We're not all pig ignorant, Miss Creech.'

'I didn't – '

'Yes, you did.'

She shrugged.

'Though we're not exactly renowned for our cultural sophistication either. Be funny if you were playing the other one. Clytemnestra, was it? Didn't she drown someone in the bath? Nothing's changed, has it? Knew a thing or two, those Greeks.'

Before Kate's mouth closed Edgley came back with two cups and some sheets of paper. He took the papers and started to read. She picked up the coffee. A cautious mouthful stayed down. *No thoughts, especially while swallowing. Silence. No thoughts.*

'Thirty-six, hn? You don't look it.'

She didn't reply.

'Lived in that nice little house three years, right?'

'That's right.'

'Alone?'

'Yes.'

'Any particular reason?'

'I like it. Correction: I liked it.'

'Living alone?'

'The house.'

'And alone?'

'It beats a horrible relationship.'

'Who with?'

'I was speaking in general.'

25

'What, in general relationships are horrible?'

'Obviously not all.'

'One in particular, then.'

'A relationship that stops working is horrible.'

'A-ha.' He seemed to enjoy this dodging and fencing, was in no hurry. His questions sounded like casual chat but you knew they weren't. 'And when this relationship did work,' he said. 'This bloke lived with you? I'm assuming bloke, I mean – '

'No.'

'Not a bloke. Sorry. Never know these days.'

'Nobody has ever lived in the house with me.'

He took a patient breath. 'Anyone ever *stayed* there with you?'

'Well, yes. Friends from time to time. My sister, my niece, when they come to London. Of course.'

He breathed out. 'And they'd have keys, would they?'

'Keys?'

'A-ha.'

'Well, yes, I suppose.'

'And when were you last in your house?'

'Eight weeks ago.'

'Eight?'

'When I started rehearsals in Coventry.'

'You never came back? Not even for a weekend?'

'Yes! Sorry, the first weekend I came back. I'd have come for others only I got this cold. It developed into bronchitis. After that I just stayed in Coventry, spent every spare minute in bed.'

'Alone?'

She didn't change her expression. 'I had a temperature of a hundred and two and a lot of lines to learn.'

'Anyone vouch for that?'

'Everyone. Almost. The company.'

'Oh, really?'

'They kept bringing me things. They looked after me.'

'Touching, isn't it, Edgley, the kindness of theatrical folk?'

Edgley looked surprised to be addressed. Didn't respond. She didn't like him, didn't trust him.

'Okay.' He took a mouthful of coffee. 'I said this was better?' Edgley's mouth formed a dutiful smile. 'Well, we'll be checking,' he said to Kate.

'Am I suspected of something?'

'We're treating this as a suspicious death. You want to be eliminated, don't you?'

'At the moment I feel annihilated. Is eliminated worse than that or better?'

He slid a piece of paper towards her. 'Make me a list of the people with keys.'

'You keep talking about keys.'

'The person in your bath got in with keys. Or was let in by someone with keys.'

'I thought – ' A hot pool of coffee filled her throat. He watched her with those little rat's eyes, all surface glitter, no feeling, no depth. She put a hand to her mouth, managed to swallow the coffee. 'I thought there'd been a break-in. A french window, I'd assumed.'

'A bobby got in over the neighbour's back wall and broke your living-room window. Until we rang your agent we were all assuming the lady in the bath was you.'

'Me.'

'You fit the description: five sevenish, dark hair. Female. Can't tell if you've anything else in common till I get the post-mortem report.'

'Me.'

'That's right Miss Creech. And now we're supposing the victim is someone known to you. But you tell me she doesn't look like anyone you know. You sure about that?'

She filled her mouth with coffee and nodded. *No thoughts.*

'In that case someone known to someone known to you.' She covered her face. 'So you'll list me the people with keys to your house.' He waited. 'Okay?'

She lifted her head. 'I don't want to do this.'

'Why?'

'People I know. My friends.'

'Who?'

'People who've never been in-involved with the police.'

'We have to eliminate – '

'You think we don't all know what that means? It means they'll be suspected and questioned and watched. They'll be – smirched.'

'Smirched?' Oh, how amused his little rat eyes were. 'Just make me the list, okay?'

A knock. The black policeman's head appeared. He and Edgley whispered at the door. Rat Eyes got up and went out leaving her with Edgley. She looked to Edgley for help but Edgley wasn't looking at her.

She felt like hell. Rat Eyes wasn't the type to give up. In the end she'd have to capitulate. She shut her eyes and prayed, to her private god and to her friends, for forgiveness. She thought of all the people she'd ever given keys to. She stopped thinking. She opened her eyes and wrote the names

27

of three safe people, three people who'd never done any harm to anyone, three people who had nothing to fear: Lizzie her sister, Aggie her best friend, and Ken her second best friend.

Rat Eyes said, 'Your friend Ken's here.'

She gave him the list. 'Three names. A-ha. Thanks, *Muz* Creech. Be seeing you.'

6

FRIEND OR FOE

Ken stood up. Michael was with him. His latest love. Small and blond with a face like a baby Nureyev. They were dressed in identical clothes, knitted black fisherman's hats on the backs of their heads, one ear-ring each, leather bomber jackets. Rat Eyes' jacket was brown and showed signs of wear. Theirs were opulent, sexy, black, with zips all over and padded shoulders and flaps. Their jeans were tight. Their boots had metal studs.

Ken said, 'Michael's shift finished at midnight. I went to fetch him.'

She walked into Ken's big arms. He said, 'It's all right, baby.' He looked at Rat Eyes. 'She'll be all right with us, mate.'

Rat Eyes said, 'Let's know if you're going anywhere, Muz Creech.'

Ken said, 'Come on, Michael. Let's get out of here.'

The little dancer opened the door. 'Gives you the willies, this place, doesn't it?'

'We should be so lucky, dear.'

He watched them all the way down to Kentish Town Road. She could feel his eyes sharp on their backs.

'Do you really not know who it was?'

'Ken, I couldn't tell if it was male or female, young or old, you could hardly tell if it was human.'

Michael said, 'Yuk.'

She said, 'I thought it was a bunch of balloons.' A sharp liquid rose in her throat. She swallowed. It hurt.

'Are you sure you want to talk, lover?' Ken always used these unlikely endearments. They made you feel cherished. He was from Birmingham way back and you could still hear it even though he'd been an actor so long.

'I have to get used to it,' she said.

28

'Was it suicide?' Michael had a sweet lisping voice. He leaned on Ken trustingly.

'I get the feeling they don't think so.'

'Oh, God!' He turned his face to Ken and back to Kate. 'Kate!'

They sat in silence taking it in.

'Why in your house, babe?'

'They seem to think it was meant to be me.'

'Ohh.' Ken disengaged Michael, went and put his arms round Kate. 'Ohh, dear.'

'Someone broke in and killed some woman in your bath thinking it was you?'

'They didn't break in. They had my keys.'

Ken's arms loosened. He sat up straight. 'I've got a set of your keys.'

'I know. I had to tell the police. I'm so sorry.'

Michael's face puckered. Ken rose up, nearly knocking him over. He rolled gracefully into the lotus position with his hands tight on his knees. Ken ran to a chest of drawers, scrabbled about in the top drawer, said, 'Shite,' scudded to the kitchen. They heard knives jangling in drawers, more scrabbling, then a long groan of relief. He came in holding three keys on a ring. 'I know they're yours, I put your name. Look.'

KC was scratched on the little flap. Kate closed her hand over them, looking up at him, not asking.

'I never lent them to anyone, love.'

She didn't mean to look at Michael but somehow there she was, staring at him. Ken turned to him too. Michael kept his superb dancer's posture but you felt him cringing inside. He shook his head and whispered, 'I didn't. Honestly. I wouldn't. Anyway, how could I? I didn't even know they were Kate's. I didn't even know they were there.'

She said sadly, 'Would you say if you had?'

They looked at each other, enquiring and rueful, shook their heads.

'No one would, would they?' Ken said. 'But I didn't lend them, sweetheart. I promise you, queer's honour, I've never lied to you.'

'And you haven't used them? Since I've been away.'

'What for, baby?'

'Yes.'

'He didn't. Honest.' Michael put his arm round Ken's waist and leaned on him; they were like one of Picasso's circus paintings, one so big and strong, the other so graceful and small. 'I'd have known. I'm so jealous I never let him out of my sight.'

Ken's arms were folded across his chest. He hesitated a second then draped an arm round Michael's shoulder. The boy smiled up at him.

*

29

She followed spirals of light on the ceiling made by passing cars. If she closed her eyes she saw the thing in the bath and the smell filled her nose and mouth, so she kept her eyes open and thought. She thought of everything except the thing she mustn't think about, till the light on the ceiling was daylight and then she slept.

'Phone, Kate.' Michael lisped, kneeling by the sofa in a short kimono. It was half-past nine.

'Muz Creech?' Rat Eyes' cheese-cutter voice. 'Woke you up, hn? I have to see you. Where's best for you?'

'Best is a thing of the past.'

'Yeah, well. It's up to you. The station or your friend's place or neutral ground.'

'Why not my place?'

'Very funny. I'll pick you up at your friend's.'

'No. I'll get to the police station.'

'Your friend's is on my way.'

'Is this called consumer choice?'

'Westbourne Grove, right?'

'Oh, all right.'

'Sorry I woke you up.'

'You sound it.'

'Yeah, well.'

She told Ken and Michael he'd be there in half an hour. They held their paws up like startled squirrels but she couldn't smile. Ken offered to run her a bath. She said fine if he could run it to Heathrow and put her on a plane.

She dabbed water on the salient points standing at the bathroom basin with her back to the bath because she couldn't bear to look at it. This was crazy, it wasn't even her own bath. She'd have to get over this.

'You look terrible, Muz Creech.'

'Thanks.'

Ken and Michael sat bathed and shaved and shiny, knees together, on their best behaviour, like two small boys visiting. No one spoke. The smell of good Brazilian mocha came from the kitchen.

'Any chance of a coffee?' Bright rattled the change in his pockets. 'I've just come from the mortuary,' he said.

Michael ran to the kitchen.

Kate handed over Ken's set of keys. 'I gave Ken my keys two years ago. He kept an eye on my place when I was away at a time when he needed a roof. He's had them ever since.'

'Why?'

30

'Why not?'

'I don't think you want me to answer that, do you, Muz Creech?'

Oh he was so amusing, he amused her to death. 'I forgot he still had them.'

'You forgot someone had your keys?'

'Yes. Well, I remembered from time to time, I suppose. But somehow it would have been churlish to ask for them back. And anyway it was a good idea for Ken to have them. I mean, it seemed like a good idea. If you're away and something needs to be done or ... And I don't know my neighbours, I'm away too much and anyway I'm not a neighbourish type. I nod at the woman opposite if I see her in the street but if I met her in the greengrocer's I might not recognise her. You know.' So she was chattering. So what. She was still in shock, wasn't she? She drivelled into silence.

'Good coffee,' he said.

Michael leapt up eager to appease. 'Have some more!'

'Sit down, mate. Relax.'

'Oh ... All right then.'

'Anyway, Ken says he hasn't used them or lent them to anyone and I believe him.'

'A-ha.' Bright turned to Michael. 'And how about you?'

Michael shot up again. 'No, no! Absolutely not!' His hands waved, fingers quivered, he looked like Ariel. 'I wouldn't. I couldn't anyway, I never saw them till last night, I mean not to recognise. I only met Kate for the second time yesterday, didn't I, Kate? How could I have known whose keys they were?'

She glanced at Bright to see how this was going down. He wasn't looking at Michael, he was looking at her. 'P'raps I'll take you up on the coffee now. Thanks.' He put his mug into Michael's tremulous hands and when he'd gone he looked at Ken. 'When did you meet him? Where? How? When did he move in?'

Ken went cold and still. Kate had seen him go like that once, just before he hit the director of a play they were rehearsing.

'If you don't want to answer, you don't have to. No problem.'

'Are we being suspected of something, because if we are – '

'Not yet. Not specially. No more than half the population of London, if not of the country.'

'Because I want to help Kate and I don't want to impede you in the course of your investigations but I have to tell you I put your behaviour down as intimidation and I don't like it.'

'Intimidation, is it?'

'The rules have changed. You're not allowed to treat nancy boys as criminals these days.'

'I can't help it if he gets over-excited at the sight of a copper.'

'So watch it.'

31

'Look, I'm not a queer basher, I'm a villain basher. If he's not a villain he's got nothing to fear from me. All I'm trying to do is find out what happened to the woman in your friend's bath. If either of you used or lent those keys and you don't tell me, you are impeding my investigation and I'll do you for it. All right?'

'I'm sorry, I don't see how a history of our relationship would help you. Michael has said he knew nothing about the keys and that's good enough for me.'

'Up to you, mate.' Bright stood up. He leaned in at the kitchen door. 'Forget about the coffee, okay? I'm off.' Michael crouched on a kitchen stool looking wretched. Bright held the door open for Kate. 'Coming, Muz Creech?'

She hugged Ken. He was trembling but not so as you could see. She engineered a smile. 'See you tonight; if you'll have me.'

'Sure.' He didn't sound it. He didn't call her babe.

7

BREAKFAST WITH BRIGHT

The sunshine was a surprise. One of those mad March days. There was something odd about this one, though. It was quiet. As though life had stopped. She said slowly, 'Oh, it's Sunday, I suppose.'

Bright said, 'Yup. It's still Sunday.'

She'd just got a whiff of a different world. Where your very nature was something you had to hide. *Ken shaking with fear, Michael crouching on that stool. I gave their names to the police. But what if all my friends have things to hide, things they've hidden from me, things ...* They were walking along Westbourne Grove. Only a few people, buying their Sunday paper, a pint of milk, enjoying the blustery sunshine. *This is how life used to be.* Suddenly she was out of energy, her face went into droop, the way it goes before you cry, from exhaustion, when everything's gone wrong and you can't see how you'll ever get it to come right again.

'You had any breakfast?' he said.

'What?'

''Cos I haven't.'

'Breakfast?'

'I've been watching a post-mortem. Not that good for the appetite but you got to eat.' He pushed open the door of a French bistro-type place, an eighties yuppie innovation, happily outlasting the yuppie. He ordered two full 'English with coffee. She said thanks but she'd just have the coffee. He said, 'Ninety per cent of vegetarians give it up because of the smell of bacon. Just concentrate on that fact.' She needed her energy to fight other things, not this. She shrugged.

A pretty waiter in black with a white apron brought two fried eggs, two rashers of bacon, tomatoes, mushrooms, a basket of warm French bread. She came down mouthful by mouthful, this out-of-control hang-glider coming in to land. She drank some coffee. She said, 'I thought we were going to the police station.'

'Food's better here.'

'I believe you.'

'When I go back there I'm into the paperwork. It's all paperwork these days. No time to do the job. Should've sent someone else for you this morning. Shouldn't have come myself. It just happened it was on my way.'

'Where's the mortuary?'

'London Bridge.'

'Westbourne Park? On your way from London Bridge?'

'Well. I got lost in a one way system. Came out in Westbourne Grove.'

'It's not easy to do that.'

'No. It's a special gift. Want to hear about the post-mortem?'

'No.'

'It's not suicide.'

She put her hands over her eyes.

'Then we never thought it was. The bash to the back of the head knocked her out. Then she was probably pushed down under the water where she drowned. Not much of a struggle that way. The plug doesn't fit too well – '

'No, I know.'

'That's how the water seeped away. If it hadn't she'd have been an even pleasanter sight. They liquefy, you know. Drink some coffee, you'll be all right.'

'But you don't know who it was,' she said, big coffee cup in front of her mouth. 'In the bath.'

'She. Not it. Adult female Caucasian, five foot seven, on the thin side.'

'Thin?' She saw the swollen rubbery thing she'd thought was a bunch of balloons.

'Before she spent several weeks in the bath. Dark hair, you know that, you saw it. Dyed.'

'Dyed?' She knew her face lit up, from a sudden flooding with the light of hope, she couldn't help it. His eyes were on her, that still mask with the smile behind it. She shut the light down but he'd seen it.

'Just in the front apparently to cover a few grey hairs.'

'How many's a few?' She'd recovered, at least on the surface. He couldn't hear the sound of her heart.

'Literally. Like six. Eight. Okay? Makes you think she was at least into her thirties but you never know. Some people are grey at twenty-five. Remind you of anyone yet? Getting close?'

'Was she pretty? Could they tell? I mean before – '

'They've got a guy doing a mock-up head from the skull. They can't tell yet.'

'Had she been raped?'

'Christ.'

'You said she'd been hit. It's what you think of.'

'It's what *you* think of.'

'I'm a woman, yes. And I saw the stains on my sheets.'

'The pelvic area spent more time in water. Hard to check for signs of sexual activity.'

He was trying her out, but her forces rallied just as they did on stage when her legs shook and her throat went dry and the sweat ran down her sides. 'The stains on the bed,' she said.

'Not established yet whether they're semen or not.'

'Ever seen stains like that that weren't semen?' She saw him taken aback, just the least little bit. 'What's the matter, women not supposed to say things like that?'

He looked at her and looked away, squinting into the distance. He signalled the waiter to bring him the bill. She got out her purse. 'Put that away,' he said.

'You can't buy me with breakfast,' she said.

'A-ha?'

'I gave you my friends for free.'

'You're not giving me the victim, though, are you?'

She went like one of those people in the fairy-tales who get put under a spell: stopped, congealed in a timeless element. 'What?'

'Even though you know who she was.'

This time she was readier. She gaped at him. 'Oh, I do?'

'Or you think you do.' His squint had intensified, the look of amusement behind the mask. 'Don't you, Muz Creech?'

She sat back, feeling as though he'd punched her. She looked perfectly relaxed. Actors, the masters of body language. 'You try your luck, don't you?' she said.

'Don't try yours too far.'

'Oh, right. I won't. Thanks.' She handed over a tenner. 'That's for my breakfast and your advice.'

He accepted the note and gravely counted out her change. 'You paying half the tip too?'

'Please.'

'A-ha. There you are.' She thought better of telling him to keep the change. 'My car's round the corner,' he said.

'Where are you thinking of taking me?'

'I hope you'll agree to come to the station with me. Where I hope to persuade you to give me your fingerprints.'

She looked at her hands, palms up, she couldn't help it. 'My fingerprints?'

'Don't mind, do you? Once we know which prints are yours we'll at least be able to tell which are not. In your house, I mean.'

She managed to speak without first swallowing the sudden saliva in her throat. 'I don't mind, no. It'll be interesting.'

'Interesting.' He gave a short laugh.

'If I ever have to do it in a movie I'll know how it feels.'

'I see, you're looking on it as research.'

'I'm trying to cultivate detachment. I'm trying to get it under control.'

'You like having things under control.'

'Doesn't everyone?'

He looked at her and looked away. She noticed he never looked at her for long. *A fish on the end of his line, he's reeling it in and then he gives it some slack, a little rest, hoping to fool it into a false sense of security. Well, he doesn't fool me.* But each time he withdrew the sharp gaze, the squinting interrogation, she felt dropped, discarded. *It's a trick. You want to get back into his attention. Don't go for it. Get off his line.* She got into his car.

8

THIS LITTLE HAND

He ran up the steps ahead of her. He said to the WPC on the desk, 'This is Kate Creech. Take her down for fingerprinting, okay?' And to Kate, 'Wait in there till they're ready for you.'

She cultivated detachment in the waiting-room for twenty minutes while a small German man told her in minute detail and a gutteral cockney accent which she tried to analyse how he'd come to lose his wallet.

'Miss Creech?' She followed the WPC down stone steps to a colder region. A brick corridor with a row of doors either side. Drunken shouts, banging on the doors.

She said, stupidly, 'Are these the cells?'

'The Saturday night haul,' the WPC said. 'This is Sergeant Bliss.' The

stocky man in uniform didn't speak. 'And this is the fingerprint room.'
Then she was gone.

An airless windowless cell. Against the wall an old table like the table
her teacher had sat at in her Victorian primary school. At one end a metal
chair with a torn canvas seat. At the other end a camera fixed in a metal
frame. 'Not going to take my picture, are you?'

He didn't smile. 'No,' he said, serious, 'the DI's instructions are just your
fingerprints.'

The fingerprinting equipment was made of mahogany and brass. 'It's
like something out of Sherlock Holmes,' she said.

'What?'

'I expected something more modern.'

'No point.'

'No point?'

'In modern equipment. This part of the job has never changed.'

'Hasn't it?'

'No.'

He pressed the middle finger of her right hand on the pad. She practised
her drama school trust exercise: put yourself in his hands, go limp; when
all she wanted was to pull away and run. She hadn't expected to feel like a
criminal but she did. She felt appalled, terrified, trapped.

He'd finished. Gave her a piece of kitchen roll to wipe her blackened
hands. She felt like Lady Macbeth. *All the perfumes of Arabia* . . .

'Enjoy that, did you? Interesting, was it? Good experience?'

'Unforgettable anyway.' She didn't pretend it hadn't shaken her.

He took her into the narrow interview room. At least it had a window
on the street. He stood with his back to her looking out of it. He turned to
face her, his back to the window now, so she couldn't see his eyes and she
knew, as he meant her to, that he could see hers. The sense of entrapment
was fresh. Like raw meat.

He said, 'You think you know who the victim is. You think you know
who did it. Someone else has your keys that you're not telling me about.'

She'd Judased on Aggie and Ken but she wasn't going to give him this.
*No thoughts. A thought in the head comes out at the mouth. Don't give the
thoughts head-room. Keep out.* She concentrated on her hands which still bore
traces of the black stuff. She rubbed her fingers against her thumbs.
Something wicked this way comes. She didn't speak.

'I see.' The voice like a twanging wire cut through her head. 'Going to
give them plenty of warning, are you? "Just in case you killed someone in
my bath I'd like to warn you that the police might be paying you a visit,
I'm telling you so you'll have plenty of time to hop it." Send them a plane

ticket to Brazil while you're at it, why don't you? Don't do it by halves, *Muz* Creech.'

'I wish you'd stop calling me that.'

'That's a good considered answer.' He nodded. 'Yup.'

'If I did – warn someone – would I be an accessory after the fact or whatever it is?'

'Impeding the course of justice.'

'Justice in this country is a bit of a blunt instrument.'

'Oh, I see, a philosophical discussion. Just what we need at this moment. Look, love, I'm just a simple copper.' She gave him a look and that invisible smile inhabited his face for a second. 'A-ha, that's right. I just catch the bastards. Justice is not my business, love. That's someone else's affair.'

'You're just obeying orders?'

The invisible smile again. 'That's right. Just getting on with the job.'

He was right and they both knew he was right about what was going on in her mind. It was no use pretending. She said, 'You underestimate what it's like my side of the fence. It's a nastier feeling than you could imagine, giving your friends' names to the police.' Something happened to his face. Without knowing how, she'd wiped the amusement off it. 'I need time to think,' she said.

'The last thing you need is time to think.'

'You make it sound as though I'm a suspect. I thought I was supposed to be the intended victim round here.'

'All possibilities remain open till disproved.'

'How can I be a suspect? I wasn't there.'

'We don't know that yet.'

She let this idea expand to fill her head while she looked at her stained fingertips and considered their implication. He gave her the time it took, then said, 'Time of death with a corpse like that is pretty tough to establish. Six weeks, seven weeks, eight, what's the difference?'

'You must have checked my movements by now, my – what I told you.'

'Not yet. It takes time. We're working on it. I haven't met your sister yet. Or her daughter. Or your friend Aggie Gutteridge. That'll be interesting. You and your friends stick together, don't you? But it's not all that hard for us to sus out the liars. It's just a matter of finding out what they're lying about.'

She was tempted to remind him of the Yorkshire Ripper, or the recent case of a kidnapped baby, where police had interviewed the culprits and been completely taken in. But then he wasn't your average 'police' and they both knew it. And anyway her heart was battering so hard it blinded and deafened her. Stuck between fight and flight she could barely hear herself think, let alone argue with him.

Then he pushed up the window. The first day of spring, after the miserable windy winter of dull grey days, and the traffic noise to add to the assault and battery in her head.

'Do I need a lawyer?' she said.

'It's never a bad idea.' She didn't reply. 'I could suggest one if you like.'

She said, 'Are you going to keep me here?'

'Do you want to be kept here?'

'What?'

'At least you'd be safe.'

Yes, keep me here, put me in a cell, look after me. 'Safe?'

'I told you, it could have been meant to be you. It's funny you keep forgetting that. And anyway where will you go?'

'I'm going back to my house,' she said.

'Er, I wouldn't advise that.'

'Why?'

'It's the scene of a crime. We freeze the scene until our investigations there are complete.'

'How long will that be?'

'A few days at least – '

'Then I'm going back after that. As soon as someone has fixed the lock on my french windows.'

He folded his arms and nodded at her slowly. 'A-ha. That's already in hand.'

'And changed the lock on my front door.'

'Er . . .' He rubbed a hand through his hair. 'Not yet.'

'Why not?'

'Well, I keep saying. The person who did this has your keys.'

'You mean you want them to get in again?'

'We don't know yet what kind of crime this is. Sometimes the dog returns to its vomit.'

'And you want me to leave the place empty so they can do that?'

'Worried you won't be welcome back at your friend Ken's?'

She didn't reply.

He said, 'For the moment we've no objection if you just want to pick things up, listen to your phone messages. If you do that, do something for me: look for a heavy thing with sharp corners. Think of anything like that?'

'I can't think what it could be.'

'It wasn't a brick. That would have left dust. Something heavy and smooth with corners.'

Her mind ranged over her house, stopped on the landing outside the bathroom, wouldn't go in. She shook her head.

'Think about it.'

She nodded. He didn't say anything else. He walked to the door and opened it. Walked through it and away from her. With his back to her, going through his pass door he said, 'Think about what I said. And keep yourself available. Let me know where you do decide to stay.'

9

LOCKS AND THE LAW

A red Astra stood outside her house. A man and a woman sat in it. She thought she recognised Edgley, the policewoman from last night, but felt threatened not protected. And maybe it wasn't a police car. Maybe this was how you went mad. *And nothing is but what is not.*

But the tiny man with a shrivelled little face was certainly a locksmith. He was dressed in overalls that had once been white and were too big for him, like an unwanted baby left on her doorstep to grow old without growing up. She was glad to see him at the front door. She needn't go in alone.

They stood in the living-room facing the garden where he slid the french window back and forth. The smell was fainter but hadn't gone. Would never go?

'Dat's a noice job, dat is. Dust loike noo, badam.' The voice was lugubrious, entombed in adenoidal misery.

It was a nice job, as he said. You couldn't tell the difference. He handed her two keys. 'Dry 'em.'

As she tried them he said, again without irony, 'Can orwise 'ave some more cut if you need 'em.'

'What a good idea. I must really think about that.'

'Yur. Don' cos' mudge.'

'No, it costs hardly anything, I know.'

He handed her his bill. 'I'll 'ave cash if it's all a sime to you.'

She paid him in coin of the realm under the eyes of the police, if they were police, in the Astra. 'Dorry, id a bid bore begod id Dunday.'

'Sunday? Oh yes, so it still is.'

He murmured a sepulchral 'Fanks,' slouched to the dirty white van that matched his overalls, and drove away.

Guilt was what she felt. She felt guilty towards the house. For leaving it alone to suffer like this while she was away. There were black marks everywhere where they'd tested for fingerprints, all up the wall by the stairs. She hadn't expected to be going upstairs but found herself doing so.

39

She pushed the door of the back bedroom. It was just as she'd left it. Undisturbed.

She pushed the front room door. No bedding. All gone. She visualised her sheets in the lab, white-coated men with microscopes. Finding out who was the Goldilocks who'd been sleeping in Little Bear's bed. *Don't think about that. Don't let that inside your head.*

Then she pushed open the bathroom door. Bare. No towels, no bath mat, no bog roll. She saw rice on the carpet under the wash-basin. That was odd. She bent down. The rice moved. It wasn't rice. She flushed the full English down the loo and leaned against the basin. Found a crushed tissue in her pocket to dab her face. She looked in the mirror and for a moment didn't know which was she: this one here or that one there.

'Can I speak to someone who is involved in the investigation into the body in my house?'

It was Edgley who came on. She recognised the posh but not too posh oh so English laid-back tones. So that wasn't Edgley outside in the red car. Or was it? *That way madness lies.* 'Listen, I need a cleaner. I need someone to clean up my house. I found a – I found some – maggots – under the bathroom sink. I can't – I've never employed a cleaner, I don't know – I can't do this myself.' She hated saying that, admitting that weakness.

'I'll look into it for you. I think we'll be able to arrange something.'

'Today. Like now. Like in the next hour. I can't – I can't – '

'I'll get on to it as fast as I can.'

'Who pays? Do you pay?'

'It's you, I'm afraid.'

'Yes, that's fine. I'll pay anything. I just wondered, that's all.' Someone got killed in your house. Then the police made marks all over it and your yellow stair carpet was ruined and you paid to clean it all up and you never could clean it up, it wasn't possible. Because the real filth wasn't on the surface. It was way down deep where it couldn't be seen. *All the perfumes of Arabia . . .* They could clean the green streaks off the bath and kill the maggots on the floor but they couldn't reach down where the real filth was.

She went out of the french window, using her shiny new key, so easy to get others cut, oh yes. A handful of sparrows threw themselves into the clear bright cold clean air. They'd been feeding on the terrace. On a mound of vomit. How practical. How resourceful. That was the attitude. Waste not want not. How she yearned for the imagination of a sparrow. And its wings. Imagine just flying out of here, over the walls, over the trees, over the roofs, and away.

She wanted to telephone – somebody. The Astra was still outside with its passengers. She couldn't use her telephone. *The police have my number.*

*It's easy these days to bug a phone. And the killer has it too. The killer has my
phone number.* Then it rang.

She jumped back two feet like someone in the third act of a farce. Then
crept forward and picked it up.

'Hello?' The tone was cautious. 'Kate?'

'Oh, Aggie!' She could have burst into tears.

'What's been going on, love? I'm just back from Sheffield. When I got in
the police were here with Daniel.'

'I'm so sorry.'

'Well, it's not your fault, Kate.'

'It is. I gave your name. They asked me for a list of people who had my
keys. I was still in shock.'

'It's okay. They were nice blokes actually. But are we sort of – suspects
then?'

'I'm afraid we are.'

'Fuckin' Ada.' Aggie's throaty giggle gave Kate a jump start. There was
this thing called normal life. If you hadn't seen. Or smelled. If it wasn't
your house. 'This is a new one,' Aggie said. 'I've been accused of adultery
by my ex-husband, child neglect by my child and my ex-husband's children
and even non-payment of poll tax for a dead hamster that one of the kids
put on the form for a joke. But accessory to murder. Well, I thought I'd
heard everything.'

'Is it really funny, Ags?'

'Oh, hilarious, darlin'. Can you imagine any actress after two perform-
ances of *Medea* or *Atheist's Tragedy* which is what I've been perpetrating in
Sheffield, one of them a schoolkids' matinée, driving down the motorway
in freezing fog to kill someone in their own house? Or their best friend's
house as the case may be? And then driving back again to be fresh for the
next performance? These policemen are out of touch with real life. They
watch too much television.'

'They did think you could get out of Coventry by train after the show.'

'Well, there you are. See what I mean? And anyway we get all our sex
and violence on stage. Why would we want any more of it in real life?'

'Can I come and stay with you? I thought I could manage to stay here
but I find I can't.'

'Oh, kid, I wasn't using my imagination. Yes. Come now. Stay as long as
you like. I'll cheer you up. I'm so impressed with the interview I gave the
police I feel quite high. It was better than *Start the Week*.'

'I can't come yet. I'm waiting for a cleaner.'

'Oh, Kate, your lovely little house.'

'I don't want to be pathetic but it is a bit tough here.'

Aggie whispered, 'Do they know who it is yet? The victim, I mean.'

'If they do they're not telling me.'

'So it could be someone we know.'

'Quite.'

'Did you think it might be me?'

'No, Ags.'

'Why not?'

'She was five foot seven and thin.'

'Oh, to die for.' Aggie groaned. 'Forget I said that.'

Kate couldn't tell her what the thing had looked like, that it had been almost unrecognisable as a human body, let alone as anyone she knew. She might have trouble telling anyone ever. She began to see that such an experience put you into a kind of isolation, like being in an air crash. No one else can imagine it. No one wants to.

But in the event Kate couldn't get out. It wasn't the locks; they were fine. It was the press. It was ironic that she should be bombarded by the press not for her work but because her house was the scene of a suspicious death. They rang the door bell. They banged on the kitchen window. They called on the phone. Kate was ex-directory. Fat lot of use. As John Clements used to say, 'Never go ex-directory. All it means is that your friends can't find you but the *Daily Mail* always can.'

She took the phone off the hook. She closed the blinds on the kitchen window. She pulled the wire out of the door bell. They used the knocker instead, and shouted through the letter box. She went into the living-room at the back and sat in the corner, huddled in the big armchair. She felt like a hunted animal. How long would this go on? Hours? Days? She ought to go out and speak to them. She couldn't. And she wasn't sure that would get rid of them. She could hear their voices like starlings roosting, questioning people in the street. 'Oh, I didn't know she was an actress,' she heard a woman say. Then a voice she didn't recognise: 'Yes, we often have a chat. Just in the street, you know. You wouldn't think she was on the telly to talk to her.'

'Does she live on her own, love? Any boyfriends, that kind of thing?'

'Oh, I couldn't say, I'm sorry.'

'You must have seen people coming and going, haven't you? After all, you only live opposite.' She was Net Curtains then. The twitcher from over the road. Kate had never spoken to her in her life.

'Well, yes. In twos and threes, though. You know. I haven't noticed anyone regular.'

'Anyone off the telly come and go? Come on, you must remember.'

'Well, I mind my own business. You know. But I think I did see some bloke once I thought was in *Miss Marple*. He left with a blonde girl, though. I'm sure she was an actress. I knew her face but I couldn't place her. I've never recognised anyone else.' *Not for want of trying.*

42

'Who was this bloke from *Miss Marple* then?' *Poor old Derek. It won't take them long to get to him. I shouldn't blame them, they're only doing their job, isn't that the phrase? Do they have to do it with such relish? Do they have to hunt in a pack? Yes, yes, and yes.*

'Come on, Katy!' No one ever called her Katy. No one had ever yelled through her letter box, *there's a first time for everything.* 'You're going to have to talk to us sooner or later, love!'

At least she was safe at the back. The garden backed on to other gardens which again backed on to gardens. They'd have to get access through neighbours' houses, climb walls, to get into hers. She went to the window. And saw a creature in a padded jacket crawling over the high end wall laden with cameras. She locked the window with her new key just as he hit the flower bed and raised the camera to his eye. She closed the curtains. *Now we are really in the dark.*

She put the phone back on the hook. It rang then stopped ringing. She picked it up. She dialled the police station. She asked for John Bright. 'If I go anywhere they'll follow me. If I stay here I shouldn't be surprised if they broke the windows, came down the chimney. They're like a virus. They spread.'

'Tried talking to them? That's all they want.'

'I somehow find I can't do that.'

'It's publicity. All publicity's good publicity in your business, isn't that what they say?'

'I just found out I don't believe that.'

'A-ha.'

'That's all you can say? Can't you give me protection from this?'

'It's not our job, Muz Creech. The taxpayers wouldn't stand for it.'

'So what can I do?'

'Issue a statement.'

'How? Through the letter box?'

'I told you you needed a lawyer. Haven't you got one?'

'Only the twit that conveyanced this house for me and I wouldn't ask him. Issue a statement? It would take six months, cost three thousand pounds and fall through at least twice.'

He didn't laugh and he didn't speak. She tried not to sound desperate. 'You said you could suggest a lawyer. Was that a joke?'

'I've got to go now, I'll call you,' he said.

'You won't be able to get through, my phone's ringing all the time – ' But he'd gone.

There was just her and the darkened rooms and the smell, and the noise outside which gradually dwindled to a murmur. And the phone ringing and ringing. She picked it up in case it was John Bright and each time it wasn't John Bright and each time she put it down without speaking.

43

Then she heard a flurry outside, different from the previous noise, sparrows flocking to the vomit. She peeped through the slats of the blind. They clustered round him, so she couldn't see him well.

But she heard him say her name and 'shock' and 'for the present'. And then the beaks opened wide and the harsh cries issued forth: 'Is your client under suspicion?' *His client?* 'Do we know the identity of the victim yet?' 'Is there a description available?' 'When will Kate be able to talk to us?' She couldn't hear what he said. His back was to her. His hair was thick, coarse, greyish brown like his sweater. He was short but strong-looking. Big shoulders like a rugby winger. Neat arse, in jeans. He knocked on her door with his fist.

She let him in through a crack. He heaved the door shut with his shoulder and said, 'Hello, I'm Ted Adams, I'm a lawyer. Just come out and stand with me. I'll do the talking. Then they'll piss off and leave you alone.'

She was on a rock face, paralysed with vertigo. She said, 'I can't.'

He said, 'In one minute's time it'll be over. And they'll be gone.'

She said, 'All right.' It was high diving board stuff. She shut her eyes and went out.

She'd been right to be scared. She was food. A carcass. She'd be torn to shreds by teeth, by beaks. Ted Adams held her arm to keep her close, to keep her upright. He said she had nothing to say at present, the investigation was going on and she knew as much as they did which was very little, she'd returned home to find this shocking thing and was under treatment for shock, she'd talk to them when she was feeling better. The bulbs flashed, the machine gun cameras peppered her.

And all of a sudden they were gone. Again like a flock of birds, a mass migration. Some jumped into cars, others ran, macs flapping. Onlookers scuttled out of their path, or ran after them. Mustn't miss the next instalment. She and Ted Adams stood watching them go. 'Hey, Kate!' A flash went off, a straggler. But Adams pushed her in and had the door shut before you could say cheese.

'John Bright sent me. Hope that's okay.'

'You got rid of them.'

'Not bad, eh?' He had a hoarse voice, rough like his hair, Northern slightly smoothed out, and a face like a street kid, ready for mischief, the possibility of a joke.

'Where have they gone?'

'Round to the station to see John Bright. I told them he had a statement for them. Didn't you hear me?'

'And has he?'

'No.' His face creased up, his body folded round his laugh.

'He doesn't know they're coming?'

'No.'

44

She shook her head. 'He's going to love you.'

'Yeah.' He screwed up his face again. 'I like the air freshener. New brand? For the recluse, p'raps? How to discourage visitors.'

'Come in.' She led him to the living-room. 'The smell's not so bad back here. I couldn't even open a window while they were here. Thanks.'

He said, 'Listen, if you want to go somewhere now's the time to do it. My car's round the corner. They didn't see me arrive.'

She yearned for Aggie, the comfort and warmth of her down-at-heel kitchen and her politically incorrect cooking.

'Incidentally I'm Kate Creech.'

'You don't say? How d'you do.' His grip nearly twisted her hand off. 'Do you want me to represent you, by the way?'

'Yes.'

'How do you know?'

'You don't play rugby by any chance?' she said.

'Only on Sundays. There wasn't a game today. Too many injuries from last time. It keeps me in shape. Well, in a manner of speaking.'

'What position?'

'On the wing.'

'Like a bird.'

'Yeah!' His face creased again like a gargoyle.

'My brother was a winger.'

'Oh?'

'He looked a bit like you.'

'Yeah?'

'He died.'

He stood there a minute, face all creased up. 'I don't think this is a great method for choosing your lawyer.'

'How else do you suggest? The Yellow Pages? A blindfold and a pin?'

'Well, put like that.'

'Anyway, look at the way you dealt with the opposition.'

His face and body folded in two. 'John Bright is going to love me, you're right.'

'And you're cheerful.'

'Oh, well, that's a better reason.'

'To answer your question, it's a kind offer but wherever I go won't they find me? And if I go to my friend Aggie which is where I'd really like to go I'll be inflicting them on her. So I think I'd better stay here and learn to deal with it. The press and – everything else.'

He held a handkerchief up to his nose. 'It's up to you. But I don't see how you can even deal with the smell. Let alone the – rest of it. This place has got to be cleaned, fumigated. How can you have a bath even?'

'I've been peeing in a bucket.'

'That's what I mean.'

'A police person said she'd try and organise a cleaner.'

'I'll make sure they do.'

'I don't know what to do.'

'Why do it the hard way?'

'I don't know!'

'Will your friend – Aggie is it – mind?'

'No, she's invited me. Also my car's at her place.'

'Well, what are you waiting for?'

'It seems so weak to go, not to stay here and face it.'

'So be weak. What's so terrible?'

She stood doubtful.

He put on a breathy earnest transatlantic voice. 'Sometimes you know, Katie, it's strong to be weak.'

She gave a breath that was nearly a laugh. She squeezed a look round the edge of the curtain. Padded Jacket was still on the wall. He looked frozen, his camera between his knees. He saw the tiny movement and put the camera to his eye. She said, 'Okay. Let's go.'

10

HOME FROM HOME

His car was a Saab, quiet and comfortable. 'Unlike mine,' she said, 'it's got room for human legs.'

'What is yours?' he said, polite. As if he felt awkward now they were in the car.

'A Beetle. Looks like it's been a few rounds. I've had it for ever. It was my brother's so I can never get rid of it even if I could afford something else. Daniel, Aggie's son, works on it for me. He's crazy about cars. That's why it's at their place. Something goes wrong with the electrics just when you need it. It refused to take me to Coventry. I should have listened to it. It was right.' It felt good to be weak, looked after, driven about. She said, 'You wouldn't like to be my chauffeur as well?'

'Sorry, guv, a bit busy with the day job.' He let a scruffy Rascal truck out of a side road then moved fast to stop a Jaguar taking advantage. 'They're a tough bunch,' he said. 'The gentlemen of the press.'

'You feel an idiot, being so petrified.'

'Thought actresses fancied all that. Picture in the papers.'

'I thought so too. Only it seems to depend what for.'

He nodded, zoomed round a bus before it left the stop, across the lights at Camden Road just as they changed.

'But I don't want them to turn me into a fugitive.'

'Yeah, but you shouldn't be on your own. And you know what? You are suffering from shock.'

'Am I?'

'Yeah.'

'Can you draft me the things I should say to them?'

'Sure.' He braked to let a girl cross the traffic with a baby buggy. 'Silly cow,' he said.

'Me?'

'Her, but if the cap fits.' He looked at Kate. 'John Bright says you're withholding information.'

'Oh, I see. Let me out of this car.'

'If you'd like to wait till it stops moving. Traffic's a bit thick in this three-lane race track, even on Sunday. Never like to lose a client that way, especially on the Sabbath. And till I drop you can I say a few things?' He glanced at her stony profile. 'I've got to say these things. As your lawyer, which I'll pretend I am till you get out of the car. Withholding information from the police is not a good idea. It's like with the press. You say nothing, you look guilty.'

'I haven't done anything except leave my house to go away to work – '

'Not a question of what you've done. Question of how it looks. Bright says there's someone you're not mentioning to him.'

'So he sends his lackey. Soften her up.'

'What you say to me is confidential.'

'Yeah?'

'Until you give me permission to repeat it.'

'Yeah.'

'He says you know someone who fits the description of the woman in the bath. And you won't say. Now why won't you say? If it is the woman you think it is, then she's dead. If she's dead, why wouldn't you want to say who she is? There's an obvious implication of course.'

Kate put an elbow against her window, leaned her cheek on her fist. 'Yeah?'

'That if you know who the woman is you have a good idea who might have killed her. And you want to protect that person.'

The traffic had slowed but she wasn't making any jumping out gestures. Just gazing out sideways as though Dillon's bookshop was the most fascinating thing in the world. She made a big heavy sigh, clasped her hands in her lap and lowered her head on to them.

He said, 'Think about it.'

She thought about it all the way to the Aldwych then she sat up and

47

leaned her head back against the head-rest. She felt tense as a tightrope. They were crossing the river. She turned her head towards the irresistible beauty of St Paul's. Then, passing the National Theatre, she made a decision. 'There is one person actually. That it could be. We – we've been out of touch for a while. She kind of moved off into the New Age scene. It's not for me, that stuff; sweat lodges, brown rice, communities on top of mountains. Last I heard it was some kind of commune in Wales. Look, she's – she fits the description.'

'Of the woman in the bath.'

'She's thin and tall and she's always worried about these few grey hairs just here, in the front. She never used to dye them but – ' Kate put her hand over her mouth then took it away. 'The thing is, she has my keys. I always said to her my home is yours because I was always worried she'd end up on the skids, I don't know why. I always wanted her to know there was somewhere she could go. I'd badly wronged her once and – So you see, I'm scared to ring her. I'm scared to find out. I don't even want to say her name in my head in case – I'm just so scared.'

'Give me the number, I'll do it.'

She pulled a battered Filofax out of her bag. She didn't open it. 'What you find out – '

'Anything I find out I have to disclose. I mean to you. I have to persuade you to disclose it to the police. You understand that. If the information is relevant, could be relevant to – '

'But you'd tell me first. I have to know first.'

'Of course. I'm your mouthpiece. I'm your glove puppet. I'm your Spitting Image.' His face did have that rubbery quality, twisting itself into grotesqueries, but he couldn't make her smile.

Her hands had made sweat marks on the cover of the Filofax. She tore a page from the notes section and wrote down a number. She didn't have to look it up, she'd done that already. She said, 'Her name's Tess. Tess Harbour.' It was no easement, saying her name. Now she was going to discover the worst. *If I haven't already discovered it.*

'Good,' he said.

'Don't give me grades. There's nothing good about any part of this.'

He turned his face, twisting it up. 'Sorry, I'll climb back down my hole. If you could just give me some directions first. This side of the river's a foreign country to me, I don't speak the language.' He went into cringe posture. 'Sorry. Honestly.'

He was just like her brother. In better days he could have made her laugh. She said, 'You take the next left. It's one of the big semi-detacheds at the end. The one with the peeling paint and the wrecked motor bike in the garden.'

He wouldn't come into Aggie's. He said, 'So if it did turn out to be your friend Tess . . .'

She scratched her forehead. Her fingers shook.

'. . . you'd know who might have had a reason to kill her, that right?'

He leaned back in fright at the face she turned to him. 'I don't. How could I? I don't know anyone she knows. She moved off into a world of freaks and head cases and charlatans. I just can't bear to find out that she's – '

He held up his hands in a cool it cool it gesture.

'I'm just scared that it's her,' she said. 'I thought I'd explained that.'

'I must have been concentrating on my driving at that point.' He dropped his hands. She gave him the piece of paper with the number. He said, 'I'll get them to see about the cleaner.' Kate said she was sorry and he said, 'I know you are.'

She didn't like seeing him drive off. She felt bereft.

11

A FRIEND IN NEED

Aggie's kitchen was a womb, that moist warmth that only comes from an Aga. Daniel, her big son, looked up out of the side of his eyes, said, 'Hi, Kate,' thought about saying something else, stopped, said, 'Your car's ready,' and put his face back into a comic.

'Thanks, Dan.'

Aggie said, 'Well, you look appalling.'

'Appalled, I think, is the word.'

'Give me that bag. And sit.' She pulled out an old half-stripped kitchen chair. 'Now drop your head. Look at you, you can hardly even move that neck.' Aggie dug her thumbs into the flesh between the shoulder blades. 'What have you got in there, iron filings? What's happened to your Alexander Technique? Breathe! You're an actress, for Christ's sake! Breathe out!'

Kate breathed out and said, 'My God, that's a new experience.'

'I feel like a midwife. I've introduced you to the experience of breathing. My good deed for the day. I'd like a coffee now. Come on, Daniel, put the kettle on.'

Daniel groaned and unfolded himself, shambled into the scullery.

The smell of coffee was amazing. Kate said, 'It's true, I have just been born, into a different world.'

Aggie took croissants out of a cupboard: 'Want yours hot?' and put them in the oven. 'Go on now, Daniel. Take your homework upstairs.' She dangled the wham-pow comic in front of him.

He said, 'That's valuable research for my combined English and Art project. Honestly.'

'Ha!'

He took the comic. 'See you later, Kate. Let me know when you finish the girl talk, okay?'

'Piss off, Daniel.'

Kate tried to tell Aggie how it was but knew she wasn't conveying the horror. Again she had that cut-off feeling. Separate from the human race.

Aggie said, 'You'll have to sell your house.'

'Who'd buy it?'

'No one you'd want to sell it to.'

'Quite.'

'Stay here till the cleaners have been in and the shock's faded a bit.'

'Yes, then maybe I could shut the bathroom up, never enter it again.'

'God, Kate. Skeletons would clank in there.'

It wasn't skeletons she feared, it was fleshy white balloons floating and bumping softly in the dark, leaving trails of red and green slime where they touched. She couldn't say that.

'Stay here anyway. We don't mind a few reporters. God knows I've been waiting all my life. "Kate Creech? Yes, she's my best friend actually. I've known her since *Six Characters in Search of an Author* at Sheffield in 1979. A popular little piece. I'm referring to the play not Kate. I mean, she's popular but I would never refer to a fellow female actress as a piece – "'

'Either I was meant to be the victim, this is what they think; or I'm the killer.'

That shut Aggie up. She made a mask of tragedy. She covered her mouth with her hand. Then she started to laugh. Her flesh shook all over. 'Well, look, it's pathetic, isn't it? It's ludicrous.'

'So what do you think the answer is?'

She stopped laughing. 'I don't know. Which would you rather be?'

'The killer, no question.'

'Hm. A wise choice, I think.' Aggie's Viennese psychiatrist voice. 'Well, stay here anyway. I've never had a murderer in the house before, it'll be a new experience. 'Yes.' Her hushed intimate microphone voice. 'She stayed here just after her first murder. And you'd never have known. She seemed just like anyone else. Still brushed her teeth and washed her tights at night. Amazing really. The only suspicious thing was the way she wandered about in her sleep wringing her hands, saying – '

'Now, no, Aggie. Enough.'

'Not superstitious, are you, love?'
'I quote that damn play enough in my head. Don't do it aloud.'

'It's Ted Adams?' Kate must have dropped into a short deep sleep on Aggie's sofa, because Aggie was now waving a phone under her nose to wake her up. 'You want to speak to him?'
'The commune's not there any more,' he said. 'They don't know what happened to any of the people. All I've got is a contact number for one of the women who ran it. It's not her number, it's her mother's. It's a London number.'
'What's the woman's name?'
'Varya?' he said.
'You might well sound unbelieving. It was Vera till she became an aromatherapist.'
'You know her, then.'
'I met her once.'
'Sounds as though once was enough.'
'You got it. For both of us, I think. Two topics of conversation: healing and money. If you strayed off into a really esoteric subject such as the arts or politics, she sat with a patient tolerant smile waiting for you to return to the serious stuff.'
'You really liked her, then.'
'Yeah. Just my type. A suburban housewife with delusions of grandeur.'
'How come a friend of yours was – is – also a friend of hers?'
'I don't know. She had some dark influence over Tess. I couldn't work it out. Once people get into all that mystery and magic stuff, a neat simple answer to everything in the universe – '
'You don't believe in mystery and magic?'
'Of course I do. But these people appropriate it, they're its self-appointed high priests. All the answers. No doubts. And they dole it out to gullible people. For money. They're mystery and magic fascists. The Mussolinis of magic.'
'Okay,' he said.
'Okay, what?'
'Okay I agree.'
'Now she'd be capable of . . .'
'Don't stop. What were you going to say?'
'Forget it. Find Tess for me.'
'Doing my best.'
'I know. I'm sorry. I'm grateful. You woke me from a weird doze.'
He gave her the number for 'Varya's' mother, but sitting dazed with the phone in her hand she thought of Ken. He didn't know yet she'd decided

to stay at Aggie's. She was afraid to speak to him. Hoped to get the answering machine but got him.

'Ken?' Silence. 'Ken, it's me!' She could hear his breathing, a flutter, like someone trying not to cry. 'Ken?'

He said at last, 'They've taken Michael in for questioning.'

'Oh no.'

'They've had him there five hours.' He started to cry in big gulps. 'The thing is Michael used to deal a bit of dope. Nothing heavy but he was in that world, you know? He did time. When he was eighteen. He never told me before. Only six months but he's got a record. He hasn't been involved in any of that for years. Five years. He's doing a catering course!' Ken laughed making a shaky noise then blew his nose. 'Did you have to tell them I had your keys?'

Kate felt ill. 'It's possibly a murder, Ken.'

'Yeah, but Michael hasn't committed a murder. Oh Christ, how can I get him out of there? What if they're knocking him about? You know what they're like. They hate us. And the prettier you are the more they like to duff you up.'

Kate gave him Ted Adams's number. 'He seems a good bloke,' she said. 'He'll find you somebody.'

'Why did Michael lie to me?'

'He was scared you'd stop loving him.'

'I can't stand being lied to. I told him that from the start.'

'Call Ted.'

'Er, Kate? Your car keys.' Daniel sheepishly handed them to her.

'Dan, you're an angel.'

'Done your homework, Angel?'

Daniel rose to his great height and sighed. 'Mum, I never thought I'd have to say this but you could get to be a bore, you know that?'

'Even car mechanics need to be able to do joined-up writing.' Aggie whacked a tea towel at his departing back.

Kate put her elbows in the crumbs on the table and her head in her hands.

'Kate, this business might have nothing to do with you.'

'Already they've got Michael in for questioning. Next it could be Dan. See how you feel about it then.'

'Well, my Daniel didn't go and murder some woman in your bath, did he? So he's got nothing to fear.'

'I thought Ken had nothing to fear. Now he doesn't know if he can ever believe Michael again.'

'Well, he ought to have more sense. If he loves him he should trust him.'

'He's only known him a few months.'

'Well . . .' Aggie sounded unconvinced. 'Maybe that's different.'

'I can only see how easy it is for trust to disappear. I can't trust anything any more.'

'What, not even Dan and me?'

Kate didn't say yes and she didn't say no. The skin of Aggie's face seemed to tremble a moment. 'Kate.'

'See what I mean?' Kate stood up. 'There's someone I've got to see.'

'You've got to leave that stuff to the police.'

'Me first.'

'Are you trying to protect someone? Because that could get other people into a lot of trouble, Kate. My Daniel for instance.'

'It's someone who might know something she wouldn't tell the police. I've got to ask her a few questions before they get to her. I'll be back tonight.'

'Oh, right, in that case I'll give you the keys.' Aggie had recovered. 'Have a nice hot bath when you come in.' She laughed. 'Don't lose your sense of humour, Kate.'

'Oh, Ags, remind me. What sense of humour was that?'

12

ON THE SCENT

Ted Adams was right, South of the River was a foreign country. It made her depressed. Those endless lines of roofs. All those people in all those houses in all those streets. All their lives. All their deaths. It made her want to howl.

Number thirteen. Naturally. It would be. Cabalistic signs outside and those circles of dusty stained glass hanging in the window. The front garden was a mess. In the thicket of dead thistles and bearded rose bay willow herb Kate saw the rusted remains of a toy pram.

Vera opened the door. She wore an embroidered band round her forehead and an Indian cotton frock from the seventies. She wore too her smug unseeing smile till Kate said hello; then Vera saw her and the smile stopped. 'Oh. Kate. Your lawyer phoned me. Come in.' She swayed along the dusty hallway, barefoot on the bare boards. Kate followed into a sunny room with a massage table and a lot of earnest slogans on the walls: *You*

Can Heal Your Life; Find Your Sun Inside You; Let Your Sun Shine Out. The back garden contained a sort of tepee and more dead thistles, tangled in the brown tentacles of a rampant bramble.

'Your lawyer wanted to know where Tess was,' Vera said.

'Where is she?'

'I don't know.' She saw Kate's face. 'It's the truth. I've been meditating. I've been sending messages. She's usually a really strong presence, you know? But I just can't feel her. I'm just getting this big absence. It's weird.'

'When did you last see her?'

'After the Welsh commune broke up she and I started this place in Glastonbury because two ley lines crossed exactly where it was built. Only we found that the male and female forces in the place were just in too much conflict, it was so bad the building was actually developing these big cracks. The conflict was of earthquake force. So the place had to break up.' She sighed.

'When was that?'

'Over a year ago. Nothing heavy. It was all meant to be. The cosmic cycle was complete, you know?'

Kate sighed. She was getting tired of the breathy one-note voice. 'Where did Tess go afterwards?'

'She didn't say.'

'You had no idea?'

'It was her life, you know?'

'She went to that Welsh commune because of you. Presumably she started this Glastonbury place for the same reason. You were close, weren't you?'

'Oh yeah. But you know love is a source of energy. Its glow has to spread around. Concentrating love in one person is a kind of disease. Tess has a tendency to do that which she hasn't worked through yet.'

'She was jealous? That what you're saying?'

'Well, yeah ... I like to welcome many people into my aura. I realised Tess had a problem with that. She had to work that through or leave.'

'But she sold up, didn't she, burnt her boats, to set up that Welsh place with you?'

'We pooled our resources, yes, both spiritual and financial.'

'For the Glastonbury place too?'

'Yeah, well, I don't want to speak ill of anyone, but when the place had to break up Tess got really heavy about having her share back again.'

'Did she get her share back again?'

'Well, some. But, you know? It was a tough time. A period of transition. A new era had to be birthed.'

Kate looked round the treatment room. It was clean and smart compared with the outside of the house and the hallway. 'You own this place?'

54

'Yes, I do.' Vera's smile was benign.

'So you got your share.'

'Now please. You must be calm. The energy in this room is a healing energy. Be open to it.'

'If you still owe Tess money you must be in touch with her. You must at least know where she is.' The foolishness of this idea struck her as she spoke: if Vera owed you money, in touch was the last thing she'd be.

'I last saw her at the Glastonbury festival. But the size of the crowd, you know? I couldn't get near to speak with her.'

'I bet you couldn't. Was she with anyone?'

'She seemed to be alone.'

'When was this?'

'The festival?' She rounded her eyes at Kate's ignorance, revealing the edges of her startling blue contact lenses. 'The summer solstice of course.'

'Of course.' *June? July?* 'About eight months ago?'

Vera lowered her head graciously and swept her eyelids down over the light-bulb eyes. 'Now you'll have to forgive me, I'm expecting a client. I thought you were she. The work of healing is never-ending. There is so much disease in the world.'

'Vera – '

'Varya. That's my name.' The gracious smile.

Kate gritted her teeth: forget the battle; go for the war. 'Varya,' she said, 'it's very important that I find out where Tess is. I can't tell you how important. You must have read the reports about what happened in my house – '

'I don't read newspapers. When you are tuned in to the eternal you lose the attachment to ephemera.'

Kate swallowed and gave a brief run-down of recent events. It appeared Vera really hadn't known. Her pale freckled skin seemed to tighten.'You believe this – dead person – might be Tess?' She focused her bright blue eyeballs on some inner space for a moment then refocused and said without obvious concern, 'This could be the reason that I have been getting a sense of absence. I shall concentrate and if anything comes through I will contact you.'

Though she might be thinking of making contact by some esoteric act of spiritual communication, Kate gave her Aggie's number. 'Or call Ted Adams,' she said.

Vera said, 'Of course,' in an unctuous breathy voice. On the doorstep she put her palms together Indian-style over the paper with the phone numbers on it and bowed her head. Kate said, 'Yeah,' and walked down the path.

She walked, to get rid of the over-sweet smell of incense that clung to her clothes, her skin. She came upon a vast grey space: overpasses, underpasses, a multi-storey car-park, a shopping mall of concrete and glass, the howl of traffic, not a person in sight, and darkness coming down. Croydon, like Coventry, seemed the result of an accident of war. She imagined blackened deformed creatures creeping out of holes but she saw only a charming Indian family who smiled at her. The rest of the population was still sleeping off Sunday lunch.

She got in the car and sat there, hands on the steering wheel, banging her head on her hands. She lifted her head and stared emptily at the bleak street. *Oh God – I've never been alone like this.* Her head began to expand and contract with fear, a sensation like pins and needles in the brain. *One of my friends has betrayed me, has used me, has killed – Stop this, cool it. What have I got? I've got Glastonbury. If Tess had no money then maybe she stayed around there, nowhere else to go. Like me now: can't go to Ken's, I've screwed up his life; stay away from Aggie's so's not to screw up hers; can't go home, all the perfumes of Arabia will not sweeten this little house.* So she started the car. First time, thanks to Daniel. And headed for the M4. She stopped only once before the motorway, to get the maximum cash out of a hole in the wall. *Ah, modern technology.*

This sure as hell wasn't the summer solstice: a bitter slanting sleet swirled across deserted streets. She had to find somewhere to stay. Somewhere cheap. On the road out to Shepton Mallet a sign said *BedNBreakfast*, a light in the darkness. She parked the car and rang the bell.

A drooping wet mouth with a damp cigarette. He grunted, then wheezed up the stairs ahead of her. His hand on the banister rail was yellow, misshapen, the nails thick and brown like something out of the sea.

There was an odd smell. Her olfactory sense had altered, so that all smells were now forceful, invasive. The chief elements of this one were bacon fat and drains. She tried not to inhale.

He opened a brown door on the dark landing. The room wasn't so bad. The furniture was British 1950s, stuff no one but a landlord could love. But a big window looked out on the hills. He told her it would be fifteen quid for the night. 'Breakfast seven to 'alf-past eight.' She thought she'd give breakfast a miss.

When he'd shuffled off – she christened him The Mortal Coil – she opened the window and drank the icy air like spring water. She pulled back the bedclothes. The sheets were clean and were not nylon; things were looking up. She left the window open when she lay down. Feeling cold distracted her from the images that assaulted her when she closed her eyes.

13

BRIGHT ON MONDAY

'Hear our chief suspect's done a runner, guv.'

  'Disappeared, has she, sir?'

  'You're kidding? No one knows where she is?'

  'How'd we lose her, guv?'

Bright was weary. He'd gone back to his ma's in South Norwood last night. Had to look in on her once a week. Even after a weekend like this. Now it was Monday morning, time for the big chief to show his team he's on the ball but, because every major road in North London is being dug up, and because his heart's not in it, he's late.

  'Where d'you think she's gone, guv?'

He ignored the grins criss-crossing the table, sat down to fill them in. His team. The neat little sergeant in the corner. Barton his name was, so they called him Dick. Then DC Dai Gwylim. Naturally called Taff. Big lad, short back and sides, got on with the job, nice, clean, correct. Then Atkins, a mean crafty little East Ender, make a better crook than a copper. Called Tommy, why ask? Then The Cat, Cato, stinking out the place with his pansy little pipe.

He introduced Edgley. 'Constable Edgley's been seconded to us for this investigation as a trainee.' Sidelong looks, gender assessment mingled with resentment: the only uniforms who got to be trainee CID these days had a double first from Oxford or a dad who was a chief inspector. 'You'll be okay with us, love.' Atkins winked. Edgley sat there, straight-backed, po-faced. More sidelong looks, deciding she was a pain. Bright had already discovered this. He would decide in the course of the meeting whom to assign her to this morning.

  'We know where Kate Creech was last seen. Croydon. The Croydon woodentops sighted her car. Parked in a residential neighbourhood. Only, when she turned up she did not get into her car, she decided to go for a little stroll and they decided to follow her in their vehicle. She returned to her car by a back lane where their car couldn't go and when they found her parking place again, her car had left it and so had she. If you want a thing done right, do it yourself.' More sideways looks: they thought he was too hands-on, didn't delegate, didn't sit on his arse filling in forms letting them have the fun. They were right. 'The papers have got her picture, you'll have seen it this morning, and – '

Low whistles and the usual remarks, cruder than usual for Edgley's benefit. She sat without expression. She would.

' – and a description of her car, a dilapidated VW Beetle. The Croydon uniforms owe us one now. They're doing a house-to-house in the streets round where Creech's car was parked. Someone may have seen where she went.'

'What's your theory, sir?'

'Well, Niki, I think she's gone looking for someone. I think she's upset about getting her friends involved with the police so she's gone to find this someone before we do. *Muz* Creech has decided to pursue her own investigation. She doesn't trust us coppers. She's withholding information. Thinks she knows who the victim is and won't say. Thinks she knows the perpetrator and even more won't say.'

'Haven't we got Creech as the perpetrator, guv?' They all nodded at that. Obvious, wasn't it?

'How's her statement check out, Barton?'

'It checks out, guv. People at the theatre say she didn't go anywhere after that first weekend.'

'The whole damn company of that play she was in will have to be questioned.'

'They'll be scattered all over the country by now, sir.'

'Challenge for you, Barton.'

Barton groaned. 'Yes, sir. The ones I've managed to talk to say she was definitely ill when she was in that play. I don't know why she didn't get a doctor's note and have some time off but anyway she didn't.'

'The show must go on, guv. Isn't that right?' Cato, smirking.

One of these days he'd flatten that little poser's face.

'She could've driven to London at night, couldn't she?' Atkins said. 'Who'd have known? 'S not a long drive.'

'Her car was out of action, Tommy.'

'That's what she said.'

'She could have hired.'

'Check the car hire firms.'

'Could have hitched, got a lift.'

'She could have had an accomplice. Borrowed a car.' Holmes again, the great detective, puffing on his meerschaum.

Barton looked at Bright. Bright raised an eyebrow. Barton said, 'Doesn't look like it. Only one she'd have asked is the queer bloke, Ken.'

'And he won't be lying for her now his boyfriend's been done over.'

'Not likely, is it?'

'No, but we can't rule it out completely. That she could have had help.'

Barton sighed. 'Right, guv.'

'Seems to me, guv, maybe we shouldn't rule her out too early.' Gwylim, false deference.

'I haven't ruled her out, Taff. I haven't ruled her out as the intended victim either. I want the names and whereabouts of her former boyfriends. And I want the murder weapon. The uniforms are doing a house-to-house and a garden check. Nothing yet. I want her house searched again today. Her friend Aggie Gutteridge might know where she is. Might know who she went to see in Croydon. Try to shake down her son. Daniel, his name is. He's seventeen, bound to have been up to something he won't want us to know about. You get on to that, Taff.'

Going through all this stuff he was thinking about who to take along as his partner. Decided the only one he could stand was Cato. At least he was a character; these other lads could have been under-managers in a supermarket. He also had to offload Edgley. 'Right,' he said, 'Atkins, you'll be working with Constable Edgley.' He looked round the table. More side-mouth smiles. No Atkins. 'Where is he?'

'Oh, Tommy went to the bog, guv. You'll find he's gone in the car with The Cat.' Gwylim, looking bland. 'They're partners, guv. Always work together.'

Stuck with Edgley. They'd scuppered him.

Bright didn't speak to her in the car. She knew the way they felt about her, it had been clear enough in her first job and it wouldn't get better till she was higher up the ladder and dealing out the snakes. She had the brains and one day she'd have the clout. She didn't even ask where they were going. Wouldn't give him the satisfaction.

He glided in and out of the Monday morning traffic as though on wings, relaxed, not even thinking. They turned into Westbourne Grove. He rang the bell on a door next to a shop. The small homosexual from yesterday opened it. Not in black leather now, T-shirt and jeans showing the perfection of his body. He looked terrified when he saw Bright, backed away down the hall.

'It's all right, Michael. We haven't come to arrest you. Take it easy. Your friend in?' He went lightly up the stairs after the boy. Edgley shut the door and followed them.

The big dark one stood in the middle of the room, his face rigid, his arms folded across his chest. The sofa was littered with clothes and small objects, an alarm clock, a shaver. A suitcase lay open on the floor.

'Someone going somewhere?'

The big one didn't even look at Bright. Michael said, 'I'm leaving.'

'No need for that, is there, Ken?'

Again, Ken made no response. Bright shrugged. 'Okay, Michael. Now before you go perhaps you can tell me something. Who does Kate Creech know who lives in Croydon?'

Michael looked bewildered. 'Croydon?'

'Ken?'

Ken frowned. 'How would I know?'

'No idea who she went to see there?'

'No.'

'Ever meet any of Kate's boyfriends, Michael?'

Michael gave Ken a quick look. No response from Ken. Michael shook his head.

Ken said, 'Why are you asking him? I'm the one who knows Kate; he doesn't.'

'Well, Ken, perhaps you can help me: do you know any of Kate's boyfriends, or ex-boyfriends?'

'The only one I know is Oliver and he was years ago.'

When Ken said Oliver, Michael turned his head away quick. Edgley saw Bright's eyes go into that strange unfocused squint.

'So you know Oliver, Michael?'

'I think I met him once, didn't I, Ken?'

Ken didn't look at him. 'You might have. He's been here once or twice.'

'Does he live in Croydon, Ken?' Bright's nasal rasp could get soft as a cooing dove.

Ken stared at a point on the rug, his arms still folded over his chest. 'I don't know where he lives. I bump into him here and there, that's all. I don't even have his phone number.'

'I think Michael could tell us a bit more than that. Couldn't you, Michael?'

Michael looked at Ken, got no help, shook his head. 'No. N-no. How could I?'

Bright sighed. 'Okay, we'll get him through *Spotlight*. *Spotlight* is a big book full of actors' pictures, constable, and the names of their agents. Ken is surprised I know that, aren't you, Ken? Haven't got an old copy round the place, have you?'

'Why don't you just ask Kate? She'll know where Oliver lives.'

Bright ignored this. 'What's his second name?'

'Broome. With an E.'

Bright nodded. 'Come on, Edgley.' At the door he turned. 'Be seeing you, Michael. Don't kick him out, Ken. Maybe I'll need to talk to him again.'

14

ON THE RUN

She avoided the breakfast but not its smell, seeping under the closed brown doors. She put three fivers into the misshapen hand, avoiding its touch. The thick brown nails scraped up the notes, scrunching them into a pocketable lump.

The air, colder even than yesterday, gave her a frosty welcome. She wondered if she might have to eschew 'indoors' for ever, spending her days as a woman of the roads. However, she pushed open the door of the *Wellcome Café, Breakfast, Lunch, And Tea.*

The windows were steamed up. At the next table thick brown tea came out of a thick brown pot. She ordered coffee. And waited, elbows on the red formica.

Someone had left a newspaper on the next seat. She picked it up and unfolded it. Her face stared at her. Her *Spotlight* picture, simpering at the camera with a three-year-old hairstyle. Nothing like her but recognisable. *Where Is She?* the headline demanded in bold black lettering above.

She got pins and needles in the head again. *They've all seen me, seen my face, read the article –* She raised her head, looked round, met an eye or two. No shocks of dawning recognition, nobody looked twice. *That's how recognisable I am. No wonder I never got famous.*

Shock had revealed a yawning hunger. She changed her order to 'full English breakfast' and read what was printed under her face. *Actress Kate Creech (36), five foot seven, with long dark hair, has disappeared without letting her friends or the police know her whereabouts. She is probably driving a yellow Volkswagen Beetle, a distinctive car, registration number . . .*

Why didn't I think? But I can't dump the car. There's no other way to get where I may have to go. I'll have to risk it. Damn! She shovelled the bacon and eggs and even the toast and marmalade into the void inside her. Comfort equals cholesterol.

She read the article over a second cup of coffee, paid and left, tucking the paper under her arm. Nobody leapt up to accost her. No vengeful mob chased her down the street. But she felt pursued just the same. She had to trace Tess quick. But she didn't know where to start. *Think Tess. I'm Tess. I'm the New Age magic and mystery Tess. My commune has closed down, I'm near enough penniless, destitute. Where do I go? There were two people Tess would go to, the Tess I knew: Nat and me. And Nat's in America. Why didn't she come to me?* Nat. She'd said his name. *That way danger lies.* She'd allowed his name into her head.

She saw a police car cruising slowly down the road towards her. The only shelter was a public phone. She turned her back to the police car, picked up the phone, stuck some money in, dialled a number at random. A male voice answered. She hadn't expected a reply. She said, 'Hello, I wonder if you've heard of this marvellous opportunity. We are giving away ten time-share apartments in Marbella. The apartments have a large lounge and three bedrooms with a gorgeous terrace overlooking the sea – ' The voice said, 'Fuck off.' She shifted her head minutely to search the street. The police car was out of view. She said, 'That's a very good idea. I'll follow your advice. Have a nice day.'

She dared not go back to the car. Not yet. This was crazy. Wandering round Glastonbury with nothing to do. It was like being on tour, when the days stretch bleakly until the show at night. The digs are terrible, you've seen the local movie three times, you drink so much after the show you're always hung over, so much coffee to cure the hangover you start speeding and can't sleep . . .

She turned a corner. No police car, but over the road a row of small shops, two of them closed down, stuck all over with posters for local gigs, one second-hand clothes shop with a filthy window. And a shop selling incense, tie-dyed flimsy cotton tops, bell-bottomed maroon velvet trousers, crystals, tarot cards, hash pipes. She crossed the road.

It smelled like Vera's place, sickly incense disguising incipient damp and dirt. Out of the dim light at the back a lissom lad appeared, wavy hair to the waist. He stroked the hair away from his eyes and said, 'Hi?' in a wispy voice.

Kate said, 'There used to be a sort of commune here. Just for women and their children. A semi-detached house in Franklin Street. I wonder if – '

'Oh yes! The Rainbow House. They painted a rainbow on the front. The neighbours complained.'

'They would.'

'Yeah.' He smiled.

She smiled back. 'I don't suppose you knew any of the women from there?'

'Well, they came in here, you know?'

'Oh yes?'

'You know, for essential oils, candles, stuff like that . . .'

He was getting evasive, looking dreamily into the distance, like he was pondering the sunrise; only, she knew he was wondering who she was, why she was asking. She might as well get to the point. 'Did you know Tess Harbour?' she said.

'Tess Harbour . . .'

'Looked a bit like me. From a distance. A little bit older. And beautiful, but about my height. Thin, with long dark hair that went into ringlety things.'

'Oh, was that Tess Harbour?'

'You know her?'

'Well, I saw her, yeah. I used to go to the aromatherapist at the Rainbow. Varya. She was quite influential in my life actually for a while. And – Tess? – used to be around. She seemed sad, you know? I used to feel a kind of negative energy around her.'

'Do you have any idea where she went when the commune broke up?'

He hesitated, moved stuff from place to place on the counter. He said, 'Why do you want to know?' without looking at her.

'It's okay. I'm a friend of hers. I've been away and we've lost touch. I'm worried about her.' But he'd withdrawn, like the head of a tortoise, into his shell. 'Look, please, I'm not a debt collector or anything. I'm a friend. She was my closest friend before she went into that commune. I'd never do anything to harm her. I'm afraid something's happened to her.'

He seemed to be examining her aura or something with his eyes closed. She waited. He opened his eyes slowly. 'All right,' he said.

'You mean you know where she is?'

'I only know where she went. There's this caravan site. It's full at festival time, pretty empty in the winter. But there's always a few vans. She went there. I heard she was broke, and that's the cheapest way to live if you've got no bread.'

'What about her kids?'

'She has kids? I never saw her with any kids.'

The car was still there. And there was nobody about. Or so it seemed. Anyway, she had to take the risk, it was too far to go on foot. *Please start. Just please start first time. Please don't get up to your tricks on me, not now. Oh, thank the heavens for Daniel.* The comforting familiar noise of the old VW engine. But till she was on the main road with nothing behind her but an old truck she expected to be accosted, accused, sirens, handcuffs. *This is me? I'm a fugitive! I'm on the bloody run!* She let the old truck pass her, saw the sign for the caravan site, checked in her mirror, no one behind, and turned in. The Beetle bounced over the frozen ruts.

One caravan stood alone in the field. Rust licked along its every join and chewed the edges of its door. Dead silence all around. Her friend in the New Age boutique would have said negative energy in a big way. Kate knocked. The silence intensified. She knocked again.

The van began to heave as though a huge animal had woken and was lurching about inside. Something pushed at the door and pushed again. At last the door surged open, forcing her back off the step. The huge animal stood there, hair all over, bushy, coarse and black, just small round eyes and a big nose visible in the bush. A complexity of smells came with him, the chief component stale cannabis. He was dressed in a thick green sweater and green cords. He was the Green Man.

'Yuh?' A hoarse grunt. He wasn't used to human speech or she'd woken him or both.

'I, er – Tess. I'm trying to find Tess Harbour. She lived here for a while, I believe, after the – the Rainbow Commune – '

'Uh. Yuh.'

'You know her?'

'Yuh.'

'She's not here now, I suppose.' Stating the obvious, she smiled.

'Nuh.'

'No. Do you have any idea where she went?'

'Why uh wunna nuh?'

They were all so suspicious, these people. Now, with her small experience of police intrusion, she didn't blame them.

'She's an old friend.' She told the same story, the truth, though felt she was lying. Why was that? *When you use the truth for a purpose, it becomes a lie?*

'Uh-huh.' Out of the beard came forth a word she vaguely recognised.

'Did you say Oulton?' she said.

'Ou'ton. Yuh. Woman nime Aura.'

'A woman called Aura? In Oulton?'

'Mm.'

'You wouldn't happen to have an address?'

'Nuh.'

'Thanks anyway.'

'Uh.'

He watched her make her self-conscious way back to the Beetle, tottering over the iron-hard ridges of mud. She waved as she drove off. He didn't respond, just stood in his doorway, slowly scratching his hairy stomach under the green jumper.

15

BRIGHT GETS A BREAK

'How'd he seem?'

'In what way, sir?'

'Any way you like.'

'He's thirty-eight.'

'He look it?'

'No. He looks younger.'

'How much?'

'Oh. Well. I suppose I might have thought thirty-five but his – demeanour – is younger than that.'

'Demeanour, ha?' She didn't go on so he said, 'What about pulling-power? Fancy him, did you?' He glanced at her. She presented a stony profile. 'Okay,' he said, 'go on.'

She took her time, getting her notebook out of her bag. Her notebook. She said, 'I gathered he's not very successful as an actor.'

'Why not?'

'Perhaps because he's not very good, sir.' She sounded patient, way this side of insolence, putting the philistine in his place but not so's you could get her for insubordination.

'Now, there's a thought,' he said. 'So how does he live?'

'He does other things. He mentioned cleaning.'

'And we suspect he does that for cash while signing on for the dole, do we?'

'I have no reason to suspect that, sir.'

'And you didn't find out.'

'I understood that this enquiry was not into DSS fraud, sir.'

'Handles, love. You get handles. On suspects. That you can turn to open doors when you need to.'

Again she presented a smooth set profile, perfect English pebble off a perfect English beach. How had he got stuck with this? He was the boss of this outfit and they'd fobbed him off, they'd put one over. He didn't like this investigation. From the corpse to the actress. He wanted no part of it.

She said, 'As I understand it, no one is a suspect until there is evidence to support one's suspicions. Sir.'

He sighed. 'A-ha. Yes, that's right. Come on, love, give me a picture, come on, I want a snapshot, talk to me.' She turned a page. 'Put the prayer book away.'

She pulled her top lip back between her teeth. He noticed she did that when you really got up her nose. She was really really cross. He enjoyed a fantasy of her taking it out on her teddy bear. Teddy would get a good battering when she got home tonight. She said, 'He's five foot eleven, dark-haired, bright brown eyes, charming, without the necessary ambition probably to succeed in his profession. His flat is a bedsit on the top floor of a house which is owned by an actress. She is a widow and he seems to run errands and do odd jobs, clean the house, mend things for her, in return for paying her a very low rent.'

'That's better.' She thought she could make him feel small? 'Now, still in your own words, constable, tell me how he seemed about the girlfriend.'

'Are you referring to Kate Creech, sir?'

'I am, constable. I am referring to Kate Creech.'

'They split up years ago.'

'Yes. We know this. Why?'

'He didn't say, sir.'

'Well, how does he feel about it now?'

'I don't know.'

'You don't know?'

'I was trying to fix his whereabouts at the time of the death, sir, and whether he has keys to the house.'

'Oh yeah, that's right, so you were.'

'He said . . .' She elaborately referred to her notes. '"I never had keys. I never went to the house. She bought it after we split up. She wouldn't give me keys."'

'Bitter. Sounds bitter.'

She didn't rise to that. 'I asked him if he had met anyone at the house while Kate Creech was away.'

'Now, let me guess what he said to that.'

She didn't move a muscle. 'He said he had not, sir.'

'Now, there's a surprise.'

'I asked him how often he saw Kate Creech now. He replied not often, they met for a drink now and then. I asked if they had many friends in common. He said not now but people in their business tended to bump into the same people over and over.'

'He got a girlfriend now?'

'I didn't ask him, sir.'

'A-ha. No use asking for your personal impression, I suppose?'

She didn't speak. She put away her notebook.

It was a classic Islington street. Looked as though it had come up maybe in the seventies and then gone down again. Several doors had brass door knockers, one had a dinky coach lamp, but the windows of two were blanked out with corrugated iron.

Number thirty-eight was a smart one. Four floors, white stucco up to the first floor, repointed brick above, original stripped pine shutters, shiny black basement railings. Edgley rang the top bell.

'Oliver Broome?'

He looked puzzled as Bright showed his ID, but he smiled at Edgley like an old friend. His teeth were a startling white and she was right about the charm. Not that the charm affected her. She didn't smile back. This seemed to puzzle Oliver. He hesitated. 'Er, would you like to come in?' On the stairs he said, 'My place is a mess, I'm afraid. Bit of a night last night.' He was fit. Not even breathing hard when they got to the top.

Theatrical posters marched up the wall of the staircase. 'Your landlady an actress, is she?'

'Jessy? Yeah. Jessica Yates, haven't you heard of her? And her husband was Don Bradshaw, the writer. No?' He turned round to look at their blank faces. Smiled at their incomprehension, the difference between their two worlds.

He was right, it was a mess. Tumbled bed, coffee cups on the floor, papers strewn around. He pulled the bed covers straight. 'Sorry. I'm usually more civilised than this.'

'Good night, ha?'

He looked at Bright, smiled uncertainly. 'Well, okay. You know.'

'Only okay, ha?'

'Well, I mean, it was just a one-night stand. I mean, you don't know it's going to be that when it starts. But you know by next morning.'

Edgley was astonished to see Bright smile. 'Who decided?' he said.

Oliver put his hands in his pockets, moved his upper body from side to side, hesitated. 'Well, let's say it was mutual.'

Bright laughed. Edgley was finding this hard to believe. He seemed to be charmed by Oliver. Wasn't that against the rules? He was doing this to teach her a lesson. She didn't want to learn any lessons from him, thanks. She didn't like it his way. She'd do it her way. She would go by the book.

'So, no regular girlfriend around these days?'

'Not since Kate, I'm afraid. A few, you know, hopeful things, but none of them have lasted.' He smiled his charming rueful smile.

'You'd like to be shacked up, would you?'

'Oh yes. Wouldn't everybody?'

Bright's face stopped smiling. He rubbed a hand over his mouth. She'd have sworn he was disconcerted in some way, but she could never tell how calculated his behaviour was. He sighed. He looked round the room, picked up a sheet of paper from the floor. 'You writing a play, Mr Broome?'

Oliver blushed. Actually blushed. A russety apple colour spread under the olive skin. 'Well, I'm trying. A lot of actors try their hand. Plenty of time when you're out of work. It's hard not being creative. So, you know . . . Jessy encourages me. But it's really difficult. I don't think I'm any good.'

'Well, you never know.'

'No.' Oliver laughed.

'What's it about? The play.' Bright was flicking through the pages.

'Oh, it's . . .'

'I see the woman's called Kate.'

'Oh well, yes, I mean, that's just . . . It's based on the break-up, I suppose. Mine and Kate's.'

'Why did she leave you, by the way? 'Nother bloke?'

'Yes.' Oliver sighed and sat down on the bed.

'Who was it?'

'Nat Crosby.' He looked surprised at their blankness again. 'He's a big success now. In the States directing and writing his own movies. You must have seen *Lady Day*. No? Well. Kate went up to Nottingham to do a play for him. I knew there was something going on, you know how you do. Anyway eventually she told me she was crazy about him and . . .' He shrugged. 'That was that. I moved out. Jessy had just been widowed. She put me up as a temporary thing and it sort of became permanent. Kate's mum died and left her her house in Liverpool and Kate sold that and bought the little house in Kentish Town and . . .' He shrugged again.

'This Nat – what? Crosby? He move in with her or what?'

'Oh no. He was married. Kate came back to London. I don't know what happened but he went back to his wife.'

'Burned itself out, did it? The thing with Kate.'

'I don't know. I wanted to get back together, you know, give it another try but Kate said no. She wanted to live on her own. She likes it. I couldn't do it, myself, I'd go round the bend, but . . .'

'She still see this guy?'

'Don't know. I doubt it. He's more or less permanently in the States from what I hear people say. I think she still saw his wife though.'

'A-ha.' Edgley saw that odd stillness come over Bright. She was learning to recognise these moments when his ears went up like a dog hearing a sound not audible to humans. 'What she look like, this wife of his?'

'I only saw her once. I thought she was Kate actually. It was at a party. I went out in the garden. It was dark and everything but I actually went up to her and said, Hello, Kate, and she said, I'm not Kate, I'm Tess.'

There was a silence. Edgley couldn't take her eyes off Bright. His face was blank as if the features had been wiped off it but she could feel the excitement go through him like he'd stuck a finger in an electric socket and

68

received fifty volts. 'A-ha,' he said at last. A meaningless little expression. He used it for everything.

Oliver was the kind who had to fill silences. He said, 'She's the same height more or less, thin, with long dark hair. Of course the hair's quite different really; hers is that crinkly type, goes into corkscrews. And she's a bit older than Kate. A bit worn-looking, you know?'

'This Tess. She still with this Crosby?'

'Tell you the truth, I don't know. He wasn't at the party. Just Tess.'

'Kate still see her, do you know?'

'I don't know. She hasn't mentioned her in a while. But they seemed really close at that time. You know, after the thing with Nat was over.'

'That's a bit funny, isn't it?'

'Well, Kate's unusual.'

'Oh yeah?' Bright paused. 'Would she have had keys to Kate's house, do you think, this Tess?'

'Oh, I wouldn't know. I mean . . .' Oliver suddenly looked scared. 'Do you think it was Tess? Who was found in Kate's house?'

Nobody spoke.

'Oh Christ,' he said.

'You're sure you don't have a set, Oliver?'

'God, I'm certain, man. I never – I'd never cross Kate like that, I promise you she'd be livid, furious.'

'If you could take Tess for Kate once . . .'

'What are you saying?'

'And if you could get into the house. Well, we're just wondering . . .'

'Are you saying that I might have – ? Why would I want to kill Kate? I adore Kate, she's . . .' He stood up and took a deep breath in.'I adore her, okay? I wouldn't harm a hair of – ' He suddenly stopped, changed tack. 'Is that what you think? That they thought it was Kate? Someone thought they were killing Kate? No, man, it's not possible. Oh God.' He sat down again. He was shaking. 'Oh God.'

Bright said, 'Look, Oliver, don't jump to conclusions, okay? We know bugger all at the moment, to be honest with you. But I'd like you to keep yourself available, all right? I might want to talk to you again.'

'Oh God.'

'Don't get in a state about it, I'm not accusing you of anything. Get on with writing your play here.' Bright took the piece of paper to the scruffy utility-style desk. The desk was covered with papers, cups, a vase with dead daffodils, letters, photographs of Oliver with various moody expressions in atmospheric lighting, coins, tissues, a bunch of keys. Bright picked up the bunch of keys. He dangled them. 'Sure none of these is the key to Kate's house, Oliver?' The nasal rasp had gone very soft, Edgley could hardly believe it, confiding as a cat's purr.

69

'Listen, take them with you, try them, I've got a spare set, somewhere
... Christ.' Oliver started to rummage through a desk drawer. 'Oh. Here.'
He gave the bunch of keys to Bright.

Bright calmly compared them. 'Thanks, mate.' And handed them back.
Oliver said, 'Look . . .'

'Listen, mate, don't worry. You get on with that play and don't give it
another thought. You've given me the best break I've had in days.'

As they came down the steps he said, 'Oliver Broome has had keys to Kate
Creech's house.' Edgley looked at him. 'Course we'll never prove it,' he
said. 'He hasn't got them now.'

16

A BED FOR THE NIGHT

She knew about Oulton. A writer friend of hers had lived there for a while.
He'd been driven out by the hordes of New Age travellers who invaded
every year at festival time. He'd gone back to Bath now, civilisation.
Couldn't stand the pace.

The sky was that white cold that might mean snow. Driving there
through the lanes, she knew that no one had followed her, and also that
she was lost. Then a sign on a small cottage said *Launderette and Video Hire*.
She stopped. A light was on so she went in. The three machines were quiet
but a tall man with a long nose came out from the back. 'Yes?' He sounded
suspicious. She was a stranger, after all. And perhaps he had some funny
videos under his counter, there wasn't much entertainment out of season
in a village in the wilds of Somerset.

'I'm looking for a woman called – Aura?'

'Aura?'

'She lives here. I'm a friend of a friend who asked me to drop in. I'm just
passing through.' Passing through? Why would anyone pass through
Oulton out of festival time? How would anyone pass through? You'd have
to find it first. Still, people tend to think their own place is the hub of the
galaxy, he might believe it. He did. But he didn't know anyone called
Aura. 'Aura?' His voice rose at the end of a lovely Somerset arpeggio.

Inspired she tried, 'Laura perhaps?'

'Laura? Oh, ah.'

'Yes?'

'Ebenezer Chapel. Oh, ah.'

'Ebenezer Chapel?'

'Downa lane, winds about a bit, can't miss it, ona right. Says Ebenezer Chapel overa door.'

It did wind about a bit. And dark was coming down. But you couldn't mistake the chapel. Victorian Evangelical. Grey stone. *Ebenezer Chapel* in Gothicke lettering over the peaked double doors. A small front garden with a gate.

She didn't stop outside. She drove a little farther and tucked the car under some heavy trees that overhung a grassy lay-by next to the road. In the dark it should be quite hard to spot. *Who am I kidding? If they've traced me this far they'll have no trouble at all.*

She walked back the way she'd come. A single street lamp on the approach to the village gave a thin ring of light round an inadequate bulb. She heard rustlings and whirrings in the hedge that brought back her childhood fear of the dark.

A lamp hung from the corner of the chapel, a long pale oval with a shade like a downturned saucer. She opened the gate. It creaked. There was no door bell. She knocked. The door was so thick the knock had no resonance. She knocked again.

'Yes?' The woman stood at the corner of the chapel. She must have come from round the side.

'I'm sorry. I'm looking for – Laura?'

'Yes?'

'Er, actually I'm looking for Tess Harbour. I believe she – '

'You know Tess?'

'Yes. I was in the area so – '

'Come in.' The woman disappeared. Kate followed her down a narrow path round the side of the building. Light from an open door showed a patch of cultivated land to the left. She stepped through the doorway into a lobby where coats, hats and bags hung from big iron hooks, boots and wellies flopped in corners. The woman wasn't there but a door to the right stood open, heavy oak, panelled and arching to a point at the top. Kate approached it.

She'd been expecting a gloomy revivalist tomb, but she saw lamps, sofas, rugs, colourful hangings on the walls. She stood next to an oblong dining-table and a wall of comfortable kitchen things: an Aga, a fridge, a big porcelain sink.

The woman stood in the middle of the room. She was small, not more than five foot two, and slight. A broad face, and short uncontrollable mousy hair going grey. The eyes were huge, heavy-lidded, the mouth set hard as though under the cheekbones the flesh was sucked in to keep it that way. She wore an old sweater and jeans. Her hands hung by her sides.

71

'Close the door, please.' A posh strangulated voice.

Kate went back and shut the outer door, returned to the big room and shut the pointed door too.

'You know Tess, you said.' The woman ground the words out.

'Yes.'

'You don't know where she is now?'

Kate shook her head and though the woman stood just as straight and still, she seemed to collapse somewhere inside.

'Want some tea?' she said.

'Er . . .'

'Only herbal I'm afraid.'

'That's fine.'

'Sit down.'

Kate went to the middle of the room and looked round. The kitchen area was under a gallery, with a balustrade carved in oak. Indian embroidered hangings closed it off from the room. There was no sign of a staircase up to it. The roof was vaulted with thick brown beams like the ribs of a ship.

Kate stood next to a big loom with colours threaded on it that jolted her eyesight. The wall hangings were tapestries the like of which she'd never seen, containing rope, stones, bits of coloured cloth; their colours as stylish and startling as tropical fish.

The woman brought the tea in big mugs. She sat in an old bed-chair with cinnamon-coloured cord cushions. Kate sat on the edge of a big sofa with an Indian embroidered cloth thrown over it. The tea smelled weird. 'What is it?' she had to ask.

'My own mixture. For shock.'

'Who's in shock?'

'I am. You are.'

'How do you know?'

'I know because you've come about Tess. You – I don't know. You look – haunted.'

'Okay,' Kate said.

'How do you know Tess?'

'We go back ten years. Her husband was directing a play I was in at Nottingham Playhouse.'

The woman paused before she said it: 'Husband?'

'Well, not officially. A sort of private religious ceremony of their own devising. Nat didn't believe that the state should interfere in people's private arrangements.'

'Nat.' She tried the name. It was new to her.

'That's how I got to know her. Later when she and Nat split up we remained friends.'

'They split up?'

72

'That was when Tess went to a commune in Wales, an all-female thing.'

'Yes.' She'd heard about that.

'That broke up. Nat went to America. He took the children for a time.'

'Children.' She got up and walked about, stopped at the loom, stood there a while with her hands on the coloured strands of wool, then turned and came back, sat and picked up the tea. 'Yes?' she said.

'She and another woman, an aromatherapist called V – Varya, started a new commune in Glastonbury. That broke up last year. I traced her to a caravan site near the Abbey, then to you.'

'She was in the caravan a short time. Then she came here.'

'To Oulton.'

'To me.'

'She lived here?'

'With me.'

'For how long?'

'Five months. She left last September.'

'Where did she go?'

'She left no forwarding address.'

'You're kidding.'

'I'm sorry?'

'She stayed with you for five months then left without telling you where she was going?'

'I had to go to Oxford to arrange an exhibition.' Laura carelessly indicated the tapestries. 'When I came back she was gone.'

'No message?'

'A note. Saying she'd be in touch. She has not been in touch.'

'Oh God.' Kate's head hung on her neck heavy as an anvil. She gazed at the rug, an intricate pattern of giraffe-like figures, pentacles, many-branched candlesticks, blue, crimson, ochre, black.

The woman said, 'Why do you suddenly want to see her now?'

Kate didn't look up. 'It's hard to say.' That was true. And she didn't know yet how much she should tell. 'Did she have any money?' she said.

'She lost everything when the commune broke up.'

'So you were keeping her.'

The woman gave her a look like a fist in the face. Kate had to get this on a better footing. She said, 'Did she never mention me? Kate Creech?'

'Not that I recall.'

'She knew she could go to my place if she needed to. I told her that. Even if I was away. She had my keys.'

'Where is that?'

'London. Kentish Town.'

'She never mentioned it.'

'What did she mention? What did she talk about?'

73

'The commune. The betrayals. She felt much betrayed.'

'Vera? Varya.'

'Among others.'

'I think she was much betrayed.'

'Yes.'

Silence fell on this point of agreement. Kate waited for the atmosphere to cool a little. 'Somebody can't just disappear off the edge of the planet.'

'People do.'

'She should have come to me for help. We were friends. She could depend on me.'

'It's taken you a long time to come looking for her.'

'I thought she was still in the women's compound. Not my scene.'

'No.' This point seemed to placate the woman a little. They both sipped the fragrant brew.

'How did you meet her?' Kate asked.

'I teach some adult education classes in Glastonbury. It pays the rent. Almost. She came. She had some talent. She had an eye. She gave the impression of being in some way – on the run. A sort of fugitive. In hiding almost. As though afraid of being caught.'

'By whom? From what?'

'I didn't ask questions. She was in need of rest. She was "getting herself back together", as she put it.'

'For five months you asked her no questions?'

'She was in a fragile state.'

'That's nothing new.'

'I didn't have the benefit of your experience.'

Kate was sick of the fencing and sparring, the woman's bitter tone. She said, 'Look, in the past she'd had some drug trouble. She's always had to keep clear of the – of officialdom. She could be deported back to the States. Nat saved her from that once. He said he'd take care of her, marry her. He did. In his way. He got her off the drugs too.'

The woman looked at her. 'You knew about that.'

'I wouldn't normally mention it.' The woman relaxed a little. *What's her problem? Is Tess in some new trouble? Is this woman protecting her? She's hiding something. But then so am I.* 'Listen, there's no reason you should trust me. I'm worried Tess may be dead, that's all.'

'Dead?'

'You don't have to tell me where she is or anything. Just tell me she's alive.'

The woman had risen and was coming towards Kate, she seemed suspended, moving through air. Above her head the roof ribs met. A message round the top of the walls read, *Suffer the little children to come unto me* in red, black and gold. She was saying, 'Dead? Dead?' Kate thought she was going to shake her or hit her; she put her hands to her face but the woman stopped and said, 'Why should she be dead? What do you know?'

So then Kate knew: *Tess isn't here, the woman isn't hiding her, she doesn't know where she is. So it was Tess, squashed into my bath. Killed. That's it, then.* So she said, 'Haven't you heard what happened in my house?' and told her the story.

The woman said, 'I heard an item on the news. You're the actress. You think it was Tess. In your bath.'

Silence. The woman looked at her hands. They were clasped round the cup. She put the cup down. The hands clasped each other. She breathed in. She let the breath go. She didn't look at Kate.

She went to an Edwardian day bed. She threw off some cushions, pulled out a drawer in its base and extracted a duvet, a pillow, a sheet. 'Sleep here. The bathroom's through there. I sleep in the gallery.' She went through a door under the gallery to the right of the kitchen area.

Kate felt dismissed. She looked at her watch. It wasn't eight o'clock yet. Had this Laura really gone to bed? She waited. Laura didn't come back. Kate made up her bed, sat on it for a while, heard the lavatory flush and footsteps on stairs, then some movements in the gallery, then silence. She crept to the door.

The bathroom was small like a galley on a boat, wood-panelled, and it smelled of rosemary. *Rosemary. There's a bush outside my front door, its medicinal smell extinguished now by* – She thought she'd never be able to sleep. Not so early and not in this strange place. She looked for a bookshelf. There was none, in this otherwise artistic room. She found a copy of the letters of Van Gogh on a table and got under the duvet, without much hope that this would stop her thinking.

17

ENTER THE NEW AGE

His mobile shrilled. He listened. Nodded. 'Number thirteen, right? That figures. Well, I said they owed us one.' He put the blue light on the car roof. 'Got to get a move on, constable. In case those Croydon woodentops lose the house.' He started to drive like Concorde through the rush hour streets.

Edgley said, 'They've found out whom Creech was visiting, sir?'

'Well, they think it's whom she was visiting, constable. But don't count your whoms before they're hatched.' He screeched twice round the mini-roundabout on to York Way. Then, siren squealing, he raced a red light, cars cowering either side to let him through, and headed down towards King's Cross and all points south.

'Vera Bradstock?' He showed her his ID.

'My name is Varya.'

'And this is WPC Edgley. Don't mind if we come in a minute, do you, Vera?' He slid past her in one smooth movement and sent Edgley upstairs. He looked into the cluttered front room, then went into the clean consulting room at the back. Varya followed protesting.

'Just a few questions to ask you,' he said. 'Do something about that stink, would you?'

'That is jasmine and orange incense.'

'I don't care if it's roast lamb and two veg, I'd rather have some good honest Croydon pollution.'

'It's important for the atmosphere of my work. I am an aromatherapist. Scents have a deep ontological effect on my clients' – '

'A-ha. Yeah. Let's have a window open, do you mind?' He went to the thick curtain and grabbed it.

'No! You'll ruin the energy! My lighting is carefully arranged!'

The curtain with its signs and symbols came off the wall in a micro-smog of dust and plaster flakes. The window was grey, greasy, stiff on its hinges. He jerked it open and stuck his head out. 'No wonder you didn't want your clients to see the garden, love.'

Her carefully modulated voice had changed. The pitch rose. The accent became pure Croydon. 'You bastard. This is my livelihood. I'll report you.'

'No, you won't.'

'It's freezing in here.'

'Who owns this house, Vera?'

'I do.'

'Your mother does.' Her mouth closed when he said that. 'She's in a council home in Esher. Isn't she? Where the sun sets on geriatrics. Isn't she? This is her house. Isn't it, Vera?'

'I look after it for her.'

'That what you call it?' Through the crack of open window he watched the back door of the house open cautiously. A boy of perhaps eighteen put his head round and looked out. A grubby head band, long lank locks of hair, an embroidered waistcoat and torn jeans. Bright stepped back, watched the boy do a crouching run into the undergrowth, making for the tepee. 'Come in here, lad.' The boy stopped as though he'd been shot in the head. The pupils of his eyes were pin-points. 'Don't think of doing a

76

runner, I've got people outside. Come on.' The boy slowly stood upright and turned back to the house. Bright opened the door of the room on to the hall. 'Your son, Vera?'

She said nothing.

'Varya?' the boy said. He was blinking like a mole in the unexpected light. 'Varya?'

There was something about the way the boy said her name. 'Or some other kind of dependant?' Bright said. The boy looked scared as well as bewildered. 'Come in, son. Sit down.'

She had sunk on to a cushion. The boy slid down next to her on the floor and took her hand. He said, 'Is he a cop?'

She nodded without taking her eyes off Bright. He said, 'You his supplier, Vera?'

She said, 'I'm his lover actually.' They both looked absurdly proud.

'Well, congratulations. Good job you're not an old queer, Vera, or we could probably get you for corruption of a minor.'

'I'm eighteen,' the boy said.

'Yeah. But that's not what I asked. I asked is she supplying you?'

The boy's eyes went out of focus. 'I don't know what you mean.'

'Yes, you do, don't mess me around.'

'I'm getting him off it!' Her voice was tight and high. 'You could put my work back years, interfering.'

'You bet I could.'

Tears were gathering on the startling blue eyeballs and spilling out on to her freckled cheeks. 'I help people,' she said.

'Well, now you're going to help me, Vera. Kate Creech was here yesterday. What did she want?' The tears stopped mid-stream. Her mouth opened. Bright said, 'That's right, yes. We've been watching the house.'

The boy's body pressed against her side. They sat like two floppy dolls, legs straight out. Their hands gripped. Two parallel lines of mascara painted her face from eyes to chin. Bright said, 'What did Creech come here for?'

The boy turned to Vera, mystified. Vera let go his hand and put her arms round her own knees. She looked at Bright, dead cool, unaware of her sad clown face. She considered her choices, letting him wait.

He watched her a bit then opened the door. He called up the stairs, 'Edgley?' He could see the footprints in the dust on the stair carpet. Edgley appeared on the landing holding a piece of rubber tubing, a syringe, a small foil package. He said, 'A-ha,' and went back into the room. He said, 'Well, we found the gear, some of it.' The boy turned to her and she took his hand again without taking her eyes off Bright. 'Going to tell me what I want to know now, Vera? Eh? Or you want me to book the pair of you for possession? Just for starters, that is.'

She considered then sighed. 'What do you want to know?'

'I told you. I want to know what she came here for.'

'A friend of hers. She hadn't been in touch. She wanted to know where she was.'

'Name of this friend?'

'Tess.'

'Tess.' He gave Edgley a quick look. 'Tess what?'

'Tess Harbour.' She spoke barely opening her mouth like she wanted to swallow the words back again.

'Not Tess Crosby?'

Vera paused a moment. 'Crosby? No.'

'And what did you tell Kate about her?'

'I was a member of a women's commune in Glastonbury a couple of years ago. So was Tess. It broke up. I came back here to look after my mother.'

'Oh yeah?'

She ignored that. 'Tess stayed on in Glastonbury as far as I know. I haven't heard from her since.'

'You sure about that?'

'Yes.'

'Why did Creech want to know?'

Vera shrugged. 'She and Tess were close till the commune.'

'She think Tess Harbour is alive or dead?'

'I think that's what she wants to find out.'

'And what about you, Vera? What do you think?'

'I don't know.'

'You heard what happened at Kate Creech's place.'

'Kate told me.'

'She thought Tess Harbour was the body?'

'I don't know.'

'Vera.'

'Yes. I think she was afraid it could be.'

'So Tess Harbour was tall and thin and dark. How old?'

'About forty, I think. I don't enquire people's ages, they're irrelevant in the spiritual cycle of birth and growth – '

'Cut the crap, Vera, it annoys me, love. This Tess married, single, kids, what?'

'I believe she was married once. But she'd put all that behind her. I met her at the women's commune in Wales.'

'What, dykes?'

Varya sat straight up and he felt Edgley move behind him. His amused look intensified.

'This was an experiment for women who needed to discover if they

78

could make a life without men. It was a journey of exploration and discovery.'

'A-ha. So you went on exploring and discovering at this other place in Glastonbury. You and Tess Harbour.' Varya sighed and said nothing. 'You part on good terms, Vera? You and your friend Tess.'

'I'm afraid not, particularly. That's why – '

'You haven't been in touch, yeah. You sure you haven't seen her recently? Say in the last couple of months?'

'Yes. I told you.'

'Oh yes, so you did. You didn't have a meet at Kate Creech's house for instance, while Kate was away?'

She hadn't expected this. She said, as though her lungs had suddenly shrivelled, 'No.'

'So why did you fall out, Vera?' He could make that nasal rasp of his as soft as syrup when he wanted to. 'You and Tess.'

'I owe her money, if you must know. She doesn't know where I am.'

'A-ha. Well, that's a big admission, isn't it, Vera? How much do you owe her?'

'Her share of the – We all put money into the commune. Several thousand pounds.'

'How many thousand pounds?'

She muttered something.

'I didn't quite catch that, love. How many thousands did you say?'

'Thirty.' She turned her head away from the boy, leaning her cheek on the wall.

'Just as well I'm not fraud squad, isn't it, Vera?'

'I have the intention of paying back the money in full. I didn't have it at the time. I have been trying to build up my business.'

'A-ha. I see. Yes. So in the meantime your friend Tess has to wait. What's she living on, air? Tess Harbour have keys to Kate Creech's house, did she?'

Varya turned her head slowly towards him. 'How would I know that?'

'Kate must have said, didn't she?'

'I don't recall.'

'If she did have keys you could have got hold of them. You could have got into Kate Creech's house. Be funny if you'd met Tess Harbour there and she threatened you about the money you owed her and you lost your temper and bumped her off.'

Varya stood up. She said, 'This is harassment. You have made insinuations against me which are intolerable. I'm going to call my lawyer.'

'Hang on, Vera, hang on.' He caught a look of satisfaction in Edgley's eye. He'd overstepped the mark. 'I've made no accusations, I've just presented a hypothesis. Calm down. Forget I said it. I apologise, I got

79

carried away. Okay?' The blue eyes speared him. 'Don't forget,' he said, 'we've got a lot of stuff on you. If you're lying to me – '

'Of course I'm not.' She'd got all her dignity back. He'd blown it. But only for now. Never mind. He'd got enough. To be going on with. 'We'll be keeping an eye on you,' he said. 'If you hear a word from Kate Creech, or from this Tess woman, you let me know. DI John Bright, Kentish Town. That's the number. You hear anything and don't ring it you're in deep shit. So is boyo here. If you really want to help him tell him to have a go at your mum's garden. Give him something to think about.'

He was out of the room, making footprints in the dust in the hall before Edgley knew the interview was over. Behind him she said, 'The gear was in a cupboard in the back bedroom, sir.'

'A-ha.' He went out of the house ahead of her.

18

LOST LOVES

She woke to find Van Gogh unopened still in her hand, sunlight slanting through the high greenish windows and the smell of coffee in the chapel. But there was no sign of Laura. The yellow coffee pot on the Aga was hot and next to it stood a pan of warm milk. On the table a bowl, a fresh brown loaf, a pot of home-made marmalade. Kate ate like a woman who hadn't seen food for a week. Then she dressed and took a look outside.

The strip of garden, ten feet wide and topped with crumbly compost, was planted even at this stage of winter with vegetables: spinach, broccoli, land cress, even lettuces under plastic cloches, in rows meticulously neat. The path led down the side of the house and opened out at the back to rough grass. Clumps of early daffodils surrounded a pond where swords of iris stuck up like so many Excaliburs. Thick evergreens stopped you seeing to the hills beyond. If you had rural yearnings this place was the business. Kate didn't, but she got a sudden inkling of why someone might.

Laura was emptying buckets on to a big compost heap in the corner. She didn't turn at Kate's approach. Didn't seem to notice her presence. She walked to the pond and stood staring at it, the empty buckets dangling from her hands. Kate felt like a spy. She shivered and crept back into the warmth.

The chapel was quite a sight with the sun coming in those long narrow windows. You could hear seagulls crying not far off. She wandered down the room still feeling like a spy, picking things up, putting them down. She seemed to be looking for something but didn't know what. She picked up an exhibition catalogue from a Bristol gallery: *New Tapestries by Laura Reynolds*. Such burning raging colours, such original ideas, from this small insignificant-looking woman. She read the biog: *As the child of military folk Laura Reynolds spent her childhood travelling in the East. She thinks this is what gave her her rather un-English sense of colour* ... That explained some of the incongruity, the strangulated voice and stiff back, with the sensuous surroundings and the exotic work.

'Did you sleep?'

'Oh God!'

'Sorry. Didn't mean to alarm you. I've been outside.'

'I was absorbed in your catalogue.'

'Oh, that. Yes. Have you had breakfast?'

'Sorry, I should have washed up.'

'Not at all.' She ran water into the sink.

Kate was looking at a row of strange little dolls standing along the base of an easel. She picked one up. About six inches long, it was almost oblong in shape, with black wool hair and a heavy dark face. Its clothes were made of thick reddish kelim-like cloth. She came down to the table holding it. 'What's this?'

Laura looked round. 'A Peruvian grave doll.'

'Grave doll?'

'Peruvian Indians bury them with their dead. I'm trying to make them. Or something like them. That's a real one. To work from.'

'How could you?'

'I'm sorry?'

'I don't see how you could weave in the weird feeling they give you. They look like something you'd stick pins in at midnight under a full moon.'

'They are to comfort the spirits of the dead.'

'They don't look all that comforting to me.'

'No. They look like the repositories of dead souls.'

'Yes.'

Laura wiped her wet hands and held them out. Kate gave her the doll. She looked at it, smoothing it as though its spirit needed comforting. 'I gave one to Tess,' she said.

Kate watched the broad strong hands press the doll till it vibrated. 'Yes?'

'When she first came to my class she was sad, thin, damp-looking, like a stray cat. She said a few things in passing – how you can't really know anyone, can there be something about a person that makes others behave badly towards them, strange how you can think you've found something then find you've lost everything – so I gathered that things at the commune were bad. She asked me a couple of times could she spend the night here.

81

"Things are a bit heavy at the Rainbow just now," she'd say. She told me about Varya, the woman who tricked her. She was completely under her influence. "She's a witch," Tess said. Varya had told her this and Tess believed it. When I met the woman I saw that she was no witch. She's a common little woman, a hausfrau, but she believed she was a witch and could make others believe. Such a craving for power. Petty power. And money too. She had all Tess's money sewn up in the commune. They were supposed to be self-sufficient, get what they needed by barter, but Tess appeared to be starving. Most of the other women had left by then. There seemed to be just Varya and a young pale girl obviously in her thrall. I threatened her with legal proceedings if she didn't sell up and give Tess her share of the proceeds. She behaved in a silly way like a schoolgirl ticked off by teacher. She wasn't used to being on the receiving end. Tess told me the mortgage company were repossessing the house. Varya disappeared. I asked Tess to come here to live. She said she refused to be a burden on me. A burden on me! She went to that caravan site. She worked in a little New Age shop – '

'She worked there?'

'For pennies, I think. The caravan had a paraffin heater that never really took the edge off the cold, just caused condensation. Water dripped off the ceiling, down the windows, the walls. Her stuff was piled in damp bags. All her worldly goods. It was unspeakable. She got flu and didn't have the strength to resist. I brought her here.' Laura wiped her eyes again with the back of her hand.

'Were you lovers?' Kate dared.

She nodded, shrugged as if to say yes but so what.

'I thought Tess was a man's woman,' Kate said. 'She used to be.'

'Not after the Welsh commune.'

'Oh.'

'Categories.' Laura dismissed the gender stereotype.

'How long was she here?'

'A few months, that's all. For me it was the best few months of my – ' She stopped a minute, pressed the doll to her mouth.

'Yes,' Kate said.

'So that I didn't see. I simply didn't see. How much she must have wanted to get away from me. She must have hated me.'

'No.'

'Oh yes, I think so now. I think now she saw me as Varya's replacement. Taking advantage of her. I made such assumptions, you see, based on nothing but my own feelings. I think Tess is capable of hate, don't you?'

'I don't know – '

'Though not of doing anything with it. Except run away. Escape.'

'Are you capable of hate?'

'I don't think I am. Of myself, perhaps. No one else.'

'So you didn't trace her to my house, find her with a man and kill her, then?'

She looked at Kate. 'Find her with a man?'

'Someone had ejaculated. In my bed. They don't seem to know if it was the same occasion as the murder or even if anyone else was present at the time. Semen stains. On my sheets.'

The great eyes stared. Not at Kate. Not in sympathy.

'I don't know what to tell the police,' Kate said.

'Why?'

'The repercussions. Two friends have already broken up. And Daniel, the son of a friend. Just a boy. He's been questioned. Because I gave their names to the police.'

'I see.'

Kate said, 'Can I tell them what you've told me?'

'What does it matter now?'

'Now?'

'If it's Tess they found in your house.'

'It would make you a suspect. And there's this horrible little inspector. He's like a terrier. Once he gets his teeth in he doesn't give up.'

'Then he'll find out who killed – who killed Tess.'

The phone rang. They jumped like frogs. Laura picked it up from the big desk by the loom. 'Yes. Yes? Who? She's not – she's not – she's no longer staying here. No, I have no forwarding address. Who did you say you are? Just a moment.' She said to Kate, 'It's Nat.'

'Nat?' Kate leaped up. 'Nat? It's Kate!'

'Kate? What are you doing there? Have I rung your number by mistake?'

'No. Where are you speaking from?'

'Philadelphia. My kids live here now. With Tess's parents. Listen, Kate, I've got to get hold of Tess.'

Kate felt such relief she couldn't speak.

'Kate, are you there?'

'Yes.'

'I thought we'd been cut off.'

'Why do you want to get hold of Tess?'

'Oh Christ, that's a long story too. I had a row with Sally.'

'Sally?'

'Yeah, my girlfriend Sally, you remember her!'

'Sally. Yes . . .'

'Yeah, anyway she said something about Tess helping her to move house. At least I think she did, things were a bit confused. Well, Sally hasn't been in touch. Her number doesn't answer and I don't know where she is. You haven't heard from Tess?'

'Why did you call this number?'

'It's the last one Tess gave me.'

'Are you thinking of coming over, Nat?'

'Yes. I'm coming tonight.'

'Tonight! You'll arrive early tomorrow morning then. I'll meet you somewhere.'

'Your place?' he said.

She swallowed. 'No, Nat.'

'Sally's then?'

'Okay.'

She took down the address, a flat in Primrose Hill. She'd have to get there without Bright knowing. Some hopes, but she'd do her best. 'I'll meet you there tomorrow around midday,' she said, 'but don't go out till I get there.'

'You haven't been in touch with Tess, then?' He sounded sad.

'Nat, I'm looking for her. No one knows where she is.'

'You think she and Sally could be together somewhere?'

'It's possible. See you tomorrow. Don't worry, Nat.'

She put the phone slowly down. She'd lost her sense of time and place. Then Laura said, 'Sally,' and she came back.

'Did you ever meet her?' Kate asked.

Silence. The woman stared.

'Laura?'

Laura smoothed the doll and put it on the table. 'Sally turned up here. That's when Tess went off.'

19

BRIGHT TURNS A CORNER

'I want her on a loose rein. If she's spotted I don't want her stopped, questioned, brought in. Just tailed at a safe distance. I want her to feel free. I want her to feel safe.'

They shifted, shrugged, shared sceptical looks.

'Why's that, guv?'

'She's more use to us that way.'

'How do we figure that?'

'She knows more than we do. She knows who she's looking for. So let's play follow my leader.'

'And if she's done a runner because she's the perp?' Atkins was always the one with the nerve to speak out.

Round the table no one looked at him. 'How do her friends' statements check out?' Bright said.

Barton wasn't there but Gwylim answered. 'Sir?' Like he was putting his hand up in class.

'Yes, Taff?'

'They checked out, sir. We talked to all of them. They all say she was ill the whole time.'

'And what about her story that her car was out of action?'

'That's true as well, guv.'

'How do we know?'

'The lad, Daniel Gutteridge. He was seen driving around in it. With a few mates and a ghetto blaster. Someone filed a complaint at Croydon nick and he was given a warning. When I questioned him he was scared stiff, admitted he fixed the electrics in a few minutes but hung on to the car. Said he thought it was okay 'cos his mum said Creech was too sick to be driving. He's been usin' it the whole time she was away.'

'You believe him?'

'Yes, guv.'

'She had no car the whole seven weeks she says she was in Coventry?'

''S right, guv.'

'Hire firms?'

'Checked.' Atkins doodled on a notepad. 'All the Coventry car hire set-ups. Only three hirings for London in the period and none of them her.'

Mitchell, the big DS on the crime desk, called over. 'Guv! Member of the public saw a yellow Beetle on the M4 Sunday evening.'

They all groaned. 'That's the fourth one of those, Mitch. But none of them saw it come off the damn M4!'

Then Barton trotted in taking off his jacket. He panted. Hadn't moved so fast in years. 'A bloke in a transport caff in Glastonbury. Monday morning. Says he saw Creech.'

'Glastonbury?' Bright sat up. His eyes lost their dead look.

'Yes. Thought he recognised her off the telly. Then we've got two geniuses from uniform branch in Somerset. They got a definite on the car in Glastonbury then decided to drive around a bit, see if they could spot Creech. Which they didn't. So when they came back they'd lost the car as well.'

'Must have been taking lessons off that pair in Croydon.'

'Right, guv.'

Bright was on his feet.'No sightings since?'

'Not a sausage.'

'The sighting we have got. Was she with anyone?'

'She was on her own in this transport caff.'

'When's the Glastonbury festival?' Gwylim was asking round the table.

85

Cato took the pipe out of his mouth long enough to murmur 'Summer solstice' in a bored voice.

'She's not a New Age type, is she?'

'Where's her sister live?'

'Bristol. We've got that covered. Hasn't been in touch, the sister says.'

'So what's in Glastonbury, guv?' Atkins, challenging.

Bright stood up, started walking round the big table, rattling the change in his pockets. 'Tess Harbour's in Glastonbury, Tommy. Or that's what Creech thinks.'

'Eh?' They looked at each other, looked at him.

'Tess Harbour. Answers the description of the victim. Got her from an out-of-work actor in Islington, Creech's former bloke, Oliver Broome. Oliver tells me he once mistook her for Creech.' He watched them digest that.

'Maybe Oliver mistook her for Kate in the bath, guv.'

'Hardly,' Edgley said. 'If they'd just had sex.'

An astounded silence then Atkins said, 'You don't necessarily look at the mantelpiece while you're poking the fire.' He grinned at Edgley. 'Oh, sorry, love.'

'It could have been dark,' Gwylim said.

Cato murmured, 'It could have been rape.'

'Oliver's not the type,' Bright said. 'Would you say, Edgley?'

Edgley said, 'All males are the type.'

'Hey! Hey!' A laugh. And a silence.

'Get Oliver to give us samples, guv.'

Bright said. 'The sex and the murder could have happened on separate occasions. Two separate perps. They might not be connected.'

A silence then a groan. Then he watched them weighing it up. His theory. The one they'd taken the piss out of, that someone had intended to kill Kate and got the wrong woman. He watched them turning around. 'It's what Creech thinks,' he said. 'That it was Tess in the bath.'

'Did she have keys to Creech's place, this Tess?'

'We don't know.'

'What do we know, sir?' Sherlock Holmes with his little eyebrows up.

'We know they were friends, her and Creech. Even after Creech screwed her bloke.'

'What bloke was that, sir?'

'Nat Crosby. He's a movie director. Lives in the States these days. His agent's trying to get in touch with him. hasn't managed it so far. Or so she says.'

'When was he last here?'

'Good question, Sherlock. Seven weeks ago.'

That got them on their hind legs.

'The time of the crime?'

'And he's involved with Creech and married to this Tess?'

'Has he got the keys?'

'Why can't his agent find him?'

'He finished a job in LA and he decided to go drive-about.'

'Oh, did he?'

'Just like Creech.'

'We got a right lot of weirdos on this one.'

But they were excited. They had two fresh suspects and a possible victim. For the first time he saw them show in his presence some emotion other than hostility. He sighed.

20

KATE MOVES ON

'You're welcome to stay, you know.'

'I'm tempted, believe me. But the longer I stay, the likelier the police are to catch up with me.'

'I have nothing to fear from police.'

'But I have,' Kate said.

'You're not going to find Tess now.'

'No. But I've got to – There's just one thing I have to do before they catch up with me.'

'If you think Nat Crosby may have killed Tess you should – '

'I don't. I don't.'

' – you should give the police all the information you have.'

Kate shook her head. She felt as close to howling as she ever had in her life, so she didn't risk speaking. She shoved stuff into her bag. The Coventry bag. Never unpacked. Pathetic. Like her. She zipped it up. 'Laura, if you're thinking of getting in touch with the police – '

'I'm not. But if they come here I won't lie.'

'Could you please not mention Nat?'

'I don't know.' She stood there, tear-stained but stiff-backed.

Kate gazed at her helplessly. 'Okay. Well, look. I can't go to my sister. The police will definitely be watching for me there. Do you mind if I phone her just to tell her I'm all right?'

Laura gave a small movement of the shoulders indicating a reluctant yes.

'*Kate?* Where the hell have you been? I've been frantic. So has Maisie. How can you do this? We thought you'd been killed. It's so irresponsible.'

'What, getting killed?'

'And facetiousness in these circumstances is particularly tasteless.'

Kate started to laugh. The pleasure in hearing Lizzie's voice and hearing her sister unchanged. The one unchanged thing in the world.

'Oh, be quiet. Where are you?'

'I can't tell you that, Lizzie.'

'Kate!'

'But I'm all right, I'm fine. And I'll come and see you soon. Lots of love to Maisie. Take care of you both.'

'Kate!'

'Bye, Lizzie.' She put down the phone, the laughter in danger of spilling into tears. She picked up her bag and went outside.

Laura was shovelling compost on the rows of spinach. She stood straight and nodded.

'See you again, perhaps,' Kate said.

'Yes.'

'If I get any news of Tess, I promise I'll tell you first.'

Laura nodded then turned away quickly. Kate let herself out of the front gate. The chapel was on the edge of the village. There were no more houses and she passed no one in the lane. *Who's a lucky girl then?*

She hunched in the car under the dripping trees. The early sunshine had not lasted. Glad to get away from Laura and her grave dolls, she was yet at a loss. She had one more night to spend in the wilderness before London and Nat. Where could she go? As short a distance as possible in the car. Leave the car somewhere they wouldn't expect and get to London by train. But not today. The car was easy to recognise, had probably already been recognised by someone in the village and she'd find a squad car lying in wait outside the video launderette.

But she didn't. And no one followed her.

The Glastonbury Arms. Not in Glastonbury but the irony appealed to her. It looked okay. Covered with creeper, leafless now but giving the Georgian brick a gently hairy appearance, it wasn't one of those modern chain hotels where every room is exactly the same, right down to the pictures on the walls. And it wasn't a motel, where they'd ask for the car registration number. The blinding rain was her greatest luck. The sky a premature night.

The room had a brass bed, two windows overlooking the car-park and some hills, but not the Tor, a point in its favour. Again she'd tucked the car in a corner under trees. She stood at the window for a while getting up her courage, then abruptly opened the door to her bathroom.

Pink and grey tiles, a shining clean empty bath, the smell of good clean soap. She turned on the taps. Water gushed out in the kind of torrent peculiar to posh hotels. Steam rose. She emptied a bottle of complimentary bath essence into it, unwrapped a miniature soap. The pleasure these actions always aroused, generally connected with a well-paid job on the telly, enabled her to slip into the bath with hardly a qualm. *If I don't close my eyes I'll be all right.* God, it was bliss. Her limbs relaxed, for the first time since – *Keep your eyes open. That's finished now. You'll never have to see it again. It's over. Think about your next step. You're meeting Nat tomorrow. Think about that.*

She rested her head on the smooth porcelain edge and started to walk her mind through London streets. Only it's not winter any more. It's summer. She's going to meet Nat but not at Sally's flat. And it's not tomorrow either. She's only twenty-seven years old and she's never met him before. And when he opens the door . . . Her mind goes slowly black like a TV screen turned off. Then she's at home. Oliver's not back yet. She runs a bath and just as she's about to get into the water she sees that Nat's wife Tess and his baby are in the bath and they are melting, congealing into a swollen greyish liquid mass streaked with green and the smell appals her and she wakes up in the smart clean pink and grey bathroom and the water is lukewarm and she clambers out of the slippery porcelain and wraps herself in a huge, thick, fluffy pink bath towel and goes into the bedroom and sits on the bed, shivering.

This won't do. I have to go back in there, I have to get right back on to the horse. She went in. The water in the bath was not gluey with globules of fat, the bath was not streaked with green but she let out the water, ran the shower and made herself step into the bath and stand under the scalding stream.

Later, body wrapped in a fluffy pink towel, hair in another, she lay on the bed, started to pull out her thoughts into smooth strands, weave them into some sort of order. She needed to tell some people she was okay. She left a message on Ted Adams's answerphone. Then called Aggie.

'Oh Christ, Kate, where are you, woman? I've been out of my mind.'

'Sorry, Ags, I couldn't tell anyone.'

'We've been bloody interrogated here. They wanted to know what you'd been doing in *Croydon!*'

Pause. 'Did you tell them?'

'I didn't know!'

'That's why I couldn't tell you. You'd have spilled the beans when they threatened to pull your toenails out, now wouldn't you?'

'You bet.'

'Tell Daniel the car's working a treat, starts every time, it's a miracle.'

'He's a changed child, my son.'

'How?'

'Well, you know for two years I couldn't get a civil word out of him? I began to think he'd regressed through time to the neolithic era, he communicated by a series of grunts which over this period I have learned to decipher? Well, he has suddenly rediscovered the use of human speech, he is standing up straight, what I had come to think of as adolescent droop has fallen from him. He is six inches taller, his eyes, dulled I imagine by constant wanking and Walkman addiction, are sparkling again. You wouldn't know the boy. It's nice to have him back again. You've done me a favour.'

'How me?'

'He just seems to have adored being interrogated by the police. He's been interviewed by journalists, he's been on the telly, he's even got a girl! Excuse me a minute while I fan myself back to consciousness, even to say it makes me faint. There, I'm okay now.' Aggie gave her deep throat laugh. Kate said she'd be back tomorrow night. 'And where will you be till then, Honey Chile?'

'Unless this phone is bugged too, no one will know.'

'Come off it, Kate, my phone isn't bugged.'

'Want to bet?'

'Well, I wish the buggers'd ring the Gas Board for me instead of leaving me to do it over and over again.'

When she rang off Kate covered her eyes. Aggie was making light of it as usual but it couldn't have been a pleasant experience having Dan suspected of untold crimes. She rubbed her head hard with the towel then dried her hair with the fierce hotel drier. She ordered room service. Then she switched on her television to watch the news and saw her face.

She had been seen in Glastonbury. But she had also been seen in Bristol. Reporters hustled round her sister's door. She saw Maisie's little face at the window but no one came out. Then the TV reporter said sightings in Glasgow were being followed up and the Channel ports were being watched. She felt like the Scarlet Pimpernel, spotted in so many places at once. Someone knocked on the door. She turned the TV off.

Hoping the hotel staff were too busy to have been watching TV, she wrapped her head in the towel again and shut herself in the bathroom. 'Just put it on the table, please!' The waiter brought the bill to the bathroom door to be signed. She opened the door just a crack, out of natural modesty, and he modestly averted his eyes.

Leek and potato soup. Smoked salmon and brown bread and butter. She sat down and flapped a thick damask napkin over her knees. She was congratulating herself – no one knew where she was and no one knew where she was going – when the phone rang.

Her heart jumped into her throat. This phone? Even this phone? They'd traced her here? To this hotel? This room? The press? Or the police? Or someone else? *Nonsense, it's reception calling for some reason.* She picked the phone up and held it without speaking. A long silence. Then a voice said, 'Madam?' She didn't know the voice, a deep woman's or a light man's, she couldn't tell. Again she waited, didn't speak. Another long silence. When she couldn't stand it any more she said, 'Who is this?'

'Oh, this is reception here, madam. Only there seems to be some confusion.'

'Yes?'

'There seems to be a different signature on your room service bill from what we have in the register.'

A moment's pause, then: 'I'm so sorry. How foolish. I'm always doing it. I'm just recently married, you see, and I keep forgetting.'

21

OLD FRIENDS

Next morning paying cash and signing the bill *Mrs T. Adams*, she grinned ruefully and set off for Bath. It was six thirty. She went slowly by the lanes and wasn't followed, as far as she could tell. She left the car in a back street, no yellow lines, no meters, and had to force herself not to run.

The London train left while she queued for her ticket. An hour to wait. She spent the hour in a converted pub opposite the station at a formica-topped table decorated with pools of tea. The coffee was bitter, the Danish pastry made of laminated cardboard. Even at this hour groups of men drank lager at the bar end. The beery smell wafted across.

While she shut out the smell she argued: *Go back and get the car, Bright knows your every move anyway, you've got freedom with the car.*

Without the car I'm anonymous.

Who are you fooling? You've probably been followed here, they know where you're going, there'll be someone in London to meet your bloody train.

But she didn't go back for the car. Inertia and the fugitive's instinct to hide in a crowd kept her still. When the train came in she burrowed down in one of the so-called airline seats, piling her bag and coat next to her, and let her hair fall over her face. She opened her newspaper.

Not a word about The Event. A Conservative MP had been outed by an extreme homosexual group for voting against sixteen as the age of consent. The paper spread the story over two pages, pictures of pathetic rent boys:

He used to pick me up every Friday night, said Darren, fourteen. She closed her eyes. And abruptly opened them again. Till Paddington she stared blindly out at the racing countryside.

Which was best for dodging the law? Taxi, Tube or bus? *Is this really me thinking like this? I am going mad.*

She was on her way down to the Tube when she changed her mind, ran back up the steps and out into Praed Street. A 27 bus was stopped at the lights. She ran. She lingered at the back of the queue, no one behind her as she climbed on. But just as she tugged her ticket out of the machine a middle-aged man squeezed through the closing doors. The bus started up. He had a long nose, he was dressed in a crumpled navy flasher's mac. He didn't look like a policeman and he didn't follow her up the stairs but that proved nothing: downstairs he was in a better position to follow her off. He didn't even look at her when she got off at Camden Town. He didn't get off after her. That proved nothing either but she waited till the bus moved on, pretending to look in Marks and Spencer's window, fascinated by a display of plastic-wrapped sandwiches and some potted plants. She imagined him talking into his mobile phone, telling them where to look for her.

The whole population of the world had gathered in Camden High Street as though for Armageddon. The smell of street food, the noise of the ghetto blasters from the leather shops, the jostling, ambling, eating, ogling people blinded, deafened her. A young woman dressed in an Armani suit hailed a taxi. Kate, desperate, jumped in ahead of her. The girl, enraged, beat on the window. Kate didn't care.

No car turned into Princess Road behind the taxi but she couldn't hang about. She told the driver to keep the change and threw herself down the basement steps. 'Hey, thank you, love!' The best tip he'd had in years. At least she'd made someone's day.

'Kate!'

It was weird to feel Nat's arms around her again. Nothing had ever felt like that, before him or since. 'Shut the door, Nat.'

He looked healthier, better fed. The great mournful heavy-lidded blue eyes had lost the haunted look. What had haunted him? Fear of failure? Obscurity? That terror was scotched and with it the spirit that had moved him? She felt a kind of horror looking at him. Something was wrong.

'She's not here, is she?' His voice affected her like a touch: hoarse, with this nasal cockney edge to it, just enough to make it sexy, not to sharpen knives with like the voice of John Bright.

The place was neat and cold. It could have been empty a week, a year, might never have been lived in at all. 'Have you looked round?' she said.

92

'Yes. It's all just like this.'

The kitchen and bathroom were clean, neat, empty. Kate opened the garbage can with her toe: a nice clean plastic bin liner. *Just like mine when I got home on Saturday night. Don't think about that.* 'Have you listened to her messages?' The reason actors go away is to work. No job: no reason for going.

'Nothing from her agent.'

'That figures,' Kate said but didn't raise the ghost of a smile. Well, there were enough ghosts already. She switched the machine to replay and heard Nat's voice five times: 'Where are you, Sal? Call me, hey?' sounding oddly American on the phone and more frantic with each repetition. Nothing from anyone else. 'That's odd,' she said.

'What?'

'Just you. No one else.'

'Oh. It's not so odd.'

'Why?'

'She's always lived in this weird isolation. I've always known it.'

Kate shivered inside. Nat sat down on the sofa bed. He said, 'It's my fault.'

'What is?'

'We had a row. I wanted her to come out to the States with me. She hates it there. She said she wouldn't come. I said if you loved me you would – well, you know.' Oh yes, Kate knew. 'Well, I crashed out of here. I had meetings till late, then a plane out first thing next day. I heard nothing from her then I rang.' He gestured at the answerphone. 'That's it. Nothing. I even wrote.' He gathered up the pile of junk mail and bills. Three airmail envelopes addressed in his dashing-ahead hand. 'She said something about Tess.'

'Yes?'

'Yeah. Going to see Tess. Tess helping her to move. Know anything about that?'

'When was this?'

'Weeks ago, I don't know, four, five? I've been directing a movie. Six. Seven it must be.'

'Tess.'

'Where is Tess, anyway? Do you know?'

'Oh, Nat.' Her legs wouldn't support her. As her knees touched the floor she felt a shadow cross the window behind her, heard a faint ringing of the iron stair. Nat too looked at the window. Nothing there. But the door bell rang.

She didn't have to hear his voice to know. 'Mr Crosby? I'm Detective Inspector John Bright, Kentish Town CID, this is WPC Edgley, we come in please? Thanks.' Nat, no time to reply, stood back shocked. 'Hello. Muz

Creech! Fancy seeing you here. Hope you're not kneeling on my account.' Kate stayed where she was. Edgley followed Nat into the room and stood back. She folded her arms, looking round.

Kate knew what Nat expected, you could see it in his face: they'd say they had bad news and tell him something had happened to Sally. That's what you expect when the police knock on your door. But Bright's cheerful heartlessness didn't fit with that. Nat couldn't work it out.

Kate was too angry to speak. She saw now: Bright had just been giving her rope and she'd used it to lasso Nat for him. She caught his snapping little eyes.

'I did warn you, Muz Creech.' His voice was quiet. Yes, he'd warned her. She'd thought she was cleverer.

He bounced almost imperceptibly on the balls of his feet. 'Sit down, Mr Crosby.'

Nat did what he was told. Looking from Bright to Edgley, 'Is it Sally?' he said.

'Who's Sally?'

'My – This is her flat.'

'So where is she?'

'That's what – I don't know.' Nat told them what he'd told Kate. About the row and the silence since.

'And when was this row?' Bright was relaxed now, leaning back against the window sill.

'Five or six weeks ago.'

'Can you be more accurate?'

'Yes. I had to go back to the States next day. It was – Hang on.' He reached for his scruffy flight bag. Edgley handed it to him. 'Thanks.' He got out an old leather Filofax. 'It was seven weeks ago.'

'And the row took place here in this flat, that what you're telling me?'

Nat nodded.

'Sure?'

'Yes!'

'Couldn't possibly have happened at Muz Creech's place for instance, could it?'

Nat looked at Kate. Something in his look bothered her, something strange; but she didn't show it, she met his look expressionless. He turned back to Bright. He said, 'Kate's place?'

'A-ha. That's right. Kate's place.'

'No.' Bewildered. 'Why Kate's place?'

'Ah yes, he's been away, the news hasn't reached the USA. Tell him, Muz Creech.'

'You tell him,' she said.

Bright's hand went into his leather jacket, came out with a folded newspaper cutting. He unfolded it. The headline read, *The Body In The Bath* with *Who is the Mystery Woman?* in smaller lettering beneath. Nat took it. She didn't watch Nat reading it. She watched Bright watching him. The amused look was gone. The squint was gone too.

Nat said, 'You think this was Sally?'

'Well, that's what we'd all like to know.'

Nat stood, as though he'd go straight on up through the ceiling. 'Nn. Nn.' He turned round on the spot like a dog that didn't know where to settle.

Kate's mind too was a spinning top: *Sally? Sally? Why should Sally be at my place? There's no reason. But Nat thought – Why would Nat think – ?*

'Why would Sally have been at Muz – at Kate's place, Mr Crosby?'

'I don't know.' Nat shook his head. 'I don't know, I just . . .'

'You just what?'

'I don't know.' In a voice like crunching gravel.

Edgley had been looking through the mail. She said, 'How long has Sally Crowe lived in this flat?' They all turned to her as though a mouse had talked. She said, 'There's no postmark older than six weeks ago.'

'That's right!' Nat's face showed a pale gleam of hope. 'She was moving in. The place was a mess. It can't be Sally!'

'She was moving in here the weekend you had the row?'

'Yes.'

'You saw the place?'

'Yes.'

'It was definitely a mess the last time you saw it?'

'Sure. Packing cases, newspaper, things all over the place. Sure – ' Nat had been going to go on but heard himself chattering and stopped.

'Well spotted, constable.' Bright's face had its mocking look. Edgley didn't respond, just managing not to express her dislike. Bright came back to Nat. 'But it was possible to sleep here, was it?'

'Well, yes, I guess.'

'But you – didn't?'

'Didn't what?'

'Didn't – sleep here.'

'If you mean did we fuck here, no, we didn't.'

'Why not? Too busy having this row?'

'That's right and the place was a mess.'

'You didn't decide to go to – some other place to – sleep together – till this place was straightened out?'

Kate saw where the path led. Nat's head hung low, moving from side to side. 'No. We didn't. We had a row. I left.' His head came up. 'You think something's happened to her. If you suspect me of something, charge me, do the thing properly.'

95

'Now there's a thought. Shall we go down the station? We can record your answers there. Less room for mistakes. If you'd prefer that.'

'Am I allowed to have a lawyer present?'

'I'm not charging you with anything, Mr Crosby. I wouldn't know what to charge you with.'

Nat said, 'I don't have a lawyer in England.'

'I'll send you mine,' Kate said.

'*You* have a *lawyer*?'

She looked at Bright. 'I do now.'

'No, you don't,' he said.

'Why not?'

'Ted Adams can't act for both of you. Might be a conflict of interests.'

Nat looked at Kate. Ted had made her feel safe. Bright watched her hesitate, amused. 'Nat's need is greater than mine,' she said.

'You think so, do you, Muz Creech?'

'You'd know, better than me.'

'A-ha. That's right.'

'I'll send Ted to the police station, Nat.'

Nat was about to say something, but Bright handed him his coat, a ragged old tweed thing, Nat's finger-up to eighties values. Edgley picked up his bag.

As they trooped up the iron steps Bright said, 'On the way, Mr Crosby, I'd like to drop in somewhere else.'

'Where?'

'The mortuary. I'd like you to have a look at the body that was found in Muz Creech's house, see if you can make out any more than Muz – Kate here. Would you mind doing that?'

'Yes, I expect I would.'

'But you'll do it just the same.' It wasn't a question. 'Drop you anywhere, Muz Creech?'

'Thanks. I'll walk.'

'Haven't you got your car today?' He was crowing. 'By the way, Muz Creech.'

'What?'

'Vera Bradstock sends her regards.'

She didn't answer him. She murmured, 'I'm sorry, Nat.' Nat was too preoccupied to reply, or perhaps he hadn't heard. She walked up towards Regent's Park Road. There were bollards to stop cars going that way. One road Bright couldn't follow her down.

22

THE LIVING AND THE DEAD

He'd never got used to the smell, or the smell disguising the smell. Edgley was holding up well so far, not a crack in her armour. Nat Crosby was something else. Tall, bony, loose-limbed, even his feet seemed loose, making a noise on the tiled floor as though dangling not walking. Bright looked at his shoes, big distinctive brown leather jobs he'd never seen before. Handmade? The guy didn't look prosperous, but maybe the look of poverty was deliberate, assumed: a working-class lad guilty about getting rich? Edgley put out a hand, held Crosby's arm. He needed steering, seemed off somewhere, in space. Was he on something? Or was it just jet lag and shock? They waited in the lobby on a bench while the corpse was located for them.

The man in the white coat lifted back the sheet. Bright took a quick look. They'd put her back together okay, better than she'd looked in the bath. Neat stitching where they'd sewn the top of the head back on. But there was no disguising the bones where the flesh had been washed away. He preferred to watch the living on these occasions, he'd seen enough of the dead. Edgley tightened her grip on Crosby's arm. As much for her sake as his, Bright thought.

Crosby looked at the thing then lifted his head and gazed round the place like a kid at a funfair. He pivoted right round and the big hooded haunted blue vacuum cleaner eyes sucked up everything in their path, swept over Bright, round and back to the corpse. Crosby then did something Bright had never seen a member of the public do before in all his years: he lifted the sheet to see the rest of the body. It hadn't been put back together as neatly as the head but Bright had seen worse, he'd seen bodies that had been in the Thames for six weeks. The blue eyes swept the length of the thing, back and forth, sucking in the sight. Then he pulled the sheet back, covering up the whole thing, face and all.

Bright said, 'Well?' Voices sounded terrible in here, like a tomb.

Crosby's head lifted. 'Can we get out of here?'

Bright turned and walked away. Edgley steered Crosby, stumbling, big shoes scraping on the floor. The doors shut behind them. They stood in the small lobby. Edgley was green. She said, 'Excuse me,' and left.

'Well?'

Crosby whispered, 'How could anyone say who it used to be, man?'

97

'That's what your friend Kate Creech said.'

'That's the thing that was in Kate's bath?'

'A-ha. Remind you of anyone?'

'Yes. Something that used to be a human being once.'

'It's dark-haired.'

'Yeah.'

'Your friend Sally, was she – ?'

'Yes, Sally has dark hair, a lot of dark hair.'

Bright noted the present tense. 'Your ex-wife also had dark hair.'

'Tess?' The man seemed brought up short for a second.

'A-ha.'

'Tess wasn't my wife.'

'Not what I heard.'

'We had a kind of Buddhist thing, made it up ourselves, like a scene in a play. Like kids. We invited our mates. We had candles and garlands of flowers and my mate Rashid played the sitar. It was nice. But we never had a civil ceremony. We didn't like officialdom.' Bright was surprised at this long speech. So was Crosby. He stopped. He said, 'Yes, Tess has dark hair too.'

There was a silence. The smell seemed to grow to fill it. Crosby said, 'Can't we get out of here?'

'Not yet.'

Edgley came back. She didn't look at anyone. She was less green now, more the colour of wet putty. She'd splashed her face. She joined the silence. They heard footsteps in the corridor and a DI that Bright knew from Hampstead came round the corner with a solid citizen in a suit who looked as though he'd lost everything. Bright and the DI nodded as they waited for the doors to open. No one spoke.

Crosby's eyes swept over the new people. At last he said to the solid citizen, 'Who have you come to see, mate?' The man said, 'They think it's my daughter,' as though his mouth was full of something his tongue couldn't get round. 'She's twelve,' he said. Crosby's bony hand touched the man's arm. The man nodded. Bright and the Hampstead DI swapped a glance. The doors opened and they went in, Crosby gazing after them with that bewildered gentle look.

'Come on, out of here.' Bright had had enough.

The thick brown London air tasted good after that place. They didn't speak in the car, not till they turned into Kentish Town Road. Then Crosby's sepulchral whisper came from the back. 'Tess and Sally are alike. I never realised before.' He sounded shocked.

'Same height, same build?' Bright watched him in the mirror. He nodded. 'But you can't make a positive ID?'

Crosby shook his head. Then he started to sob, a sound like fingernails on sandpaper. Edgley gave him the box of tissues. He blew his nose. He said, 'I hope to Christ it wasn't that guy's kid. I've got two daughters of my own. Thanks.' He handed the box back to Edgley. 'Zoë and Rose.'

They stopped in the car-park round the back of the station. He said, 'Give me a minute, mate,' and wiped his face.

When they at last got him into the room and sat him down he said, 'Could I have a cup of tea?'

Bright nodded at Edgley. She went out.

Crosby said, 'Sorry, mate.'

Bright wished he'd stop calling him mate, it put him on the wrong foot. He wished he didn't like the guy too. He wished life was simple.

'But if anything happened to my kids.'

'Your kids are in the States, aren't they?'

He nodded. 'To get them away from Tess.'

'Why?'

'They weren't safe with her.'

'A-ha?'

'Oh no, she wouldn't have hurt them on purpose. No. But she wasn't stable. She had a breakdown. Well, more than one. And she was always finding a new craze, you know, a new religion. When I met her it was Buddhism. Well, that was okay. Oh, thanks, love.' He took the tea from Edgley and drank half of it in one go, Adam's apple jumping. He breathed out, wiped his mouth, put the cup down carefully. 'Then she got in with those orange people, you know? Are they still around? The Bagwan Razhneesh or something. That was a pain. She went on this macrobiotic diet just after Zoë was born and Zoë nearly – ' He put his hand over his eyes then took it away. ' – nearly died. We didn't know what was wrong. It turned out to be malnutrition. The diet wasn't suitable for babies. Tess had post-natal depression, but I didn't know. I was busy working, you know? I knew she wasn't happy but I didn't know she was ill. I didn't know she wasn't fit to look after a kid.'

'What's her address?'

'I don't have it.'

'You don't have it? Come off it. Don't you have to get in touch with her about the kids?'

'She doesn't like to be in touch with me.'

'Why not?'

He shrugged and sighed, shook his head. 'She fears my influence, she says.'

'Aren't the kids in touch with her?'

'It's a post box address in Dorset. I don't have it. You can get it from her parents. Here.' He fished a battered old notebook out of his pocket. Pulled a rubber band off it. Scraps of paper showered out of it. Edgley picked them up.

'Is this it?' she said.

He peered. 'That's the parents' number, yes. You dial 215 for Philadelphia.'

'Have you got her dental records?' Bright said.

'Dental records?'

'A-ha.'

'Her parents'd have those, I guess. Maybe. Their dentist. Oh, Christ, you don't think . . .'

'We don't know, mate.' There, he was doing it himself. 'Edgley, get on with that, will you?'

Crosby stared at the wall then swung the searchlight eyes to Bright. 'Ah, Jesus.'

'Yeah. Where would we find your girlfriend's dental records? Do you know?'

Crosby shook his head. 'Sally. No.' He picked up the cup then put it down again. 'Ah, Jesus Christ.'

Bright said, 'I'm getting a warrant to search Sally's flat. You know her folks?' Again Crosby shook his head. 'How long have you known her?'

'A few years. Three, four.'

'And you never met her folks?'

'She's a mystery woman, Sally. She'll never talk about her life before she came to London. She was born in the West Country somewhere but I don't know where. I stopped asking. It wasn't a guessing game with her; she didn't want me to know. I figured that was her business.'

Now Bright said, 'Christ.'

Edgley came in.

'Have we got the warrant yet?' he said.

'Yes, sir.'

'Get over there. I want her address book, diary, anything. Mystery woman my arse.'

'Me, sir?'

'Yes, you, constable. With Cato. Tell him I said to take you.'

She looked as though he'd goosed her, but recovered fast. 'Yes, sir.'

'And get me someone else in here, whoever's free.' He scraped a chair away from the table and sat on it. 'So. How long since you've seen Tess?'

'Tess?'

Why did the guy always ask *Tess?* like that whenever you mentioned her name? As though she was an irrelevance, in the past. 'Yes, Tess. Your ex-common-law wife. Mother of your kids. Remember her?'

'We were talking about Sally.' His tone was puzzled, mild.

100

'Well, now we're talking about Tess, okay?'

'I haven't seen Tess for over a year. Since she went to that commune in Glastonbury. When I took the kids.'

'That must have been an unpleasant business.'

'She couldn't support them. She'd sold our house and put the money into it. She had nothing.'

'You weren't sending her money for them?'

'I didn't like the set-up. I didn't want my daughters being brought up by a pack of lesbians.' His voice and his body shook suddenly, but subsided again. 'I've got nothing against anybody living how they want. But when my kids are involved . . .'

'So it was unpleasant.'

'I just said I was taking them for a holiday.'

'But you both knew that wasn't true?'

'No. We both thought it was true.'

'Hey?'

'She never asked for them back. It got bad in the commune. That Vera woman was a snake but Tess wouldn't believe it.'

'Vera?'

'Yes. Tess met her at some women's consciousness-raising group after we split up. She had this power over Tess. It was Vera got her to go into the commune. When it fell apart Tess said keep the kids till things get better. We got them into school in Philly. They stay with their grandparents. They like it. Well, Rose likes it. Zoë? I don't know.' He covered his face again, close to tears. 'I don't know.'

Bright felt glad to have no kids.

Atkins looked in. 'You want me, guv?'

Bright introduced him. 'Detective Constable Atkins.'

'Hello, mate,' Crosby said, like he was welcoming him to a tea party.

'Why would her parents' dentist have her records?'

Crosby looked blank. 'She'd have her teeth fixed when she was over there to see them. They'd pay. We weren't rolling in it in those days.' The big eyelids came down and up again as if he might pass out. 'Dental records. Christ.'

Bright stood, folded his arms, said, 'I've got to explain to you. We can't identify the woman in the bath. We thought we had one missing woman. Now we have two. It could be either of them. It could be some other woman, unknown. The only thing going to tell us anything for sure is the teeth.'

'I got that.'

'Now, you haven't seen Tess for over a year. Haven't you even talked to her?'

'She called the girls. Sent them postcards. Called me once. That woman

101

Vera – Varya she calls herself now – was making trouble. Tess was miserable, broke. She had nowhere to go. Then she moved in with that painter in Oulton?'

'Painter? In where?'

'Place near Glastonbury. I've got the number. Laura? Yes, that's her name.' He took a wrinkled scrap of paper out of the notebook and handed it to Bright. 'I never spoke to Tess there. I don't think she stayed there long. I called it before I flew out. That's how I got in touch with Kate.'

'Kate Creech was there?' So that's where Creech had gone after Glastonbury. He glanced at Atkins. 'And Sally?'

'I told you.'

'Oh yes. You had a row the day she moved into her flat. The flat was a mess, now it's neat. Meaning it looks like she was alive after the row.'

His head rolled as though he'd been punched. 'She was alive after our row. I left her there. She was crying.' He made that scraping noise again in his chest. Bright didn't offer the box of tissues.

'You hit her, Nat?'

'Hit her?'

'That's right, hit her. Did you get a little bit upset, a little bit carried away and bash her about a bit?'

'Me?'

'It can happen to anyone.'

'I don't hit women!'

'No?'

'No!'

There was a silence. Atkins offered Crosby a cigarette. He didn't notice. His great eyes were staring at Bright. Atkins lit it for himself. Crosby said, 'Someone hit her?'

'Hit who?'

'Sally.'

'Well, we don't know because we don't know if the woman is Sally. Do we?'

Nat's eyes closed. He sighed. His chin dropped on to his chest. Sleeping or praying.

'Now, Crosby, when was the last time you were in Kate Creech's house?'

The eyes opened slowly, fixed on Atkins. 'I'm a suspect, then?'

'Well, that's what we're here to find out,' Atkins said. 'Isn't it, guv?'

Bright said, 'We're trying to eliminate you, Nat. Let's say we need your help with a few aspects of the case.'

Atkins said, 'We ask the questions, Mr Crosby. You're here to answer them.'

Crosby picked up the tea and drank it cold. He wiped his mouth. The knuckles on his long hands were big knobs. He said, 'I can't remember the question.'

Atkins said, 'When you were – '

'Oh yes. I've never been to Kate's house.'

'Sure?'

'Yes. Oh.'

'Yes oh?'

'Yes. Once. When she first moved in. I was sitting in my car. Near the church in Lady Margaret Road. There was a – I was just sitting there, I was on my way to visit Tess and just – stopped a minute. I saw Kate coming down the street. We talked and she said she'd bought a little house just round the corner, come and have a cup of tea. So. It's a nice little house. It was a – not so much a mess but new. Smelled of paint and wood shavings. Nice.'

'It doesn't smell of paint and wood shavings now,' Bright said.

Crosby shook his head. 'I never saw Kate again until today.'

'I didn't ask you if you'd seen Kate. I asked if you'd been to her house.'

'How could I?'

'Tess had keys.'

'I haven't seen Tess.'

'Sally saw Tess.'

'How do you know?'

'You said Tess helped her move.'

'Oh yes!'

'Can I have a word, guv?'

Bright turned an expressionless face to the DC, got up and went out. Atkins followed. They watched Crosby through the glass. His big hands came up to his face. Then he stretched his arms straight out across the table and laid his head down on his arms.

Atkins said, 'Your time's up, guv. You've had him longer than you should already for one session.' Bright was watching Crosby and didn't answer, didn't even show he'd heard. 'He's punch drunk, guv. Better give him a break, right?'

'Mr Nice Guy,' Bright said.

'Me or him, guv?'

'Take your pick.' Bright went back into the room. Atkins had to follow him. 'DC Atkins is right, you're jet lagged, mate. But before we give you a break I want you to listen carefully and tell us what you want us to do. Right?' Crosby came up from the table and looked at them.

'Semen stains were found on the sheets of Kate Creech's bed. She doesn't know how they got there, she says. They can't be placed at the time of the killing but it seems logical there could be a connection. With me so far?'

103

Crosby crossed his arms over his chest, trapping his hands in his armpits. He breathed in and held it like he couldn't manage to breathe out, couldn't move, locked up.

'Right. Now, if you haven't been in Kate's house in what, three years? you won't mind giving us a sample, will you? This DNA stuff's pretty accurate these days, so if those stains are nothing to do with you, you'll be cleared out the picture, won't you? And we'll be able to move on.'

The silence went on. Then Crosby breathed out. He said in a voice that was almost no voice, 'I think I've got to wait until – Kate sends this lawyer. I'm sorry, mate. I think I've got to wait.'

Pretty acute intelligence for a bewildered innocent matey suspect deep in jet lag and shock. 'A-ha.' Amusement returned behind Bright's impassive mask. 'Well, we've got no objection to that but you'll understand if we keep you on the premises until he gets here, okay?'

'You're going to lock me up?'

'Just till he gets here. Shouldn't be too long. Should it, Atkins? You'll be able to get a bit of rest, have a kip, should think you need it.' And Bright left the room.

Atkins caught him up in the corridor. 'Guv, there's nothing to go on, we got no evidence, you know we haven't, not till we get the samples.'

'You left the suspect alone in the interview room, Tommy?' Bright's eyes were focused on the middle distance.

Atkins wasn't phased. 'We got nothing but circumstantial.'

'Thanks for the advice, Tommy. Keep an eye on him, eh?' Bright prowled off, head down, shoulders up.

'We've got semen stains on the bed at the scene. Two possible women the victim could be. This bloke is connected to both the possible victims and to the woman who owns the house. He was in this country at the time the pathologist's report places the crime.'

'So you need samples.' The DCI raised an eyebrow. 'Has he agreed?'

'Asked for his lawyer.'

'Well, wait for his lawyer.'

'It's Ted Adams. He's a belligerent little bastard.'

'Get the samples if you can. You've got just about enough circumstantial for that.'

'Thanks, guv.' Bright meant it. He was grateful. A lot of DCIs were so scared of PACE these days they forgot you were there to catch villains.

23

SWAPS

Coming through the pass door he saw Kate Creech in the waiting-room, her hair tangled in a black cloud round her white face. A small tough-looking guy sat next to her.

'He's come to see Nat Crosby.' Her mouth quivered a bit.

'Hello, Ted.' Bright stuck out his hand. Adams shook it. Quite a grip. Bright remembered. He caught Kate Creech's eye. She looked away.

Adams said, 'Kate's filled me in. Can I have a few minutes with Crosby alone?'

'If I can have a few words with Muz Creech.'

Ted looked at her. She shrugged. Ted said, 'Help yourself.'

'You saw this Laura,' Bright said. Her face looked paralysed. 'She tell you where this Tess is?' Kate in despair shook her head. 'Come on, Muz Creech.'

Her voice was like fingernails on silk. 'Tess left her five months ago. She hasn't been in touch. Laura knows nothing.'

'You telling me the truth?'

'You'll check anyway.'

'Write the address.' He gave her a memo pad. She flexed her fingers as if they were brittle. She wrote Ebenezer Chapel, Oulton. He watched her. 'Yes, we'll check.'

Her eyes looked despair. 'I've given you everyone now.' She sat. He stood looking. Neither moved.

Ted felt he was interrupting. 'Okay, inspector?'

Bright seemed to come back from somewhere. 'Er, yeah. A-ha.' He turned back to Kate. 'Thanks.' It sounded like an apology.

Her mouth moved, without sound.

'Come on, then.' Bright ushered Ted through the pass door, then kept ahead of him, fast as a fox and as light on his feet. He opened a door. 'Here's your lawyer, mate.'

Atkins stood up, all surprised green eyes. Bright jerked his head to get Atkins out. He said, 'You've got five minutes, that's all.'

Atkins said, 'But, guv – '

'Go and get a cup of tea, Atkins, and get me one while you're at it.'

Atkins shut his mouth on a protest and went. What his mouth hadn't said, his back did.

Bright said, 'I've got permission to take samples. See if you can persuade him to co-operate,' and shut the door on them.

'I'm Ted Adams. I'm Kate's solicitor. She thinks your need is greater than hers apparently.'

These great blue searchlights swept over him for a second. 'Nat Crosby,' he said. 'Thanks for coming.'

'*De nada.*' Ted sat on the edge of the table.

Crosby said nothing. His big bony hands hung between his knees and his head hung over them.

'Listen, I've come here to help you if I can, advise you. I don't want to know if you – er, did it or not – the crime, I mean.' Crosby's head came up. The eyes were curious, an incredible blue and big under the heavy lids. They looked bruised like kids' eyes when they're being punished and don't know why. 'What I want to say is, if you weren't there you've nothing to fear, obviously – '

'They want me to give samples.' Crosby was shaking. 'They want me to jerk off in here or what?'

Ted gave a short laugh. 'Don't imagine you'd be capable just at the moment, would you?'

Nat's face relaxed.

'Not exactly inspiring, is it?' Ted said.

Nat breathed in deep, and out. Shook his head.

'No,' Ted said, 'They'll settle for hair, probably. Saliva.'

'Haven't got much of that either.'

'They'll be getting the doctor lined up.'

'Doctor?'

'Bright's given us five minutes alone. So anything you want to tell me, tell me now.'

Nat said slowly, 'I never thought I'd find myself in a position like this. In here like this. I'm scared. People talk about shitting yourself, you can see how that could happen. All your controls go.' He held out his hands. 'See that?' They shook. 'But the coppers are interesting. That little guy who's in charge? Bright, is his name? He has his problems. I'd guess he's new. They don't like him. They don't trust him. It's getting to him, except he's not letting it. Keeps his eye on the ball. You do any sports?'

'Spot of rugby.'

'Thought so.'

'Why?'

'You can always tell by looking. You know everything in one look. That's why real love is always at first sight – '

'Listen, Nat – '

'I don't want to say anything.'

'Do you object to giving them samples?'

106

'Yes, I object.'

'Might I ask why?'

'Because – ' He swung sideways on the chair, bent his back like he might throw up.

'Nat, if the samples would clear you – '

The door opened. Ted looked at his watch.

'A-ha, not quite five. Well, you can't have everything, can you?' Atkins's face appeared over Bright's shoulder, beaming satisfaction. 'Go and get another chair, Atkins. If you want to sit down that is.' For a second the lad's face mutinied then he left. 'Get anywhere?' Bright said. No one answered. 'You going to give us samples, Nat?' Silence. 'See, I've got permission to take them, so – '

'I'd say you don't have enough evidence against my client to insist against his wishes.'

'Not tonight, mate, but by tomorrow I will have.'

'You're keeping Mr Crosby overnight?'

'That's right. Come in, Atkins, make yourself at home.' Atkins didn't look at him.

'On what grounds? He says he wasn't there. Without samples you have no evidence he was there.'

'You know I can keep him for twenty-four hours and I'm doing that. Unless you'd like to talk to us, Nat? It might be easier in the long run.'

They all looked at Nat. His eyes were weird. They seemed to pull all the light in the room, fill with it. They had no middles to them, that was it, no dark bit in the middle, that was what gave them this blind look, seeing not what was in front of them but something beyond. He said, 'I didn't kill anyone. I've never even hit anyone. Not since I hit my best mate. We were nine. This pig sports master made us put the gloves on and hit each other. I couldn't see the sense in hitting my best mate, you know? Anyway, he hit me then I hit him then he hit me a bit harder because the sports master said to, so I hit him again and he went down. He was out. I thought he was dead. I thought I'd killed my best mate. I asked God to make him alive again, I said I'll never hit anyone again if you make him alive. And He did. My mate opened his eyes and said Hello Nat. So you see I can't hit people. And never a woman. I can't understand that. Sally's fragile. She's so fragile. How could anyone hit her?'

'But you were there, Nat. You and Sally were in Kate's house. You had it away on Kate's bed, Nat. You did. You had a row with her in Kate's house.'

'You don't have to say anything,' Ted said.

'That's right, Nat, you don't have to say anything. But if you didn't kill her it won't help you to keep stumm now. I don't want to arrest you. Matter of fact I don't think you did kill her. But I think you were there.

And if you were, that means you were the last person to see her, you see? Apart from the killer. You see? So if you can give us what you know, the quicker I can get on with this investigation and find out what happened to her.'

'You don't even know that the body is Sally Crowe, do you?' The lawyer's tone was neutral.

Atkins didn't hide a gleam of satisfaction. Bright's look hardened. 'I asked for some stuff from the lab, Atkins. Go and see if it's arrived, will you?'

Nat was watching Bright like an imprinted duckling now; he didn't even see Atkins leave the room.

'May my client know what evidence you have got?'

'I don't see why not. DC Atkins has gone to pick up some sets of fingerprints. From Kate's house. From Sally's flat. The lab has been doing a spot of mix'n'match. Nat's fingerprints are going to be in both places.'

'Were you to prove that to be the case, it would only tell you that my client – '

'A-ha. I know. It won't say he did it. But it will place him in the house.'

'Place me,' Nat murmured.

'And until you do have at least matching prints you don't have enough evidence to keep him here.'

Bright leaned back in his chair. Its front legs came up off the floor. He crossed his arms over the scruffy leather jacket. Darts of amusement jumped under his skin, his face was alive with it. Ted wanted to kick him. Nat watched him as though he were an animal in a zoo that he'd paid to see. They waited.

Atkins came back and handed a folder to Bright. Bright looked through it. Silence but for the paper flicking. Bright looked up from the folder straight at Nat. Silence. He closed the folder. He stood up. He said, 'Okay, Atkins, take him down.' He left the room.

Ted caught up with Bright at the duty officer's desk. In the interview room and the corridors you forgot there was daylight outside. Now they saw it, and themselves reflected in the window of the pass door. They were the same height but didn't look it, Ted so stocky, Bright so wiry.

'I don't have to remind you this doesn't make him guilty, John.'

'No, you don't, Ted.'

'Twenty-four hours. That's your limit.'

'And another twelve if I need it.'

'You won't need it. He's shitting himself, he could confess to anything.'

'I don't need him to confess to anything. Not once I get samples.'

'Samples would not prove him the killer. They would only place him at the house.'

'At the house with a woman.'

'Possibly with a woman. Possibly is supposition, I don't need to tell you. Possibly isn't evidence.'

'Probably at the time the woman was killed.'

'*A* woman was killed.'

Bright gave him a sideways squinting glance sharpened to a point like a knife. He was dangerous in a way Ted found hard to handle. He resisted you with his metallic stare, his humorous mask, slid out of your grasp, eluded you, then popped up somewhere else, behind you, taunting you. He'd be hell on the rugby field.

Edgley came up. She handed Bright an armful of papers. Bright said, 'You can see your client in the morning. He'll be safe with us.' Ted was left standing. The pass door was opened for him. He went through.

Kate was still in the waiting-room. But for the open eyes staring he'd have said she was asleep. He stood right in front of her before she focused. She said, 'Ted?' as though she'd ceased to believe in his existence. 'They've kept him in?'

'Yes.'

'Does that mean they've arrested him?'

'They can only keep him thirty-six hours without charging him with something.'

'How can they charge Nat?'

'They've placed him at your house.'

'How?'

'Fingerprints.'

'But he's only been to my house once. Three years ago at least. He never went upstairs even. He just had a cup of tea, standing at the kitchen sink.'

'That's what he said.'

'Well, it's true.'

Kentish Town Road, stiff with traffic, knee-deep in litter, hectic with people. He piloted her into Tolli's, the Italian coffee place. She sat down but she didn't speak.

'Your coffee's getting cold.'

She took a sip. 'You know why he came into my house? He was afraid of death.'

'What?'

'Yes. I found him sitting in his car just down from the church in Lady Margaret Road. There was a funeral. All these black cars, the hearse, flowers, people in black clothes. He got out of his car and came round the corner with me, he looked terrible. When we were standing in my kitchen he said, "I couldn't drive on to Tess's because of that funeral." I didn't know what he meant, I mean it wasn't blocking the road or anything. He said, "I've got this fear of death. My kids are going to die. I've got death in me. I'm a carrier. I've got this dread all the time. I'm sure I'm going to die." I said well, you're not dying now, you're having a cup of tea in my kitchen. He didn't laugh; he looked the way he does, you know, as though he's pulling an idea towards him slowly on the end of a long string. "Oh ye-es!" he says.'

Ted hadn't met people like these before; it was like being with kids. 'Is he all there?' he said.

'All there?' She looked offended. 'He's gifted, he's – I was going to say clever but that's not it. He hears a different music. He was a marvellous actor. Then he started to direct. Then to write. Now he writes and directs his own stuff.'

'He directs?' Ted expressed disbelief. The guy came across a hand's breadth from thoroughly simple. 'He directs other people? Tells them what to do?'

'He's excellent. Finds out the real core of meaning in the play. Knows how to get the actors to dig deep, knows how to pull it together. And he's not solemn, he's playful, like a bossy kid having a ball.' She shivered. Or rather a kind of ripple went over her skin.

'You fancy the guy?'

'I was crazy about him once. It was quite something. Took me a while to get over it. Long time ago.'

She was over it, then. But retained more than a touch of tenderness in the area, that was bloody blatant. 'So why did it end?'

'The play was over. I had to come back to London. He wanted me to stay on in Nottingham.'

'Why didn't you, if you were so crazy about him?'

'Well – you always come back to London when the job's over. It's where you live. It's where the work is. I'd have felt a right pillock, you know, spare prick at the wedding, just hanging around, being someone's *woman*.'

'How did Nat feel about that?'

'Nat just couldn't see it. If a woman loves you, she's your woman, she stays with you, you know? Our last tryst – if you could call it that – was in my old flat in Islington. The electricity had been cut off.' She smiled. 'In all senses. There was no heat. It's always cold when I see Nat. Cold rooms. It was cold in my house that day when he thought he was dying. Cold in Sally's flat this morning.'

Ted said, 'He wanted Sally to go to the States with him.'

'Yes,' she said. Then sipped some coffee. Then put the cup down. 'Yes.'

She didn't want him to see the thought in her eyes, but he did. She said, 'He couldn't kill anyone.'

'No?'

'I'm sure you're a good lawyer, Ted.'

'Why?'

'Well, like I'm sure you're a good rugby player.'

'You haven't seen me do either.'

'I'll come to your next game.'

'Looks like I might be a bit busy for rugby the next few weeks.'

Her mouth moved oddly. 'Yes.'

They'd finished the coffee. There seemed nothing else to stay for. He said, 'Where are you going now?'

'Oh. I'll go back to Aggie's, I guess.'

'She's your friend in Tulse Hill?'

'Yes.'

'Okay, I'll take you to Aggie's.'

'Thanks. Where's your car?'

'Lady Margaret Road. But I think you should go to your house first.'

'What for?'

'Listen to your messages.'

'I'd know from the police if there was anything important. I'm sure they hear everything before I do.'

Ted made no comment. They reached the corner of her street. 'I'll come in with you,' he said.

'Are you suggesting I'm afraid to go in alone?'

'Give me your keys.'

'Get stuffed.' She opened the door herself. And then she opened her eyes. The place was neat. The smell had gone. It was hard to believe in the recent presence of bodies, alive or dead. Now the house was dead too.

'The cleaner did a good job. Thanks.'

'No sweat.'

She picked up the post. The usual junk and an A4 envelope that felt like a script. A script? It aroused about as much interest as a gas bill.

'Is there anything you need?' Ted said.

'What?'

'To take to Aggie's.'

She shook her head, standing over the answerphone. A voice was speaking. A man's voice. A light voice. 'Kate? Hello. So sorry to hear about this thing. Are you all right? Give me a ring, if you'd like to. I'm on . . .' While she wrote down the number a woman's voice followed. 'Hi, Kate. This is Allie at Diana Sutcliffe's.'

'My agent,' she said.

111

'Will you give me a ring please. It's about the Bristol script. Thanks.'
That was all, just the scrag ends of old messages after that. So the script
was from Bristol. Well, that was nice.

'Let's go,' she said.

'Who was the bloke?'

'Oliver.'

'The guy you used to live with, the guy you were living with when you
and Nat – '

'Yes.' She didn't say anything else.

In the car he said, 'Will you call Oliver?'

'I don't know. I might.'

'Could he have had keys?'

'I told you, no!'

'Okay, okay.'

It wasn't till Camden Town she said, 'Sorry.'

'It's okay.'

'So you said.'

He said, 'Bright seems to have dropped you as a suspect.'

She turned in her seat to face him. 'I can't make it out. Can you? He says
I'm off the hook. But I don't see how I can be from his point of view. Not
completely. It's not a long drive to London, I could have been back in
Coventry before morning. Who'd have known? Even with bronchitis,
sweating cobs, hoping for death as a merciful release, I was playing Medea
every night. If you can play Medea with bronchitis, believe me, you can
drive to London and back, no problem.'

'But who did you kill?'

'Ah, now there I do have a problem.'

'And why did you kill her?'

'Oh, fuck knows.'

They laughed silently. She wiped her eyes. Later she said, 'He gets me
to lead him to my friends. I refuse to tell him about people so he just hangs
about till I take him straight there.'

'Clever little bugger, isn't he?'

'So sharp he'd cut himself. That's why I won't call Oliver.'

'I see.'

'I won't give him Oliver.' She wiped her eyes again. She wasn't laughing
this time. 'I gave him Nat.' Ted said nothing. She said, 'I thought I was clever.'

'You are clever. But – '

' – I'm not as clever as him.'

'That's right. Don't underestimate him.'

'Believe me, I don't.'

*

112

He'd polished off the lasagne and salad. Aggie had changed into her old embroidered kaftan which had a deep V-neck. She leaned over the table and said, 'Hot sponge and custard?' with her throatiest rising inflection.

Kate found herself irritated, and surprised to have feelings not entirely connected with The Event.

Ted was into a second helping of sponge and custard. Aggie was flushed, glowing globes of breast squeezed in the V of her kaftan. 'Have a glass of wine, Kate?'

Kate said, 'I'd like to phone Oliver but I can't.'

'Why not? I keep telling you this phone's not tapped.'

'How do you know?'

'Anyway you don't have to do it from here.'

'No.' She sipped. Even the oaky Rioja tasted sour.

Ted looked up. 'Unless you *want* them to check out Oliver.'

To Kate the lights seemed to flare then dim. Silence crept round the kitchen.

Aggie said, 'Look, what the hell, kid? They'll check out all your mates anyway. They've got to. You can't do damn all about it. Might as well send them your address book.' A heavy drumbeat blared from above. 'Danny!' The beat marginally diminished. 'Come into the other room. It's not as deafening in there. He never starts it till after dinner, it's our deal, so I can't complain. I'll bring the coffee.'

Kate and Ted crossed the wide hallway, dabbed with splashes of coloured light from the stained glass of the front door. They went into the room. Kate stood behind the sofa, too preoccupied to go further, or sit. Ted shut the door. He stood beside her. He took her hand. She turned to him and he kissed her. His lips tasted of custard. Comforting. She smiled. He said, 'That's better.'

'What is?'

'Everything.'

'Oh?'

'You smiled anyway.'

Aggie felt the difference when she came in. She was aggrieved but she didn't sulk; Aggie never sulked. She looked sideways at Kate and said with a wicked eye, 'Coffee, *dear*?' Then she said, 'You're bushed but it's no use trying to sleep till Dan's gone to bed. Midnight, I'm afraid. That's the rule.' She looked at Ted, put her head on one side and said in a light little husky little voice, 'Do you want to sleep here too?'

A sudden stillness came over him and Kate. They were both looking at their hands side by side on the sofa cushion. Nothing happened, then he said, 'No. Thanks, Aggie. I've got to be getting back.'

After she'd seen him out Aggie said, 'I wish you'd told me he had the hots for you. I wouldn't have gone to all this trouble. And expense! At

113

least half an ounce of the perfume Dan brought me back from his school trip to Boulogne.'

'Does he?'

'He does.'

'I didn't know.'

Aggie sat down on the sofa. Kate leaned on her. 'I'm so tired, Ags. I didn't know you could feel this tired.' Suddenly she sat up. 'Ken sees Oliver sometimes. They questioned Michael. What if – Aggie, I've got to see Ken.'

24

WITH FRIENDS LIKE THIS

He looked even bigger when he was sad. He loomed in a towelling dressing-gown with pulled threads and coffee stains, his face was black with three days' growth of beard. When she said it was all her fault he shrugged and shook his head. He didn't have the energy for anger or denial.

'Ken. Have you eaten at all?'

He shook his head again. She went into the kitchen, opened the fridge, found a cauliflower, a green pepper, two tomatoes and a limp carrot. She started chopping. John Bright's influence spread far. Food, the answer to life's little problems.

When she took the bowls of salad in, Ken sat where she'd left him, drooped on the sofa. He ate in an absent-minded way. She said, 'Has Michael been in touch?'

'He rings every night.'

'What does he say?'

'He cries and asks if he can come back.'

'Don't you want him back?'

A shrug. He shovelled the crunchy bits of vegetation into his mouth.

'Ken? You hate living alone.'

'I can't be lied to, Kate.'

'Oh, you are a fool.' His face became mutinous but she persisted. 'A lie is just a lie. It isn't a murder, Ken.'

'That's where you're wrong. A lie is a murder. I can no longer trust him. If you can't trust a person there's no future there, no hope.'

'You're making a tragedy out of a little mistake.'

'He saw Oliver while I was away.'

'God. Did he tell the police that?'

'No, but he told them we knew Oliver.'

She let this information seep through her veins. Michael saw Oliver. Michael could have borrowed her keys. Oliver could have been in her house. Oliver could have – The police must already be on to him. She put her hand in front of her eyes a moment. 'Ken, it's me you should cut out of your life, not Michael. It's me who told them you had keys. It's my fault Michael was questioned. It's my fault – '

He banged the bowl down and stood up.'It's not your fault Michael lied to me!'

'No. It's yours!'

'Mine? How?'

'You frighten him. Like you're frightening me now. You're a great big strong bloke with a great big horrible temper. And you're stupid. You're thick! Someone's offering you love but that's not enough for you, you want perfection. What makes you think you deserve it, you asshole? None of us deserves anything. We should all be grateful for what we can get.' She stood at the door. The salad had shot out of the bowl and was spread on the carpet like sick. 'You love him, Ken. He loves you. For heaven's sake. Save something. Don't make me responsible for this too.'

'You're wrong. There's no love where there are lies. There's no possibility of love. If you'd been lied to as much as I have you'd know.'

'You're just addicted to being betrayed.'

'What?'

'"Look what they've done to me, me the big innocent, poor old me." You don't want love; you *want* betrayal.' She hadn't known she was going to say this, but as she said it she found that it was true. Ken also found that it was true. He gaped. He began to bluster then stopped. She said, 'If you love him, get him back and teach him not to lie. Teach him it's safe to tell you the truth.'

When she banged the door he was staring open-mouthed, a fork dangling, miniature, from his hand.

She shut herself in the phone box, hesitated then dialled. 'Oliver?'

'Kate!' His voice was as familiar as a glove. They'd been such mates before the misery of the split.

She said, 'Oliver, I won't talk but let's have a drink.'

'Sure.'

'I'll meet you where?'

'The French Pub?'

'Too noisy,' she said.

'I'm on the Radio Rep now.'

'Great.'

'Yeah. So how about one of those mews pubs near Broadcasting House? The Dover Castle?'

'Okay.'

'I've only got an hour for lunch.'

'I'll be there at five past one.'

'It's good to hear you, Kate.'

Was it? She didn't know.

He hadn't changed. She'd always thought his name suited his appearance: smooth olive skin, smooth black hair, smooth slim body; even his eyelids drooped over his eyes in smooth olive ovals. But his smile was innocent. He always looked a little apprehensive, though relaxed, and trusting. He was a younger brother and it showed. She was touched to see him sitting there by the fireplace waiting for her.

She said, 'Listen, I may have got you into trouble. I may have been followed here. I shouldn't have arranged to meet you. If I go now – '

He pulled her hand and she sat down. 'Say hello to me, Kate.'

'Hello, Oliver.'

He kissed her lips lightly, gravely. 'Hello, Kate.'

He went to get her a drink and a sandwich. She looked round the pub. Office parties, mainly young men in suits. A few old codgers at the bar, regulars. She hadn't been followed, she was sure. But then she'd been sure before.

Oliver said he liked being on the Radio Rep. 'They're nice people. And I'm lucky, I'm getting good parts, all different, I'm always busy. It's not badly paid either, really. At least it comes in every month. I'm so relaxed! For six months I can breathe easy, pay the bills. And I'm learning. It's not easy working with the microphone. Well, you know, better than most, don't you, Kate? I haven't got the hang of it yet. But I'm getting there.' She hadn't said a word. 'Kate?'

'Why did you get in touch, Ollie? Why did you leave a message on my machine?'

'Well . . .' The brown eyes gave her an apprehensive look. 'You know the police came round to see me?'

'*No*? Already?'

He put down his Guinness and pressed all his fingertips splayed on the edge of the table. He said, 'Well, I didn't tell them but – I've been in your house.'

She didn't speak, just stared at him.

'Yes,' he said, 'I was curious, you know? I knew you'd moved, bought your own place. I was round at Ken's – '

116

'Ken?'

'Michael, you know, his friend, was there. We'd been smoking some dope. Just pleasantly mellow, you know? Not really stoned or anything. And I said come on, let's go round there. To your place, I mean. I knew Ken had keys. You were away, you'd never have known.'

'Surely Ken said no.'

'That's right, Ken said no. But one night a week or so later I went round and just Michael was there. He thought it was a gas. We went round and let ourselves in.'

'When was this?'

'When you were doing *Duet For One* at Plymouth. You'd just opened. That's how I knew it was safe.'

'That was six months ago.'

'Yes.'

'Oliver – '

'I know, I know. I'm going to tell the police. I've got to.'

'No. You don't have to. Please. Leave it alone. You've no idea what it's like. I wish you hadn't told me.'

'I know they've questioned Michael.'

'Yes.'

'He didn't tell them because he didn't want to put me in it.'

'Or himself.'

'Sure, yes, but – '

'I gather Michael is not unknown to the police.'

'Yes, he said something to me. No details, you know?'

'So don't stir things, Oliver. Don't. Leave it alone.'

He drank some Guinness. 'I never went back again after that. To your house. I felt a bit terrible actually, once we were in. You not there, you know? It's a lovely place, Kate, you've made it nice. That gorgeous yellow carpet. Coming down from the dope, I felt like a thief. I've been feeling bad ever since. Thought I ought to have let you know.'

'So you should've. But it's different now.'

'Okay.'

'So don't, please don't, Oliver. Don't go to them.'

'What if they've got my fingerprints or something? From your house.'

'If they haven't got you, they've nothing to compare them with, idiot.'

'Oh yes. Oh no.'

'Oliver, just stay out of it. As long as you can.'

'I don't know if I can.'

'Why?'

'They've said they might want me to give samples.'

'For DNA?' She saw a tiny face of horror mirrored in each of his eyes.

'I don't see how I can refuse. If they do ask.'

117

She stared into her drink. Oliver writhing on her bed with – Whom? Tess? Sally? Michael? Person or persons unknown? These images too were tiny, clear, distant, wrong end of the telescope, seen from above. She covered her eyes. Much time seemed to pass. Oliver was silent. She looked up. Into the gentle fearful brown eyes.

'You tell them one thing, Ollie, and this is where it leads.'

'I know, I am an idiot. I got in a bit of a panic. This police guy was so friendly and everything, I was just telling him about – well – us, you know?'

'Who was this police guy?'

'Detective Inspector John Bright.'

She groaned. 'How did I guess.'

He gulped at his drink. 'Who's this bloke they've taken in for questioning? Anyone we know?'

'What?'

'It's in the *Standard*.' He fished in his folded overcoat and brought out a crumpled newspaper. '"A man is helping with enquiries in connection with the murder of a woman at the house of actress Kate Creech . . ."'

Kate couldn't speak, seeing it in print. She shook her head.

'Don't you know who he is, Kate?'

She swallowed some Brakspear's to wet her throat but still couldn't speak.

He said, 'Is it Nat?'

'Nat?' She stared at him. 'Why should you think that?'

'I don't know. Just came into my head.'

She shook her head as if to say this was a crazy notion of Oliver's. 'Just don't let the next one be you, okay?'

'See, I told them about Nat and you and – all that.'

She swallowed. 'All what?'

'Nothing really, just about the split and how I once took Tess for you and – '

She stood up to put on her coat.

'Stay, Kate. Just stay and finish your drink.'

'No, Oliver, I've got to go.'

Even his stricken face couldn't keep her there. After all her refusal to betray them, her friends, Nat and Tess. All the secrets she had tried so hard to keep, released like doves from a hat. Just a chat with your friendly neighbourhood copper. Sweet confiding Oliver. She had to get away from him.

She sat on a bench in Regent's Park, in the avenue that Roy Strong had ruined. It suited her state. The herbaceous border, a perfect windbreak, had been ripped out, so now a gale sliced across the suburban plantings of garish Technicolor polyanthus and the silly imitation stone urns. It cut in under her skin. She crossed her arms over her chest.

Oliver. One of nature's innocents. That's what she'd always thought. But Oliver had been in her house. Oliver could have cut more keys. Oliver had told John Bright about Nat. Nat and her. Nat and Tess. She put her hand over her mouth. *Oliver wants Nat to be guilty. Mentioning Nat to the police is his revenge. But just a minute: telling them about Nat makes Oliver a suspect himself. Possessiveness. Then taking Tess for me: if he could do that once he could do it again; if he thought he was killing me, that would be the ultimate revenge. But surely if he had done it he'd never have mentioned it at all. But then John Bright's clever, he'd have wormed it out of Oliver. How can I know? How do I know anything about anyone? What does Ken know about betrayal? I now have no one in my life I can trust.*

Except Lizzie.

Lizzie?

Lizzie has never been less than nasty to me; the perfect sister she ain't; but she'd never betray me, she'd never do anything behind my back.

And I'm without a home. I'm out of places I can go. She wiped some wet off her face. The wind had made her eyes water. She was way beyond tears. She got up off the bench.

25

TWO FOR THE PRICE OF ONE

'The samples match, Nat.'

The great heavy eyes swept over him.

'It was you in Kate's bed.'

Nat nodded slowly, resigned.

'Why didn't you tell me? You knew the samples would match. Why?'

'I hoped, I suppose.'

'What for? A miracle?' Nat smiled. He was so pale. They talk about the ghost of a smile; this was the smile of a ghost. 'Listen, mate, this does not look good for you. Does it?' The eyes stayed on him, blue light bulbs in the white face. He looked like some peasant dragged in off the fields, barely able to read and write. Hard to recall he was meant to be this clever bloke, writing plays, directing movies. You had to be tough to make it in Hollywood, that's what they said. How did he manage? What was the truth of him?

119

'But,' Nat said in his hoarse whisper, 'I didn't do anything.'

'You screwed someone in Kate Creech's bed.'

'Yes.'

'So tell us about it.'

'Yes. Well, I didn't have long in London.'

'When was this?'

Nat gave the date, a Saturday seven weeks ago. 'Sally was moving house. Her place was a mess, I told you. Packing cases, newspaper, things piled up. She said Tess had been helping her to move.'

'Tess?'

'Now you're doing it.'

'What?'

'Saying her name like that.' The smile of the ghost again.

'A-ha. It's catching. Get on with it.'

'Sally told me Tess had the keys to Kate's place. She'd lent the keys to Sally, said Kate was away and wouldn't mind.'

'You believed that, did you? That Kate wouldn't mind? She was an ex-girlfriend of yours, right?'

'I didn't think. I just wanted to be with Sally. We had to talk. I wanted her to come back to the States with me. She didn't want to hang around the mess in her flat. So we went to Kate's.'

'Together?'

'Yes, in a cab.'

'In a cab. I see you're going to spare us no details.'

'We went to bed.'

'A-ha.'

'We hadn't seen each other for six weeks.'

'Excuses, excuses.'

'I asked her to join me in the States, come out there and live with me. I told her she'd like it. She would. I rent this white house with a green roof in the hills. There's a pool. Imagine. I couldn't see why she wouldn't come.'

'Her work is here, I suppose?' Edgley said.

The men turned to her, in equal astonishment at the fact that she'd spoken and at what she had said.

'She could get work there if she wanted to work,' Nat said.

'Don't you think women should work?'

'I think some things are more important than work.'

'For men? Or just for women?'

Nat looked at her. He gave a shrug you could hardly see, and said nothing. Edgley turned to Bright with an expression of defiance and trepidation mixed. Bright gave the subject a moment to drop. 'So she refused to go?'

120

'Yes. She had all kinds of objections: her new flat, her career. She doesn't *have* a career. Just jobs. One after another but just jobs.'

'Isn't that what you make a career out of in your business: jobs?'

'No, a career's more than that.'

'What's the difference?'

'Talent, seriousness, commitment to the work. Sally doesn't have those things. She'll drift and get old and – ' He looked at Edgley's set mouth. 'She'd be better off with me, honestly she would.'

'You told her all that?' Bright's eyebrows lifted.

'I don't know what I said. I asked her how she saw her future. She got wild and told me to' – he looked at Edgley – 'leave.' He looked at Bright. 'I felt really violent, mate.'

No one spoke now. Till at last Nat put a long bony hand over his face and sighed. 'So I put my clothes on and left.'

'You hit her, didn't you, Nat?'

'No. I never hit a woman in my life, I told you that.' His hoarse voice rose in pitch.

'Okay, okay, but I bet you wanted to.'

'She screamed at me: how I despised her, thought she was around just for my benefit, how I despised women, just used them. Something about fantasy, used them for my fantasy or something. I didn't understand. It was all crap, you know. She'd been talking to Tess, she couldn't have thought of that by herself, she's a simple person, Sally.'

Bright could almost see the smoke coming out of Edgley's ears, if she spoke now she could screw up everything. 'What then, Nat?'

'I couldn't make her see sense. I told her that was it, then, I couldn't see her again. She said why was it always all or nothing with me. I said if I go now, that's the end. She said you don't love me, you just love your fantasy of me. I felt so angry when she said that, man, I thought I *was* going to hit her. So I went. I put my clothes on and went.'

'You left her in the house on her own?'

'Yes.'

'What did you do then?'

'I walked. Round those streets. Nice streets. Nice houses. I passed the house where Tess had lived before the commune. That made me think a bit. I was still angry but I thought I'd go back and make it up with Sally. I didn't want to lose her, mate, believe me. I rang the bell, I banged on the door, I called through the letter box. Nothing. Not a sound. She'd got dressed and gone.'

'Maybe she just wouldn't let you in.'

'I'm sure she'd gone. I know Sally: if I came back she'd let me in.'

Edgley looked sceptical.

Bright said, 'How long were you walking the streets?'

'I don't know. Half an hour. Well, maybe more like an hour, I can't say.'

'A-ha.'

'So I didn't make it up with her. I went back to her flat in Primrose Hill. There was no reply there either. Then I had meetings till late. I kept phoning, got the answerphone, and I was out on a plane at crack of day. I couldn't do anything.'

'Was her flat still in a mess?'

'What? Oh. Yes. Yes, it was.'

'What happened to her handbag, Nat?'

'Handbag?'

'Did she have it with her?'

'I don't know.'

'Women don't go anywhere without their handbags. Do they, constable?'

'No, sir.'

'I guess she had it then, I don't know. She was wearing a white thing.'

'We found no clothes at Kate's place, no handbag.'

'Well, that means she walked out of there, doesn't it?' His face filled with a pale hope.

'So who's the body, Nat?'

'It's not Sally, it can't be.'

'So you're saying Sally killed the woman, whoever she is.'

'Sally? No!'

'So who did? You?'

'No.'

'Then disposed of her things. What did you do with them? Stick 'em in a litter bin? Not in Kentish Town, they're all full to bursting, junk flowing out like lava over the streets. Canal at Camden Lock? What did you do with her stuff?'

Nat looked at him unbelieving. Bright felt foolish, as though the guy was criticising his performance. He could see Edgley was pleased though. That's more like it, she was thinking. Her back was bristling with pride, like his ma's cat bringing in a mouse to show it off. As if the mouse had ever had a chance.

At last, Nat's hoarse whisper: 'Sorry, mate, but where's this lawyer of Kate's? Ted, is he called? I reckon I need him.'

'How about answering the detective inspector's questions first?' Edgley said.

But the game was over for the moment. The mouse had died. Nat looked at her sadly. 'I've answered. I can't go on answering the same questions the same way. Can I, love? It's a waste of time. Everyone's time.' He said this without aggression. Even Edgley moved her head as though her collar had got uncomfortable. He looked at Bright and said gently, 'Have you got people looking for her?'

'For who?'

Wearily: 'For Sally.'

'How about Tess?'

'Yes ... Tess ... They could be together, you know. It was Tess who gave Sally the keys.'

'And you never saw Tess that day?'

'Oh, mate, I've told you. No. Where's Sally? Where is she, man?'

'Anything in her flat?'

'No, sir.'

'There must have been something. No address book?'

'No. Only one handbag. Empty.'

'She had her address book with her, then.'

'It looks like it, sir.'

'Or someone took care to remove it. No medical records?'

She held out a thin folder. 'No passport, no insurance. A six-month tenancy agreement on the flat. A few cards saying good luck on your opening night. A few photographs.'

He picked up a glossy eight-by-ten with an unnatural shine. Limpid eyes, wet mouth, a froth of dark hair. 'Beautiful girl,' he said. He turned the print over. On the back was her name, *Sally Crowe*, and the name and number of her agent, *William Morris UK*. 'Speak to the agent?'

'Yes, sir. They haven't heard from her for a while. She's not the kind who's always ringing up, they said.'

'Not the kind that's always working either.' He took out another picture, a blurred snapshot of a tall thin dark woman among trees. 'Who's this?' He turned it over. On the back it said *Tess, Wales, 1990*. 'So that's Tess,' he said.

'It seems so, sir.'

He looked at the pictures side by side. 'Tess's dental records arrived yet?'

'They'll fax them, they said. A couple of hours, perhaps.'

'What do you think of him, Edgley?'

'You're asking me, sir?'

'I'm asking you, Edgley.'

'Well ...' She felt his sympathy with Crosby, but she couldn't compromise her opinion. 'He's a male chauvinist,' she said.

Bright sighed and gave her one of his most squinting looks. 'Yeah?'

'I believe it's relevant, sir.'

123

'I'm not asking you if he has a few minor character defects, I'm asking you if he's a killer, constable.'

She swallowed her objections. 'If he couldn't get his own way, if a woman wouldn't do what he wanted, if he was angry enough. Yes, sir.'

'That what you think happened?'

'He was there!' Her face was red. 'He admits he was there. He's the only one who was there! As far as we know.'

Bright looked at her till she'd quietened down. He put his hands on the two photographs. He said, 'Two women are missing. We don't know which one of them is dead.'

They kept coming back to that.

The dental records had not yet been faxed. Pictures of the two women were circulated to police forces all over the country. Five tall dark women had been reported missing. None of them was Sally or Tess.

26

BLOOD IS THICKER

On the train she pulled the script out of its envelope. A Bristol Old Vic compliment slip clipped to the front page said, *Dear Kate. This is a weird play but I think it's possibly brilliant. Will you have a look at the part of Miss/Mismo and let me know? You'd be perfect for it. Hope you agree. Lots of love, Colum.*

She laughed when she read the title: *The Mask and the Face*; then shivered. Colum was right though, it was a good play: eight characters – extravagant in these days of artistic penury – enmeshed in a web of betrayal. Each character had two personas, one the face, the other its mask. The masked and unmasked stories increasingly overlapped. The features gradually disappeared from the face, transferred themselves to the mask, so that by the end the mask became the face, the face the mask. It was dramatic, surreal. It gave her the creeps.

And work was a crazy notion, something from the past, the other life. Life before The Event. And even before The Event she'd finished with acting. Her hunger was gone. Her desire was dead. But it went against the grain still to turn down a job. They weren't that thick on the ground these days. And directors like Colum who knew their jobs an endangered species. And she had a living to earn and as yet acting was the only way she knew how. And Bristol was where her sister was. And she needed to see her sister. She groaned. She supposed she'd do it.

She finished reading just before Bath. Looked up to see PREPARE TO

MEET YOUR GOD in big white letters on a black roof. Hoped *not just yet* as the train drew in.

But the Beetle was just where she'd left it, like a faithful dog. It hadn't been towed away. It hadn't been clamped. It didn't even have a parking ticket. These were good omens. All might yet be well. She stopped at a phone box to call her agent and got Allie who dealt with Theatre these days. 'Kate!'

'The Bristol script, Allie. Can you call and tell them yes?'

'Kate, where can we reach you? We keep getting your answerphone.'

'Don't worry, I'll reach you.' She put down the phone, forestalling questions about The Event.

Maisie stood in the doorway at the top of the front steps. Tall, skinny, hair frizzed into spirals, face made up. Only six months ago she'd been a child. Kate was appalled but didn't show it.

'Oh hi, Ankate! Haven't seen you for yonks! She's in the garden.'

'In this weather?'

'She's talking over the wall to Sarah Next Door. They've been at it for hours. They never do any gardening, neither of them. No wonder the garden's a mess. Ex-husbands, I expect.'

'What?'

'That's what they'll be talking about.'

'Oh well, an engrossing topic, I imagine.'

'Yuh.'

'How is he by the way, your dad?'

'He's having a great time. Course, that makes it much worse for mum. Drives her up the wall.'

'You see him much?'

'Nah.'

'Why not? He's only down the road.'

'Yuh . . . Well, I don't like it there much actually. All these dolly students in and out. They think he's, like, their guru or something, you know? He smokes spliffs with them and that, it's pathetic. Anyway mum hates me going, so . . .'

Normal life. Ordinary problems. For once maybe Lizzie would do her good. 'Is it okay my staying for a bit?'

'Yuh!'

'Sure?'

'Yuh, brilliant. I'll get mum.'

'What, interrupt her gardening? I'll get my stuff out of the boot.'

*

'Kate, you're so thin!'

'Only in contrast to you, Lizzie.'

'Oh, I know, it's awful. Maisie says I should go on a diet.'

'Yuh, you should. I'm going now, mum. See you later, okay?' Maisie lounged down the steps and pecked the air near Kate's cheek. 'Bye, Ankate.' She wore skin-tight jeans and a nearly transparent white Indian cotton top. She pulled on a padded silk bomber jacket and strolled off down William Street swaying her non-existent hips. The sisters stood watching her.

'She can't be as grown up as she looks,' Kate said. 'Can she?'

'I hope not, that's all.' Lizzie's voice was at its most sepulchral. 'She's not thirteen yet.'

'Makes me feel a little elderly. A veritable maiden aunt.'

'What do you think it's like for me? Makes me feel a hundred. Ripe for the compost heap.'

'She can't be as confident as she seems, Lizzie. Remember what it was like at that age?'

'No. I don't. Maisie's blanked it all out. She's blanked me out.'

'Lizzie!'

'I can't bear it, Kate, I really can't.' Lizzie's eyes overflowed.

Kate picked up her bags from the pavement with an inward sigh. 'You're really in a bad way.'

Lizzie followed her up the steps dabbing her eyes. 'I've just had nobody to tell,' she said.

Kate didn't say what about Sarah Next Door. She sat at the kitchen table, covered with bright red oilcloth. Such a gay kitchen for such a sad woman. The teapot was a clown's head. The lid was his hat.

Lizzie poured the tea. 'It's all right for Dave. New life, no responsibilities, all these nubile students draped all over him. And you know how unscrupulous he is. And he doesn't seem to see the pathos of it. Forty-year-old man having his second youth.'

'Or his first.'

'What? Oh yes, his first. Of course you'd sympathise with him, you the big career woman. What about *my* first? When do I get mine? I've got the responsibility of Maisie. His daughter. He hasn't. He got out of that.'

You'd never think, Kate thought, I'd had a murder in my house. You'd never think they'd found a body in my bath, that my life had been turned inside out. 'Does Maisie miss him?' she said.

'Yes,' Lizzie admitted. 'But he embarrasses her. Those girl students of his aren't that much older than she is. It doesn't bear thinking about.' She shivered. 'It gives me the creeps.'

Kate suddenly drooped. She had no more energy for this. Though it was only tea time, she longed for sleep.

126

'Oh poor Kate, you always get this when you arrive. Me moaning on.'

'I don't mind,' she lied.

'It's because I hardly ever see you.' She had to get that dig in. 'You're sleeping in the front room, by the way. Maisie refuses to share with me any more when someone stays.'

Kate said, 'Um-mm,' but thought, *If I'm sleeping in the living-room I can't go to sleep before bedtime. Hell.*

Maisie returned. They ate dinner. Lizzie nagged: 'You're so late, you ought have some consideration, what will Kate think?' Maisie rolled her eyes at Kate: see what I have to put up with? and shovelled in the vegetable curry. Another odd thing about Lizzie: she was a good cook, tasty spicy comforting food. 'We're completely vegetarian now,' she said. 'Only men really like to eat meat.' She sent Maisie upstairs to do her homework. Kate begged for bed.

On the landing outside the bathroom Maisie waylaid her. 'Mum says I'm not to talk about it.' She rolled her eyes. 'It must have been awful, Ankate.'

'It still is awful.'

'Do they know who did it yet?'

'No, they don't even know who the body is.'

Maisie's eyes were round. She'd scraped the make-up off and wore a long T-shirt that came down to her thighs. She looked ten years old. 'I expect you'll never go back to your house.'

Kate found herself on the edge of tears. She shrugged.

'Never mind. You can come and live with us.'

'Would you like that?'

'Yuh! Brilliant. 'Night, Ankate.'

The twiglet arms came round her neck a second, then Maisie was gone. Lizzie ought to be more grateful. *I should be, too.*

Standing in the front room, arms full of duvet and pillows, Lizzie at last said, 'What about this murder, then?' as though accusing her: what have you got up to this time, naughty Kate?

'What about it, Lizzie?'

'Well, what's happening? Have they found anyone?'

'They've arrested one of my best friends.'

'That Nat?'

Kate looked at her, stupefied. 'That Nat, yes. Why should you think him?'

'I don't know. You brought him to our place once.'

'Did I?'

'He seemed a bit barmy.'

'Did he?'

'Yes. I didn't say anything 'cos you were obviously crazy about him. I could tell right off he was married though.'

'How?'

'The way he took to Maisie. She was three then.'

'Oh.'

'Those were the days,' she said. Lizzie's mind moved in mysterious ways.

Unfolding the sofa bed Kate decided to find some digs. Family was all very well. She was fond of Maisie and even of Lizzie deep down but she needed to concentrate and not just on the work. Questions nagged at her. Her friends sat on the merry-go-round in her head, bobbing past her eyes: Nat, Tess, Ken, Michael, Oliver. Even Aggie and Dan. Sometimes their faces smiled at her open and innocent, sometimes they turned away, hiding, hurt or betrayed. Sally was there, right at the end of the line. The lights of the hurdy-gurdy changed colour, tinting the faces red, green, blue. Except for Sally whose face stayed blank, a white featureless mask.

The street lamp shone through the curtains. Cars slushed through rain. The last face she saw was Nat's in a greenish glow then the carousel swept him out of her sight away into the dark.

She drank her coffee in the garden under a deceptive blue sky. No birds sang up here in Totterdown, apart from the gulls screaming. Her Kentish Town garden was always alive with birdsong. A pang of homesickness hit her, but Sarah's face appeared over the wall. 'Hey, Kate!'

'Hi, Sarah.'

'Lizzie late again?' They both worked in a small pottery in Clifton. Sarah had got Lizzie the job.

'She's nearly ready.'

'She's always keeping me late. It's just as well I like her. How are you anyway?'

Kate shrugged. She could have lain on the terrace face down and howled but she didn't say so.

'Awful thing,' Sarah said. 'Funny though.'

'Funny?'

'Yes, you see the pictures in the paper this morning?'

'No.'

'Two girls.' Sarah fished in her big bag. 'Got it here to show Lizzie.' She handed it over the wall. 'Quite alike in a way, aren't they? Dark hair, bit like yours.'

'Yes.'

'Do you know them, Kate?'

'Sally and Tess.'

'Sally and Tess? Oh.' Sarah's voice slid down into disappointment.

'What?'

'Only, one of them's the spit of a girl used to work in the restaurant down the road.'

'The Glasnost?'

'Not called that any more.'

'Which girl was it?'

'That one.' Sarah pointed to the picture of Sally.

'When was this, that she worked there?'

'Years ago. Before Lizzie moved in. When it was the Glasnost.'

'What did she do there?'

'Waitress. She was nice. Said she grew up round here.'

Kate felt dizzy. Falling, Alice down the rabbit hole. 'Have you called the police?' she said.

Sarah looked amazed. 'Oh no!'

'Why not? They want information.'

'I didn't think it could really be her.'

'Christ, Sarah.'

Sarah's round eyes looked ashamed, shifty, like a child ticked off. 'I didn't think. You know. Well, you don't, do you? I mean, it was London it happened. It was in your house. I mean, you just don't think – And her name wasn't Sally.' As though that was the clincher.

'What was her name?'

'Erm, oh Lord, ohh . . .' Sarah's eyes stared, she sucked in her cheeks, she pushed out her lips.

Lizzie came out and stood on the terrace. 'Sorry, Sarah, I'm a bit late – '

Kate cut her off. 'Shh.'

'Linda,' Sarah said.

'Linda?'

'No. Not Linda.' Sarah's face creased up again.

'Who?' Lizzie said.

'The girl at the restaurant.'

'Oh, you talked about her. Lilian, wasn't it?'

Sarah's face opened like a flower. 'Lilian! Yes! They called her Lily. She hated it. Lilian. That's it!'

'How many years ago did you say it was?'

'Lord . . . Five? I should think five. She wasn't there long. A few months.'

'So they might not know her there now.'

'Some of the same people are still there. Jenny who does the desserts.'

'Jenny who does the desserts. Thanks.' Kate was at the top of the steps to the kitchen door.

Sarah's breathless voice followed her. 'You don't really think it could be her?'

'It couldn't possibly be. Too much of a coincidence.' Lizzie occupied the doorway, cutting out the light.

'Thanks, Lizzie.'

'You don't really think it could be?' Lizzie said.

Kate pushed past her out of the room, out of the front door, leaving her staring in the hall at an oblong of empty air and the horrible frosted glass replacement front door of the house opposite.

27

JENNY WHO DOES THE DESSERTS

The restaurant wasn't open yet. Blinds down over the windows. She rang the bell, heard it echoing. No reply. Should she call John Bright? No. She had nothing to give him. Lizzie was right. Hundreds of girls fitted Sally's description. It was too much of a coincidence. But she had to find out. What could she do till the place opened?

She went down the hill to the river, curiously depressing always, the banks of chocolatey mud, and the thick brown water. She walked along to the iron bridge and crossed into the dock area: houseboats, cinemas, smart boutiques, galleries. From here it was only a step to the theatre. Well, why not?

This was how she always felt in a theatre she wasn't working at: grotesquely out of place. Even front of house like this, in the bar, the Laura Ashley ladies from Clifton sipping their coffees had more right to be there than she. She wished she hadn't come, was about to turn tail when Sandy came through the pass door from backstage. Sandy worked in the scene shop. He'd painted an eerily authentic Italian renaissance ceiling for a play Kate had done here last year. 'You're coming back,' he said.

'Next week.'

'That's nice.'

'I'm looking forward to it,' she lied.

'I'm designing it,' he said. 'My first show.'

'Sandy, that's great.'

'Only 'cos Debbie Locke walked out.'

'Why?' She forced some interest into her voice.

'Colum wanted her to do something less expressionist. She refused. Big rows. So you're stuck with me.'

'Oh dear, Sandy, how will we bear it?'

The moment came. He lowered his voice. 'How are you, Kate? Are we allowed to ask?'

She answered briskly as depression swooped down again. 'I'm okay.'

There might be someone at the restaurant now. She stood up. 'I've got to go, Sandy. See you next week.' Suddenly she turned back. She pulled the newspaper out of her bag.

'Yes,' he said. 'I saw that.'

'Doesn't ring any bells, I suppose?'

'Well . . . See this one?'

'Sally?'

'Sally? No, that's not the name. But a girl quite like her used to hang about here a bit. Nat used to give her lessons.'

'Nat?' She felt punched in the throat.

'Nat Brenner.'

'Oh.' She breathed out. Sat down. 'Oh.' She looked up at him. 'Nat Brenner.'

'Yes. Dear old Nat. God rest his soul. He'd such a heart. Once he retired from the theatre school, if someone gave him a sob story, he couldn't say no. Taught this girl for free, I think. Felt sorry for her. I can't remember her name.'

'Lily?' she suggested.

He shook his head. 'Couldn't say.'

'Do you know anything else about her?'

'Nothing, Kate.'

'Might anyone else know anything?'

'I'll ask around.'

She scribbled Lizzie's number along the newspaper margin and tore it off. 'I'm at my sister's if you hear anything. Let me know.'

The blinds were up. She pushed the door. The place was empty. 'Hello?'

Footsteps. From the back a boy appeared, tall, thin, with a chrysanthemum of russet hair. He sounded breathless. 'Yeah? Hi. Coffee?'

She hesitated. 'Yes. Thanks.'

He disappeared again. She didn't sit. She wandered. Looked at the pictures on the walls. Didn't see them. He came back. She stood at the little counter. 'You the only one here this morning?' she said.

'Yeah. We don't get many customers in the morning.'

'You don't seem like a waiter.' He seemed a student doing it part time.

'I'm everything, from chief cook to bottle washer.'

'You're the owner?' She tried not to show her surprise.

'With my wife, yeah.'

'I must be getting old.' They both smiled. 'I suppose you've had a complete change of staff from the Glasnost days.'

'Oh yes.'

Her heart sank. She tried not to show that too.

131

'Well, actually,' he said, 'not a complete change. We still have Jenny who does the desserts. People come from miles for Jenny's almond cake.'

'Oh, Jenny!'

'You know her?'

'No, but a friend of mine does. Is she here now?'

'No, she bakes in her own kitchen. She comes in in the evening to help serve sometimes.'

'She live close by? Only my friend said say hello to her.'

'Just there.' He put her coffee on the counter and pointed across the narrow street. A terrace of little houses curved round the corner and climbed up the hill. 'The one with the yellow door,' he said. It was right opposite. The yellow was just the yellow of Kate's front door in Kentish Town.

'Do you think she'd mind if I were to visit now?'

'I'll pop over and perform formal introductions, if you like.'

'That would be grand.'

The coffee burned her mouth but she had no time to waste. Two cups in a morning. She'd be buzzing all day. She was buzzing now but not because of the coffee.

She didn't look like a dessert maker. Or like a Jenny. She was bony and severe with scraped-back greying hair and a face like Virginia Woolf. She wore an efficient white starched apron and her fingers were white with flour.

Kate said, 'I'm staying up the street with my sister. Sarah who lives next door said to say hello.'

'Oh.' The woman looked puzzled. 'Yes?'

'Do you think I could come in?' She sounded like a lunatic. 'I'd really like a chat.'

The woman must have heard the desperation. Her heavy lids drooped a little then she looked at the bloke. 'It's all right, Andy. Thank you. Yes, come in.'

Andy loped back over the road to the restaurant. Jenny Who Does The Desserts held the door open.

The hall was dim and cramped, living-room one side, kitchen the other, stairs in the middle. Jenny went into the kitchen. She washed her hands letting cold water run over her wrists. Kate said, 'My mum used to do that.'

'Yes, you should have cool hands for baking.' She stood over her mixing bowl, the traditional English kind, white inside, biscuity beige outside with raised lozenge patterns. Women had been using these bowls for centuries. The smells in the room, vanilla, almond, sweet hot baking, were making

Kate almost faint with nostalgia. She wished she could forget why she'd come.

Jenny's fingers, crumbling the butter and flour, moved fast and light. She didn't look at Kate and didn't question her, didn't even seem to be waiting for her to state her business.

Kate said, 'When the restaurant was the Glasnost a girl worked there as a waitress. Her name was Lilian, I think. They called her Lily.'

'Yes, she didn't like it.'

The clock missed a tick. In this moment Kate nearly changed the subject. Nearly didn't go on. The moment passed. She took the paper out of her bag. 'Did she look like this?' Kate held the picture up.

Jenny's fingers paused. She was looking at the headline, *The Body In The Bath*. The Adam's apple moved in her bony throat. The heavy lids lifted. 'Are you saying – ?'

'I'm just asking – '

'Yes, the answer's yes. It could be her.'

They stood in silence. Something suddenly screeched and Kate's heart jumped against her ribs. Jenny looked bewildered then murmured, 'Oh, the scones.' She switched off the strident oven timer. Took two trays of pale golden scones out of the oven and slid them on to a wire rack to cool. In the context of the conversation the cosy smells suddenly became a little sickening. Jenny wiped her hands on a damp cloth. 'Come into the other room.'

A grandmother's room. Dim light through lace curtains, over-stuffed Victorian furniture. Jugs of dried flowers. The room smelt of pot pourri, papery, spicy, sweet. Kate sat on a velvet sofa, Jenny on a chenille-covered armchair, long thin hands clasped on her knees. She said, 'I saw the paper. I thought, it looks like Lily. I didn't do anything. I didn't think it possible.'

'Everyone's the same.'

'I suppose so.'

'And it's probably not her. But if I could trace this Lily at least I'd know.'

'Of course, you're the actress. It happened in your house.' She looked round her snug room as though imagining it defiled. 'How can you bear that?'

'I can't.'

'No.' Her voice moved in beautiful wavery cadences, words in water.

'Did she tell you anything about herself that might help?' Kate said.

The hands unclasped and came up to her mouth in a prayer position. The fingertips touched her lips. 'Lily made a mystery of her life.'

'Sally did too.' They used the past tense for both without noticing.

'She made up stories. They were blatant fabrications: her parents were rich, they owned a big house in Clifton; she wanted to break away from

133

her privileged background, earn her living; she was going into show business against their wishes; the head of the Bristol Old Vic Drama School was giving her lessons and said she had great talent. No one was very convinced.'

'The last bit was true.'

'No? She came over here once. I was baking just like now. She sat in the kitchen watching me. We didn't talk. I hardly noticed; I'm used to silence, indeed I prefer it. Then I turned round from the stove and saw she was crying. Tears were pouring down her face. She was ashamed and put her hands up to hide them. It was most pathetic. I'm not a demonstrative person but I put my arms round her because she was in such a helpless state. Sobbing, you know.

'Eventually she calmed down and washed her face and I made some coffee and she told me her real life story. Well, a version of it. Even then I sensed she was – editing. The gist of it was her mother was unmarried and had to give her up so she had been taken into care. She had been fostered a couple of times, not for long, had been brought up in a series of institutions. She was desperately ashamed of this and swore me to secrecy.' The heavy lids lifted and she gave Kate a look of ironic guilt.

Kate replied with a shrug of helpless complicity. 'Did she tell you which institutions?'

'No, but mostly in Bristol, I believe. That was the impression she gave.'

'Sally's accent had a trace of Bristol, I thought.'

'Here, of course, it sounded like no accent. Lily's, I mean. But I don't have a good ear.'

'Did she say anything that might give me a clue as to where I might start to look?'

'What are you looking for?'

Kate paused a moment. 'The police need Sally's dental records.'

The Dürer hands came up to her mouth again. 'Oh dear no.'

'Yes.'

The heavy eyes gazed at the dried flowers in the grate, the deep blue of delphinium, yellow of corn, the crimson and gold of helichrysum and little white rosettes of feverfew. She broke off a head of helichrysum and crumbled it between her fingers, red and gold specks scattering. 'She left a phone number.' Jenny stood up. 'I tried it once or twice after she left. A woman answered but said Lily had left Bristol and left no forwarding address. I asked the woman to get in touch with me should she hear anything but I felt she wouldn't.'

'Who was she?'

'I'm afraid I was too reserved to ask. I've had a frightfully English upbringing. A feeble excuse, I realise.' She was rummaging through a drawer in a small walnut desk. 'Here.' She held out a piece of paper soft with age. The writing, square and sloping slightly backward, said *Lilian Groves 344721.*

'May I keep it?'

'What will you do?'

'I'll call this number first.'

'Call from here.'

'Thanks, I will.' Even the phone was a black bakelite model from a former age.

'Hello?' A distrustful Bristol voice. 'Yes?'

'Oh, hello, would it be possible to speak to Lilian Groves?'

A silence, then the woman said uncertainly, 'Lily?'

'Yes.'

'She hasn't been yur for yurrs, Lily.'

'How long is it since you've seen her?'

'Ohh . . . Foive yurrs, I sh' think.'

'Is that – ' Kate searched fast for a name, any name. 'Is that Crosby Street?'

'No.' The woman's voice was scornful. 'It's Lasson Street, up near Kingsdown Parade.'

'What number Lasson Street?'

'Who are you? What you want to know for?'

'My name's Kate. I'm coming to work at the Bristol Old Vic for eight weeks.'

'O-oh.' She felt the woman take the bait.

'I just thought I'd look up Lily. I haven't seen her for so long.'

'She left some stuff yurr.'

'Oh?' *Be still, my heart.* 'You're a relation, then?'

'Lord, no. I was her, well, landlady I s'pose you'd say.'

'Well, I'm looking for a place as a matter of fact.'

'I've got a room free at the moment.'

'I could come and look at it now.'

'Well, I'm in the middle of my housework.'

'Oh well, I've got some other places to look at first so – '

'No, that'll be all roight. You can come now if you loike.'

Kate wrote down *Mrs Bowyer, 113 Lasson Street.*

135

28

THEATRICAL DIGS

She stood in the stuffy beige living-room, the phone squeezed between her shoulder and her right ear. The room depressed her. Bright white nylon nets with frills looped across the window. A row of china canine clichés perched along the window sill: a perky Scottie, a sad spaniel, a keen setter. Wallpaper like raw sausage meat, the fireplace put in in the fifties in place of the original, beige mottled tiles and electric coal effect fire. The beige carpet had raised bits like a badly cut cornfield. The three piece suite was beige moquette, rough to the touch with hairy fringe along the edges of the cushions. The place smelled of room freshener with the nostril-scouring pungency of lavatory cleaner. She'd rather die than live in a room like this.

Lily's bag spilled its few pathetic possessions on the sofa. A UB40 card. A scuffed address book. The brief life of Lily Groves. Kate leafed through the address book while she waited. Not many names. Just the doctor, the dentist, the DSS office, the Glasnost Restaurant. A few other restaurants crossed out one by one, places she'd waitressed then left. Jenny. Her heart jumped when she saw the name Nat.

Not Nat Crosby, she knew now, but the wonderful Nat Brenner, actor and teacher. Head of Bristol Old Vic Theatre School all those years. Mentor to streams of actors. Loved by everyone who worked with him. Nat Brenner had been coaching Lily. Was Lily Sally? Too late to ask him. A year too late. Mourned and missed. Another Nat. That was weird.

'Where are you?'

'The digs Sally had five years ago.'

'Where?'

'Bristol.'

'Jesus. Give me the address. I'll have someone sent round. Can you wait there?'

'Sure.'

'You're all right, then?'

'Yes! Why shouldn't I be?'

'Never mind.'

'How long will they be, your Bristol cohorts?'

'Cohorts?' he said. 'Christ. Minutes if I've got anything to do with it. Hours if it's your average provincial woodentops.'

She groaned.

'What's the matter, don't you like the place?'

'Let's say I wouldn't like to spend my life here.'

'Okay. Give me the dentist's number.'

She read it out. She said, 'I called him. He remembers her.' She heard Bright's breath of exasperation.

'Can't you leave anything to us?'

She ignored that. 'He knows her as Lilian Groves. So does everyone here.'

He was fuming. 'Lilian Groves?' Her eardrum quivered.

'Yes.'

'Not Sally Crowe.'

'That's right.'

'But you're naturally sure it's her.'

'Sally had a trace of Bristol accent. I told you that.'

'Oh well, that proves it then, no question.'

'Lily disappeared from here five years ago. That's when Sally first turned up in London. And her past is gruesome, I quite see why she hid it from everyone.'

'When the dental records have been found and checked with the corpse and examined by the experts we'll know whether Lilian Groves is Sally Crowe. Until then we don't know.'

'It's her.' The defiance wavered in her voice.

'We will speak further,' he said and killed the phone. Instead of killing me, she thought.

Mrs Bowyer put her head round the embossed-glass door, disappointed not to interrupt the phone call. 'Would you loike a cuppa tea, then?' Imagining the tea but needing to stay there, Kate said yes.

The kitchen was better. Blue and white units, sparkling surfaces.

'I keep a noice clean house.' Mrs Bowyer handed her a cup in which a thick brown liquid stood. 'Biccy?' she said.

The tea filled Kate's throat, preventing speech. She shook her head and concentrated on swallowing. She turned away to look at the garden, a neat square of grass with a narrow empty border.

'It's noice in the summer,' Mrs Bowyer said. 'A little sun-trap. I let my lodgers sit out there noice days.'

She'd at last squeezed the tea down her throat. She said, 'Did Lily sit out there much?'

'No. Well, she wasn't in much. Out a lot. Went to classes in the day.'

'Classes, where?'

'Didn't say. Seemed to be theatricals. 'S what she used to talk about, how she'd be a famous actress, loike, one day.'

'She didn't mention the Old Vic School?'

Mrs Bowyer pursed her lips, shook her head. 'Not that I remember.'

'Brenner. She ever mention the name Brenner? Mr Brenner. A teacher.'

'No. Now then . . . She used to talk about this Nat.'

'Nat?'

'Nat. He was giving her lessons for free, she said, 'cos she showed such promise, that's what she said. I said you don't get nothing for free in this life, moy dear.'

'Oh, you did from this Nat.' *Someone had faith in her then. Helped her.* Typical of Nat Brenner. The questions she'd like to ask him. And he wasn't here to ask.

Mrs Bowyer was saying, 'Never heard her mention anyone else.'

'How long did she stay here?'

''Bout two years.'

Kate tried to imagine spending two years here. 'And when she left – ?'

Mrs Bowyer's broad back bristled. 'She didn' even say she was leavin', gave no notice at all. Goin' up to London to meet a producer, she says, I'll be back on a late train. She had the key so she could let herself in. That's the last I ever seen of her.'

'She didn't come back at all, not even for her things?'

'No.'

'Didn't give a forwarding address?'

'Not a word, not a peep out of her.'

'You didn't think to report her missing?'

'Missin'? She owed me two weeks' rent. If I reported missin' every lodger that left owin' me rent they'd have a list as long as your arm.'

Kate nodded sadly. 'Mrs Bowyer, the police are going to come and take her things away with them – '

'Oh no, oh no! I shouldn've let you in, I shouldn've believed you. I've never had trouble with the police, never. What'll they think?' She twisted about towards the windows of each house that backed on to her garden, filled with imagined spectators of her shame.

'It's nothing to do with you.'

'Nothin' to do with me? It's my house! You're all the same, you theatricals, you got no morals. Wherever you are there's trouble.' She snatched the cup from Kate's hand and emptied it down the sink, ran the tap hard to hose away the contamination. For this relief, Kate thought, much thanks, and thought it again when the door bell rang.

Mrs Bowyer, her cheeks red blotches on a white ground, clung to the edge of the sink behind her. There'd be no moving her. Kate went to the door.

29

A BIRD IN THE HAND

His phone rang. He grabbed it. He listened. He didn't speak. The voice at the other end stopped. Silence. Bright still didn't speak. The voice at the other end spoke again. Bright came to life and said, 'Yes. Yes. I'm still here.' He started to put down the phone, brought it up again, said, 'Thanks,' and this time did slowly put it down.

Edgley stood in the doorway of the room watching him. His eyes stared past her still matt, still dead. She said, 'It wasn't Sally, then?'

His eyes slowly focused on her. The points of light came back into them. He rose out of his chair, looked like he'd lift the desk with him. He turned to the wall behind him and punched it. He went to the door and punched that shut. He went to punch the window. Didn't do that. Put both hands either side of a four-drawer filing cabinet, shook it, then, arms at full length, leaned his forehead against it. He let go of it and turned round. 'Come on.'

'We have a victim,' he said. The heads came up. 'Dr Dave just called. The teeth match. It's Lilian Groves a.k.a. Sally Crowe.' They sat straight. A breathing cheer whispered round the table. Atkins whistled. Cato took the pipe out of his mouth.

Barton said, 'What now, guv?'

'Yep.'

Atkins said, 'We charge Nat Crosby, don't we?'

'With what, Tommy? Screwing the victim at the scene of the crime? He's already admitted that.'

Cato emptied his pipe into the ashtray. 'Still no weapon. With or without his fingerprints. And no witness who saw him at the scene.'

'You'll go far, Cato.'

'We need a confession, guv.' Gwylim had a gift for stating the obvious.

'Crosby's thirty-six are up in' – Bright looked at his watch – 'three hours' time.'

A groan went round the table. 'Can we get more time, guv?' Barton being helpful.

'I'm about to have a word with the DCI.'

*

'You haven't got the evidence, John.'

'That's what I need more time for, sir.'

'You're going to need a confession.'

'Easier said than done.'

'How do I justify this to the Super?'

'Crosby's all I've got. Either he's involved or he knows who is. Up to now I've had nothing over on him. Now at least we've got a victim. If I can get the weapon as well, we're cooking. I might be able to get that out of him. I might be able to get the whereabouts of the other missing woman. If I let him go now he's off the hook. He could do a runner, to the States, anywhere, I'd never get him back. I've got to keep him hanging. Cut him down now and he's gone. I've lost him.' The DCI sighed. Bright forced himself to stay quiet. He'd pleaded enough. At last the DCI shifted in his seat: 'Okay, I'll have a word.'

'Thanks, sir.' It was all he could hope for, for now.

'It's Sally,' Bright said.

Silence. Crosby sat. His long hands on long arms hung between his knees.

'They just called from the lab. The teeth match.' Bright waited but Nat neither moved nor spoke. 'She had a couple of fillings at sixteen, then regular cleans and polishes. Under the name Lilian Groves but it's the same girl. When she first signed on with this dentist her address was a children's home in Montpelier in Bristol.'

Again he waited. Nothing. The guy could have been a waxwork. 'Any of that familiar to you, Nat?'

A longer silence. The great blue eyes looked up. Then, 'Sally's dead?' Nat's voice like ashes in a dead grate.

'Killed, Nat. Knocked out with a blow to the head, a heavy object with a sharp edge. Then drowned. Then left in your friend's bath for the water and the maggots and time to do their work. You saw her, Nat. That was Sally you saw in the mortuary.'

Crosby closed his eyes. Edgley was reminded suddenly in horror of the face on the Turin shroud. The big swollen eyelids, the long nose with a bend in it, the sharp shadows under the cheekbones in the harsh neon light. And the sorrow. A non-christian, she nonetheless felt she'd blasphemed. She pulled herself up. Cleared her throat. Cleared her mind. Looked at Bright.

He and Nat gazed at each other. 'Got anything to tell us now, Nat?' Another long silence. Bright didn't move. At last he said, 'Nat?' in his most catlike purr.

Nat said, 'I shook her.' His arms crossed over his chest, hands trapped

140

in his armpits. His head went down, his voice went up. 'I shook her. I shook her.'

Edgley took a step towards him. Bright stopped her with the slightest of movements. Nat raised his head. Gazed at Bright in hapless misery. They waited. His voice was a whisper. 'That's why I walked out. In case I – I told you I don't hit people, I'd never hit a woman, well – I was trying to be controlled, reason with her, say just come with me for a few weeks, a month, see if you like it. She wasn't listening. Just saying no, if she went out there she'd never come back, like it was the moon we were talking about, not California. I said if she loved me she'd want to be where I was. She kept saying, "What about my life?" Her life! As if her life was something separate from mine, like they had no connection. I took hold of her shoulders, I was shaking her. She looked so scared. Christ. I told you she was fragile. I saw that look in her eyes, it was like Zoë looking at me that way. A frightened kid. I felt like a murderer. I felt sick. No no, man. I got out of there. I just left. I just left her there. I got my clothes on and left her there. In case I – nnh.'

He was shaking now. Sweat stood on his forehead and his upper lip and a sudden smell came off him that was sharper than sweat, harsher, that filled the room. Bright recognised it. As a copper you got to know it well, the smell of fear. The man's breathing was shallow now, short shallow breaths. Bright waited. 'Didn't mean to kill her, did you, Nat? Of course you didn't, you needed her, you wanted her with you. She wouldn't go with you. You got wild.'

The man stood up. Edgley feared he was going to attack Bright but he didn't even look at him. He walked to the wall, put his forehead against it. Stood there, his back to the room. He took a trembling big breath in, then out, then in. 'I didn't – I didn't – do that to her head. I didn't do that. I didn't, mate. I didn't.'

'Sounds like you're trying to convince yourself, Nat.'

'Yes.'

'Yes?'

'Well, you wonder, you know?'

'What do you wonder, Nat?'

'You think, what if I blacked out or – ? But man, I remember stopping. I remember her face. I remember going out of there. I'd have had to put her in the bath and – I couldn't have done that. Could I? Could I?'

'You want your lawyer here, Nat?'

Edgley gave him a look that said about time too, but Nat shook his head. 'No yes no. I don't care. I didn't do that, you see. There's no way. Only – '

'A-ha?'

'Who did, you see, mate. Who did?'

'Well, that's the question, isn't it?' Bright barely paused. 'What did you

141

hit her with, Nat? We haven't found it. Something pretty big? Or something small but heavy. Nice and heavy, nice and sharp. We've looked for it. Dug up Kate's little garden, looked in the gardens next door, searched the local litter bins, not a hard job in this part of the world, is it? Camden Council like to keep their working class areas in a state of comfortable filth, they think clean is élitist. What did you hit her with? I know you didn't mean to hit her, you just picked up something that was to hand, something lying around. What was it, Nat?'

The nasal tree-saw voice droned on. Edgley could hear the lack of conviction in it. Crosby turned from the wall. He wiped the back of his hand across his mouth, his nose, his eyes. Easy tears, Edgley thought.

'I'm sorry, mate,' he said. He came back to the chair. 'What were you saying?'

Bright looked at Edgley. She swore he almost smiled. There was a pause. He said, 'You tell him, constable.'

'The detective inspector was asking what you hit her with.'

'Hit her with?'

'Don't pretend to misunderstand me. Don't pretend you didn't hear Inspector Bright. You've seen her head, what it looked like. What did you hit her with?'

'Doesn't Kate know?'

'Kate?' Edgley felt a surge of triumph. In a few easy questions she'd got him to say that he and Kate had done it together. 'Why Kate?' she said.

'If it was something in her house, you'd think she'd know.'

Barton handed him the phone as he walked into the CID room. 'It's the DCI, guv.'

The DCI sounded tense. 'Did you get your confession?'

'Not yet, sir.' A groan from the phone. 'But he's moving. He's admitted to shaking the victim before he left the house.'

Jubilation round the table, and the DCI impressed. 'That's something, John.'

'A-ha.' Bright waited.

'Well, you've got another twelve hours. But get it moving. I put my arse on the line for this.'

Around the table they were all agog. But Bright's face was motionless. 'Thank you, sir,' he said. He put the phone down.

Barton asked, 'What did he say, guv?'

'We've got another twelve.'

General exultation. Taff said, 'You'll be chargin' Crosby then?'

'I don't think Crosby did it, Taff.'

General consternation. 'He's all we've got, guv.'

They all assumed he'd be charging Nat. Bird in the hand. In the bag. Off our hands, on to the next one. 'He was there, guv. At the scene. With the victim. He admits it.'

'He admits attacking her, sir.'

'And he pissed off to the States right after, guv.'

Bright gave them the arguments: 'Yes but he kept ringing her number from the States, writing her letters, calling people who knew her.'

'Bluff, guv.'

'Taff, he came back to look for her. He didn't have to do that. We could never have extradited him on the evidence we've got. If he'd stayed put there we'd never have got him out.'

They weren't convinced. All sitting back, heads down, arms folded or tapping pens, fiddling with paper clips. He was tempted to call them to attention like some sergeant major. That'd go down well. No. Everyone's equal these days. They know you're the boss but you treat 'em like you're mates. All in this together. He was new, they didn't like him and the false matiness made him gag. But somehow he had to carry them along. The thought of the effort made him tired.

'Who else have we got, guv?' Barton again.

'How did Oliver Broome react to the idea of giving samples?'

'Sweet as pie, guv. Any time we liked.'

'Might change his tune if we take him up on it.'

'What about Kate Creech?' Taff said. 'Why aren't we bringing her in?'

'Loose, Tommy, Kate Creech gave us our victim. Loose, she can give me Tess Harbour. In here, she'll give me nothing. As long as I know where she is, I'm happy.'

Atkins gave a little grin. Bright watched them all round the table. Exchanging looks. Making sure he caught the tail end of the looks. He said, 'It's the other woman we've got to find.' He passed round the pictures of Tess.

'Crosby's got to know where she is, guv.'

'He doesn't. The only leads we've got on her are this weirdo woman in Croydon and she swears she's not in touch. And this Laura in Somerset. The local police have questioned her and she says the same.'

'And Kate Creech.'

'Right, Niki. And Kate Creech.'

The DS said, 'Nothing new on the weapon, guv?'

'Someone come up with something, I'm out of ideas. Apart from dragging the Regent's Canal.'

A couple of them shook their heads, shrugged.

Little Cato The Cat stopped tapping his pen, didn't look up, said in a bored voice, 'Where is Kate Creech now?'

'Bristol. Why?'

'Well, the weapon was most probably some object in her house.'

143

'A-ha?' Bright sighed. 'This we know, Niki.'

'Well, assuming she's innocent, she was in a state of shock before. Maybe that's why she couldn't think what it was, know what I mean?'

'Keep on at her sister's place and the theatre in Bristol till you get her. Good thinking, Holmes.'

Cato just managed not to smirk. Expressionless as Bright he tapped his pipe against the ashtray and lifted his phone.

Atkins said, 'How you getting on with WPC Edgley, guv?'

Bright looked at him a moment and waited. 'She's a pain in the arse,' he said. He watched the ends of all the just not hidden smiles and let them enjoy the joke. Then he said, 'But she's clever. She's learning fast. And when she becomes chief super she'll remember her time on our team. She'll remember you well, Tommy, I should think.'

Atkins actually blushed. There was a slight shifting round the table. No one looked at anyone. Someone down the far end, the DS maybe, gave a short laugh. Atkins's mouth made a downward pull.

'Still,' Bright left it just long enough, 'she is a pain in the arse.' They all laughed. Atkins's big thick face filled out again. 'Anyhow, as we've got a bit more time, let's go for it. You and Cato have another go at Crosby. You can't do worse than me.' They thought they were cynical but they went for the head prefect stuff. He just managed not to call them lads. Mustn't overdo the boyish charm. 'We want to talk to Oliver Broome and Michael Thing.'

'The little poofter?'

'When you get them let me know.'

Edgley got the big actor, Ken, for him straight away. She handed him the phone.

'Hello, Ken. Is Michael with you?'

'Why?'

'Don't worry, I'm not arresting him. Not yet. I just want to ask him a question. Or two.'

'He's not here.'

Patiently: 'This is nothing to do with his past life of crime or his sexual proclivities. I just need one bit of information from him. Where is he, Ken?'

A long silence. Then Ken said, 'All right. I'll get in touch with him and ask him to phone you.'

'That's very kind of you, Ken.'

But Ken had put down the phone.

30

HOMELESS INDEED

'Lizzie, I'm going now. I'm going back to London.'

'You can't! You're knackered.'

'I've got to.'

'Why? What can you do tonight? What are you going *for*?'

'I'm – not sure.'

'What can you do *anyway*? Tonight, tomorrow or any time?'

'Don't go, Ankate.'

'I've got to, Maisie.'

'Kate, you keep saying that but it's rubbish. It's because you're overtired and overwrought.'

'I've got to see Nat. That's a reason. They might let me. I don't know what other reasons there might be. I can't just sit here.'

'It'll be terrible on the road.'

'Yes.' She looked tired. Lizzie glared.

'Shall I make you a flask of coffee, Ankate?'

'Maisie, you're a peach plum angel.'

'Wonder why my maths teacher never calls me that.'

'Bad, is it?'

'As can be. I'm going to fail.'

'She's not.' Lizzie slapped butter on a long-suffering slice of wholemeal bread. 'She's never failed anything.'

'There's always a first time, mum.'

Yes, there's a first time for everything, for things you can't even imagine. This cosy homey scene isn't the real world any more. They're wearing masks, just going through the motions, it's not real. No. I'm the one going through the motions. I'm the one in the mask. I'm the one who'll never again be the same.

Lizzie banged the sandwich down on the kitchen table wrapped in a plastic bag.

'Thanks, Lizzie.'

'You shouldn't go. You're stupid. You've never changed, you never will. Pig-headed. Just don't blame me if something terrible happens to you.' Lizzie left the room banging the door. She was no believer in the comfortable motto: don't let the sun set on a quarrel. She didn't know you could wake up one morning and find the landscape so changed you could never find your way back. A sudden thought of Ted

145

Adams made Kate feel momentarily safer. He'd be in London. He was there.

Maisie sat down and pushed the yellow flask towards her. She leaned forward. 'Did you see the body?' She was whispering.

Kate thought a moment. 'Yes, I did.'

'What was it like?'

Well, let's see now: its hair, Sally's hair, was matted with dried blood and you could see down to the skull and maggots crawled over the gash and the policemen had even trodden maggots into the bathroom floor. Like to hear about the face? Sally's face. Like to hear about the body? Sally's body. So swollen it looked like – Maisie's little face waiting for her reply. Not so little now but behind it Kate would always see her face at three years old, six, nine. This face, made up so prettily, was just a mask. Every adult face was just a mask carefully arranged to cover the child's face underneath. *Sally's face.*

'Was it really terrible, Ankate?'

'It was pretty unpleasant, Maisie, but I didn't have to look at it for long. Just a quick whizz in and out.'

'I've never seen a dead person. I can't imagine it.'

'We're not meant to imagine it.'

'So you're not going to tell me anything.'

'It was a bit – swollen. Because of the water – that had been in the bath.'

'Ugh.'

'Ugh is right.'

Lizzie pushed the door open. 'And where will you stay anyway? You can't stay in your house.'

It was late when she got to Aggie's. But surely not too late? Aggie was a night-wanderer, raiding the fridge, watching videos, draped in an old dressing-gown that her husband had left behind in the rush to get to his pretty blonde younger new wife. However, the house was in darkness.

Kate's heart sank. *Please don't let Aggie have gone away.* She could spend a night in the Beetle but didn't fancy it. Feeling like the Traveller whose horse in the silence champed the grasses Of the forest's ferny floor, she heard the bell echo through the empty house. Not a sound. Not a light. 'Is there anybody there?' she murmured in a plaintive whisper. Then a light came on upstairs.

Through the stained glass she could make out a shape descending. *Aggie, you darling, you.* The door opened. Ted stood there, her lawyer, in a sweater and Y-fronts, strong brown legs and beautiful bare brown feet. His hair stuck up all over in tufts as though in surprise.

They looked at each other for some time. Then Aggie's voice called from upstairs, 'Who is it, Ted?' And her large form appeared at the top of the stairs, the Venus of SW11 wrapped only in a sheet. She put her hands up to her cheeks and gave a raucous gurgle. 'Oh fuck,' she said.

Ted took Kate's bag from her and Kate followed him. She shut the front door. He turned to her and scratched his head. She smiled at him. Sort of. He carried her bag into the sitting-room. Aggie was biting her lip, eyebrows up, round eyes full of laughter and mock shame.

But Kate didn't feel like laughing. She followed Ted into the room. He was pulling out the sofa bed. She watched him. It was only a few days ago he'd kissed her. Here in this room. Wasn't it? Well, she'd gone away. She was always going away. Did she care? She didn't know.

He looked up and gave her an oh hell kind of half grin. She gave him an I don't believe it shake of the head. He said, 'What can I say?'

'It was love at first bite?'

He doubled up: his trollish laughing posture. He said, 'It just happened. It was unexpected. A bit of a surprise. To both of us.'

'That's what you think, is it?' It was no surprise to Aggie, she thought. An orchestrated campaign. She hadn't decided how much she minded. Like Scarlett O'Hara she'd think about it tomorrow. Or the next day. Or never. How about that?

He said, 'You look knackered.'

She said, 'You sound just like my sister.'

'We thought you were staying in Bristol till the start of rehearsals.'

We. 'So did I. Sorry and all.'

He came close to put his arms round her. But she couldn't have that. Not with the Y-fronts and the bare strong legs, oh no. She stepped sideways. He shrugged and screwed up his face.

She said, 'Will they charge Nat now?'

'They've got a further extension of custody. They have to charge him by tomorrow afternoon or let him go.'

'Why haven't they charged him already?'

'All the evidence is circumstantial. If they had a murder weapon, with his fingerprints, that would still be circumstantial but it would be enough to charge him. Maybe. As it is . . .'

'I see.'

He hovered, wiggling his toes. He said, 'See you in the morning, then.'

'Yup.'

She heard whispering in the hall but Aggie didn't come in. They crept off back upstairs. Intertwined no doubt. Maisie's coffee was scurrying in her veins like ants. She slept after the first blackbird sang and woke again when the first journalist rang.

She lay and listened while Ted dealt with them. He said simply, 'We don't know where Miss Creech is. Yes, that is her car but she is not here.' He was pretty convincing but they didn't leave; she heard them talking to the neighbours.

Daniel poked his head round the door. 'Give us your car keys, Kate.'

'What for?'

'I passed my test on Thursday.'

'You're going to drive my car?'

'Yeah. Legally this time.'

'Daniel!'

'I'll put it somewhere they won't find it.'

'Yeah, like the knacker's yard.'

'Kate! I'm a good driver. I've been driving since I was thirteen.'

'I'm sure.'

'Kate, if they don't know where it is it can be your getaway car!'

She considered. He had a point. 'Okay.' She threw the keys.

He caught them. 'Hey. Brilliant. Don't worry about a thing. I'll give you a call later on, tell you where I've stowed it.'

She peeped through a crack in the curtains as he drove off. Three cars took off after him, the others not far behind. Only one reporter remained. Old sheepskin jacket, no hat, ears red with cold, fag on his bottom lip. He put his little dictaphone in his pocket, took out a hip flask. Rather drink than drive. He wouldn't stick it out long; he'd be off to the pub soon, to replenish supplies.

Aggie in the kitchen whispered, 'Kate, you don't really mind, do you?'

'Mind what?'

'You know!'

'You're a cow, Aggie.'

'You're so careless with your belongings. You shouldn't have left him behind.'

'What was it? Your succulent lasagne? Your scrumptious apple pie?'

'That may have had a hand in it, if you'll excuse the expression.'

'Aggie –'

'It just happened. Honestly. I didn't plan it. I didn't do anything. I didn't expect it. It was this sudden, like, heat – '

'Aggie, an old friend of mine is about to be charged with murder. Another old friend has disappeared. Do you think we could hold the girlish gossip for another time?'

The glow went out of Aggie's happy face. How could she have spoken to Aggie like that? Aggie whom she loved? Kate was sorry. Appalled. She wanted to say so. But Aggie had turned away. *We're all killers.* She left the kitchen.

31

INSPIRATION

'But I'm in the studio today, inspector! All day, yes. It's a leading role.
They can't do without me. Honestly, I'd like to help but – '
　'Where's the studio?'
　'Oh. Broadcasting House. The only drama studio still here.'
　'Do you have a coffee break?'
　'No, I'm sorry, we don't – '
　'You do today. Ten minutes, that's all I need. I'll see you in the foyer.
Two minutes past eleven.'
　'But, inspector – '
　'Don't be late, Oliver.'

Bright stood, jostled by people moving in and out, just inside the heavy
bronze doors, facing the beautiful portico of the Wren church. He saw
Michael emerge round the portico from Regent Street and approach
Broadcasting House. The lad was dressed in his black leather gear,
little black wool hat to the back of his head, moving with grace on his
strong dancer's legs. But he was pale. He was scared. He stood peering
to his right then his left. He pivoted in a circle. He held the handle of
one of the doors, peered in through the glass. Then he pulled. He'd
obviously not been here before, was surprised by the door's weight. He
pulled again with more strength and succeeded in getting it open. Bright
moved behind a stand with magazines on it. From here he watched the
pantomime.
　Oliver came out of the lift. He and Michael saw each other at the same
time. Both stopped dead. Both turned as if to go back the way they'd come.
Both turned back again to stare at each other, each with his eyebrows up
in his hair. Each stood, eyes scraping the foyer. The activity in here was
constant, people meeting and parting, crossing to and from the lifts,
showing their IDs to the guards. At the desk messengers and visitors
queued for the attention of the receptionists. Oliver raised his shoulders in
a silent question. Michael opened his hands in a mystified reply. Still
looking this way and that they carefully approached each other. Oliver
took Michael's arm, moved him over to the left, away from the reception
desk.

They didn't see Bright approach. He was good at that. He stood in front of them and grinned. 'Well, well, well,' he said.

'Inspector – '

'All right, Oliver, all right.' Michael looked like he might do a runner. Bright took his arm, guided him to a sofa against the wall. 'Let's sit down, shall we?'

Oliver didn't sit: 'Inspector, I've only got five minutes.'

'Oliver, don't push your luck.'

Oliver sat.

'That's better. Now. What I want to know is when you two went to Kate's house.'

He loved watching them, Oliver's facial expressions, Michael's whole body a-quiver as though a bolt of lightning had shot through him. They didn't look at each other. Bright sat with his arms folded. At last Oliver sighed, swallowed, pushed a hand through his hair. 'We've got to tell him, Michael.'

The little dancer nodded, incapable of speech.

'We did go to Kate's house,' Oliver said.

'Well, I am surprised.'

'We used Ken's key.'

Michael spoke, dry mouth: 'Ken didn't know, inspector, honestly.'

'But it was months ago. Ages before – '

'Can you prove that?'

They looked at each other. 'No.'

'Okay, okay, I knew you'd had Kate's key, I knew you two had been to the house at some time. What I want to know from you is this: is there anything you saw there that could have been used to kill the girl? Heavy, with sharp corners – '

'Inspector.'

'Yes, Michael?'

'I just thought, yesterday actually – Do you think it could be an iron?'

'An iron? Now that's an idea. Why didn't any of my blokes think of that?'

'P'raps they don't do a lot of ironing, inspector.'

'You might have a point there, Michael.' Michael looked slavishly grateful for this crumb of praise. 'However, I believe they found an iron in the house and it wasn't implicated. Cleared of suspicion.'

'Oh.' Michael drooped.

'But I know exactly what you did in that house, the pair of you. You went all over, didn't you? Exploring. Up the stairs and down the stairs and in my lady's chamber. Yes you did. You opened drawers, cupboards, wardrobes. Went through her clothes, didn't you, Oliver? Sniffed her perfume? Listened to her messages on the answerphone?' Oliver's shame

150

filled his face. He got up and moved towards the wall as if to hide himself. Bright got up and joined him, still holding Michael by the arm. His tone altered. 'Now look, somewhere in the house, probably out in the open, ready to hand, lying about, on a window sill, chest of drawers, mantelpiece, just around the place somewhere, there was a thing that someone could have just picked up, on the spur of the moment maybe, something maybe you'd never even think of as a weapon, it was there to hand, maybe close to the bathroom, and they just picked it up and – ' He stopped. Michael's mouth had dropped open. His eyes were fixed on something beyond Oliver's head. He touched Oliver's arm. He said, 'Oliver.'

Oliver turned. On the wall behind his head there was an exhibition of photographs. Winners of Awards for Excellence in Radio. Twenty-odd years of them. Immediately behind him hung a picture of three people: Roger Cooke in the centre with Gabriel Woolf on his right and a young woman on his left. 'That's Kate Creech,' Bright said.

'Yes.' Oliver had calmed down. 'She won the best actress award, in 1979 I think, for – '

'No, Oliver – ' Michael pointed. 'Look!'

Oliver gasped like he'd been punched in the chest. He turned to John Bright. 'Oh, inspector,' he said. 'Oh my God.'

Michael said, 'It could be, couldn't it?'

In the car Bright tried Aggie's number and got Kate. 'Muz Creech? Will you do something for me?'

32

LOST AND FOUND

The traffic was setting like concrete. It looked like her future. No way out. 'Even if someone buys it,' she said.

Ted seemed to follow her thought. 'No one's buying houses now anyway.'

'Even when they start buying again, no one will want a house where – Some property dealer will have me over a barrel. I'll have to sell for peanuts. I can't afford to sell for peanuts. It'll be squatted while I wait.'

'You'll need a lawyer to evict the squatters.'

'I'll need a chauffeur if Daniel totals my car.'

'Where will you live?'

'I'll live in my car if that child ever returns it to me. On the day when London actually stops, do you think they'll actually do something about the public transport system?'

'The car has that unique advantage: you couldn't live on public transport.'

'P'raps I'll be a bag lady. That's how it happens, you know. You lose your house, then because you get scruffy you lose your job, then because you don't have an address you can't get another job so then you take to drink. And the drink fossilises your brain cells and you get the shakes and you start pushing your belongings round in a pram and that's that. You die in a shop doorway. Found frozen stiff at 3 a.m. by the bobby on the beat.'

'Pretty good scenario except for the bobby on the beat.'

'Okay, two police officers in their squad car.'

'More like it.'

'Joking apart, I am going to have to start again from scratch.'

'Absolutely no way you can go back and live there?'

'Could *you*? Want to buy it from me? You and Aggie live there happily ever after?'

His face screwed itself into a grimace. 'P'raps a pervert will buy it. A ghoul who'll keep the bathroom intact, slime on the bath and everything.'

'Ted.' He looked mock shame. 'It's my only hope,' she said.

'Is there anything that could happen to the place, be done to it, that would make it acceptable to you again?'

'A fire?' she said.

'Would you like me to arrange that?'

For a second she thought he was serious but he slid his eyes sideways and grinned at her. 'I wish you could,' she said.

The house was still cordoned off with tape but there were no journalists to be seen. She put her key in her lock and opened her front door. Things are supposed to be easier the second time around. She discovered this was not the case. She knew she'd be shaken going in again, but this shaken? She wanted the foetal position and a dark room and she wanted it now and she wanted it for the foreseeable future. She felt scattered like beads off a broken necklace, nothing left of her but a bare string. 'Hold my hand, Ted?'

They went up the stairs like children, hand in hand. On the landing outside the bathroom the chest of drawers stood unchanged but for the gathering of dust. On it untouched the bowl of dried delphiniums, the bowl of dried pink roses, the photograph of her mother, her sister her brother and herself taken twenty-something years ago. A pottery ashtray made by an actor friend and ex-lover to commemorate the production of

Mrs Warren's Profession in which they had met. She kept beads in it. There they still were, covered in dust.

'Yes,' she said, voice as dry as the dust. 'It's not there.'

'Sure?'

'Yes. I'm sure.'

Downstairs she couldn't stop talking: 'It was just an object to them, I suppose. A nice heavy object, easy to hand. Part of the jumble on the chest of drawers. Just outside the bathroom door. So convenient. The only award I ever got. Best Actress in Radio 1979. Two vertical wavy metal rods about ten inches long, meant to represent sound waves or something I guess, on a heavy green marble base, square, heavy, with sharp corners. Just the thing. Just what was required. Get a good grip on the wavy rods and the marble base would be just right. Always knew it would come in useful one day. Used it as a doorstop before I got a lock on the bathroom door but since then it's been a bit redundant. I was proud of it actually but a bit embarrassed too. That's the trouble with awards: where do you put them? The mantelpiece is too much like showing off; the loo is just inverted showing off, backing shyly into the limelight, after all, everyone who comes to your house eventually goes to the loo, don't they? Whatever you do with it seems an affectation. That's why it was in that jumble on the chest of drawers, waiting to find its final resting place. Now it's found it, I suppose. I wonder where.' He let her ramble on, didn't stop her. She said without a pause, 'I wish you hadn't got involved with Aggie.'

'I know but . . .'

'But it just happened.'

'It did.'

'Is it nice?'

'Yes, it is.'

'Will it last?'

'Who knows?'

'Do you think it was just accident they used my award, or design?'

'Accident. Like you said, it was there to hand, just outside the bathroom door.'

'Is everything accident? Crawling like insects from one accident to another?'

'Running not crawling.'

'Yes. Generally trying to run away.' She picked up the phone and dialled.

'Think I was running away from you?'

'I think it's a possibility, Ted. But then I'd already run away from you. Inspector Bright, please,' she said.

'And where are you running to now?'

153

'Well, I can't stay at Aggie's any more.'

'Why?'

'Why? Did you say why?'

'I could piss off back to my place,' he said.

'That would make everyone happy.'

'Be serious. You can't stay here; where will you go?'

'How about if *I* stay at your place?' she said.

His hand came up and plucked at the corners of his mouth. 'My girlfriend's there,' he said. 'Things are a bit tough at the moment.'

'Ted!'

He shook his head. 'Don't, don't.'

'Does Aggie know?'

He nodded. 'She says it's the story of her life.'

Kate gave a shiver. Another narrow escape. 'Inspector Bright? Kate Creech. You were right. It was there and now it's not.'

'We've got the weapon, guv?'

Bright squinted at Cato and sighed. 'We've a good idea what it is.'

'We just don't know where it is?'

'Got it in one, Sherlock.'

'So we can't charge him?'

'We've got no weapon, with or without his fingerprints, even though we're pretty sure what it was, we've got no witness saw him at the scene. Edgley thinks I could have got a confession, don't you, constable?' They all looked at Edgley whose face set like stone. 'But I haven't got a confession – and nor have my colleagues here' – Atkins and Gwylim shifted sheepishly – 'and we're not going to get one. And shall I tell you what we have got? We've got PACE rules telling me we've got to let him loose, and we've got his brief downstairs insisting on his release.'

Edgley handed him a fax: 'This has just come from the lab, sir.'

Bright read it, lifted his head and laughed. 'Well now we really got lucky. You know what this tells us? The victim was not Tess Harbour. Ah, the miracle of modern communications. So you know what else we've got? We've still got a missing woman. Isn't that a surprise?' He poked the blurred photocopy of the face of Tess Harbour.

'It's been on the news enough, guv. She'd have to be deaf and blind not to see it.'

'Or abroad.'

'Or dead,' Bright said.

33

THE WORLD IS WIDE

'Five minutes.' Bright opened the door for her. 'While Adams completes the formalities.'

'It's good of you.'

'I make a deal, I stick to it.'

'Thanks anyway.'

He looked at Nat and looked at her, briefly. 'Be careful,' he said and shut the door.

Nat clattered towards her in his big shoes in his loose-jointed way. He put an arm around her and she rested her head on his chest a moment. Not long; the feel of that hand on her back raised memories. She didn't want to go back there. She backed off and they stood not speaking. She didn't know how to mention Sally but the thought of her was a barrier that wouldn't let anything else through. He looked haunted but then he always had.

'They're letting you go,' she said. *Making conversation. With Nat. In a police cell.*

'Yes,' he said. 'A few hours now.'

Pause. 'You'll go to a hotel,' she said.

'Yes. Ted has to vouch for me. I'm on a short rein.'

Pause. 'But you'll be glad to be out of here?'

'No.'

'No?'

He thought a moment. 'Safe. I've felt safe here.'

'*Safe*?'

'They feed me. They even talk to me. I'm writing. What will I do outside?'

'You're writing?'

'I've – removed myself. I've become the – recorder. I'm the recording angel.'

She wondered if that was the same as the angel of death and still dreaded raising the subject but had to. 'It's unbelievable that it's Sally,' she said.

He turned his face away. He pulled some tissues out of the box and wiped his face. 'I saw her body.'

'So did I.'

'Someone did that, Kate.'

'Yes. I'm sorry, Nat. I'm so sorry it was Sally. But, you know, I didn't know her well and all I keep thinking is: it wasn't Tess, it wasn't Tess.'

A sheath seemed to cloud the blue of his eyes. He was about to speak, but didn't.

'Don't you have any idea where Tess might be, Nat?'

'No.'

'Can't you even make a guess? What if her disappearance is connected with Sally's death?' He made a noise half whinny half groan, put his head down on the table. But Kate had no mercy. 'Where might she go, Nat?'

Another long groan. 'Vera, maybe.'

'Vera owes Tess money. She'll keep out of her way.'

'Tess depended on her, that's all I know. They were lovers for God's sake, can you fathom that? Tess had two kids to look after. My kids.'

She dragged him back to the question. 'You've no suggestions apart from Vera? Nothing and nowhere that occurs to you? Nowhere she mentioned? Nothing at all?'

'The last number she gave me was that artist. Laura. The place in Somerset.'

'She wouldn't go back there.'

'Another dyke, is she?'

'Nat. You don't sound like you.'

'They're my kids, Kate. They're my kids!'

He lifted his tragic face to her. He said, 'Kate?' and held out his arms but she couldn't go to him. She wasn't afraid but she didn't want to be here with him. She felt death coming off him like a smell. His picture of things, that's what he needed, that's what he imposed. But if you get sucked into another person's picture of things, that's death. It's death of your spirit. Sally had been trying to get out of his picture. He couldn't let her go. Sally was dead. Tess had got out of his picture. Maybe Tess was dead. Kate kept the mask on her face, she hoped. The cool mask. But she wouldn't go to him. He saw that. The great eyelids came down like blinds. Then he lay down. Face down. On the floor.

She knocked on the door to be let out.

'Thanks,' she said.

Bright's face had a curious expression, the squint pronounced but the hard light gone from the eyes. 'No use asking you what he said.'

She couldn't manage a smile. 'He said you have him on a short rein.'

'A-ha.'

'Like you have me.'

The corner of his mouth moved, as near to a smile as she'd seen. 'That's right, Muz Creech.'

'So whatever he's planning to do, you'll know.'

'A-ha,' he said. 'And what are *you* planning to do now?'

'I'm fresh out of plans. I'm going back to spend the evening at Aggie's. Then, who knows? The night is young, the world is wide. You probably have a better idea than I do. P'raps you could ring me later on and tell me what my plans are.'

He suddenly laughed. These startling white teeth. She saw a kind of beauty, charm, a capacity for joy? Something anyway that she hadn't seen before. And all at once they were stuck there, he and she, nothing to say, nowhere to go. Just standing. In this dim brick corridor outside the cells in a sudden silence that bound them like rope.

'Sir.' Edgley's face appeared round the corner. 'Sir, the custody sergeant would like to speak to you.'

34

WHAT FRIENDS ARE FOR

Rich smells filled the kitchen. Aggie glowed in the golden light, wine bottle squeezed between her knees as she yanked on the corkscrew. 'Shouldn't the bloke be doing this?' she said.

'The Bloke is getting Nat out of the nick.'

Aggie laughed, then said, 'Pity he can't bring him round here. Awful to come out of the nick and have to stay in a hotel on your own.'

And Kate suddenly couldn't bear it. This cosiness; that chill. This happiness; that misery. She went out across the hall into the cooler front room. A scrap of exercise book paper on the mantelpiece said *Yellow Beetle. 35 Despard Street. Love Daniel.* And her car keys lay under it.

'Where the hell's Despard Street?'

'A few streets away,' Aggie said. 'Near the railway arches.'

She put her arms round Aggie. 'I'm sorry for being a cow. I'm very happy for you. And for Ted. And I won't be in to dinner, Ags. Have a good time.'

The forecourt of a Volkswagen dealer. Beetles of every year and colour but hers the only yellow one. There was a light on inside the railway arch. The proprietor was bemused. 'A kid,' he said. 'I thought he'd nicked it. "Matter of life and death," he says. "If it's not collected by closing time tomorrow, ring this number."' He read out Aggie's number off the torn scrap of paper. 'That you?'

'That's me.'

Stuck fast in the traffic she thought about kids, people's kids. Daniel. Maisie. And Nat's kids, Tessa's: Zoë's face at two, at five, at seven, a little flower face, fair like Nat with a little round chin and Nat's great haunting blue eyes. The other one, Rose, had been only a baby, dark like Tess and afraid of the world like Tess. *Don't think about Tess, you don't know where she is and you can't do anything about her. And don't think about Nat. And don't go to Nat. Don't think about the places you are not going to spend the evening. Think about where you are going. Though this also might not be a whole lot of laughs.* And all the time she had this uneasy feeling, something nagging, something about Nat that was separate from her remorse at failing him. Something else.

Ken answered the door wearing only his old towelling dressing-gown. Just like the last time she'd seen him. But this time the dressing-gown was clean and he looked better. In fact he looked good. He pulled her into the hall and put his arms round her. Stood there holding her then let her go.

'Ken, I'm sorry for the things I said to you.'

'What things, babe?'

She gaped at him. People were weird. You said things you thought they'd never recover from and then you found they either hadn't heard or couldn't remember. She shook her head. 'Never mind.' He led the way into the room.

The place was a mess. Articles of clothing and cushions lay strewn about the floor. And Michael, naked except for a pretty pair of boxer shorts, stood in the middle of it, hastily pulling on a sweat shirt. 'Michael, you're back!'

He gave her an uncertain smile. 'That Inspector Bright rang Ken up so Ken had to get in touch with me. Isn't that right, Ken?'

'And you've been celebrating, I see. Maybe I should go.'

Ken smiled at Kate. 'Don't be daft.'

'I never would have had Inspector Bright down as a matchmaker. Would you, Kate?'

'Was it you who told Bright about the award, Michael?'

'Well, Oliver helped.'

'Oliver?'

Ken said, 'He's coming round in a minute. When he's finished work.'

'Oliver is?'
The door bell rang.

You'd have sworn nothing bad had ever happened. Old mates round the table like old times, Michael tripping in and out with food. Only, to Kate they seemed unreal. Innocent children. Like Lizzie's house. Aggie's. They didn't know life on her side of the screen.

Oliver said, 'Once we told him we'd been in your house, we were off the hook, you could feel it.'

'I felt just like a fish actually, whoop, the hook came out of my jaws and plop, I'm back in the water waggling my little tail.' Michael was high but only on happiness.

Kate was not high, in spite of wrapping herself round half a bottle of Chilean Cabernet Sauvignon.

Oliver said, 'Don't be sad, Kate. Just for this evening. After all, it wasn't Tess.'

She turned to him. Her eyes opened wide. He smiled at her, his sweet sad smile. 'I know that's what you were scared about.'

'Where the hell is she, Oliver? If she's okay, why hasn't she come forward? Bright thinks she's keeping her head down in order to protect Nat. Or is that only what I think?' She rubbed her eyes. 'I don't know.'

Michael sat, leaning back against Ken. Ken said, 'Is Bright getting anywhere?'

'He's pretty desperate, I think. He's had to let Nat go. And he'll never get anything out of Vera. Even if she knows something. Which I don't think she does. He strikes me like someone waiting for a phone call.'

'Like me waiting for Ken to call.'

'You know what I mean,' she said. 'A miracle.' And then she remembered. The fear nagging at her brain. The thing Nat had said. The important thing. 'Talking of calls, I have to make one, Ken.'

'Feel free, love.'

She used the bedroom phone for privacy, dialled, and got the answering machine. She looked at her watch. It was after 2 a.m. Of course, the rest of the world was asleep. The moment the message began in that tight constrained voice the place came back to her: the Gothic arches, the amazing tapestries, the grave dolls. 'Laura! It's Kate! It's two in the morning, I'm sorry. I just have to tell you that they've let Nat Crosby out. I think he may try to get in touch with you. I just wanted to – ' *What? Warn her? Against what? Against whom? Against Nat? But surely she didn't think – ?* And then a shrill squeal shocked her rigid, until she realised it was the message being interrupted. Laura had picked up the phone and was saying, 'Kate?'

159

'Laura, I'm sorry to wake you – ' *The crazy things we say.*

'You didn't wake me. I've been calling you all evening.'

'Calling me?'

Pause. Kate waited. Laura said, 'I've heard from Tess.'

Kate's stomach turned over. Her eyes saw red. Her life went into freeze-frame.

'She phoned me,' Laura said.

'When?'

'At six o'clock this eve – well, now, yesterday – evening.'

'Where is she?'

'She wouldn't say where. She doesn't want to see me.' The constricted voice faltered but only for a moment. 'She didn't want to speak to me. She wants to speak to you.'

'You have a number?'

Laura spelled out the number. Kate's shaking hand wrote it down. 'Have you phoned the police?'

'She asked me not to. So I have not.'

'Thank you, Laura.'

'You will get in touch with me? When you've located her? I won't contact her against her will. I just want to know how she is.'

'I promise you I will.'

'Thank you.'

She sat with the receiver in her hand. You weren't supposed to ring people at this time of night. Even a Lazarus just risen from the dead. She was laughing weakly, silently, and tears were running down over her hand which clutched her mouth. She dialled the number Laura had given her. It rang and it rang and it rang and it rang and nobody came to answer it.

Ken found her half an hour later asleep with the phone in her hand. He replaced the receiver on its rest and picked her up. He carried her into the other room and laid her on the sofa. He tucked a duvet round her. She didn't wake.

35

ON THE ROAD AGAIN

But she was awake at six. Morning was the best time in Ken's living-room, sunshine billowed in there, dust danced. Michael had cleared the mess from last night. She sat and shook. Then she got up and walked in the sunshine of the room. She dragged deep breaths in, pushed long breaths out. The light was too bright, everything over-exposed. She dialled the number Laura had given, and shut her eyes. She had a kind of propeller in her chest, whirling round, causing turbulence, whoomf, whoomf, whoomf.

'Hello? The Barnabus Community. How may I help you?'

The Barnabus Community? Kate couldn't speak.

The voice persisted: 'Who is speaking, please?'

In spite of the propeller at last she managed to say her name and ask for Tess.

'I'll see if she is free to come to the telephone.'

'It's urgent, quite urgent – ' but the woman had gone. She had a precise, old-fashioned utterance: 'the telephone'. Who called it that these days? Was the Barnabus Community a nunnery? Had Tess joined a contemplative order? How else could she have been unaware of the terrible events, the hunt for her?

'Kate!' Tess's voice. That light, fading music with its dying falls, the trace of America floating through it. 'Kate, is it you?'

'Oh, Tess.'

'Kate, what is it?'

But Kate couldn't reply. She hadn't expected ever to hear this voice again.

'What is it, sweetheart?'

'Oh, Tess, where have you been?'

'Well, I've been here, I guess.'

'Where's here?'

'It's this wonderful community in Dorset.'

'Tess, haven't you heard what's been going on?'

'Kate, we don't have TV, we don't have news. Yesterday someone gave Simon a newspaper with my picture in it.' *Simon? Who's Simon? No time now. Find out later.* 'He showed it to me. That's why I called Laura. I'm so shocked.'

'I thought it was you,' Kate said.

'Oh no! But, Kate – ' She stopped.

'What, Tess?'

'It could be Sally, couldn't it?'

'It is Sally, Tess. She's been identified.'

Tess drew a fast breath. 'I gave her your keys. I'm sorry. I'm so sorry, Kate.'

'I must see you.'

'Can you come here? Are you free?'

'Will they let me in? Are visitors allowed?'

'Oh, sure.' Her shaky leafy laugh. 'It's not a prison.' She gave directions.

161

Kate made marks that trembled like words in water. Tess said, 'I'll expect you then.' And then was gone.

She knew Bright would be after her. But she no longer cared. She had to see Tess. Had seen her dead so often she had to see her living. Had to see she wasn't just a bunch of fleshy grey balloons streaked with slime. And had to find out what she knew.

The village of Abbotsbury was as perfectly preserved as a façade in a film set, sea on the left, hills rolling up behind. She had Tess's directions by heart: 'Follow the signs to the Swan Farm. Take a right, then a left at the next intersection,' but she still got elaborately lost. The lanes narrowed. In the summer they'd be green tunnels; now the black branches showed the sky, skeleton arms linked to block the way or beckon her on. Her mind went into horror movie mode. Her mouth was dry though saliva collected in her throat. *All our emotions: fear, shock, lust, love, hate, anger, all create havoc in our bodies. Heartbeat, pulse, sweat-glands, tear-ducts, bowels, bladder, they all react. We shake we shudder we cry we sweat we shit ourselves dry mouth or dribbling. And when we're dead all that stops. Just a thing. In the bath. Liquefied. But a thing that wasn't Tess.*

Gateposts with stone balls on top, in a crinkle-crankle wall. No gates. A lodge house with boarded-up windows. She drove in. The drive wriggled through woodland. Pines and evergreens grew among the bare trees thickening the winter woods so that the house surprised her, appearing as though from nowhere. Narrow pale bricks; stone window frames and terrace. It threw a long dark shadow towards Kate. She drove into this shadow. The sun was low. Three o'clock. She got out stiff into the shadow's chill, and went up the steps.

The bell didn't clang in distant halls and passages, in fact she couldn't hear it and was thinking of trying another door when a small woman opened it. Grey hair cut short like a boy, tweed trousers, an old sweater and a scarf. She looked up at Kate.

'I've come to see Tess Harbour,' Kate said.

'Oh, you're the person who telephoned.' As though a phone call was an event here. Her smile was sweet, trusting, a child's smile. 'I'll tell her you're here. Come with me.'

She hurried ahead. She was just like Sister Veronica, the little nun who'd kept the door at Kate's school. The room she showed her into was large, rather bare, with cheap fifties furniture all in brown. She switched on one bar of an enormous metal electric fire. 'You'll need some heat. You won't be used to our rather Spartan conditions.'

'Thank you.'

'We're all at tea. But that would overwhelm you I fear. I'll send Tess to you, shall I? With some tea?'

'Thank you.'

'Both then. Tess and tea.' She beamed then tiggywinkled away on fast little feet.

The room too reminded Kate of a convent, going back to visit nuns who'd taught her at school. Did poverty chastity and obedience always go with depressing furniture? A deliberate deprivation or what? She was keeping her mind off Tess, and the cold, and the delay which seemed grotesque.

A bang on the door, and a huge tea tray pushed it open, piled with pots, cups, jugs, plates, cake. Thinner than ever, Tess looked too frail to carry the load. Kate watched her lower it carefully on to the spindly coffee table.

She wore a long brown dress in fine wool, a tunic over it, also in fine wool, of a kind of greenish grey. She'd always had amazing style. But when she bent to place the tray you could see every knob of her spine and imagine her ribs like a bare fish bone. She stood and they gazed at each other then took each other's hands. Tess's hands were colder than Kate's and thin and narrow. Kate gripped them and felt a tremor.

'Tess?'

'Oh, I can't understand it. I lent her the keys. I'm so sorry. I'm so sorry, Kate.'

'Let's have some tea.' Kate too was shaking. The cup rattled in the saucer just the way it does on those opening nights when you have to look unshakeably calm, and nothing is under your control. The tea was some lovely China stuff, hot and smoky, Lapsang or something. It did you good, settled you down. 'I thought you were dead, Tess.'

Tess shook her head. 'But, Kate, that it's Sally. How can that be?'

'They think it's Nat who killed her.'

Tess whispered, 'She wanted to be with him there.'

'They were there together. He says so. They haven't charged him. Not enough hard evidence. They've let him go. Yesterday.'

'Where is he?'

'A hotel. I don't know where.'

Tess's long trembling hands covered her mouth.

'You don't know anything that could help, Tess? You didn't go to my house yourself?'

'No.' Her hair shook out, wiry tendrils round the thin face.

'You see, all the woman's – all Sally's – belongings were removed: her bag, her clothes, everything. It makes it look like the killer was trying to cover up.'

'Yes. It can't be Nat. She must have met someone else there, mustn't she? After Nat had gone back to the States. Isn't that possible?'

'Yes, it's possible, but – Do you know of anyone? Did she have some other man in her life?'

'She didn't tell me of anyone. She only ever seemed to talk about Nat.'

'And there's the sheets.'

'The sheets?' Tess's mystified face was drained, no colour under the skin.

'They'd used my bed. All her clothes were taken away but he didn't think to change the sheets. If Sally had gone back, or stayed there to meet someone else, you'd think she would have changed the sheets. I would. Wouldn't you?'

Tess nodded, silent, swallowing. Her hand came down to her throat. Kate heard the scraping noise in her chest. She took an inhaler out of a pocket and dragged on it. 'I thought Nat had cured your asthma.'

'He did,' Tess said. 'But it came back.'

This time Kate heard the door bell, a tinny warble, and knew who had arrived before the little nun-woman showed him in.

She said, 'Forgive me, Tess.'

36

BIRD IN THE NET

Tess put out her hand and said, 'Hello,' in her floaty childlike way. Bright shook hands with her but Edgley backed off and stood against the door, she wasn't letting anyone out of the room. Bright said, 'Sorry, Muz Creech.'

'I expected you,' Kate said. 'Just not quite so fast.'

Tess looked puzzled.

Bright said, 'Wherever your friend Kate goes, I turn up.'

'Oh?'

'As the investigating officer in the case you've no doubt been discussing. The Body In The Bath as the tabloids are calling it. Well, at least we know now the body isn't you.'

Tess turned slowly to face Kate. 'I know that's what Kate thought.'

'A-ha. That's what she thought. Sit down.' Tess, startled, obediently sat, her cup between her hands. 'What did you want her to think?'

'I'm sorry?' She didn't get his point.

He spelled it out: 'You've lain low for a long time.'

'Lain low?'

'You must have heard about this. Why didn't you come forward?'

'No.' Tess's head shook slowly from side to side. 'No.'

'I'm sure you heard what she said on my phone,' Kate intervened. 'They get no news here.'

'I wasn't talking to you, Muz Creech, you shouldn't be here at all, don't push your luck. And I don't believe it. No one can escape the news these days. It's everywhere, every hour of the day. Someone here's got to have a radio.'

'Yes, there's a radio. But we only have it on Radio 3 if there's a recital or something that some people want to hear. I'm not musical. I don't listen. We try to think about the good things in the world, not saturate ourselves with the bad things. The news only tells you the bad things.'

He sighed. 'Someone here must have heard it, even if you didn't.'

'But there would be no reason to tell me.' Her voice lilted up with puzzlement. Bright shot her a look, quick as a flick-knife, there then gone. Kate felt alarm but Tess seemed not to notice; she gazed upon him with her trusting eyes.

'No,' he said. 'You're right. There'd be no reason to connect it with you. A lot of women answer your description. As we have found.'

A knock. The little nun-person handed two cups and saucers to Edgley. Edgley thanked her and shut the door in her face. Tess poured tea.

He went to the window, stood with his back to the room, rattling the change in his pockets. 'What is this place, a nunnery?'

Tess smiled shakily. 'Just a community.'

'What for?'

'Peace. Healing.'

'How'd you end up here?'

'I heard about it. I can't remember how. I need to be part of a community, to feel useful, to have a purpose to my life, give my life a – shape.'

'This place does all that, does it?'

'You work so hard you don't have time to think about yourself. We grow our own food, we freeze and preserve things. We keep goats, we make yogurt and cheese. We make our own clothes, we do everything. And if you get worried or upset there's always someone to help you. Simon is wonderful.'

'Simon who?'

'Oh, Langdon.'

'He's the boss, is he?'

'He wouldn't say that.'

'What would he say? Priest? Guru? Bagwan?'

'Oh, he'd say he's just trying to be a human being, I think.'

Bright bounced a glance off Kate. He pushed a hand through his hair. 'A-ha?' he said.

'He's a searcher, I guess. He says he tried many things in many places and finally came home, to his own country and his own religion. This was his family's house.'

'Where is he now?'

'Oh, he's out in the boat. He works with local young people. Teaches them sailing. He won't be back till late.'

'Okay, he can wait.' Bright turned round. 'I want to know everywhere you've been, everything you've done, everyone you've seen, the last eight weeks.'

'But I've been here.'

'Except when you went to London to give your friend Sally, your husband's friend Sally, the keys to your friend Kate's house.'

'Yes. Apart from that day.'

'Day? You didn't even go for the weekend?'

'Well, no. Just the day. I don't like to be away from here too long.'

'What date was this?'

'Sometime in January. I don't know the exact date. Here, we don't – '

'Yeah, yeah, yeah. Okay. Edgley, make a note to ascertain this date. Sometime in January.'

Tess said, 'Claire might know.'

'Claire?'

'The person who showed you in. She writes things down for Simon. I know it was a Friday though. Sally said so.'

He rubbed his forehead. 'How long have you been here?'

'Since – Oh, since November. That's when I first came.'

'You didn't let your friend Laura in Oulton know where you'd gone.'

'No.' She looked hunted, her eyes went sideways. 'I – Things had gotten a little heavy for me there, I – can't explain.' A little faint colour showed under the papery whiteness of her skin. She drank some tea.

Bright shot Kate a look. 'That where you got your information, Muz Creech?' She didn't respond. He didn't pursue it. 'Go on,' he said.

'I came here to see Simon and he – took me on.'

'And you've never left. Not for a weekend, not for a day? Apart from this day with Sally. How come you were in touch with Sally and not with anyone else?'

'I was always in touch with Sally. She kind of – depended on me.'

It was hard to imagine anyone depending on Tess, this frail reed. Bright showed his doubt then said, 'Okay, okay. So Sally calls and you go to London. Sometime in January.'

'Yes.'

'You go by train?'

'Yes, I don't drive.'

'That figures.'

'When I got there everything was nearly packed up. She was throwing away a lot of stuff. We tied up these big plastic garbage bags and took them down to the bins. The removal men came. We met them at the new flat.'

'She talk much?'

'She was worried. Nat wanted her to go back to the States with him. To live. She didn't want to burn all her boats like that. She loved him, she really did, but it was a big step he was asking of her.'

'That was the first you'd heard of it, was it? This idea of her going to the States.'

'Yes.'

'And what did you think of it?'

'I said she should go.' She caught Kate's reaction and said, 'It was never any use arguing with Nat, was it, Kate? I said she should go for, say, three months, I think that's the length of a visitor's visa anyhow, then she could see how she felt. She was so worried. Nat frightened her.'

'Nat frightened her?'

'Kate knows. Don't you, Kate?'

Kate looked as blank as she knew how. She wanted to hit Tess. All this damned floaty innocence, just as though she wasn't speaking to a rottweiler in plain clothes. Had she forgotten who he was? Why he was asking these questions? 'No,' she said. 'I don't know.'

'Oh well, you wouldn't feel it p'raps in the same way; you've always been so independent. I just mean – Nat's will.'

'Nat's Will.' Bright said it like the title of a play.

'You see, Inspector Bright, Nat has this strong will. It's like a – I don't know, a – force of nature or something. As strong as a hungry baby. It only sees one way. His way. If you won't go along he just can't understand. You just get mown down by it. Well, people like me and Sally do. Kate is strong, a stronger person. Aren't you, Kate?'

'That right, Muz Creech?' She shrugged, irritated, confused, feeling his eyes on her. He turned back to Tess. 'So why'd you give her Kate's keys?'

Tess looked apologetic. 'She had to have a serious talk with Nat. He was only there for a short while and in meetings all the time and then he was going back to the States. She was in such a state at the mess in her new flat. There wasn't time to get it straight. Then I – ' She stopped and looked at Kate. 'I'm so sorry, Kate. I remembered I had your keys and how pretty and peaceful your little house was. I just thought – I guess I thought you wouldn't mind, you know?'

'How did you know Miss Creech was away?' Edgley's voice surprised them coming from over by the door. They all turned to her then back to Tess.

'Oh, I telephoned. Kate's answerphone said, if you want me urgently call this number.'

167

'Why didn't you do that?' The hardness in Kate's voice shocked Tess. She made a softening gesture with her hands.

'I did! It was the theatre in Coventry. They said you were on stage. It was the matinée. I asked were you coming home that night, they said no, you were really sick, so I thought, oh I guess it'll be okay. It was only for a couple of hours, Kate. That's all they needed. Till she got her new flat straight. I meant to call you afterward but I . . . I should have done that, I should have done that.' She put a long narrow hand up to her face and tears ran down it into the sleeve at the wrist. No one spoke or moved till Kate said, 'It's okay.' At last Tess groped at the tea tray for a paper napkin and mopped herself up with it. Her big brown eyes looked washed clean. Her fragile body had a slight tremor. She pushed the mass of hair away from her face.

'So you gave this Sally the keys.' Bright spoke as though the storm of crying had not occurred.

Tess nodded, not able to speak yet.

'You go to Kate's place with her?'

'No, Nat knew how to get there, didn't he, Kate?'

'He'd been there once.'

'Just once?' Tess was taken aback. 'Oh. I thought – '

'No. Just once. For a cup of tea.'

'Oh.'

Bright's eyes followed this exchange without moving. He wasn't a rottweiler, Kate thought; he was one of those dogs that stands with its nose up and its tail straight out, absolutely still, scenting the prey. A pointer. 'What was the arrangement?' he said.

'I'm sorry?'

'About the keys.' Tess didn't get it. 'She'd give them back that day, post them to you, what?'

'Oh. I guess we didn't – well, she'd give them back next time we met, I guess. I wouldn't need them.'

Kate looked unbelief. 'Tess – '

'I know, Kate. It sounds kind of casual. But we were friends. If you'd been there to ask you'd have said yes, sure. Wouldn't you?'

'Would I?'

'Wouldn't you, Muz Creech?'

'I don't know, frankly.'

Bright said, 'You were pretty casual yourself the way you handed your keys around.'

'I gave my keys to people I trusted.' She was so angry she forgot about protecting Tess, she was so angry she could barely contain it. 'And yes, I wish I hadn't.' She got up and started to walk round the room, she couldn't keep still. 'And yes, I'd have said yes. Yes, sure. Yes sure use my house,

use my bed, use my sheets, use my bath – ' She stopped, shocked at the state she was in, her voice down an octave with emotion. Just like Medea. Only Medea suffered the loss of everything she held dear: husband, children, country; this was just a house she was talking about. Wasn't it? She breathed out slowly, getting it under control. She stood close to Tess. 'Tess, they could have gone to a hotel like anyone else. Nat's rich these days. I still go about thinking everyone's as poor as me. Or you. Yes, I'd have said fine, sure, go ahead, use my place, but I wouldn't have wanted them to really. And you should have known that, Tess. You did know that.'

Tears filled her eyes again. 'I didn't, Kate. I couldn't know how you felt.'

'No?' She'd never before spoken harshly to Tess. People didn't, she looked so breakable: *this way up, handle with care.*

'Kate, you know me. I don't have a feeling of ownership, it's a thing I can't understand. Anything I ever owned I've let go.' Like belongings were caged birds you could set free.

Kate gave a narrow smile, all she could manage. She sighed. 'No. I know that. I'm sorry. I'm the one to blame.' She looked at Bright. 'You don't want people to use your place? Don't give them the key. You're right. See, I'm ashamed of my desire for ownership. I think we should all be like Tess. We should want to share.' He had an odd expression, looking at her, she couldn't work it out. 'Especially a house. A house! Just bricks and mortar. A roof.' He still looked at her steadily with this expression she couldn't get a handle on. Like yesterday outside the cells. Feelings she couldn't control punched like fists in her stomach. She didn't know why she was so upset. She'd think about it later. Now she said to Tess, and to Bright, 'I would have said yes. Tess is right. It's not her fault.'

'Oh, well, glad that's settled, now we're all happy. Sit down, Muz Creech. Edgley, get away from that door and give her some more tea. What did you do then?' He was looking at Tess. No trace of the squint, just the hard points of light, straight at her.

'Me?'

'A-ha. You. After you'd lent the keys.'

'I left Sally because I didn't want to bump into Nat, and went to catch my train.'

'What time?'

'Well . . .'

'What time?'

'I'd meant to catch the two thirty but I – well, I saw a poster in the Tube. It was for an exhibition of tapestries. At the Craft Centre in Covent Garden. The picture on the poster was of a Peruvian grave doll. Laura had been making those. So I just thought, well, as I'm in London, you know? I knew I wouldn't be there again for ages. So I went. It was a very good exhibit.

169

And Covent Garden was fun, you know? All the lights and people. So I just missed a train, I don't know what time. I caught the last one, I think. I didn't get back till late anyhow. So late. Everyone was in bed here, asleep. We go to bed early here.'

Bright folded his arms. He rocked on his heels. He never took that hard stare off Tess. He nodded. He said, 'A-ha. I see. So you didn't go to Muz Creech's house that day? You didn't go there, that what you're telling me?'

'No.'

'No, you didn't go there or no that's not what you're telling me?'

'No, I didn't go there.'

'And you didn't get the keys back.'

'No.'

'And you haven't heard from Sally Crowe since?'

'No.'

'And you didn't see Nat Crosby?'

'No. I told you. I left Sally before Nat arrived. I told you, Nat and I – because of the children – we don't get on so well. Not just now anyway. I need a – an interim – to rest, become whole again, reshape my life. Then I'll be able to stand up to him. He overrides, me you see. Kate knows. He overwhelms people, he's not wicked but it's just like wickedness the way he can't see – '

'Tess,' Kate warned.

'Oh yes, I'm sorry, I shouldn't. I've said it all before and it's not what we're talking about here, is it?'

'Isn't it?' The lights in his little eyes seemed to quiver. 'What if Nat couldn't cope with Sally refusing to go to the States with him? Think he'd be capable of killing her?'

'Oh no! No! No!' Tess stood like a sapling in the wind, then ran. Edgley in her guard dog position restrained her at the door. Tess was taller. They struggled. In the struggle she looked stronger than her fragile appearance would suggest. Edgley was getting the worst of it. But Edgley was skilled. She made a grab for Tess's waist, got a grip and did a sideways half-turn. Tess seemed to collapse in the middle like a sack of bones. Kate looked on astonished. Bright grinned at her. Those surprising white teeth. She wondered why he'd allowed her to come here, why he wanted her here. He was still looking at her. And she suddenly knew. *He still suspects me. Of course he does. Of being in cahoots with – first he thought Nat, now he thinks Tess.* He was still watching her.

Edgley escorted Tess back to the tea table. Bright said. 'How come you're so friendly with your husband's girlfriends, Tess?'

The clear-washed eyes gazed at him. She didn't know what he meant.

'Eh? That's a bit funny, isn't it? You're friends with Kate here. And you're friends with Sally. Both of them pinched your bloke. Most women don't take kindly to that, now do they?'

She looked pleadingly at Kate but Bright moved to block her view. 'Look at me, Tess.' His voice went soft. 'Tell me about it.'

'I don't know – I don't know any other way. I never felt I should own anything. Anybody.'

'Even your kids?' His voice went softer still.

'My kids?'

'A-ha. Your kids. He took your kids too, didn't he? Nat. He took everything.'

She stood. 'The children are only on vacation! My parents have them. Until I get my life straight. Then I'll have them again. They write me! Look!' She fished under the grey-green tunic into a pocket in the brown wool dress. 'Here.' Her hands were full of pieces of paper covered with crayon drawings and jumpy lettering. 'Look at these. They write me every week. Look at them!'

Bright rubbed the back of his neck, moved his head to one side and back again. 'Okay, okay. I believe you. Put them away.'

She carefully, tenderly folded each of the drawings one by one and one by one hid them again in the folds of her soft wool garments. In the unbearable silence Kate watched. *What a psychological gesture. What a moment. Wish I'd used it in Medea.* This was what it was like, being an actor. Constant bloody detached observation. This was one of the reasons she was fed up with it.

Bright seemed suddenly to have lost heart. 'Okay. Thanks for the tea. Thanks for your help. We'll be back. In the meantime tell that nice little woman – Claire, did you call her? – to give you a sedative and put you to bed.'

'We don't have drugs here.'

'That so? Tell her to give you a cup of herbal tea, something to knock you out. You staying, Muz Creech? Or coming with us?' He held the door open, not giving her a choice.

She was knackered anyway, needed a hot bath and a drink. She didn't hesitate long. 'I'm staying at the village pub, Tess. I'll see you tomorrow, okay?' They kissed, lips to cheek, this side then that side, like pigeons. The narrow hands pleadingly gripped Kate's arms but she pulled away. 'Tess, I've got to go.'

37

THE SILKEN THREAD

She followed the red Golf GTI down the drive, through the dark tunnels of the lanes, into the disturbing village that looked like a painted canvas backcloth, till it stopped outside the pub, a dignified stone house covered with some kind of creeping plant.

The bar was full of people, many of them elderly men in cloth caps. Kate was surprised, from this smart village she'd have expected a different clientele. A hush fell as she and Bright walked in: of course, out of season it would be odd to see strangers here. They found the reception desk and booked rooms. Kate put out her hand to pick up her key. Bright put his hand on hers. An odd shudder went through her.

He said, 'Don't go to your room yet. Hang on.'

Not propositioning her then, just police instructions. 'I need a bath and a drink,' she said. 'You think I'm going to run away if I'm out of your sight for half an hour? I haven't the energy, I promise you.'

'Half an hour?' he said. Her hand stayed under his, holding her key. 'Okay,' he said. 'See you in half an hour.'

'Where?'

'In your room,' he said.

'What for?'

'Some things you've got to fill me in on.'

Edgley appeared at his shoulder. She should have been a comedian, her timing was so good. He removed his hand. 'Get through?' he said.

'Yes, sir. They're bringing her in for questioning.'

Kate felt the roots of her hair pricking her scalp like spikes. 'Who?' she said. 'Tess?'

'No, Muz Creech, not your great friend Tess. Not yet anyway. Go and have your bath.'

The hot steam surrounded but didn't soothe her. *Who have they brought in for questioning? Female, not Tess. Not Tess yet. He's so sharp he'll cut himself, he has this fast motor inside him, you can feel it rev, see it in the way he bounces on his feet, jangles the change in his pockets, yet he has this air of having all the time in the world. Like an angler sitting on the bank with his rod and line. Waiting.* She felt her hand on her key and his hand on hers. She shut her eyes and saw

172

her bath at home and the thing in it. She opened her eyes. She wasn't cured yet. She turned on the shower and stood under the fierce hot jet till she felt clean. She rubbed her body with towels till she felt flayed. She dried her hair fast on the hottest setting of the drier, burning the bad thoughts out of her head. She'd just got dressed when he knocked at the door.

'I've ordered room service,' he said. He was cradling a bottle of scotch and a glass.

'Room service? Here?'

'Salmon, new potatoes, peas. Bottle of Australian plonk.'

'This is just a pub.'

'A-ha, yeah. But for the police, anything. They're used to touching the forelock round here. It's all owned by some lord, you know, the whole village. He tells them what colour to paint their front doors. He came into the bar while I was down there. They all did this.' He put the glass into his left hand and with the other he tugged a front tuft of his short dark hair.

'Come off it.'

'They did, I'm not kidding. The old guys, yeah! Pulled the peak of their caps. Like this. Feudalism is not dead. Yeah, the food'll be shit but you got to eat. Can I come in?'

'I'd prefer to be in the bar, with people.'

'You'll have to pretend I'm people.'

'I don't think my imagination is up to that.'

'We got to talk.'

'I've told you everything I know.'

He grinned and walked past her into the room. 'That's a corny line.' He picked up her tooth glass from the bedside table, poured whisky into it. 'You haven't told me everything you know by any means.' He held out her glass. She found herself taking it. He poured his own. 'Cheers.' He clinked his glass on hers. She found herself drinking a mouthful.

She said, 'Everything I know about what?'

'Everything you know about these people.'

'What people?'

'What people.' He sighed and drank some scotch. 'She on the level? That Tess.'

'"That Tess".'

'A-ha, that Tess, yeah. She for real?'

'You're the policeman. What do you think?'

He shrugged. 'I don't know. She's American.'

'What's that got to do with it?'

'I don't understand them. Maybe it's just the accent. I can't believe they're not putting it on. They always seem like something off the movies. Get behind their screen you'll find there's nothing there, they were just a mirage, a trick of the light.'

173

She looked at him. The sudden poetic vein threw her. She didn't show it. She took another mouthful of scotch. It tasted so good, heat in the throat. She went to the window. Darker trees against dark sky. Old street lamps made small yellow circles like rings round so many moons.

'Come on, Kate!' His voice as sharp as his eyes sliced into her thoughts. She jumped. 'Come on. Wake up. I'm trying to have a conversation here.'

'I'm sorry, I was, I don't know, drifting off.'

'You're hungry, that's your problem.'

'Oh yes?'

'A-ha. Low blood sugar, you start to space out. You'll be all right when you've eaten.'

'Are you an expert on everything?'

For a moment he looked like a sad dog. 'Not on everything, no.'

A comfortable woman arrived with a tray. He took it from her. 'Thanks, love.' She dimpled for some reason, said shyly, 'I hope everything'll be all right for you,' and went out closing the door softly behind her. They were alone again.

'She seemed overcome with your charm.'

'Wish I had that effect on a few other women.'

'Where's your lady policeman?' she said.

He gave her a look. 'In the bar. Putting herself about a bit. They always know stuff, places like this. They wouldn't tell me but they'll tell her. Feel her up with their eyes and tell her things. Their eyes are bigger than something else as my ma used to say. But she was talking food. Eat.'

The salmon had been heated up but she'd tasted worse. 'Better than I expected,' he said. He poured the wine and tasted it. 'So is this. Cold anyway. Cheers.'

She ate in silence. Thought about Tess, about Nat, about Oliver, Ken and Michael. About Aggie and Ted. About betrayal. About how she wasn't going to talk to Bright.

'You're feeling better,' he said.

'How do you know?'

'You're a different colour.'

'What, a lighter shade of pale?'

He got up. Poured wine into her glass, then into his. Took his to the bed. Lay on his back on the bed. Her bed. She stayed where she was, in the chair, on the other side of the room. Her room.

'So tell,' he said.

'There's nothing to tell.'

'Oh Christ.' He rolled on to his side, drank some wine.

'And even if there were, I wouldn't. Betrayal of friends is not my scene. I can't live with it. It's not something I am prepared to go further with. I've told you this.'

174

'Who's betrayed who, Muz Creech?'

That was the point. That's what she couldn't face. Someone she loved had betrayed her. She stared at him. She got up. She went to the window again. Saw her reflection there. Then her breath clouded the glass so she couldn't see her reflection any more. She turned her back to the window. 'Also I do not want to be questioned in my hotel room without witnesses.'

'So let's go for a walk.'

'If you want me to tell you things about my friends, do it officially.'

'This is off the record. I promise you.'

She laughed.

'You going to turn me down, Muz Creech?'

'Didn't you hear? I just did.'

He got up, picked up the scotch bottle and his glass, went to the door. 'You don't care. That Sally's dead. Or who killed her. Nothing.'

'I can't put the lives of innocent people who are my friends into your hands.'

He looked away. His strange sharp squinting eyes wandered the room. All the tautness in him went loose. He shrugged and opened the door. He said, 'They're in my hands whether you like it or not.'

'Well, I don't like it.'

Suddenly he was back in the room with the door shut. 'For your information neither do I. Neither do I. Matter of fact I like these people. They're not wicked people, they're not villains, not even manipulative amateur crooks like that Vera-Varya. They're not conventional, right? but they're not evil. But one of them killed somebody. Or knows who killed her. Whoever did this thing, somebody knows. You understand me? One of them knows.'

'I don't believe that, you see. That's where we differ.'

'Tell me another scenario.'

'Say Sally was two-timing Nat. Say another man turned up after Nat had walked out on her.'

He spread his arms, bottle in one hand, glass in the other, and pushed his head forward. 'You really think that?' He spoke in a shouting whisper. His hands gripped the bottle and glass like he wished they were hand grenades. 'Stop giving me this bullshit. Use your brain.'

She'd thought he was a cold-blooded animal. She was shocked. 'Look – ' She stopped. To draw breath. To think. She said, 'I cannot believe that Nat or Tess, or anyone else I know, killed Sally. By accident, in anger, or any other way. I cannot believe that. But I do believe that if one of us knew who had killed her we would tell you.'

The little brown eyes stopped their snapping and snarling. They looked at her with a doggish sadness. 'You've just been playing Medea,' he said.

'So?'

'They test us before we become policemen, Muz Creech, see if we can read and write.'

'You're not telling me you've read it.'

'Thought I'd give it the once-over. See what you'd been working on.'

'Oh, I see. You think I was type-cast. If I could play a woman who killed her children I might be a woman who killed her friends.' He grinned. She said, 'You really read it?'

'So you ought to know, Muz Creech, that the nicest people are capable of the nastiest things.'

'But there's not a lot of point locking up a person who did one bad thing by accident and will never do it again.'

He raised his head and gave a muffled howl. 'Why am I always getting into philosophical arguments with you? Listen, I'm not a priest, I'm a policeman. An investigating officer. It's my job. To investigate. People's souls are their own affair.'

'But you want me to tell you about their souls.'

'And yours, Muz Creech. And yours.'

'And mine?'

'Maybe telling the tale would reveal too much about you. Maybe that's the reason you're not telling. Hn?'

'You don't get me with that kind of unsubtle challenge.'

'Aw shucks, it works with everyone else.'

She almost smiled. She shook her head. She sighed. She said, 'Who's this woman you're taking in for questioning?'

'Vera.'

'Vera? Why?'

'I think I can put pressure on her.'

'Well, you can't put pressure on me.' She opened the door.

He raised the bottle and glass in a short sharp salute. He went out.

She'd expected to feel relief. She didn't. She felt deflated. Bereft.

38

TELLING TALES

When the knock came he lurched to his feet. She'd changed her mind? He opened the door. Edgley stood there. Bright looked amazed, at her then at his watch. 'It's gone midnight,' he said.

'I've come to give you my report, sir.'

In disbelief he said, 'Your report?'

'Yes.'

'A-ha.' He nodded three times slowly. 'Well, in that case I guess you'd better come in.'

She stood stiffly just inside the door. He wandered across the room, poured a scotch, held the bottle up. It was almost empty. 'You?' he said.

'No, thank you, sir.'

'Not while on duty,' he said. 'Quite right, constibule. Exemplary. Well, get on with it.'

'The locals say that the Barnabus Community is a weird place.'

'Surprise, surprise. You hung around till midnight to tell me that?'

'They think all the people, sorry not all, some of the people are on drugs.'

'Help me, I'm going to pass out. Why do they think they're on drugs?'

'Because of the way they look, sir.'

'What, they've got long hair and don't wear suits?'

'They say when they see them in the village they seem spaced out.'

'But no shooting up in the men's bog? Leaving syringes scattered round outside ye oldee worldee cottages?'

'No.'

'Just hearsay then, no evidence. Any other hearsay? Satanic rituals surely, they can't have left them out?'

She was about to say yes but changed her mind. 'They think it's a free-love place.'

'Never! Everyone doing it, stoned out of their heads, twenty-four hours a day? Their idea of paradise. A-ha.' He sounded weary. 'As I said, it's after midnight.'

'That Tess,' she said.

'A-ha?' He sounded not quite so weary and for the first time he stood still.

'She's been to London more than once since she's been here. Three times, they say.'

'Do they now?'

'Yes, sir.'

'And how do they know?'

'One time she was seen getting out of a cab at the station. Once someone behind her in the queue heard her say return to Paddington. Once someone on the platform saw her get out of a London train – '

'A-ha, I get the picture. Do they have dates?'

'No exact dates but two visits were before Christmas and the third was probably the one she told us about near the end of January. A man called Donkin – '

'A man called what?'

'Donkin, sir.'

'I thought that's what you said.'

'Yes, sir.' She looked nonplussed. 'He says he thinks the January trip was on a Saturday.'

'She told us it was a Friday.'

'Mr Donkin's not sure but he thinks it was the day he went to visit his mother. She's in a nursing home in Weymouth and he generally visits her on a Saturday.'

'Why?'

'He's too busy the rest of the week, he says.'

'What does he do?'

'He's on the dole.'

He looked at her. Screwed up one of his eyes, the one with the squint. 'A-ha,' he said.

She suddenly made a noise that was almost a laugh, a short one, quickly curtailed.

He nodded. He said, 'That all you've got for me?'

She consulted her notebook. 'That's it,' she said.

'Good work, Edgley.'

'Thank you, sir.'

'You're welcome. Now can I get some sleep?'

She looked at the carpet then put the notebook into her pocket. 'Certainly, sir.'

'See you at breakfast, Edgley. Eight o'clock.'

'Yes, sir.'

She left the room with a straight back. When she closed the door he clicked his heels and gave a military salute. 'You'll go far, love.' He groaned and sat on the bed. He took off his shoes and lay back.

'First time I slept in my clothes for a year or two.'

'Why did you, sir?'

'I guess I was knackered, constable.'

'Oh.' In front of her was a plate of fried eggs, bacon, sausage, tomato, mushrooms. She broke bread over it and went into the attack. The plate began to look like a traffic accident.

He poured a second cup of coffee. He said, 'We're going up the Community again. Nine o'clock.'

She nodded, chewing. She swallowed and wiped her mouth. She said, 'Kate Creech went out at seven, sir.'

'What?'

'Yes.'

'Where to?'

'I don't know, sir. I couldn't follow her as I was to meet you here at eight.'

178

He groaned. 'Was she on foot or what?'

'In her car, sir. It was the noise of the engine that alerted me.'

'Alerted you, nn?'

'Yes, sir. The Volkswagen engine has a distinctive sound.'

'Does it now?'

'My room overlooks the car-park. I looked out of the window as she drove off.'

'Which direction did she drive off in, constable?'

Edgley pointed to the road that led through the village. 'That way, sir.'

'You know she's gone back to see her friend before we do?'

'That seems possible, sir, yes.'

'Ah shit.' He stood up, went to the window, rattled his change, came back to the table, sat. He rubbed his eyes. 'Well, never mind. She'll probably find out more than I could.'

'Would she tell you?'

'She tells me everything, constable.'

'Does she, sir?'

'She does, yes. Why d'you think I give her so much rope?'

'I hoped that was the reason, sir.'

'Oh, you hoped that, did you?'

'Yes, sir.'

'It'll all be in your report, of course.'

'Yes, sir.'

'A-ha.'

'Aren't you going to eat anything, sir?'

'Er. Yes. Give me a slice of that toasted cardboard.'

She pushed the toast rack in his direction. He began to open a small packet of butter, sighing. 'You have any hobbies, Edgley?'

'Yes, sir, I belong to a historical battle society.'

'What's that when it's at home?'

'We do simulated battles. Reconstructions of the real thing.'

'What, the Civil War and that?'

'That sort of thing, yes.'

He'd given up on the butter. 'And what are you, a Roundhead or a Cavalier?'

'Sometimes one, sometimes the other.'

'I see. Don't take sides.'

She looked at him but didn't reply. He said, 'They tell me you've got a degree. From Oxford.'

'Yes.'

'What in?'

'In? Oh. Classics, actually.'

He put on his thick copper look. 'What, Latin and Greek and that?'

'Yes.'

'Lot of use to a copper.'

'That's what everyone says.'

'Get the piss taken much?'

'Yes. Especially in my first posting. In Hackney.'

''Cos of the way you speak or what?'

'Partly that, I think.'

'You didn't try to rough it up a bit, to fit in with your average woodentop, then?'

'I didn't see the point.'

'No. Well, you won't be hanging round in the ranks all that long, will you?'

'I intend to have a decent career, sir, yes. Do you have some objection to that?'

He shrugged. 'I wish you'd said you were a Roundhead, that's all.'

She looked at her watch. 'I'm going up to get my things. I'll be down in five minutes. If that's all right, sir.'

'Or at least a Digger or a Leveller,' he said. 'That would really be the world turned upside down.'

She looked nonplussed for a moment. His look was bland. He watched as she decided the reference to Christopher Hill was a coincidence. Then she went.

39

TILLERS OF THE EARTH

You'd have thought it was the middle of the day, not ten past seven in the morning. Two women were mulching the border. And a boy with long hair was clipping the lavender hedge that ran along under the terrace. He pushed the hair out of his eyes. 'Hi, can I help you?' His voice was wispy, thin, pale, like him.

'I'm looking for Tess Harbour.'

'Oh, you're her friend who came yesterday.'

'Kate, yes.'

'Hi, I'm Ben. I'm the one who fed the goats for her.'

'The goats?'

'When she went to London.'

'In January?'

It took him some time. 'January . . . Oh, yes! That's right. It's her turn on Fridays.'

'Her turn?'

'Yes, we take turns to feed the goats. It has to be done early or they eat everything in sight. Well, they do anyway but, you know . . .'

'What day is your turn?'

'Saturday.'

'So she did it for you on Saturday?'

He looked puzzled for a moment. Pushed his hair behind his ear again. 'I suppose she must have. I don't remember, quite honestly. It's ages ago.'

'And a lot must have happened here since.'

He missed the irony. 'Yeah, sure.'

'*Does* anything happen here?'

'Oh sure, yeah.'

'Like what?'

'Oh. Well. It's more, like, internal, know what I mean?'

'Internal?'

'Yeah. Well, we all have things to, like, deal with. You know? I mean that's kind of why we're here. We're – you know – kind of wounded people, you see.'

'Wounded,' she said.

He shrugged his bony shoulders, looked confused. 'Well, yeah. So we spend a lot of time – dealing with that. That's why we don't have distractions here, you see. So we can deal with those things.'

'Do you have psychiatric help here?'

'No. We help each other.'

The blind leading the blind, she thought. But she didn't say that. Instead she nodded sagely. 'Yes. I see.'

'Tess helps me a lot,' he said shyly.

'Does she?'

'She seems to understand so much.'

'About what?'

'You know. Life?'

'What was – is – your problem, Ben?'

He looked startled by this question, pushed his hair back, breathed in, raised his shoulders, waved a vague hand, the one without the shears. 'Phoo . . .' He breathed out. 'All kinds of heavy stuff. Baggage. Hard to leave behind, you know?'

The front door opened and Ben went guiltily back to his lavender. Claire stood in the doorway. The sun was straight in her eyes. She put her hand up like a visor to see who her visitor was. Kate ran up the steps.

'You're here early.' Claire didn't look at her. She was taking a tin of metal polish and dusters out of her big apron pocket.

181

'Yes. Do you know if Tess is awake yet?'

Claire started to rub vigorously at the lion's head handle. 'Someone else is doing her work this morning. She seemed quite shaken by your visit yesterday.'

'Not me so much as the police, I think.'

Claire put her head on one side like a robin and looked up at her. 'You were with the police, surely.'

'No. That's how it looked, I know that. But it's – He keeps me in his sights, the inspector. That's why I came early today, in the hope that I might get ahead of him. I didn't get a proper chance to talk to Tess on her own yesterday. I've got to explain to her and apologise for bringing them on my heels.'

'You're going to wake her up just to clear your conscience?'

Kate grinned. 'No. I want to talk to her. She's my friend. It's so long since I've seen her. Of course, if she's – '

Claire put the polish on the step and the dusters back into her pocket. 'Come along.' She trotted in front of Kate, not into the house but down the curving stone steps. Sloping shoulders, round bottom, short sturdy legs. She ignored Ben and he ignored Kate, dealing with his internal problems, she assumed. Claire at her brisk pace led the way along the house to wide wooden gates in a high wall. She pushed a gate open. It creaked and she made an exasperated noise. 'Someone should oil this, it would waken the dead.'

A broad cobbled courtyard with a long stable building on the left. Claire trotted to the second stable door where she stopped and turned to Kate with a finger to her lips. Kate followed her inside on tiptoe.

In the gloom after the bright sun outside she could see the two rows of original stable stalls on either side of a wide cobbled alleyway. Posters or paintings were pinned to some of the doors. Claire still on tiptoe stopped at the fourth stall down on the right. She gave a neat quiet little knock. Kate heard a groan from within. Claire pushed the stall door. 'Tess, dear?'

'Mmm?'

Kate made out a narrow low bed along one side. A cheap supermarket metal lamp stood on a wooden box. A few clothes hung from the original tackle hooks. A thin rush mat covered the cobbles next to the bed. Tess, thin, pale, in a white Victorian chemise, sat up, her hair wildly splayed out against the whitewashed wall behind her.

'Oh Claire, I'm so sorry, am I late for – ?'

'No, Tess. No work this morning, remember, dear? Simon is coming to see you at eight.'

'Eight?'

'Yes.'

182

'Simon?' She clutched the duvet to her chest.

'Yes, but in the meantime here is your friend Kate to see how you are.'

'Oh, Kate!' Tess held out thin arms in the long white sleeves.

Claire trotted off clip clop down the cobbled avenue, outlined in a halo of light in the doorway, then gone.

'Kate!'

Kate sat on the bed. 'I hoped we'd have longer yesterday before Bright caught up with me. I didn't have time even to warn you. I'm sorry.'

'I'm so afraid, Kate.'

'Of what?'

'Nat?'

'Of Nat or for Nat?'

'Oh . . .'

'Look, I think Bright is – unusual. He looks just like you imagine a bent copper, just out for a conviction, you know? But actually oddly enough he seems interested in the truth. If Nat's – clear – he'll find out. I think.' She wondered when she'd changed her mind, and why.

'Oh.' Tess's voice was a breath. Her eyes stared past Kate. 'But who could have done it except Nat?'

'Yes, I know it looks terrible.'

Tess still stared at something only she could see. There was nothing more to say on the subject. To lighten things up Kate said, 'I was just talking to Ben.'

'Ben?' Tess's head came round, so fast Kate heard her neck crack.

'Yes, Ben. The one who milked the goats for you.'

'Fed them.' Tess rubbed her neck.

'Fed them, yes.'

'Oh?' Tess waited for more with an intensity Kate couldn't understand.

'He's nice. Seems nice. He says you're all dealing with internal problems here. Don't notice much else that goes on in the world.'

'Oh.' Tess's eyes cleared. She gave her wide old smile. 'Oh yes, I guess that's true.' The smile went. 'I guess your policeman will question everyone about me.'

'Not my policeman.' She felt a liar as she said this and wasn't sure why.

'Don't worry, Kate. It doesn't matter. I don't mind.' Tess suddenly got to her knees then to her feet. Standing on the bed she reached over and grabbed a hanger with some jeans and a sweater on it. She pulled off the linen shift. Her body was skeletal, hip bones like jug handles, the breasts empty little purses. But Kate thought she saw something in the dim light that scared her more than the thinness. She went to the swing gate that served as a door to the stall, her back to Tess to hide her face. She said, 'This is where you all sleep? I imagined you in elegant rooms in the house.'

183

'No. Only the permanent people live in the house. Claire. Sharma. Eleanor. Simon of course. The rooms are mainly used for activities. Yoga. Meditation. Massage. T'ai Chi.'

When Kate turned round Tess was pulling on a pair of boots. 'Not much privacy in here is there?'

'No.'

'A sort of glorified dormitory.'

'If it's privacy you want you don't come and live in a community.'

'I suppose not.'

Tess stood up in jeans and a big grey-green sweater. She pulled her hair back and fixed it with a rubber band. She reached for a jacket. 'Let's go for a walk.'

'But you're supposed to see Simon,' Kate said.

'I don't want to see Simon.'

'Why?'

'Kate, come on. If we don't go now the day will begin. Simon, then your policeman again, then lunch, then – I haven't seen you in so long. Let's just go.'

'You'll have to face all these things later.'

'Yes, but that's later; this is now.'

She loped with the long strides Kate remembered down the cobbled aisle to the sunlight, through the door at the rear of the courtyard, into a huge walled vegetable garden: rows of spinach, cauliflower, broccoli, in beds edged with low tight hedges of parsley; greenhouses down the left-hand side. People were already at work in the greenhouses. Kate could see them clouded by the steamy glass.

'Tess, this is idyllic.'

'It's hard work.'

'It reminds me of Laura's garden.'

Tess stopped abruptly and turned. 'What did she say about me?'

'Well, she's worried. Wants to know where you are.'

'You know why I had to get away?'

'I gathered – '

'It was like Vera all over again. Taking me over.'

'Yes. She said Sally came to see you just before – '

'She saw Sally?'

'I assumed she did.'

'I asked Sally to help me get away from her, I couldn't have done it alone.'

'I think you should get in touch with Laura. Just to tell her you're okay. She thought as I did, that it was you dead in my – ' Kate stopped.

Tess looked at the ground. 'I don't want to get involved again.'

'You could just give her a ring.'

Tess gazed into the distance. 'Yes. I guess I should.' She looked at Kate. 'Okay. I'll call her.' She strode down a brick path dividing the beds to the end wall where fruit trees were espaliered against the sunny bricks.

Two boys forked crumbly black compost out of a huge heap into a wheelbarrow. A short square person with curly red hair pushed the barrow to a fallow bed where she tipped out the muck, and an athletic-looking girl with a shaved head and several nose rings forked it into the ground.

No one took any notice of Tess and Kate. They might have been invisible. A small green door in the far wall took them into a field fenced with elegant iron rails. Tess set off across the field. She negotiated a stile with ease and waited for Kate to catch up. The grass was wet.

A footpath took them across the next field where they climbed another stile into a lane. A row of five goats gazed at them over the hedge with their curious yellow eyes. Tess slowed down now they were in the lane, out of sight of the house. She stroked the nose of a goat.

Kate said, 'Are these the goats Ben fed for you?'

Tess stared. 'What do you mean?'

'Well, nothing, just, are these the actual goats? That's all. What do you mean, what do I mean?'

Tess gave a breathy laugh. 'Oh, I don't know, I'm so worried about everything. I feel so bad about giving Sally your keys. I guess I keep expecting you to be angry with me or – suspect me of something.'

'Suspect? You? Tess! No!'

Tess looked at her. Doubt. Then a sad nod. 'Yes, they're the goats. I love them.' The long eyes filled with tears. 'I love this place. I need it. I don't ever want to leave.'

'Don't you want the girls to live with you?'

'But they could live here too. It's a great place for young people. So innocent. So good.'

'How old's Zoë now?'

'She's twelve.'

'Teenagers tend to want something different from innocence and goodness.'

'Don't *say* that!'

Kate was startled by her fierceness. 'Okay, okay.'

'Sorry, Kate. Only I want them here with me so much. And yet I don't feel I'm a fit mother just yet.'

Kate didn't stop to think. She said, 'You will be when you're cured.'

'Cured?' Tess stopped and turned to her.

Kate swallowed. Took courage. 'I saw the marks on your arms.'

'Oh.' Tess gave a laugh on an intake of breath. 'That's my diabetes. I'll never be cured of that.'

'Diabetes?'

185

'Sure.'

'I never knew you had diabetes.'

'No? Oh, that's right. It was diagnosed when I was in the commune in Wales. I was so ill then. And this great doctor discovered why.'

'Oh.'

'Kate, you thought I'd – '

'Well, it's what one thinks these days, and – '

'Oh, thank God no. I'd never get my girls back if anyone thought – '

'No.'

Tess walked on. Kate caught her up. 'I'm sorry, Tess.'

'It's okay. Natural to think that, I guess, with my past.'

'We seem to do nothing but apologise to each other.'

'Do you forgive me for lending your keys?'

'I forgive you. Do you forgive me for thinking you were . . .'

'A junkie? Never.' She spoke lightly and smiled her widest smile.

Kate saw behind her head high on a hill a small chapel. 'What's that?'

'They call it St Barnabus. The community is named after it.'

'It's very small.'

'Barnabus was a hermit. He worshipped there alone.'

'I see.'

'He lived there too. In a hut. But that's not there any more.' She turned to Kate and said lightly, 'Shall we walk up to it?'

Kate shivered. 'I don't like the look of it somehow.'

'Why?'

'I don't know. It gives me a bad feeling.'

'What kind of bad feeling?'

'I don't know. Evil.'

'The locals think that. None of them will go there.'

'I know it sounds stupid.'

'Well, some local satanists were said to be using it at one time, I guess that's why. We did find some odd stuff there once or twice. But we cleaned it up and blessed it with our prayers. It's not evil, it's beautiful.'

'Who's we?'

'Oh, Ben. And the girls in the garden: Ginger and Sam. Come on, come up there with me. You'll like it, Kate, you will.'

Kate hesitated. A powerful feeling warned her off the place. But she was rational, wasn't she? She didn't believe in such things, did she? Could evil events change the spirit of a building? *Does a building have a spirit? Is my house changed for ever? It is, for me.*

'What is it?' Tess's voice was gentle.

'I don't know. Wondering if I can ever live in my house again.'

'Oh no? You think you can't?' She spoke with an eager sympathy.

'I think I can't.'

'Oh no.' Tess's arms enfolded her, but Kate remained stiff in the embrace. She wasn't sure why. Was behaving oddly altogether and didn't know why.

Tess let her go. 'You haven't forgiven me, have you?'

'Tess – '

A white VW camper came round the bend of the lane. Tess gasped and turned her head. The camper braked. Tess hesitated then slid open the side door and climbed into the back. Kate followed.

'Kate, this is Simon.'

'Hello.' He didn't turn to look at her. She saw only the back of a shaggy head and in the mirror two green eyes. He backed down the lane to a place where another lane crossed it, then turned into a narrow alley between evergreen oaks. Tess sat on her hands staring ahead, angry or scared, Kate couldn't tell which. Simon had said nothing.

'Beautiful trees.' Kate's words dropped into the silence.

Simon said, 'It's a beautiful place.'

'Your home, I believe.'

'Yes, put to some use at last. My pa used to come down here to shoot things. I used to think of these acres as the killing fields. Now we nurture here, and protect.' He had the kind of accent that made Kate feel working class.

'I see,' she said.

He stopped the van on the gravel in front of the house. Ben had finished his work; the lavender looked barbered. Simon got out and opened Kate's door. His eyes were small, his nose round, his mouth disguised by a free-form beard. His body was tall, thin, hard. She felt a dislike for him that almost overwhelmed her.

Tess hadn't moved. He said, 'See you in my office, Tess. When you've said goodbye to Kate, of course.' He walked off towards the house. He wore a many-coloured thick sweater, old very expensive corduroy trousers, and green wellies. Tess didn't get out of the van. He stopped and turned. 'Tess?'

She said, 'Oh yes,' and climbed out. She stood near Kate, not looking at her. Not speaking.

'Well, Tess, you'd better say goodbye to me as he told you to.'

'Told me?'

'Oh, come off it, Tess, that was an order: get your friend off the premises.'

Tess looked at her toe scraping the gravel. 'I wish I didn't have to see him just now.'

'Come away with me.'

'Oh no! I can't do that.'

'Tess, I'll stay on tonight. Come and see me at the village pub later. If you like. If you can. If he lets you out.'

'Sure. I'll try. I'm meant to be leading yoga this evening but maybe Ben will – Ben will do it for me.'

'Okay. Give me a ring.'

Driving off, the house in her wing mirror receding in miniature, she felt she'd had a narrow escape. From what, she was at a loss to know.

40

SIMON SAYS

Four huge windows floor to ceiling looked out over the garden full of vegetables and young people working. 'Slave labour,' he said. 'Nothing like getting the serfs to believe they're doing it for God.' He bounced on the balls of his feet, jangled the change in one pocket, keys in the other. 'You could get the whole of my ma's house into this room. With space to spare.' He paced to the next window. 'I suppose you fit in fine with this kind of aristocratic bullshit.'

Edgley looked perplexed. 'Me, sir?'

'Oh, these types as far above you as you are above the rest of us, that it?' He looked at his watch again. 'Where *is* this toffee-nosed git?'

The door opened. 'Tess is on her way. Just saying goodbye to Kate Creech.' Simon Langdon loped to his big desk in thick hand-knitted socks and Birkenstock sandals. They always had everything of the best, these types, Bright thought. Even when they'd renounced the world, the flesh and the devil they still shopped in Burlington Arcade.

'So sorry to keep you waiting.' The languid tone. Even apologising they were doing you a favour. Bright didn't reply, went on looking out of the window.

Two oddly matched girls, a short square redhead and a tall bald one, had put down their implements and were standing entwined in the fresh dug furrows. The little redhead leaned her head on Baldy's shoulder. He became aware of Edgley standing near to him. She watched the girls too, something wistful in her expression. 'They look happy,' he said.

She jumped. 'Oh!' and blushed. 'Yes, sir. They do.'

'That's the idea.' The patrician voice from the desk. 'The reason people come here. Most people can achieve happiness. It's a technique. One can learn it.'

'Oh, can one? That right?' Bright was still looking at Edgley.

'Certainly. It can be taught.'

'And who does the teaching? You?'

188

'We teach each other here. Discover our capacity to give happiness to others.'

'You a vicar or what?'

'This is not a question of religion, but of enlightened self-interest.'

'You're not a parson, then.'

'You belittle things you can't understand.'

'Yeah, well, I'm just a simple copper, you know.'

'One of our ways of achieving happiness is to keep you people out.'

'The police? Most people would agree with you.'

'Not the police. Or not necessarily the police. The philistines.'

'A-ha. Oh, right, yeah.' Bright scratched his nose, he was starting to enjoy himself. Edgley was still watching the two girls who now held each other round the waist and were swaying together down the brick path towards the door in the garden wall. He suddenly didn't want them to disappear through that little green door. He said, 'Go and talk to them.' She turned to him, surprised. 'Go on. Quick.'

'Yes, sir.' She shot out without reference to his lordship.

'Where has your assistant gone?'

'Just out for a breath of air.'

'I have made it clear, I hope, that you are not to have the run of the house simply because you insist on questioning one of my – one of our members.'

A touch like a dry twig stroked the door.

'Come!' Langdon called.

Bright grinned. 'I thought people only said that in the movies.'

Tess came in reluctantly and stood with her back to the door. She looked transparent, like a lacewing hovering.

'Sit down,' Bright said.

'Please don't give orders in this house.'

'Give it a heave, mate. The girl looks like the walking dead.'

Simon said, 'Sit down, Tess.'

'Oh, I see,' Bright said. 'It's not orders you object to; just who gives them.'

Langdon ignored this. 'There.' His manner was solicitous.

Tess seated herself as though contact with the chair might hurt her bones and Bright remembered with surprise the struggle Edgley had had to subdue her yesterday. He watched Edgley now hurry down the path and the odd girls turn as she called them. He wanted to go on watching them. He'd have liked to be down there with them.

'Okay, Tess?' Simon leaned over her. She nodded without looking at him. He went back behind his desk.

Bright approached. He cleared a space on the corner of the desk and rested his backside on it. The desk was big enough for a family to live in, but the lord of the manor recoiled, considered a reproof, thought better of

189

it, sat straight with folded arms. Tess's fear was palpable. Fear of what, Bright couldn't tell. 'You went for a walk with Kate?' he said.

'Yes.'

''Cos I was coming?'

'I didn't know what time you would come.'

'Doesn't answer my question.'

'Oh. Yes. I guess it was, partly.'

'What was the other part?'

She smiled briefly. 'Simon.'

Langdon sat up.

'You were scared to bump into Mr Langdon?'

'A bit.'

'Tess!' The very beard seemed to quiver with surprised distress.

'Yes, Simon, because I've been so stupid and so bad.'

'Tess, there is no badness in human beings, only thwarted goodness – '

She turned to Bright, the long blue eyes full of water. 'I can't stand to go over what I did. Lending the keys, putting Nat in this mess. I was trying to help Sally. And him. But – ' She pulled a crushed Kleenex out of a sleeve and blew her nose.

'That's okay, Tess. I don't want to go over that again.'

'Oh?' Her face came up slowly, wondering.

'No. No, there's just a bit of a confusion I need to straighten out. Nothing much, I'm sure you'll be able to clear it up without any trouble.' Bright spoke in his softest nasal croon. 'You told me that, until that day in January, you hadn't been up to London since you first came to live here last November, that right?'

Langdon didn't move and neither did she. The stillness was of the kind Bright knew well. It meant he'd touched a nerve.

Langdon put out his hand to a smart fountain pen on the desk. He rolled it under his saintly fingers. 'What can that possibly matter?' he said.

'Well, it might not matter at all. On the other hand why lie about it?'

'Lie? I see no justification for an accusation of that sort.'

'I was talking to Tess, mate. Eh, Tess?'

Her face was still lifted to him like one of those pale daffodils growing at the foot of the wall out there. She came to a decision, seemed to be using Bright for protection. 'I didn't tell you, Simon. I went up two other times. Once in November and once before Christmas.'

'Now, that's just what I heard,' Bright said.

She didn't ask where he'd heard. She said, 'I didn't tell you because I hadn't told Simon.'

'And why didn't you tell – Simon?'

'Because I went to see Varya.'

190

'A-ha.'

Langdon stopped fiddling with the pen. He sat very still. Bright's tone was still soft. 'And why wouldn't you want him to know you'd seen Varya?'

'Because I didn't get any money from her either of those two times. I didn't want Simon to know that I'd failed.'

'And why did you need to get money out of Vera?'

Tess looked discomfited. 'I need to pay something for my keep here.'

Langdon sat back and folded his arms. He turned his head in the direction of the windows.

'How much?' Bright said.

'We each pay according to our means.'

'A-ha. And you haven't paid a sausage since November. And his lordship here was getting impatient.'

'All of us here see money as an evil necessity.' Langdon sounded a little rattled. 'Apart from that we have no interest in it.'

'Simon has to keep the building in good repair. We can't always barter or do the work ourselves.'

'So you lied to me because you were frightened of him?' Bright spoke softly. 'Or because you'd been to see Varya and didn't want me to know?'

'Don't put words into her mouth.'

But Tess answered. 'Because of Simon.'

'And why would you be frightened of his lordship? I thought he was a holy saint, wouldn't harm a greenfly.'

'But that's it! He's so good he thinks it's easy for others to be good. To be perfect. You do, Simon.' She wiped her nose again with the small soaked ball of tissue. 'You do.'

Langdon rolled his head down to one shoulder and up again. He gave a heavy sigh, modest, self-deprecating. He spoke in a muffled voice. 'Perhaps we do make heavy demands here.'

'A-ha.' Bright's expression of enjoyment deepened. He took in a deep breath, held it a second, blew it out. 'Okay.' He stretched out his legs, crossed his feet. 'Now, Tess, I just have one other little problem p'raps you can help me with. You went up to London for a day, late in January. The twenty-seventh probably. Anyway, a Friday. That's what you told me, right?'

'Yes.'

'A-ha, I thought so. It's just that this bloke who saw you at Weymouth station thinks it was the Saturday. The twenty-eighth. I've talked to him this morning and he's pretty adamant. Now, it's easy to get these things mixed up and it's a good while ago, he might have it arse over tip. But I'm sure you can clarify that. Can't you, Tess?'

She said in a stronger voice, 'It was Friday. It was my day to feed the goats, Simon. That's Friday, isn't it? I got Ben to do it for me. He'll tell you.'

'Ben?' Bright looked to Langdon.

'I'll take you to him later,' Langdon said.

'That's very big of you. But everyone here would know what day you went, wouldn't they?'

Tess looked at Langdon.

'Not necessarily,' Langdon drawled.

'How come?'

'We try to keep our awareness of time to the minimum. We don't wear watches, we don't have clocks. We rise with the sun, we fit our rhythms to the rhythm of the earth. All time is gathered in the present. As it is for a child. For a child there is no yesterday, no tomorrow. We try to become as little children here.'

'Great. You're telling me no one here knows what day it is.'

'That would be quite possible I hope.'

'In that case we'll have to question everyone here just in case somebody who hasn't quite achieved this state of nirvana might have just carelessly noticed whether she went to London on the Friday or the Saturday, won't we, Tess? Or' – his voice became a seductive murmur – 'even went on the Friday and stayed over till the Saturday.'

She shook her head slowly. 'But they wouldn't know. Because Saturday is my day away.'

'Your what?'

'Each person here has a day away each week. A day without duties.'

'I see. Friday's your goat day, Saturday's your away-day but no one knows what day it is. How do you manage this double-think?'

'We each know what our duties are.' Langdon was patient. 'That's how we define – deduce, if you like – the days.'

'Okay, on goat day – Friday to the rest of us – you get Ben to do your duties and you go to London. But on Saturday, your away-day, you're also not here, that's what you're telling me, right? But you're not in London either. So where are you?'

'Am I allowed to say, Simon?'

Langdon gazed over towards the windows. They waited. He gave a slight shrug, then a sigh and a resigned nod.

'Well, that Saturday I was meant to go into Weymouth and meet Simon.'

'A-ha?' He looked at Langdon's profile. 'What for? A spot of nookey out of sight of the other inmates?'

That brought him up, vibrating. 'I find your tone and your choice of words objectionable.'

'Oh, I'm sorry about that, sir. Which words in particular? Inmates, maybe?'

'And your prurient suggestion. Tess and I had matters to discuss and since it was her "day away" it seemed a good idea for me to have an "evening off" and join her for a meal in Weymouth.' He was talking too much.

'Oh, you do eat then, like the rest of us. What did you eat? Where?'

'As it happens Tess was late for our appointment. We didn't eat in a restaurant, we had fish and chips in the van.'

'In the van, ha? Why were you late meeting his lordship, Tess?'

'I was walking on the beach. I forgot the time.'

'Walking on the beach?'

'Yes.'

'In the dark? On the twenty-eighth of January? In the freezing cold?'

'Yes.' And then she suddenly gave a great breath out. 'Oh, Simon, for heaven's sake!'

Langdon stood up, head bent as though in close study of the papers on the desk. He rolled the pen this way, that way, to him, away from him. Bright waited. No point rushing things. Langdon muttered something he couldn't catch.

'Say again?' Bright said.

He raised his head, looked straight ahead. 'If you must know, Tess was visiting my brother.'

'Where?'

'The prison.'

'What, Portland Bill?'

'He refuses to see me. Tess kindly goes in my place.'

'What's he in for?'

'A drugs offence.'

41

THE GARDEN GIRLS

They swung round, each with an arm round the other's waist, and looked her over in a friendly, curious way. The little ginger one said, 'Hi.'

'Great garden you've got here.'

They didn't reply.

'Must be nice living in the country like this.'

They turned their heads to each other and smiled, then looked back at her. Waited.

'Especially if you've had a rough life,' she tried, looking at the girl with the shaved head. She felt her stiffen, defiance and fear in her eyes.

The little redhead said, 'It's nice even if you haven't had a rough life.' Posh voice, private school. Stockbroker-belt; not top drawer. 'I'm Ginger. This is Sam.'

'You the police lady?' Sam's accent was broad cockney. John Bright would probably be able to identify the borough. Her voice was deep and coarse. 'Bit posh for a copper, ain't you?'

'Well.' Edgley looked embarrassed. 'I'm new.'

'Could have fooled me,' Sam mocked.

'I've been sent out to kick my heels in the garden till my boss has finished.'

Sam smiled, scepticism in her eyes. 'Oh yeah?'

'What's it all about?' Ginger had a round freckled face like a child. She didn't look a day over seventeen.

'I don't know. I'm just a trainee. They don't tell me anything.'

'You're not CID?'

'No. I just asked for the assignment. Trying to get experience.'

Sam looked her over, more relaxed. 'Trying to get promotion more like.'

'That too, I hope.'

Ginger said, 'Has Simon done something, or what?'

'Not as far as I know.'

'Tess, then.'

Bright had issued no instructions. Was she to question them or just keep them talking? How much was she to tell them? What would he do? She said, 'A body was found in a house in London. You may have read about it.'

They looked at each other. 'A body?' Ginger put a small dirty hand to her chest.

'Tess may know something about the case, that's all.'

'Why should she?'

'The house belongs to a friend of hers.'

'Woman who was here this morning?'

'We thought she was her sister, didn't we, Sam?'

'Yeah, she looks like her.'

'Is Tess a suspect then?'

'Oh no, I don't think so.'

'He in charge, the little bloke in the leather jacket?'

'Detective Inspector Bright, yes.'

'And he's come down himself? Must be a big deal.'

'Well . . .' She was floundering, being side-tracked. 'He's rather hands on, for a DI.'

'Oh yeah?'

'Have you lived here long? In this lovely place.'

Sam said, 'Who wants to know?'

'Oh, I'm sorry, no, I was just curious, I didn't mean – '

Sam said, 'I've been here two years. So has Ginger. Haven't you, Ginge?'

'Yes. We met at the Glastonbury festival. We were searching. You know? Amazing grace? Was lost but now am found, was blind but now I see?'

'That's where you heard about this place?'

Ginger nodded. 'I think so, yah. People were just, you know, talking about it. It was kind of in the air.'

'I see.'

'I doubt if you do, mate.' Sam's eyes gave her a sceptical smile, from under the lids.

'No, you're probably right. I've been too busy studying then working ever to go anywhere like the Glastonbury festival.'

'Aaah,' they said in mock sympathy. She laughed and so did Ginger. Sam did not.

Edgley said, 'Did you do gardening before?'

'Why?' Sam looked threatened, threatening.

'Oh. No. Only the garden looks so good, that's all I meant.'

'Yeah. I bet.'

'Sam.' Ginger looked up at her friend.

Sam glared, stopped glaring, gave a growl. 'Okay. Look. So I've done time, right? I was a garden girl at Ascham Grange. So what? I was a naughty girl and I paid for it, all right? So what's it to you?'

'It's none of my business, you're quite right. I wasn't trying to – '

'Oh no.'

'Sam.' Ginger sounded like she was rebuking a naughty kitten.

Sam's hard tight face loosened. 'Okay, so I was in for GBH. This bloke was beating up on my friend, right? So what am I supposed to do, just stand there watching? He's trying to rape her, right? He has a blade. I got it off of him and cut him up a bit. So I went a bit far. But I was mad, right? I wasn't going to stand for it. So I done my time and I don't regret it, okay? He recovered. He ain't dead. He ain't even crippled. He just ain't quite such a pretty boy no more.' She laughed.

'Didn't he come after you or threaten to? After your release?'

'He'd have a job to find me here, right? Unless you lot was to tell him, that is.'

'Never. It sounds as though justice was done.'

'Oooh!' Sam made mocking round eyes but, with a curious innocence, seemed pleased with this statement of solidarity.

'She'll never get in trouble again,' Ginger said. 'I'll make sure of that.'

'She's my minder. Ain't you, Ginge?' Sam put a strong arm round the

195

little redhead's shoulder, towering over her. 'I'm safe with her. What d'you reckon?'

Edgley smiled. How friendly were you supposed to get? These might be witnesses for the prosecution, they might even be suspects. She suddenly said, 'Listen, do you like Tess? Is she a good person, do you think?' She was sure the question was out of order, and silly too.

But they spoke together. 'Yeah!'

'She's really sad, you know? She wouldn't hurt a fly. Would she, Sam?'

Sam smiled her teasing smile at Edgley. 'No.'

'She just desperately wants her kids back,' Ginger said. 'That's all she thinks about.'

42

COHORTS AND BROTHERS

'And what sort of drugs offence would that be?'

'He had been using my boat at night. Picking up packages offshore. Cocaine, amongst other substances. He received a light sentence under the circumstances. Eighteen months. It was a first offence. Foolish. He is young, my junior by thirteen years.'

Bright sat letting the silence breathe a little. He looked at Tess. 'What time's visiting on Saturdays?'

'It finishes at five.'

'And what time did you get there?'

'Five minutes to.'

'Bit late.' Silence. 'No trouble about letting you in?'

Langdon gave the question a lordly dismissal. 'One of the officers is a friend.'

'Oh, is he, now?'

'He and I do a lot of work with young offenders. He appreciates the exigencies of our life here.'

'The exigencies? Does he now? And why were you so late, Tess?'

'I lost track of time.'

He sighed. 'Come on, love, we've had that one.'

The long eyes looked darkly at him, then at the desk, then at Langdon who did not look at her. She came to a decision. Took a breath. Her words came in a rush. 'All right. I hate going there. I hate the prison. I go for Simon's sake but I really loathe it. I hate seeing those men locked up in there. I hate the doors, the electronic locks, the keys, the searches, the noises. I hate the atmosphere. I can't bear it, Simon.' She lifted her face to Bright. 'You know, at Christmas some of them, especially the young ones, are so desperate to see their families, their mothers, that they jump into the sea? The sea is dangerous there. Some die.'

'So you spent Saturday wandering round Weymouth putting off going to Portland Bill to see his lordship's drug smuggler brother. Not in London like our witness thinks. And that's why you were nearly too late for your charitable prison visiting.'

'That's right, inspector.' She didn't notice his irony.

Langdon did and began to object. Bright interrupted his objection. 'And there won't be anyone who saw you wandering round Weymouth, will there?' She shook her head. 'I bet you didn't even have your lunch in a caff.'

'I don't eat in the middle of the day.'

He eyed her bony wrists. 'There's a surprise.'

'We live a frugal life here.' Langdon again. Bright ignored him. Pompous prick. He said to Tess, 'So that's two drug dealers you know.'

A moment of dense stillness. He was on the nail. He let the silence creep about a little. Let it ooze. Let it fill the space.

At last Langdon said, 'You had better clarify your insinuation. What precisely are you trying to say?'

'What do you think I'm saying, Tess?'

'Don't answer, Tess. Say nothing. This is intimidation. He's trying to frighten you.'

Bright's head came round swift as a striking snake. 'This is a murder investigation, mate. A woman has been killed.'

'That is no reason for intimidation of witnesses. Either behave in a civilised manner or leave.'

'Are you intimidated, Tess?'

'It's all right, Simon. Inspector, are you saying that Varya is a drug dealer?'

The very room seemed to let out its breath, though nobody had moved.

'Oh, Vera. That's who you think I mean. Now why would you think I meant her?'

'Oh, because she helps people who are addicts.' Tess spoke simply. 'But she's not a dealer, inspector. I lived with her, I'd have known.'

'A-ha. I see.' He let a silence hang. 'You see, Tess, if you stayed over in London till the Saturday. To see Vera for instance. See if you could get some money out of her this time. That would make sense, wouldn't it? Only where would you stay, you see? Sally's new flat?'

'I left Sally's flat before Nat came there. I told you. I didn't want to see him. I couldn't go back.'

'How about Kate's house? You had the keys.'

197

'No. Sally had them.'

'Oh yes. How could I forget? So Vera seems to be the only other possibility. How did you know where to find her, by the way?'

'I knew from before where her mother lived.'

'So there was no way Vera could hide from you. Was there? You had a bit of a hold over her, didn't you? That's a lot of money she owes you. Thirty thousand quid.'

'How can you know what this woman owes Tess?'

'Oh, didn't I mention it? We have Vera in for questioning.'

Langdon stood. Seemed about to speak. Didn't. Strode over to one of the windows.

'Varya?' A tremor shook Tess's face as a breeze shakes the surface of water.

'Your damned assistant is interrogating my people!' The patrician voice cracked like a whip. He flung the door back and strode out, shouting, 'Claire? Claire!'

Bright and Tess sat and looked at each other. His squint was intense so she hardly knew whether he looked at her or through her. He said, 'You did stay in London till Saturday. This bloke is ready to swear he saw you getting off the London train at Weymouth station on Saturday afternoon. That would explain, you see, Tess, why you were so late getting to the prison. Wouldn't it?'

'I may have wandered about in the station, inspector, I just don't recall. But I did not get off a train.'

'Yeah.' He sighed. 'So to recap: you wandered all over Weymouth including the deserted beach till near 5 p.m. on a freezing cold day with no witnesses who saw you except this bloke who saw you at the station. This is what you're telling me?'

'Yes, that's right. I'm sorry.'

'And you're sorry.'

'Yes.'

'What for, Tess? What are you sorry for?'

She looked at him a moment. There was a hiatus.

'All the trouble I've caused,' she eventually said.

'Your cohort is waiting.' His lordship was back. 'I've had her escorted to your vehicle. I'd like you to join her there.'

'My cohort. A-ha. Right. I've finished here. For the moment. I'll be seeing you, Tess.' He let that prospect hang in the air while he strolled to the door. At the door he stopped a moment. 'Cohorts,' he said.

'I'm sorry, what?' Lordly exasperation.

'Cohorts. That's what you ought to call them.'

'What are you talking about?'

'Your people here. You didn't think much of inmates. Patients isn't great.

Guests? Not quite right, is it? But cohorts now. Cohorts and brothers in exile. Did that at school. *Twelfth Night,* isn't it? No, the other one, Forest of Eden, Garden of Arden. Forest of Arden, that's it. The banished duke. You are a duke, aren't you, mate?' Something in Langdon's expression made him decide not to wait for a reply. He went.

43

EDGLEY GETS EXPERIENCE

Claire was cold, hugging her little brown cardie to her, but she refused to move inside off the steps. She appeared to be guarding Edgley, a yorkie guarding a labrador, ensuring that she didn't question anyone else.

With the air of filling in time Edgley said, 'What do you do here?'

'Oh, we all work very hard – '

'I meant what do *you* do? You personally. You seem to have a lot of responsibilities.'

'Oh, me?' She blushed. 'Oh, I just – do what I can to help, you know.'

'You seem to run the place single handed.'

'Oh no. Mr Langdon does that. I just – '

'Mr? I thought he was an Hon. Or a Right Hon.'

'Oh no.' Claire lifted a serious face to her. 'His father was a younger son. Mr Simon was not in the direct line. But if he had inherited the title he would have refused it. He says we are all equal before God.'

'That's very unusual in one of his class.'

'Yes. But Mr Simon, Simon, is an uncommon person. He always was.'

'You've known him a long time, then?'

'All his life.' She raised her chin. 'I was his nanny. I was young to get such an appointment, but I think I must have proved satisfactory because I stayed until he was quite grown up. He wouldn't allow me to leave. He told his father, if you let Nanny Claire go I shall never come home again. I left in the end because there was nothing further for me to do here and I like to be busy. I like to be of use.'

'I can see that.'

'Yes, when Simon returned here he told me his plans and I left my employment, a very good family in the Cotswolds, to come here. I was the first person to come and I shall have to be carried out feet first. I shall never leave. We are all so happy here. And he brings such happiness to others.'

'Yes, one can feel the atmosphere, so peaceful.'

'And such joy.' Claire glowed.

'Yes.' Emphatic, lying shamelessly.

'As for what I do, well, where shall I begin? I'm absolutely on the practical side. I should be no good at yoga and that sort of thing. Meals, you know. Cleaning rotas. Allotting tasks.' She gave a naughty smile. 'I'm afraid even the best intentioned of young people do forget their allotted tasks if not reminded.'

'So you do a lot of reminding.'

'Well . . .' She pursed her lips again in a little smile. 'Let us say a little.' They both laughed.

'You're probably the only person here who ever knows what day it is.'

'Oh, I don't.' She was serious. 'No. We try not to know the day nor the hour as Simon says. No, I only know the day by its appointed tasks.'

'I expect Tess is rather absent-minded.'

'Tess? Oh no. When Tess can't do her tasks she always deputises. A couple of months ago, oh dear, I shouldn't think like that but it's so hard, I should say seven or eight goat days ago she had to go away and she deputised Ben. Now I *often* have to remind Ben.' They laughed.

'And I expect Mr Langdon doesn't often need reminding.'

'Oh.' She raised her hands. 'I have to remind Simon all the time, his head is so filled with great thoughts. And of calls he has to make, appointments. And I answer letters and generally, well, help.'

'I don't suppose you'd consider coming home with me?'

Claire laughed gaily and hugged her woolly closer to her. 'Oh no, my dear, I'm afraid I'm needed here.'

Bright came down the steps light as a cat, a sleek black sure-footed urban cat. He ignored both of them, slid into the car. Edgley shook hands with Claire; she wasn't going to scuttle after him. She strolled round to the passenger side. Claire watched them down the drive.

'Seeing us off the premises,' Bright said. 'Learn anything?'

She reported the chat with Claire.

'Old family retainer,' he said. 'That figures. He likes loyalty, doesn't he? She afraid of him?'

'I didn't get that impression. Protective more, I'd say.'

'But nothing concrete out of her? Times, dates?'

'She was aware of Tess being away on her goat day because Ben was feeding them.'

He groaned. 'If I hear once more about Ben feeding those goats . . . Okay. What about the lezzies?'

Edgley went stiff. 'I'm sorry?'

'The garden girls. Dykes, aren't they?'

Her face was red. She struggled. 'If you're saying they're lovers, yes, I

200

should say they are. I didn't ask them. It's not a crime and is none of our business.'

'A-ha.' No expression. Small capable hands on the wheel. Relaxed. Alert.

She had to get her anger under control. Be detached. People were always annoying her. She was always annoying people. She would not tell him, however, that Sam had done time. Let him find out his own way, he was so clever.

'What happened to Kate Creech?' he said.

'She left, before your interview with Langdon and Tess. Langdon told her to go.'

'Told Creech to go?'

'That's what she said.'

'Likes giving orders, doesn't he? Goes with the territory.'

Edgley didn't reply.

He said, 'You think I'm prejudiced.'

She said nothing.

'You're right. I am. And we better be. They got friends everywhere, these bastards. They know how to work the system. They should do, they invented it. Never get yourself on their side.'

'No, sir.'

'You taking the piss?'

'No, sir.'

'A-ha. Okay.' He paused, then said, 'His brother's a drug smuggler. Doing time. In Portland Bill.'

Her head turned, first sign of real life he'd seen from her. 'Sir!'

'A-ha.'

She didn't say anything else, she asked no questions, just sat there considering this news.

They were on the M3. The morning sunshine had given way to a sharp sleet that drummed on the car roof like nails. After a mile of silence he said casually, 'Where'd Kate Creech go?'

'She said London to pick up some things then Bristol to start this job.'

'She said.'

'Yes, sir. She said.'

He didn't say a-ha. He didn't say a word for some time. Then he said, 'What do you think of her?'

'Who?'

He slid a glance towards her then away. 'Kate Creech.'

'She's not involved.'

'With what?'

'This case.'

'The murder case or the drugs case?'

'You think there's a drugs case, sir?'

'There is a drugs case. But is it our case? That's the question. At some point I'm going to have to call in drug squad. But not just yet. Okay? Just for now, it's ours.'

'Yes, sir.'

'Yes, sir,' he said.

She swallowed and looked at the sleety rain, the endless flux of traffic, visibility almost nil. He was an arrogant bastard but he was a nimble driver. They might have been in a speedboat, zooming through waves of blinding spray. She discovered suddenly that she trusted him. 'Where are we going, sir?'

'Prison visiting,' he said.

44

VILLAGE LIFE

No call from Tess. Kate waited till it was almost dark, then phoned. The inevitable Claire answered at last. 'I'm sorry, Miss Creech. Tess was questioned by that policeman and then she was with Simon for an hour afterwards. She was very tired and went to lie down. I'm sure she's sleeping now.'

'Only she said she might come over to see me this evening.'

'Oh, I doubt that she could go out. She's quite exhausted.'

'Oh well, give her my love. Tell her I'll be in touch.'

She stood at the window. Diagonals of sleet out of a thick grey sky. Didn't fancy driving in that. Anyway, driving where? *Where does a homeless person go nights?*

She thought she saw a faint glow from that spooky chapel on the hill. You could imagine anything about that place. She closed the curtains and went downstairs to eat. Bright wasn't joking. A willowy chap in tweeds came in and all the old blokes touched the peaks of their caps. Afterwards she settled her bill, to get an early start in the morning, then came back up, sat on the bed and opened the script. She began to think about masks and faces. About how little you knew about the people you knew.

She woke at dawn. Birdsong drilling a white sky. But they rose early at Barnabus, Claire's voice sounded bright as noon. Tess was off at the goats, she said, and then had other duties out of doors, she wouldn't be back till lunch. 'Of course I'll ask her to telephone you then.' So that was that. Tess didn't want to see her. Or Simon Langdon didn't want Tess to see her. Either way she'd wasted enough time here.

202

She knew where she should go. She should go back to her big sister, stay quiet in Bristol and get to grips with the play. And she would, she would. There was just somewhere she had to drop in first. She'd promised. And after all it was on the way.

The village was a storm of activity today: two whole living people chatting in the doorway of the video launderette. But the lane was empty except for a lean long-legged dog rummaging in the hedge. The Ebenezer Chapel looked like night. The sunlight stretched to reach it, tucked back there off the road.

She went down the side path to the back garden. No sign of Laura. She heard a faint step behind her and a breath. She jumped, turned, her heart in her throat. The rangy dog stood a few feet away on the path. 'Don't do things like that to people,' she said. He stuck his wet nose into her palm and came back with her to the side door. The door was open a crack. 'Stay,' she said. He sat on bony haunches making small whimpers in his throat.

She pushed the door. 'Laura?' No answer. She stepped into the cluttered lobby. The arched inner door was closed. She knocked lightly, called, 'Laura?' and waited. Then opened it. She expected to see the small upright woman working at her loom, but the room had no occupant, just the fierce tapestry colours vibrating in the morning light.

She heard a whimper behind her and the light clip clop of toenails on the wooden floor. 'Where is she then, Dog?'

He sat again, looking perplexed, making his muffled whimpers. Then he jumped up and made for the door under the gallery.

'Dog! This is not your house. Come back.' She ran after him to the dark staircase. He was ahead of her, waiting at the top, panting, his big tongue lolling red.

The bed was a mess. The slant of sun from the greenish glass lay like a blessing on the broad face with its huge heavy-lidded eyes. The eyes were closed, though the face was turned towards the window as though reaching for the last of the light. She appeared to be wearing a red rose in her hair. Only, it wasn't a rose. Her pillow was red also. One of her arms stretched out across the other pillow. That pillow was white. On it lay a Peruvian grave doll like the one she had once shown to Kate.

The dog stayed with Kate in the doorway. Neither of them ventured in. *I have supped full of horrors.* 'Come on, Dog, let's go down.'

She phoned John Bright first. He didn't speak for some time. Then he said, 'Stay there and don't touch anything.'

'Shall I phone the local police?'

Pause. 'No. I'll see to everything. Don't phone anybody. Wait for me.'

She sat on a stone by the pond. The dog stretched out by her, his nose on his paws. The sun took the edge off the cold, though she was impervious to weather. And to time. And to her surroundings. She heard no footsteps when they came.

She saw Ted Adams first. She said, 'What are you doing here?' And he opened his arms but she didn't walk into them. Bright stood behind him by the door. She got up, nearly fell, her legs were so stiff. And went to Bright.

'This the way you got in?' he said.

She nodded.

'Was it open?'

'Just a crack.'

'Like that?'

'Yes.'

'And the pointy door inside?'

'That was closed. I opened it.'

'Why did you go upstairs?'

'The dog went up. I followed him.'

'Dog?'

She looked around. No dog. 'There was a dog . . .'

Ted said, 'The horde of blokes coming up the path must have scared him off.'

'As Dog's my witness,' Bright nodded. 'A-ha.' She couldn't fathom the expression on his face. 'Stay out here,' he said.

He and the men disappeared into the chapel. She and Ted stood looking into the pond. Ted said. 'Bright called me. Said you might be needing me. He wanted me to bring Nat Crosby too.'

'Why didn't you?'

'The hotel I booked for him? He checked out.'

'When?'

'Yesterday midday. I don't know where he is.'

'Oh Christ.'

'Yeah.'

'He didn't know Laura,' Kate said.

'He had her phone number.'

'Oh God. Yes.' Silence. Seagulls. Screaming. *He'd only have had to tell her he had news of Tess and Laura would have said yes, come! But why? Why would Nat – ?*

Ted said, 'Was it horrifying up there?'

'No. Quite peaceful. I don't even know how I knew she was dead. It was quite clear though. There was no presence in the room. Even when a person's deep asleep there's a presence. The dog knew too.'

'Cerberus.'

204

'Yes.'

'Who's Cerberus?' Bright had come up without a sound.

'The hound of death.'

'Guards the gate of hell,' Kate said.

'Well, when you've finished making classical allusions the local fuzz need to search your bag and search your car, Muz Creech.'

'Why?'

'She was killed with something very similar to the thing that killed Sally Crowe. And again we can't find this thing.'

'Oh God.'

'You keep being connected with nasty deaths, Muz Creech.'

She looked at him wearily. 'When did she die?'

'It looks recent. Last night. Maybe early this morning even. Where were you?'

'The hotel in Abbotsbury.'

'When did you leave?'

'Very early this morning. Five-ish?'

'Someone up to check you out, were they?'

'I paid the bill yesterday evening.'

'A-ha. So's you could get an early start? And your friend Nat Crosby. Where did you arrange to meet?'

Kate wanted to lie down on the stiff cold grass and go to sleep. She didn't reply.

'The local police want to question you,' Bright said.

'Yes. Sure.'

Bright was present while they questioned her. Where was she last night? Why? And this morning? Why? And why was she visiting Laura? At this point Bright intervened. He asked the Somerset policeman outside for a chat. The Somerset man came back and told her she could go.

'Go?'

Bright's squint was at its most intense. 'I've told the inspector I'll vouch for you. You're coming with me.'

'Where?'

'London. You've been on a loose rein long enough.'

Bright, driving fast, had just reached the bend when the dog appeared in the lane. He braked and the dog skittered sideways on stiff legs. That was when they saw the car. It was a silver Nissan, tucked in where Kate had tucked the Beetle on her first visit here, almost hidden by the overhang of ivy-twined branches. A man was slumped over the wheel. The man was Nat.

Kate and Bright silently got out. Bright opened the Nissan's door. Nat didn't stir. Bright touched his shoulder. Even then he didn't move. Bright shook him. 'Nat?' he said.

Nat grunted. His head turned on the wheel. His eyelids flickered then opened. He looked up at Bright. Recognition dawned.

'Get out of this car,' Bright said.

In the dim gallery he stood and stared. Tears ran out of his eyes. He wiped them unheeding with the back of his hand. He whispered. 'Who did this? Who's doing this?'

'You are, aren't you, Nat?'

But Nat couldn't take his eyes off the body with the blackening blossom of a wound in its hair. And when Kate saw him come into the downstairs room she thought his eyeballs had turned over to look only inwards. He appeared blind. He was shaking. He held on to walls, door-frames, table, chair-backs and Bright held on to his arm. 'Good job the place has already been dusted. You've put your signature everywhere.' He handed him over to Ted. 'See he doesn't abscond this time, Ted. Think you can manage that?'

'You all right, mate?' Ted said.

But again Nat whispered, 'Who's doing this?'

'It looks like the same weapon. Or something damn like it. They're dragging the bloody pond, searching the bloody village. Tell them to scour the bloody Nissan. Hired, is it, Nat?' Nat gave a bewildered nod. 'When did you arrive?'

Still the hoarse whisper. 'Last night. It was late. I knocked at the chapel but there was no answer. I was knackered. I thought I'd kip in the car, get up early, see her this morning.'

'Why didn't you phone before coming all this way?'

'I was phoning all evening. Four or five times? I got the answer machine.'

'Leave messages?'

'Three, I think.'

Bright went to the phone and pressed replay. They listened to the tape go round. No messages. 'All wiped, Nat. Now there's a funny thing.'

Nat's eyelids closed over the blind blue orbs.

'And what did they say, Nat, these messages?'

'Said I was coming to see her about Tess. I wanted to talk about Tess. I had a message from Tess.'

'And did you?'

'Have a message? No. Want to talk? Yes.' His voice became suddenly desperate. 'She had to know where Tess was!'

'She didn't,' Bright said.

Nat's head drooped, too heavy to support.

Bright looked at Kate. 'Well, which of you am I going to charge? Or shall I charge you both? Did you arrange to meet here? Get here in the middle of the night, did you? Bump her off? Only, then what? Why on earth would you stick around? And why bump her off anyway? Rage 'cos she wouldn't tell you where Tess was? That would rule you out, Muz Creech. Why did you come here, by the way?'

'I promised I'd tell her how Tess was. I thought I owed it to her to come – '

Nat's head came up. He turned so fast that Ted momentarily lost his grip. 'You know where Tess is? You've seen her? You! Where is she? Where?' He was shaking Kate, long strong bony hands gripping her upper arms, so hard she thought her eyes would fall out of her head.

'Come on, mate, now come on.' Ted and Bright prised him off her and into a chair. Bright said, 'Well, that's the answer to one of our questions. You two had no arrangements.'

Edgley said, 'They're actors, sir.'

Nat seemed not to hear. Kate looked impassive. Bright slowly turned his head to fix Edgley with an expressionless stare. 'Thank you, constable. And why did you want to get in touch with Tess, Nat? You never showed a blind bit of interest in her before.'

'She was the last one to see Sally alive.'

'Oh? We thought that was you.'

Nat ignored this. 'Where can I reach her, Kate?'

Bright's mobile trilled. He walked down the room answering it. 'Bright. Yeah. You're having me on. A-ha. A-ha.' He slowly put the phone away. He said, 'You can't reach her anywhere, mate. None of us can. She hasn't been seen since yesterday morning. She's disappeared.'

After that the chapel emptied. The body was brought down on a stretcher. Nat was put into the police van and driven off. Kate was put into the garden with Ted. She sat on her stone by the pond. 'Why am I not in the van with Nat?' she said.

'I think he's still checking your – version of events.'

'Why not Nat's version?'

'No one saw him after he hired the car yesterday afternoon. Hours and hours going drive-about. He could have been anywhere.'

The dog sat on his haunches and leaned on Kate.

'Okay.' Bright's raven voice behind them. They turned. He spoke to Kate. 'You were seen leaving the hotel in Abbotsbury at half-past five this morning. The lady who brought us the food? She thought you were a burglar, got up to check and saw you go. She also remembers doing your bill last night and seeing your car in the car-park when she locked up well after midnight. Even I don't think you'd have had time to get here, bash Laura's head in and get back there in time to leave again at the crack of dawn. Not in that old German jalopy. Sixty miles an hour if you're lucky. Downhill.'

'I could have hired a faster car.'

'Kate.'

'Don't worry, Ted.'

'That's right, Ted, don't worry. She couldn't hire faster roads. I'm not going to arrest her. Not just yet.'

'He just has to give me enough rope, he knows I'll hang myself. And my friends.'

'For Christsake be careful, Kate.'

'Time you were getting off, isn't it, Ted? Your client's going to need you.'

'Will you be charging Crosby?'

'Looks like it this time, doesn't it?'

'Will you come with me, Kate?'

'No. I've got questions to ask her. She'll go when I say she can.'

'I'll be okay, Ted.'

'I hope you're right.'

Ted gave her a sad salute from the gate. They heard his car rev up the lane. She stroked the dog's head. Her hand took comfort from his warmth. Bright came close to her. 'Here.' He held out her bag. 'It's been searched.'

'Thanks.'

'I'll hang on to this.' He had started to leaf through her address book when Edgley appeared at the door of the chapel.

'Sir? Can I have a word?'

He joined her.

She said, 'I've had a phone call.'

'This is news?'

'From the Barnabus Community.'

'A-ha?'

'From Sam.'

'Who's he?'

'One of the garden girls.' She flushed a little.

'The bald one with the nose rings?'

'Yes. They have something to tell me.'

'You, hn?'

'They wouldn't tell me over the phone.'

'Sound serious?'

'I think so. I thought so.'

'What you going to do?'

'Sorry?'

'You heard.'

'I thought you – '

'The call came to you.'

'Yes.'

'And I'm tied up here for a good while yet. So decide.'

'Oh.'

He waited. She started to speak then stopped. Then said, 'I'd like to go over there and hear what they've got to say.'

'Why?'

'I think there might be something to be found out that we need to know.'

'Why not have them brought to London?'

'I think Sam would do a runner.'

'I'd have to send one of the local constabulary with you.'

'She'd do a runner.'

He didn't say anything. Just stood there. Then he fished in his pocket. 'Here.' He put his car keys into her hand.

She looked at them dumbfounded. 'But what will you do?'

'I'll manage,' he said.

'Thank you, guv'nor.' She heard herself say it. No effort whatever.

He raised an eyebrow, that was all. 'Keep in touch. Don't get into trouble.' She gave him a scornful look. 'And don't for fuck's sake crash my car.'

He went back across the coarse grass towards the pond. He stood looking a second at Kate and the dog. The dog leaning on her. She with an arm round it. Forlorn wasn't the word. He stood next to them. She said, 'Vera might know where Tess is.'

'We let Vera go. Yesterday afternoon.'

'Did they get anything out of her?'

'Bugger all.' He groaned. 'And I'll need a warrant to search her place.'

'I can't think of anywhere else she'd go.'

'Except here.' He glanced at her and she shut her eyes.

'She didn't do that,' she said.

'After we left yesterday she said she was going to the stables to sleep, so no one disturbed her. She didn't appear at supper but that wasn't unusual, they say. This morning they assumed she was feeding those bloody goats. But when she didn't turn up for lunch they started to get a bit jumpy and went to look. No sign of her and her bed all neat and tidy. They don't *think* any belongings have gone. They're not sure, natch. They don't take account of worldly possessions, you see.'

209

'Simon Langdon must know where she's gone.'

'Apparently he doesn't have a clue.'

'I don't believe that.'

'Oh, don't you? Why's that, then?'

'He seems to have her on a chain. He has this weird control over her.'

'Did you know that his brother is doing time for smuggling heroin?'

'Oh Christ.' Her face held some unexpressed horror he couldn't fathom.

'A-ha. But Simon Langdon is Mr Big. I'm sure of it. His brother took the rap. Other people will always take the rap for his lordship. That's the way things should be in his world. As long as he holds on to his big house and his big position. His birthright. That's how he sees it. I'm gonna nail him. Only I'm gonna have a hard time getting proof. He's in with all the bigwigs down there. All his charitable doings with the local lads.'

She held her head with both hands. 'Oh Christ.' The dog licked her fingers and whimpered.

'So what is it you haven't told me, Kate?'

She looked up at him, closed her eyes then opened them. 'Tess is a user,' she said.

Torches wavered about the grounds and the fields. Ben was crying, rubbing his nose over and over with his sleeve. The garden girls huddled under the same rug on the front steps. They looked up when they saw her but gave no sign of recognition. Edgley introduced herself to the man in charge. He said, 'They've found no trace of her yet. And it'll be dark soon.'

'May I ask how long you expect to continue the search, sir?' He looked sharply at her. It was her accent. He thought she was taking the piss.

'I expect the search to continue until I call it off, constable.' He stomped off towards the house. Edgley and the garden girls eyed each other warily. She sat down on the steps. A Land Rover drove across the gravel and stopped. Langdon got out and ignoring them went up the steps two at a time into the house. Sam said, 'He's been drivin' around all day. Conductin' his own search.'

'Doesn't he know where she is?'

'Nah. He's havin' kittens, isn't he, Ginge?'

'Yeah.'

'You got a mobile, love?'

'Yes.'

'Can I have a look at it?'

Edgley hesitated.

'Don't you trust me, then?'

Uneasy, Edgley handed it over. Sam took it, looked at it, said, 'Ain't that nice?' and put it somewhere inside the blanket.

Edgley sounded calm. 'Someone might need to get in touch with me.'

'I'll give it back later,' Sam said. 'It'll help me to trust you. It's hard to trust a copper, you see.'

When new men arrived and started to drag the pond she and the dog stood by the gate. Bright came out of the house with the local inspector and started to call people on his mobile phone, someone named Cato, then Edgley. From Edgley he got no reply. 'That's weird,' he said. He put the phone away. Stood a minute thinking. Went back to the inspector and shook hands. Came back to Kate. 'Let's get out of here. It's getting dark. What happened to the damn day? Give us your keys.' She handed them to him. For once he seemed to miss the irony.

The dog came with them down the path. 'Goodbye, Dog,' she said. She held his wet nose a moment then climbed into the passenger side. Bright started the engine first time. The dog watched mournfully as they drove off. Bright said, 'They'd break your heart, dogs.'

'Dogs?' she said.

'I didn't say only dogs.'

The thick grey sky began to hurl down rain, the tail lights of the car ahead of them blurred and refracted. The car was a frighteningly intimate place, water running down the windows like curtains sealing them off from the outside world. But he drove her funny little car well, speeding through the clouds of muddy spray, those capable hands relaxed on the wheel. She didn't want to like him or trust him. She felt a terror that nearly took off the top of her head.

He said, 'You knew Millie Hale.'

'Millie? Yes. How – ?'

He threw her address book into her lap. She flipped through to H. Yes, there was Millie. Crossed out with a single line, over a year ago. 'We met at Bristol Old Vic,' she said. 'I was starting rehearsals as her show opened so I didn't see a lot of her. Different hours. You know. But I liked her. And I liked her work. We exchanged numbers, meant to get in touch, but you know . . . Then she got famous, then busy. And then – it was too late, she – Oh, my God.'

'Yeah.'

'You're the policeman who – You're the one.'

'A-ha.'

She scrabbled at the buckle of the seat belt. Managed to free it, then snatched at the handle of the door. The door opened, the wind rushed in, and the rain. The car screeched to a halt. 'For fuck's sake, Kate!' She was half-way out of the car. He hurled himself across her and managed to drag

211

her, struggling, back in. She flailed her arms, tried to bring up her knees but he had her pinned down under his weight and then he got a grip on her arms. She felt brought down like a game bird. He was panting. He said, 'I should have bloody handcuffed you.' He grabbed the door, heaved it shut, and locked it.

'That why they put you on this case?' she said. 'Think you have a way with actresses, do they? You make out you're crazy about them, so they trust you completely, and then you – Now I know why all my instinct was to tell you nothing, you bastard.'

'It wasn't like that.'

'I bet.'

'I was crazy about her.'

'Yeah.'

'I still am.'

'You got special commendation, didn't you, for being such a great copper?'

'Yeah, I'd done a great job. Oh yeah.' He suddenly wearied of the struggle and stopped. 'Don't jump out the car, Kate. You want to be stranded in the wilds of wherever we are in the middle of the night? Just put up with me till we get back to civilisation, right? Or I really will have to handcuff you.' He loosened his grip on her arms. She made no move. He struggled from on top of her, back to his own seat, tangling with the gear lever on the way. 'How'd I manage to get myself *in*to this position?' he said.

She shifted a little in her seat but said nothing and didn't try to escape. He picked up her address book from between the seats.

He said, 'I'd have given it all up for her.'

'Your career? Oh yeah.'

'She didn't believe me either.'

'Who would?'

'Well, she believed me but she didn't think I could exist without it.'

'You couldn't, could you?'

'For her, yeah.'

'I see why she didn't believe you.'

'She couldn't understand someone giving up their work for anything.'

'Nor could I once.'

'That what finished you with Nat?' he said.

And without thinking about it she said, 'Yes.'

'Crazy about him, were you?'

'Yes. From the first moment.'

'What, love at first sight?'

'I was up for the part of Ellie in *Heartbreak House* at Nottingham Playhouse. I'd never heard of him before, and I wasn't sure I wanted to go to Nottingham, but I dressed in white linen and put the hair up, to look the part. He was seeing people at his house in Crouch End.'

'I've got a flat there.'

'Have you? The moment he opened the door. We looked at each other and that was it. I stayed for hours, arguing, laughing, coffee, lunch, tea and then we went to bed. Can you believe that? The first time we met? He told me he had a wife and child, I told him about Oliver, but none of that mattered. Not to either of us.'

'Got the part then, did you?'

'I was afraid he'd think that: she fucks directors, or maybe every man the first time she meets him. And even when he offered me the part I tried. I decided not to go, but of course I went. It was a – cataclysmic passion. He wanted to leave Tess. I tried to be realistic, I said he couldn't leave his daughter, I said I wouldn't let him.

'Then one day soon after the play had opened I was having lunch in the theatre bar and this woman walked in. I knew right away it was Tess. I was shocked to see how alike we were, though she was older than me, into her thirties, and much more beautiful. I was shocked that she was real, this person whose husband I'd been screwing day and night for weeks. Then Nat came in holding this little blonde girl. And the biggest shock was this *family*, wanting to be part of it, part of his life. I'd never known that pain before.

'Later on Tess came to tell me how much she'd liked my performance. She invited me for lunch. I wouldn't go to the house but she and I and Zoë started meeting in this little vegetarian place in a narrow street near the theatre. She told me that she'd had a drug problem and Nat had cured her. But then she'd had a breakdown after Zoë's birth. "Nat loved Zoë so much," she said, "I felt useless, kind of a discarded husk from which he had extracted the fruit." She said they didn't make love since her illness. "I tried," she said, "but I used to weep, because his passion for me had gone. And this weeping enraged him, you can imagine, distressed him. So we stopped. And I don't seem to mind too much. He's great to me now."

'Then Nat asked me to stay on after the play was over. I was taken aback, I mean, you go home when the job's over, back to where the work is. This was no comment on my love for him. I'd still see him, in Nottingham, in London, but that cliché a mistress, hanging round with nothing to do? Me? No. I could see he just didn't understand. He had this image of me demure in white, the perfect woman, there just for him. That was stronger than his passion for me, stronger than me. He was shocked to find I was so different from this image. He couldn't cope with it.

'I came back. I was lying to Oliver for the first time in my life, talking to Nat on the phone when Oliver was out. Then one day Nat didn't phone and then he didn't phone for a week so I knew Tess had found out.

213

'I had a fortnight of torment then he came to the flat to tell me: they were getting back together again. "Tess and I are being very middle class about this. Try to save our marriage. For the sake of the children, all that. We'd like to have another child maybe." I didn't say what about me? because it was obvious what about me, I could see where his mind was. He and Tess were together again and he was thrilled. I didn't make a fuss, I could see it was no use.

'I told Oliver. You can imagine how he felt. He had three affairs in three months then we split. I heard Tess had had another baby, another girl. Nat wrote the TV trilogy. He was famous all of a sudden. I used to see his mournful face on magazines. I carried this love around like some mammoth, huge, heavy, grey, obsolete. Invisible to everyone but blocking my view of the world. I couldn't get rid of it. I didn't know what to do with it.'

'I know the feeling.'

'Then one day soon after I'd bought my house I bumped into Nat. They'd moved just up the road and he invited me to the housewarming. I said no unless Tess invited me and he said, "Why?" Why. The past had been wiped right out for him.

'It was good to see Tess again. We became real friends after that. We used to meet nearly every day when I wasn't working, she and I and the babies. Opened our hearts, you might say.'

'So when did he meet Sally?'

'It was the party for the screening of *Lady Day*. When I first saw her it was against the light. She was coming downstairs and I said, Hi love, because I thought she was Tess. Her face wasn't like Tess but her body was, tall, thin, with the same long black crinkly hair. She was dressed in white silk that you could almost see through but not quite. Nat said to Tess about eleven, "I'm just giving Sally a lift home, she's not feeling too good." He moved in with her that night. Only came back to collect his things. Rose, the baby, was just over a year old then. Zoë was four. She just seemed to collapse inwardly, Zoë, a kind of slow implosion.

'But Tess didn't collapse. It was extraordinary. She'd already met Vera at one of these women's groups she went to. Next thing she'd put the house on the market and moved to the commune in Wales. Before she went she said, "Why didn't you just take him, Kate? It would have saved a lot of pain and trouble."'

'I expect that's what you thought.'

'No. I was glad by then. He'd have gone off with Sally just the same. That Sally or some other Sally in some other white dress somewhere sometime. Tess said, "I was wearing cheesecloth but that was the end of the sixties. You were in linen, that was the seventies. This is the eighties so Sally was in silk."'

After some time Bright said, 'Millie decided to save my career.'

'You're telling me that's why she – ?'

'But I couldn't work afterwards anyway. I took some leave.'

'How long?'

'Few months. Had it owing. Stayed drunk as much as I could. Far as I was concerned I was out for good.'

'That would have been ironic.'

'A-ha. That's why I got back in again. Stopped drinking.'

'Not so's you'd notice.'

'Oh yeah. You'd notice.'

'So you made her sacrifice worthwhile,' Kate said in a light voice.

'Believe me, I wish I'd stayed out. But I'm in and I got to get on with it. Know what I mean?'

He started the car again. Like searchlights under water car headlamps pierced the darkness a moment and were gone.

'You get over things in the end,' she said.

'That's the saddest part.'

'No, it's not. It's only a couple of years since Millie. It takes longer than that.'

'You're over him now, then, are you?'

'I think I am at last.'

'He's a pretty ruthless bloke.'

'Nat? No!'

'Oh yes. That's what you've described. I had him wrong. I think Edgley's right. If a woman tried to leave him, he could get violent.'

'No!'

'Talking of Edgley, hang on a minute.' He got out the mobile. 'I'm worried. It's not like Miss Perfect not to do it by the book.' He listened. 'Why's she not answering? I don't like this.' He called the local police and told them his problem. He said to Kate, 'The inspector talked to her when she first arrived. Hasn't seen her since, hasn't seen the car. I'm having the hotel checked. She's a pain in the arse but I don't want to lose her. Christ, why did I let her go? They're so busy looking for your junkie friend they've lost a potential chief constable.'

'Edgley?'

'You bet. That's the police force of the future, that is.'

'What can you do?'

'I can't go back to Dorset Disneyland, can I? I've got to deal with your ex-lover in London. And find his ex-common-law wife. The local force say Langdon definitely doesn't know where she is, he's nearly out of his mind.'

45

EDGLEY TAKES HER CHANCE

The girls stood outside the gates. Sam in a long overcoat, Ginger in an old mac and wellies. Sam's arm round Ginger. Edgley stopped the car, they peered inside then jumped in fast. Sam's throaty London voice: 'Keep drivin', get away from here. Quick.'

'Where to?'

'Up the chapel.'

'Up there?' She could see it in silhouette on the top of the hill, the sky behind swollen, purplish.

'We can talk there, no one'll see us.'

'We can talk in the car.'

'No.'

Her chest felt tight. She had too much saliva all of a sudden. She swallowed. This wasn't an amusing situation.

'Listen,' Sam said, 'it's where they'd expect us to go of an evening, it's normal, it's no big deal. Don't worry about it, right?'

She started the car and rolled slowly away from the gates. She felt she had no choice. No use asking what Bright would do. He wasn't here. Ginger hadn't uttered, she leaned on her big bald friend in the back like a cat on a lap.

'Anyway,' Sam said. 'It's the only door round here you can lock.'

That made Edgley feel really good. But she drove where Sam told her, along a winding lane tunnelled by trees rising with the hill. She put the car where Sam told her, in an entrance to a field off the main lane. 'No one'll see it there,' Sam said. Edgley only half hoped she was right.

She struggled in their wake, ankles rocking in the ruts, shoes sucking in and out of the mud, into a steep field full of hillocks and holes. They waited for her at the gate, closed it after her, crossed the upper lane into another field, this hardly a field, just scrub and gorse on a rounded hill, thorn trees bent in the wind like old crones pointing the way. A narrow mud path skirted the gorsy hillock. They trod it, pfluck, pfluck, their feet in and out of the mud. It was getting darker. Their long shadows joined longer shadows. Soon all shadows would merge and everywhere be dark.

It was Ginger who took the key out of the pocket of her mac. The oak door opened on to a small room. Stone walls, whitewashed, and a stone floor. Cushions scattered about, and candles. Candles everywhere, big creamy beeswax ones, small multi-coloured pyramids and every shape and size in between. The place had one round window above where the altar would once have been. The girls lit some candles and their shadows flickered now, changed and moved.

The place was cosy, a children's den. What had she expected? An altar devoted to the black mass, charred remains of animal sacrifice, a cockerel with its throat cut? She wanted to laugh at herself but couldn't. Sam locked the door with the big key.

'No need to lock it, is there?' This dead stone place thinned the voice, she might have been out on the hillside in a high wind.

Sam put the key in her pocket. 'Safer,' she said. She stood next to Ginger. Such a contrast they were: Ginger so little, face like a heart with her Harpo Marx hair and her home knit sweater; Sam so tall with her big bones, her shaved head and nose rings and her soft patterned loose cotton frock under the long coat; both in their wellies, kids after rain.

'Okay, what do you want to tell me?'

They looked at each other. They were scared. More scared than she was. Of what? Of whom?

Sam said, 'Look, there's a drug scene here, right?'

'We knew this.'

'Yeah. yeah. Well – ' Sam stopped, then went on. 'Look, we were both on the stuff, right? I started in the nick. But we went to detox. Ginger went first then she made me go. It was someone at the detox unit told us about this place. We couldn't believe it, could we, Ginge? The country and that, the garden. Anyway, we're here, right? We're settling in, learning the drill. It's cool, you know? Real easy, even the prayers and that, like it's up to you. I mean we can see there's users here, it's obvious – no names, okay?'

Edgley hesitated. 'Okay.'

'Okay. Anyway, eventually someone offers us some stuff. It's tempting, right? You think, well, I'm clean now, I'm not addicted no more, I can handle it, I've got it under control, I can just jack up every now and then, take it or leave it, right? It was Ginger stopped me, wasn't it, Ginge? She said once an addict always an addict. That's what they told us in detox, you know? So it was hard, with all the stuff going round in this place, but we didn't do it. No sweat. Anyway, then Tess came.' Sam stopped speaking. Ginger sidled up to her and stood closer. 'Okay, we're crazy about her when she comes, right? She's so good and gentle and that. Kind, you know? And she's cracking-looking, right? Even though she's, you know, not that young. And she's so *sad*, Christ, we were so sorry for her, like, that cow cheating her out of her money, and losing her kids and – I mean, everyone feels like that about her, not just us. Well, Simon goes crazy for her. Like, normally you don't see him much, he's in his office or out round the land and Claire is, like, her master's voice, know what I mean? He's always at prayers and meals and that but he's not exactly matey, right? But when Tess comes, Christ! He's turning up everywhere, stables, gardens, dairy, all hours, it's embarrassing.'

'Did they, he – did Tess . . .?'

Sam and Ginger looked at each other. 'Yeah, in the end she did. She never said but it was obvious. Like she wouldn't be in the stable in the morning, she started looking bad.'

Ginger suddenly spoke. 'I don't think she liked him really.'

Sam agreed. 'She was shit scared of him, I know that much.'

'Why?'

There was a silence.

'He made her the courier,' Sam said. 'Started sending her up to London regular, and visiting his brother in the nick. Did you know about him?'

'Yes.'

'Well, Tess was taking him the stuff to distribute round the prison, that's what we think.'

'Was Tess a user when she came here?'

They looked at each other. 'Yeah.'

'I see. So how did it work?'

'Simon would get a delivery, right?'

'How?'

'We don't know, we never found out exactly but he's got this boat. He takes problem kids out in it, teaches them sailing and that. No one'd think anything of him being out all hours and no one'd suspect him, right? Mr Big Charitable Worker. He's got this great reputation round here, right?'

'Okay.'

'Then Tess would go to Portland nick. And she'd go to London as well.'

'On the same day?'

'Usually.'

'How do you know all this?'

'We worked it out. We followed Tess.'

'Look – ' Edgley's voice took on a slight edge. 'We knew all this. More or less. You've brought me down here to tell me a whole lot of stuff we already know.'

They moved closer. Sam folded her arms across her body, looked down at her muddy wellies, shook her head. 'This is a murder case, right?'

'Yes.'

Silence. Even the candle flames seemed to stop flickering.

Ginger said, 'It wasn't till Tess went off, yesterday.'

'We got worried, see?'

'Where's she gone off to? We worried if she'd gone off to do something for Simon, or if he'd . . .' Ginger's childlike voice died away into the silence.

218

'Only we read you've got this bloke banged up for it. Tess's ex.'

There was a knock on the door.

Candle flames and shadows jumped. The women stood still. Edgley didn't know who else had a key and it was too late to ask.

'Come on, open up!'

Edgley started to move to the door, to be behind it when it opened.

'I know you're in there! I can see the light!'

The oak muffled the sound. But they couldn't risk speech, she to ask who it was, the girls to tell her. Bang bang bang, again, the door and her heart. It wasn't the physical danger, she was up to that, she wasn't big but she was good, she could handle herself, and Sam would be good in a fight, if there's one thing they learn in prison it's that. But what if it were the local police? How could she explain?

'Come on, girls!' The voice took on a plaintive tone, clear even through the oak. They looked at each other but didn't move. The voice dwindled to a sad mumble. They listened. Impossible to tell if the person had gone or was still waiting. Sam whispered at last, 'I think it was Ben.' She and Ginger laughed silently holding their stomachs. Reaction from the fear of Simon Langdon. They recovered fast. Edgley was impressed.

'Ben wouldn't harm a fly,' Sam said.

'No, but he can talk.'

'That's right, if he tells Claire – '

'We have to get out of here,' Edgley said.

'Okay.'

'Do you want me to get you away from this place?'

They looked at each other, faces full of distress. 'The thing is, we like it here. Best place we've ever been.'

'But it's going to be busted.'

'Has it got to be?'

'It's drugs money that runs this place. Langdon gets busted, how do you think it could survive?'

'We could run it without him, sell the garden stuff and that.'

'Do it like a business, you know?'

Dreamers. 'Don't you think you should come away with me just until Langdon is sorted? You might not be safe.'

They looked at each other. 'Ben won't say we were here.' They looked at her. 'And no one knows you've come here.' They shook their heads. 'We're staying,' Sam said.

'Well, I'm not. How do I get out of here?'

They stood uncertain, shifting their feet, Ginger's face creased in worry, Sam's scowl intense. Sam sat down on the little step that would once have held the altar. Ginger stood. Edgley's hackles rose, fight and flight. They were not going to let her out. They'd brought her here for some other

219

purpose. Sam had the key. She'd have to overpower Sam. But each of these girls would fight to the death to save the other. Sam stood up. Edgley tensed, then relaxed, deliberately, made herself ready. Sam said, 'Go on then, Ginge.'

Ginger moved. Edgley stood very still, ready, waiting. Ginger bent over a pile of cushions, lifted them, then lifted the stone underneath them. From the cavity under it she pulled out a plastic Tesco's carrier with something in it. Both girls walked towards her and stopped. She didn't move. Ginger lifted the bag and handed it to her. It was heavy. She stooped, put the bag on the floor, opened it. She couldn't tell what this strange object might be. She took a tissue out of her pocket and lifted it out. She was holding two vertical wavy rods which were attached to a heavy green marble base. The thing was mucky, matted with blood and hair, but on the base was a brass plaque and through the muck she could make out *Society of Authors and Pye Radio Award Best Actress 1979*, and the name Kate Creech.

He turned left on to Shepherd's Bush Green. 'Where do you go now?' he said.

'You mean I'm not in custody?'

He squinted sideways at her. 'Where are you spending the night?'

'Ah, freedom,' she said. 'I'll go to Ken's.'

'What's wrong with Aggie's?'

'It's a long story.'

'Not another one?'

She laughed. Just a short one but a laugh nevertheless.

He said, 'I'll drop you there.'

'And my car?'

'Your car too.'

'Then what will you do?'

'I'll manage,' he said.

He parked round the corner from Ken's place. 'I'll see you to the door.'

'Oh. Okay.'

He lifted her bag out of the boot and handed her her keys. 'I told you never to lend those,' he said. 'You want to be more careful.'

'I thought you hadn't noticed.'

He almost grinned. 'And after tonight?' he said. 'What then?'

'Collect some stuff and go to Bristol.'

'A-ha.'

'I'll be there eight weeks.'

'Don't lend your keys this time.'

'Not even to a policeman.'

'Will you come to the station at three tomorrow afternoon?' he said.

'What for?'

'I need a statement from you.'

'Why three?'

'I'll be there at three.'

'You're an odd sort of a policeman, aren't you?'

'You're an odd sort of an actress, aren't you?'

'Am I?'

'Maybe everyone's an odd kind of everything,' he said.

'I'm out of love with acting.'

'That's temporary. I'm well out of love with investigating.'

'That's temporary too, isn't it?'

'I don't know.'

He put her bag down on Ken's doorstep. They stood in the doorway. She thought, *I don't want him to go. What is this? What's happening to me?* 'Er, thanks,' she said.

'Yeah, well.'

She half smiled, sadly, quickly, then stopped smiling. That sudden silence wrapped them again. Just like the moment outside the cells that time. He looked at her in speculative query, then put out a hand and pushed her hair behind her ear. 'Kate Creech,' he said.

A sudden shrill sound shook them. He fumbled for his mobile. 'Yes?'

Edgley's crackling voice said, 'Sir? I'm calling in my report.'

His hand covered his face a second. He shook his head and made a sound between a gasp and a laugh. 'Your timing's slipping, constable, it's not quite midnight yet. Hang on a minute.' He looked at Kate and shrugged. 'I got to go.'

'Sure.'

She rang the door bell. He hailed a taxi.

'Sleep well, Muz Creech.'

'You too.'

46

TRUE COLOURS

'Cato, how's your car?'

'Nothing a complete organ transplant wouldn't fix, guv, why?'

'Will it get us to Croydon?'

He stood up and shook out his pipe. 'Should just about manage it, when?'

'Now. See you in the car-park in one minute.'

He could hear them taking the piss before he was out of the door. 'Puss puss puss, who's the guv'nor's little pussy, then?'

Cato might be a natty bugger, neat in his blazer and his smooth grey trousers with their perfect crease, might despise the Starsky and Hutch types, as he called them, in their scruffy leather jackets and jeans. Still, the guy had style, wasn't just a ten a penny DC. Bright suspected he might be useful in a scrap: a cat looks sleepy till the action starts, then he's in for the kill. You can but hope.

He drove his old BMW like a helicopter, complaining all the time how he'd used up his petrol allowance this month. 'Shut up and put that pipe out while I fill you in.' The Cat raised his eyebrows but put the pipe on the dash. Bright shut the window, distancing the klaxon's howl.

They arranged a few contingency plans: if Tess was there; if she wasn't; if drug squad were there; if they weren't. The Cat nodded like his mind was somewhere else, executing manoeuvres across three lanes of traffic and two sets of lights in as many seconds. Bright didn't like being driven as a rule but this was amusing stuff, brought back his time as a DC, a DS, whizzing around, not tied to the paperwork.

'This makes a change,' Cato said.

Bright remembered: they were all tied to the paperwork now; the job had changed for everyone. 'Turn right.' He took the lamp off the roof. Cato turned off the klaxon. The sudden quiet was dramatic, the car whispering down silent streets. They stopped short of the house. Both got out and walked, not hurrying, but fast.

The front door was open. 'What?' He ran back down the path looking both ways. Only a short Indian woman in a sari and a thick coat. 'Did a woman pass you, love? Tall thin dark, a lot of black hair?'

The woman shook her head cowering. 'No no no not at all.'

'Christ.' He sent Cato down the side of the house to the back. It was a narrow squeeze, and a climb over a grimy fence. That'd make whoopee with the blazer and the trouser crease. Still, the guy slid down there like his BMW, quiet and fast. Bright went into the house.

The house was just as filthy but there were now more footprints in the dust. A big lad with a pony tail came down the stairs, his pace was leisurely, his arms full of gear: syringes, bulging plastic bags, lengths of rubber. Another lad with silky long brown hair and an innocent face came down behind him, holding the boyfriend by the arm. The poor creature looked ready to pop his clogs, green, shaking.

'Where's Vera?'

'Who are you?' Pony Tail said.

'Kentish Town CID. The burk who put you on to this. I wanted to get here before you lot. You were asked to wait till I'd done. But no, you couldn't wait.' He gave a perfunctory flash of his ID.

'Oh. She's in there.'

She looked a mess, hair lank, face white, freckles out on stalks. Her lips looked chewed. So much for aromatherapy: over the other aromas Bright smelled fear again. As soon as she saw him she said, 'I'll sue you for this. I don't know what you've found but it's nothing to do with me.'

'It's your house, Vera.'

'My name is not Vera. Did you put these thugs on to me? I'm suing for wrongful arrest.'

'Have you been arrested, then?'

'I'm being held in my own house, forbidden to go up my own stairs. What do you call that?'

'Where's Tess Harbour?'

'I don't know what you mean.'

'Don't mess with me, Vera. Where is she?'

'I'm saying nothing till my lawyer advises me.'

He got out of the room before he did her some permanent damage. It wasn't often he lost his cool. They were just taking the boy out of the house. 'You.' They stopped and turned. 'Where's Tess?' The boy was shivering, even his mouth was shivering, he couldn't speak. Bright took a breath, rubbed his hand across his face. 'Get on the blower to your guv'nor,' he said. 'He'll have heard from my guv'nor by now.' He looked at the boy. 'Come here, sit down.' He took the lad's arm and led him to the stairs. The drugs guys looked at each other, shrugged, let the boy go with him, leaned themselves up against the wall. Bright sat the kid beside him. 'What's your name?'

'Chris.'

'Okay, Chris. There's a woman.' He described Tess. 'We're worried about her. There's been a murder. A woman just like her was killed. We're afraid the killer might try again, get her this time. You see? I'm not drugs squad. You see? It's a murder investigation. You help me, I might be able to help you, see?'

The drugs guys looked at each other and sighed. Bright said, 'These guys shouldn't be here, they jumped the gun, they could be in big trouble, so maybe we can all do each other a favour, hn?'

The guys didn't say anything. The lad didn't say anything. The guys unleaned themselves heavy and slow, swayed out through the door on to the path. Bright closed the door to, crouched in front of the boy. 'Chris.' He cooed the name through his nose. 'She was here, right? Tess.'

The boy nodded.

'But she's not here now?'

223

He shook his head.

'So when did she go?'

He lifted his shoulders. Time wasn't one of his major preoccupations. The only time he knew was the time between hits.

'Okay, Chris. How did she go? Just walk out? What?'

Chris whispered, everything shaking, 'A man came.'

'A man, what man? What man was this?'

The boy's head shook on his shaking body.

'Chris. Was he tall, thin, with a beard? Green welly and Land Rover type? Voice like he owns the place?'

Now the boy's head wobbled up and down, an attempt at a nod. 'They call him Simon?' The kid nodded again. 'He took her away?' Nod. 'How? In a car, a jeep?'

The boy could hardly speak. He pointed to the back of the house. Bright ran, pulled open the back door. It was all gardens to the end of the street. No sign of Cato. He turned back to the boy. 'When did he leave, this bloke? Was it when the drugs guys rang the bell?' No, the boy signalled. Bright knew: drug squad knew better than anyone to cover the back exits before you go in the front.

He pulled the front door open and shouted to the long-hairs, 'No one got away at the back here when you started your raid?'

'Eh? No!'

'Sure?'

They exchanged fuck-off looks.

'Okay, how long you been here?'

They looked at their watches, very slow. Number One said, 'Twenty minutes maybe. Twenty-five.'

Nearly an hour to get here, nearly an hour since getting the warrant. Langdon had nearly forty minutes to get her out. He was clever, he wouldn't be in his own vehicle. Shit. Shit shit shit.

At this point The Cat appeared, neat as a new pin, not a mark on the blazer, strolling along the street lighting his poncy pipe. He came up the path pulling his little beard between finger and thumb. The drugs guys' faces: he might have been ET. 'Seen in the back garden of number seventeen, guv,' he said. 'About three-quarters of an hour ago. Upper class bloke and dark thin girl. Girl's not well. Lady of the house challenged them. Bloke tells her they've just been looking at the empty house, number fifteen, and they've locked themselves out. Could they possibly come out through her place. Very charming, the gentleman, apparently, very polite. So she lets them out through her house and she tells them the best place to find a taxi on the main road.'

A pause while he pulled on his pipe to get it going, examined it to see it was working all right.

'This is Niki Cato,' Bright told them. 'Kentish Town CID.'

They shut their mouths. Pony Tail said. 'Who's he talking about?'

'Mr Big. Maybe. The one you want. Maybe.'

'How big maybe?'

'No maybe at all. And big as you like.'

'Who is he?'

'That's information for your guv'nor.'

The long-hairs looked at each other. Decided it was no use getting mad. 'Come on, mate,' Pony Tail said.

Bright jerked his head at the back room where Vera was. 'What are you charging her with?'

'She's a dealer, mate. We found a lot of stuff up there.'

'For me she's an important witness. I need her.'

'Look, mate, I'm just obeying orders, right, I can't – '

Bright strolled down to the room and opened the door. 'I'll take her off your hands for a bit.'

'What, sir?' Number Two, younger than Pony Tail, lower rank, following.

'In connection with my murder case,' Bright said.

Vera's head came up, face whiter, whites of the eyes sicker. 'I don't kill people.'

'Is that right, Vera?'

'I heal them.'

'See if you can heal my assistant here. He's in need of healing, aren't you, Cat? You tell him a few things about Simon Langdon, that'll do him a lot of good. Won't do you any harm either, Vera.' Bright went out of the room. The drug squad lad followed. The Cat stayed behind. Pony Tail was on his blower to head office. They'd have had the word from Bright's DCI by now. Pony Tail pushed his aerial down like it was Bright's head. He scowled at his henchman and hunched off down the path, didn't even look at Bright.

Bright stood in the doorway, looked at the scruffy front garden, the drab Croydon street. He bounced on his toes. He was breathing the pure air again, the icy stuff, the fiery stuff, the real thing. He was back again. He was back in. He was alive. He was going to be all right. 'Thanks, mate,' he called down the path. 'I'll do the same for you one day.'

'This interview is being recorded. Present are Detective Constable Cato and Detective Inspector Bright. Okay, Vera, Tess came to you. When?'

'Yesterday morning.'

'What time?'

'Quite early. I had my first patient. About half-past ten.'

'Where had she come from?'

'She said from Dorset.'

'How?'

'She said she'd hitched.'

'Why did she come to you?'

'I am her sanctuary.'

'Don't give me any bullshit, Vera, we've got too much on you. She came to you for money or a fix. Or both.'

'No. She wanted protection from Simon Langdon. She had run away from him. He is a very dangerous person.'

'How'd you get involved in his business, Vera?'

She looked at them out of eyes like marbles. She breathed short breaths through her nose. She swallowed.

'Come on, love. You know you're going to tell us in the end.'

'Tess told him I owed her money. So he put me on his list.'

'His list?'

'Well, you don't think I was the only one? I was small fry. I used to deal just a little, in methadone to get people off the real stuff. I – '

'Yeah, yeah, we believe you, Vera.' Bright squinted at Cato and sighed. 'And the rest.'

'He has a lot of – contacts. Local and in London. Tess would bring the – packages. He thought Tess was the ideal courier because no one would ever suspect her of anything. I had to deal to make the money to pay Tess back, otherwise he'd . . .'

'He'd blow your cover.'

Vera said nothing. She folded her arms as though to keep all words safe within the cage of her ribs.

'Thank you, Vera. That is all very helpful. Now just a few more questions. Did Tess at any time mention Sally Crowe?'

The skin of her face seemed to tremble. 'She said she was helping her to move.'

'When was this?' Bright's voice was soft.

'The last Saturday in January.'

'You saw her then?'

'Yes, I had to meet her off the train at Paddington because she had a lot to do that day.'

Cato gave a short laugh.

'How did she seem?'

'Well . . . Preoccupied. She wasn't as careful as usual making the – exchange. Apart from that I didn't notice anything.'

'She mention Nat?'

Vera's hands fluttered round her mouth. 'She said Sally knew she was a user and might tell Nat.'

Bright and Cato both sat back and breathed out hard. 'You were right, guv,' Cato said.

226

Bright turned off the recorder. 'All that bullshit about the goats and Ben and who fed them and when. All to convince everyone at the funny farm that it was Friday she'd gone to London. As if they'd have remembered anyway. Christ.'

'What's that, guv?'

'But it means she planned it, Cat.'

'Tess Harbour?'

Bright said, 'Off the record, Vera. Was Tess a user when you first met her?'

Vera's eyes were closed. In a tired voice she said, 'She'd been off it for years. But a couple of the women in the group were addicts.'

'And you were helping them, were you?'

She ignored this. 'When Nat went off with Sally she begged me. Just to get her through it, she said. She begged!' Vera opened her eyes. 'And it did! It did get her through it! She was strong then. She was magnificent!'

'Yeah, yeah. She's magnificent all right. And where the fuck is she now?' He saw Vera wince. 'Better get used to it, Vera. Where you're going, love, you're gonna hear worse than that.'

Then Atkins poked his head round the door. 'Guv? They picked up Simon Langdon near Victoria station.'

'Was the woman with him?'

'She got away, guv.'

47

A HOMECOMING

Why do you always want to pee as soon as you enter your own house? Some atavistic urge to mark your territory or what? She used a bucket and emptied it down the outside drain; she couldn't face the bathroom yet.

She would have to face the bedroom sooner or later though. Her things in the cupboards and drawers. All the hands that had been through them. All the eyes. And Nat fucking Sally on the bed, just before – *Come on, you can control this. You can do it. You just have to go up the stairs, open the cupboard. There'll just be clothes. As you left them, years ago, before Coventry. You'll be in Bristol for two months, you just have to grab things: jeans, sweaters, one posh frock for the opening night, another posh frock just in case. Shoes.*

But she couldn't go up the stairs. *I'll just tidy down here first.* But there was nothing to tidy; it had all been done. She could feel the presences, the SOCOs doing their stuff, all the people who'd been in and out, but there was no visible trace of them. Even the pile of newspapers Ted brought her had gone. She picked up a cloth and wiped it over the draining board, the tiles. *My lovely tiles. I'd made this house so beautiful.* She growled with anger and it was this anger that got her up the stairs and that got her into the bedroom without looking at the closed bathroom door.

A woman with long black hair sat on the bed with her back to Kate. *I'm hallucinating.* Newspapers were scattered over the bed and across the floor. At Kate's feet the front page of the *Independent*. A picture of Sally with the eyes gouged out. A copy of the *Guardian*: a picture of herself. The eyes gouged out. The woman on the bed. Kate's kitchen scissors in her hand. A newspaper with a picture of Nat. The woman is gouging out the eyes with the point of the scissors. Next to the picture of Nat is another picture of Kate. The eyes have gone. Pictures spread all round the woman on the bed. She has gouged out all the eyes.

The top of Kate's head opens like a tin can to release the pressure under the skull. She looks at her feet. They are standing on yellow carpet. This is her carpet. In her house. These are her feet. Therefore this is real. She is real. She is here in her own bedroom in her own house. In this moment she knew what madness was. Real psychosis where the rules of the world had changed and new rules had to be learned, new strategies for survival, and you were always a step behind the game, a word behind the breaking of the code.

'Hello, Kate,' the woman says. She hasn't even turned round.

'Hello, Tess.'

'It took you a long time.'

'The traffic was bad.' *I'm apologising for being late?*

'It's quicker by Tube.'

'That's what they say on the hoardings.' *What sort of conversation is this?*

Tess calmly, methodically goes on working her way through her friends' eyes. But Kate's moment of paralysis is over and she backs silently out of the room and along the landing to the head of the stairs. Half-way down she looks through the banisters. No movement from Tess. Still absorbed then in her fascinating task. *Why here? Why my house? What's she come for? Well, she had the key and she has nowhere else to go.* But Kate knows the reasons are not these.

She reaches the phone. It's on a long lead so you can walk round with it. She takes it into the living-room. She calls Bright's number. It rings. It rings. *Oh Christ, come on. Come on.*

'John Bright.' The nasal raven croak. The best sound in the world. Relief rises in her throat like vomit. 'Hello,' she says and the phone dies. Tess stands in the arch to the kitchen. The scissors in one hand, the cord in the other. She has cut the cord. The beautiful midwife.

Tess drops the end of the cord, comes towards her with the scissors. Kate could go backwards towards the french windows but finds herself moving forward towards the woman, the midwife, the midwife to death. The long deep pools, her eyes. The scissors. Tess stands still, watching her come without expression. No rage or fear; just the stagnant pools. Dead water. Kate makes a rush. Tess steps aside. Kate hurtles to the front door and turns the handle and pulls but the door won't come. Tess's floating voice, wind in reeds. 'I mortice-locked it, Kate. Just now. While you were on the phone.'

Mortice-lock, dead lock, death lock. 'Give me the key, Tess.'

'I can't.'

'Come on, now.'

'I pushed it out through the letter box.'

'Clever Tess,' Kate says.

'Yes, I am clever.' She sighs.

My own keys, where are they? Pocket? No. Kitchen? No. I know, straight back in my bag when I first came in for fear of losing them. Ha! Threw the bag down somewhere, desperate to pee. Yes, oh God, the living-room. Have to get back in there. Kate folds her arms, to control her heartbeat, to look as strong as she feels weak. Her voice comes out smooth, calm. 'You still had my key, then, Tess.'

'Oh yes. I had one cut for Sally. I kept the one you gave me, of course.'

'Why did you kill her, Tess?'

'She was taking Nat away. If she went to the States they'd never come back. He'd have the children for ever.'

'But she refused to go with him.'

'He'd have persuaded her sooner or later, you know how he is.'

'Yes.'

'And then she asked me to help her find a place to make love with Nat. People should know they can't take those kind of liberties. And they did make love, Kate. I was here waiting for them. I heard them. And it was never like that with him and me. It may have been that that decided me really in the end. Though there were other reasons too.'

'What reasons?' Kate's voice has ceased to work. There's barely a sound to the words.

'Sally saw me jacking up. At Laura's. Laura saw too. I thought Laura would never give me away so I wouldn't have to kill her.'

'When did you change your mind?'

'When you told me they had set Nat free. I'd made her promise not to tell. But when they let Nat go I knew he'd call her. And I knew she'd tell

229

him. No one can refuse Nat anything. Even Laura. And once he knew I was a user again, I'd never get the children back. Do you see? So I called Laura and told her I was coming back to her. That was just to make her wait. And you know too now. So you have to die too. It's okay. You mustn't be fearful. Dying's easy. It's so easy, Kate. Sally was in the bath and I picked up your award thing and came up behind her and hit her just once and she blacked out and I pushed her down and she didn't even struggle. So easy, Kate. And Laura was asleep! I hit her head with that little stone Buddha she kept by her bed. It was her most precious possession also. It's in your garden now. I buried it there.'

'Why my house, Tess?'

'Well, you know why.'

'I don't.'

'But you took Nat from me. You broke me up. Broke us up.'

So that's it. All the betrayals started with one betrayal: mine. But I can't think about that now. 'He left me, Tess. He went back to you.'

'He never really came back.'

'You had the baby together. Rose. It was going well. You said so at the time.'

'That's what I said.'

'It appeared to be true.'

'It was, for a while. Till you introduced Sally to him.'

'I did?'

'Yes.'

'Tess, I never met Sally before your party that night.'

'You brought her.'

'No. We arrived at the same time, that's all.'

'That's what you say.'

'This would be a funny time to lie to you.'

'I don't believe what people say any longer. You shouldn't either, Kate. How could you ever have believed that I had forgiven you? That is so naïve.'

'So that's why you killed her in my house?'

'Sure. I wanted them to think you'd done it.'

'Thanks.'

'They ought to have thought that, really.'

'Yes, they ought.' *Anyone but John Bright would have thought that.*

All this time she's moving, little by little, to get back into the living-room to the keys which are in her bag on the big armchair. Tess stands with her back against the arch that divides the living-room from the kitchen. Kate has got herself as far as the arch. She rests her back on the opposite wall. They stand facing each other either side of the arch, two caryatids. If she can just get to the chair. She takes a step sideways and suddenly the floor's gone, nothing's there, she's falling into an abyss. She's forgotten the step down to the living-room. Forgotten the step down in her own house. She's sprawled backwards across the step and when she gets herself together and sits up Tess is silhouetted against the french windows, the garden blowing behind her, the scissors in her hand. Kate can see her bag where she flung it down, over on the blue chair, right next to Tess.

I could get a knife from the kitchen drawer behind me. I couldn't use it, this is Tess. Get the knife. I can't. Kate sits on the step. She's shaken. The fall was nightmare, packed like real nightmares into a few seconds, your life passing before your eyes, or you falling past your life. She's panting. And sees her watch. It's way past three. John Bright said three. Her only chance is his coming to look for her because she's late. *He doesn't know I'm here. I could break the kitchen window. No, I can't, it's strengthened glass so that burglars can't get in.* She would laugh if she could. She seems to be stuck here on the step, bemused, anaesthetised. If someone touched her she'd fall all one way like a stone image. This is what they mean by petrified. If Tess would rush at her she might come to life, overpower her, get the scissors. But she recalls Tess's fight with Edgley, how strong Tess is inside that fragile appearance. Life down home on the farm. She tries to gather the ends of the conversation. *Keep her talking. Where did we leave off? Oh, yes, they should have thought I'd done it.* 'But they didn't think I'd done it, Tess.'

'No.'

'They thought Nat did it.'

'Yes. That's so good. It's so just. I hoped they'd think that too.'

'What, that we were in it together, Nat and I?'

'Why not? You still love Nat.'

'I don't still love him that way.'

'That way.' A little laugh. This laugh makes Kate feel stupid. In such a situation you can still feel stupid, humiliated? This surprises Kate, makes her angry again. *Anger. That's better.* She starts to think. Without the keys her only hope is the bathroom window. It's a casement window. It opens on the street. She can shout. She can even jump. She winces: she suffers from vertigo. The bathroom's behind her, up the stairs, away from Tess. She'll have a twenty-foot start. If she can just lock herself in the bathroom with Tess on the other side of the door. Tess has started to open and close the scissors in a dreamy way. *Keep calm. Don't let her see me think.*

'You know, I came to your house one other time. After the Welsh commune broke up.' Tess says. *Open, close, light on the blades.*

Kate feels sick. 'Yes?' she says.

'I had nothing. I had lost everything. Varya had taken my money, Sally had taken Nat, Nat had taken my children. You were so happy in your pretty house in your pretty street. The cherry trees were just about to come into blossom. Like now. Dark red blossoms, aren't they, just like – And you had started it all, all the taking away. You had set the standard for the rest. Well, I wanted to defile your house, I wanted you to feel the way I felt, that everything had been taken away from you and made filthy and spoiled and defiled and – '

'You succeeded, Tess.'

'I did, didn't I?'

'And are you going to kill me now too?'

'Oh yes, I don't want you to go on living and be happy. See, you've come to be friends with Nat again over this, haven't you? You see? He hasn't got Sally any longer so he'll turn to you. Well, I can't have that, can I, Kate?'

'He frightens me actually, Tess. Almost as much as you do. You both have a very odd way of seeing the world.'

Tess is moving towards her. Her hand looks so strong round the scissors. She's holding them like a knife now, closed: more strength that way.

'Tess, they know everything now, the police, they know it's you. Why go on with this? Haven't you done enough? Shouldn't it stop now?'

She says dreamily, smiling a little, 'You and he together and you'd get my children the both of you. You and Nat, Kate. My children, you see. I can't have that.'

Tess steadily comes on. Kate backs through the kitchen. The distance hasn't closed. *When I get to the stairs I'll turn and run.* The thought of turning her back on Tess makes her sick, already feeling those scissors between her shoulder blades. *Scissor blades, shoulder blades.* But she's through the kitchen, she's in the hall. She feels behind her for the newel post. *There. Now.* She turns. She takes the stairs three at a time. *Don't let me trip, don't let me trip.* The scissors jab her ankle, the back of her calf. Tess's breath behind her. She thinks *At the top I'll turn and kick*, but she doesn't, she keeps on running. *The bathroom door's shut!* She barges at it. Tess is there, behind her, but Kate's in. She presses with all her body-weight and power and fear and anger, yes, against the door, and it's closing, closing, and Tess's foot is in the last four inches of space and Kate kicks at the foot and stamps hard on it and the foot moves and the door's shut and she shoots the bolt which might hold for a few moments while she gets to the window and oh, God, the window is locked shut and the key is in the bedroom. She grabs the bog brush in both hands and bangs the window. She can hear the scissors jabbing at the door. The window shatters, jagged glass everywhere, she's bleeding, there's blood on the walls, her own now. And suddenly she's aware that there's silence and she turns.

Tess stands in the open doorway with the scissors and John Bright stands behind her and someone down in the street shouts, 'Here! Are you all right

232

up there?' And she looks through the jagged hole in the glass and hears her voice say, 'Yes, thanks. Fine.' He's a small man with a florid face. He looks dubious. He'll go now and call the police. She wants to laugh.

Bright has got hold of Tess and of the scissors in a red handkerchief. *Red handkerchief?* 'It's okay,' he says. 'Just a little nick.' Blood is pouring from his arm. Tess's eyes are on the blood as though that's all they'll see, open or shut, day or night, from now on. She's sitting with her back against the banisters, her long thin legs outstretched. She looks elegant, relaxed even, but her eyes are only on the blood.

Bright crouches in front of her saying, 'You don't have to say anything but anything you do say . . .' and Kate is scrabbling in the bathroom cupboard to find something to stem the blood.

48

THERE'S NO BUSINESS LIKE SHOW BUSINESS

'Let me go, guys, please, or I'll be late for rehearsal. I can't be late the first day.'

'Just turn this way, Kate.'

'How did it feel to be attacked like that?'

'Is it true you once had an affair with Tess's husband?'

'Is it true that Tess was your best friend?'

'I've got to go!'

Maureen bolted the stage door behind her. 'They were here when I arrived this morning,' she said. 'I think they'd been here all night.'

'I hope so, it was freezing last night.'

'Aren't they dreadful?' Maureen said. 'I never realised.'

'I'm really late.'

'Only ten minutes, don't fret. They'll understand, they've all had it this morning.' She leaned forward and laughed. 'Some of them loved it, they were revelling in it, I thought they'd never come in.'

The rehearsal room is right at the top of the building. The stairs keep you fit. She opens the door. Six, seven faces turn to her. Blank, white, expressionless, featureless. They're not faces. They're masks. All masks. She's had some shocks in the past few weeks. She's survived them all. Maybe it's the stairs and being late, the scary start of a new job, but this freaks her. She feels round for something solid to hold on to but she can't find anything. She can feel herself going. She can't help herself.

233

Someone puts her on a chair. Sandy holds a paper cup of water to her mouth. 'I didn't know the masks were that effective, Kate. It's quite a compliment.'

She sees Colum. 'Colum, I'm sorry I'm late.'

'For heaven's sake, Kate,' he says.

The faces are curious, concerned. The real faces. The masks are under their arms now or dangling from their hands. She takes one and looks at it. A smooth white chalky thing. She imagines it with features. Tess's features. *Betrayal. That's what the play is about. The play and life both.*

'Are you going to be okay, Kate?'

'I'm fine. Now I'm here, I'm fine.'

Sandy laughs. 'It's the first time I've had to fight through a gang of reporters at the stage door since I worked as a stagehand on a Joan Collins show.'

'It's because they couldn't find me the last few days.'

'Where were you, Kate?'

'It's a secret, I'm afraid.'

'Come on, Kate, tell.'

'No.'

What a surprise it had been. His mother in her wheelchair. Books on the shelves. The beautiful garden. His mother was called Lily. That was odd, another Lily. 'You're the girl with the lovely voice,' Lily had said; not 'You're the girl whose friend tried to murder her.' If it ever got out a witness had stayed at the investigating officer's mother's house . . . Lily had got her through it. She hadn't seen much of Bright. He stayed at his flat in Crouch End.

Kate liked read-throughs. Each actor has a different approach. Hers was to go for it, full-throttle, with a kind of freedom she never felt again till the show had been open a week. After ten minutes she was over the nerves. She had a scene out. She looked round the table. Eight actors. All prepared. All in their different ways. All open to the surprises coming from all sides, all responsive, all hungry for the play, and hungry to be good, to be the best, to make it work, to make it the best show ever. She thought, where could I find anywhere else a group of people like this? And it's always like this. Always this generosity. And always the jokes, the laughter. And I was going to get out of this? Give it up? No chance. This is my world. I'm an actor, whether I like it or not. It's the air I breathe. It's the food I eat. It defines me. It's what I am.

She stayed in the theatre at lunch time. Sandy brought her a sandwich from the bar and she ate in the scene dock with him and the stage manager, Lin, with whom he lived. They concocted a plan.

At six when rehearsals finished Sandy went out of the stage door and got into his VW van. There was a pause while he got the engine running. Then the stage door opened again. Eight actors, director, assistant director, stage manager and assistant stage manager walked out in convoy, each face a dead white chalky oval blank. This phalanx moved inexorably forward, the walking blind, the walking dead. Silence fell. The reporters parted ranks, open-mouthed, and let them through. They moved smoothly into the van and were out of the yard before the press gang recovered their wits.

And after that first day they didn't bother her. Another day another scandal. The show was a success, booked up, queues for returns, but not because of Kate's notoriety. Until Tess came up for trial, Kate was yesterday's chip wrapping.

She was in the dressing-room putting the used tissues and cotton wool into the bin; the eye-liners, lipsticks, mirrors, good luck cards into her big make-up box. She was rolling up the make-up-stained towel and dressing-gown when there was a knock.

'Phone call, Kate!'

With a sick sense of *déjà vu* she plucked the phone from its rest. Wary. 'Yes?'

'Muz Creech?'

'Oh, Christ, it's you.'

'Is it over, then?'

'Is what over, detective inspector?'

'The show.'

'Oh, that's over, yes.'

'When are you coming back to London?'

'Tomorrow, I suppose.'

'Where will you go?'

'My house to pick up the mail. Then Ken's again for a while.' She sounded forlorn even to herself so she laughed. 'Back to real life,' she said.

'Will you go to your house first?'

Pause. 'Well, I have to, don't I? Yes.'

'What time will you be there?'

'Why?'

'Well . . . I thought you might like some company.'

'Oh, I see.' She was touched. How thoughtful could you get? 'Okay,' she said. 'One o'clock.' And suddenly she was profoundly nervous. 'If you're not too busy.'

'Too busy? One o'clock on Sunday afternoon?'

Jenny Who Does The Desserts said, 'Why are you going so soon?'

'Got to face it again, I suppose.'

The ascetic face smiled. 'Best of luck.' She shook Kate's hand.

Maisie didn't hug these days either, too sophisticated. But she did mutter, 'You were great in the play, Ankate.'

Lizzie said to Jenny, 'She and her friends saw it four times.' They stood in the street waving. Sarah Next Door came out to wave too. Kate waved from the car window till the hill behind filled her wing mirror and blocked them out.

Leverton Street, Kentish Town. Pretty in the sun. Cherry blossom finished, the trees in leaf. She got out of the car. The curtains opposite twitched. Some things don't change. No sign of John Bright. Well, it was only just past one and no one is punctual like actors.

She couldn't just hover outside in the street. She had to go in some time. She got the bags out of the boot, put them down. Found the keys in her old leather shoulder bag, took them out. Misery fell on her like rain, the dripping kind that chills you and goes on and on. The mortice was already unlocked. He'd arrived early? Let himself in? She opened the door, picked up the bags and went in backwards, watching the twitching curtains over the street.

'Way-hey!' Aggie and Ted stood in the kitchen. Aggie came into the hall and enveloped her in soft flesh. 'We thought you'd never come in!' she said. 'You can open it now, Ted.' She scooted back to the kitchen and held the glasses while Ted eased out the cork. The champagne frothed. Kate could barely manage a smile. It was good of them, she was glad to see them, and she wished with all her heart that they weren't there. She and the house needed time alone together, to see if they could get on. What about John Bright, who was meant to be here now? He was different. He'd be quiet, he'd let her be. He'd help her get things straight.

'We're getting married,' Aggie said. 'Can you believe it?'

'Frankly, no.'

'Go on, you can if you try.'

'Okay, I'll try.'

'You're the first to know.'

'What, before Daniel?'

'No, after Daniel, of course.'

236

'Daniel pleased?'

Ted looked modest and proud, like a real father. 'Mmm. Seems so, yes.'

'D'you think we're crazy?'

'No. I know you are.'

'Aren't we? Isn't it fantastic? We both said never again.'

Ted looked sheepish, Aggie laughed and poured more champagne. Kate needed to pee. The bucket trick was out. Not with a house full of people. She waited as long as she could but a trip upstairs became inevitable.

The bathroom door was shut. She pushed it open with her eyes closed, didn't open them even when she was sitting on the bog. But something felt different. Smelt different. Paint. She could smell paint. She opened her eyes.

This wasn't her bathroom. White tiles, so white they hurt your eyes. A white bath panelled in old pine. The basin, the bog she sat on like a burnished throne, all new, all white. They'd even matched her yellow carpet, and the blue of the tile edging matched the blue of her Provençal tiles downstairs. She sat there for some time. Then stood and went to the window. Even that had been replaced. It now matched the original sash window in her bedroom. She touched the shiny clean white surfaces. She breathed in the shiny clean smell of paint till it hurt her lungs with a pleasant pain. Nothing was as it had been.

They were standing on the landing when she emerged, like the Startrite Kids, hopeful, eager to please, hand in hand.

'Who did this, you bastards?'

'It's a wedding present,' Aggie said.

'You're the ones getting married.'

'You introduced us,' Ted said without a flicker.

'Oh, that's right, so I did.'

'Do you like it, Kate?'

'It's incredibly beautiful. It's a sort of visible time warp. A wipe-out. I can never thank you – It's too much.'

She went downstairs slowly. They stayed up there. God knows what they were doing, canoodling on her landing she supposed. This desolate feeling might go away in time, perhaps. She stopped in the hall.

John Bright was standing in the kitchen. He was striped like a tiger with the bars of light that came through the slats of the venetian blind. He regarded her with his unfocused squinting look and no smile. He said, 'Hi, Kate.'

She was so pleased to see him she felt quite weak. She had a great desire to put her arms round him. But she didn't. She picked up a glass. He slowly poured champagne into it.

'How's your ma?' she said.